Dear Reader,

There was an ongoing debate between the Silver brothers of Silver Town about their heritage and the notion that anyone in the family could find their mate in dreams. It happened to Darien, the oldest of the triplet brothers. Tom, the youngest, was sure it would happen to him. Jake, the middle brother? No way.

Some of my readers had hoped Tom would be the one to be dream-mated, but life tends to throw us curve balls, so I felt the doubting Thomas—Jake, in this case—should be the one to find his mate in his dreams, since he totally didn't believe in it. But it had to be really different from the story about Darien. And that's what makes storytelling so much fun for me.

Do canines dream? Sure. We have no idea what they're dreaming about as they whimper and woof and kick their feet as if they are running after their prey or maybe even a mate in play. What do we know?

And that's the fun of fiction and the paranormal element of wolves in love—finding the balance between the real and the unknown.

Wolves are real. Dreams are real, as in people and animals dream. Since werewolves are real—work with me here—then dream-mating is perfectly real too.

Readers have been asking me for more stories about the Green Valley wolf pack, mentioned in *Destiny of the Wolf* and *Wolf Fever* and other Silver Town books, and so my treat to you is to write novellas about the continuing stories of the Green Valley wolf pack—because they tie in with the Silver Town wolf pack too—in tenth anniversary Silver Town book releases. I hope to one day write Rosalind's full-length story also. She is Ryan McKinley's sister, and he is the pack leader and mayor of Green Valley. Should she end up in the beloved Silver Town? Or are we going to take over Green Valley and turn it into a wolf-run town?

Ryan has always wanted to do that and has studied Silver Town's success. He just needs to increase his pack size and fill key positions in Green Valley to do it.

Silver Town has captured the imagination of readers for years. It's based on silver-mining towns I've skied at when I've visited Colorado in winter that I fell in love with. I love old, historical towns anywhere I go, but something about the ones in Colorado really resonated with me. Even so, their home is unique to the wolves of Silver Town.

Green Valley will be its own unique wolf haven, if it comes to that. It would need special places—like maybe a drive-in movie theater—that Silver Town doesn't have. It would have to come alive, just like a character in a story, just like Silver Town has, to make it the kind of place where wolves would love to settle down.

So to you with much love, the world of wolves continues.

Terry Spear

Welcome to Silver Town, where the shifters are hot and the romance sizzles

"Intense and swoon-inducing… The chemistry is steamy and hot."
—*USA Today Happy Ever After* for *Dreaming of the Wolf*

"Terry Spear weaves paranormal, suspense, and romance together in one nonstop roller coaster of passion and adventure."
—*Love Romance Passion* for *Destiny of the Wolf*

"Riveting and entertaining…makes one want to devour all of the rest of Terry Spear's books."
—*Fresh Fiction* for *Wolf Fever*

"Another great story sure to amaze and intrigue readers… Terry Spear's writing is pure entertainment."
—*Long and Short Reviews* for *Wolf Fever*

"Nobody does werewolf romances like Terry Spear. The romance sizzles, the plot boils, the mystery intrigues, and the characters shine."
—*The Royal Reviews* for *Silence of the Wolf*

"With nonstop action, thrilling suspense, danger, a beautiful setting, [and] well-drawn characters, this story will keep readers guessing right up to the very satisfying ending."
—*Romance Junkies* for *Silence of the Wolf*

"Essential reading for werewolf romance fans."
—*Booklist* for *Alpha Wolf Need Not Apply*

"A thrilling good time…teasing banter and delicious sexual tension."
—*Fresh Fiction* for *All's Fair in Love and Wolf*

Also by Terry Spear

DREAMING
OF THE WOLF

TERRY
SPEAR

sourcebooks
casablanca

Published by Sourcebooks Casablanca, an imprint of Sourcebooks
P.O. Box 4410, Naperville, Illinois 60567-4410
(630) 961-3900
sourcebooks.com

Originally published in 2011 in the United States of America by
Sourcebooks Casablanca, an imprint of Sourcebooks.

Printed and bound in Canada.
MBP 10 9 8 7 6 5 4 3 2 1

I dedicate Dreaming of the Wolf *to our frontline workers all across the world who are working every day during the fight against the deadly COVID-19 virus at risk to themselves and their families and friends. A heartfelt thank-you.*

CHAPTER 1

ANNOYANCE WELLING UP INSIDE HIM, JAKE SILVER STARED AT the *Closed* sign taped prominently to the glass door as he parked in front of the Cliffside Art Gallery in Breckenridge, Colorado, his framed photography neatly stacked in the back seat of his pickup truck.

Hell, he didn't want to be here in the first place. But now this?

The Victorian charm of the place reminded him of his own hometown of Silver Town, where he *should* have stayed!

The sign pronounced: *Closed until 11:00 a.m. due to unforeseen family emergency.*

With so much work to do managing the leather-goods factory and running the town and pack as his older brother Darien's subleader, Jake had only intended to drop off his photography and then drive the three hours back home. He hadn't originally planned to display his photography at all. But Lelandi, his brother's mate, had finally persuaded him, despite Jake having balked at the notion. He had to admit sales of his photographs in a Denver art gallery had exceeded expectations. Still, he had half a mind to forget the whole damn thing and return home. But he knew Lelandi would be upset if he didn't go through with this, and in her pregnant state, she could easily shed a bundle of tears with the least provocation. He really didn't want to see her break down again.

Hell, he would have eaten breakfast with the family first had he known of the delay. All business all the time, Jake glanced around the town, wondering what to do with himself until the gallery opened. He hated wasting time like this.

Then a woman caught his eye as she stopped briefly to

surreptitiously take a picture of the license plate on a black Mercedes parked across the street at a restaurant. Dressed in a businesslike short-waisted suit jacket, a modest-length skirt, and three-inch heels, she was a real looker with her thick, dark-brown curls piled on top of her head in an elegant twist. Her actions, combined with her appearance, grabbed his attention. He photographed wildflowers as a break from work, while she was photographing a license plate *for* work? Undercover job maybe?

He wondered what color her eyes would be: smoky gray, chocolate brown to match her rich, thick hair, misty green, oceanic blue—or something in between.

The wolfish side of his curious nature was piqued. She didn't look like the type he'd picture working undercover. And he wondered who her target was. Maybe she was a private investigator checking on a wayward wealthy husband, *not* a cop after a criminal.

Then the woman slipped her small camera into a little black purse and entered the restaurant, her high heels clicking on the pavement.

As soon as the door shut behind her, Jake considered the place, a burgundy-red Victorian house with white gingerbread millwork fitted into gables and dormers, ornately carved corbels clinging beneath beams, and lacy fretwork running across the length of the house. The restaurant looked a lot classier than those where he was used to eating. The meals probably cost a fortune.

But he couldn't quit thinking about the slip of a woman and what she was up to. He didn't really want to eat at such a high-class joint and waste a lot of money on a breakfast that he was sure he could eat for a fraction of the cost somewhere else. But he still headed across the street to the restaurant, telling himself it had nothing to do with the woman, that it was just a way to kill time, and that the restaurant was the closest one to the gallery. He tried to ignore the steak-and-eggs place just down the street, which was more like what he was accustomed to and where the meals were probably much more at his price. Not that he couldn't afford the higher prices. He just wasn't inclined to pay them if he didn't have to.

When he entered the restaurant, he found it filled with talkative customers seated at lace-covered tables or tucked into booths where the tables were bare, which suited him better. But the woman who had garnered his interest was nowhere to be seen. Tiffany-style light fixtures hung over the tables, while large windows faced out onto the street, their lace curtains tied back to permit the view of the snow-tipped mountain in the distance. Royal-blue velvet swags hung above them, fringed in gold. Feminine and floral. Nothing that appealed to Jake.

He preferred Silver Town Tavern's more rough-and-tumble, old silver-mining town appearance. But then he considered the floral landscapes hanging on the walls and thought his work would fit here nicely.

A young woman wearing a Victorian gown and a lace-trimmed apron quickly showed him to a booth with too bright a smile and a wayward perusal of his physique. But the overly tanned blond didn't garner his attention like the woman with the dark hair and creamy skin had. The sway of her hips in the fitted, black pin-striped skirt, the way her hands had lovingly held the camera while she quickly took the picture she needed, and the way her full peach lips had parted as she concentrated on getting a good shot still lingered in his thoughts. He had to admit part of his interest was because she carried a camera, the way he often did, even if she didn't use hers in the pursuit of a hobby. Maybe when she wasn't working, she did.

"Sir, is this booth all right?" the woman asked, breaking into his ruminations.

"This will be fine."

He wanted to ask if the hostess had seen the woman who had entered before him and could seat him where he could further observe her. He normally photographed strictly wildflowers, but in her case, he would have made an exception and taken her portrait. But not in a sterile studio environment. On a high, sloping field at the foot of the mountains with soft natural lighting. Wearing faded blue-jean short shorts and a skimpy tank top, barefoot and braless, the object of his fascination would sit in a field of pale-purple daisies with their gold-button centers facing upward and lacy, towering firs providing the backdrop. That was the portrait he wanted to take of her.

A waitress, dressed in a Victorian gown and apron similar to the hostess's, hurried over with a menu and a glass of water. She was just as friendly and just as unabashedly bold about giving him the once-over. He was sure that had more to do with feminine interest than with a bigger tip since he was the only male around the age of thirty who was seated alone in the establishment. Then again, maybe she *was* sizing him up to see if he fit the usual clientele— rich resort visitor—or if he was an off-season ski bum who had mistakenly found his way into this place.

He'd dressed up a little more than usual because he would be meeting with the art gallery owner, although he probably could have worn anything and the gallery staff wouldn't have cared. Artists were artists, after all.

But he wore a vest with his stonewashed jeans and a pin-striped dress shirt, although he'd rolled the sleeves up to his elbows and left a couple of the buttons down the front of the shirt undone. And he hadn't bothered to shave for a couple of days, giving him more of a rugged appearance. Dressy just didn't suit him much.

Light, fluffy music played overhead, while the aroma of coffee brewing and steak sizzling on a grill wafted through the air. Jake's stomach rumbled in anticipation as he considered the menu, narrowed his eyes to study the prices, and nearly had a stroke.

"Highway robbery," he muttered under his breath. He would have walked out, but he wanted to see the woman again and learn what she was up to. Then he waved to the waitress, told himself he only lived once—if paying exorbitant prices meant he was living—and placed his order.

When the waitress left, Jake saw her—the woman who'd caught his eye outside the restaurant—sitting in a booth across from his. His heartbeat quickened, and he sat up a little taller. She was observing a man in his midfifties who was seated at a nearby table and wearing a fitted dark-gray suit. He was swarthy, fat-faced, and fat-lipped, with a bulbous nose, receding black hair, and dark, cold eyes. Something about the man warned Jake that he was a threat, not someone to anger. Not just a man having an affair on his wife.

The fact that she was watching the man bothered Jake. He saw it as a case of her flaunting danger. She was maybe five foot five in stocking feet with a small build and tendrils of curls spilling from her upswept hair to tickle the back of her neck. She was not nearly big enough or mean-looking enough to take on whoever the man was and win the confrontation. Now Jake could see her eyes—the color of rich chocolate, just like her hair. Her eyes were narrowed a hint and her brows knit into a small frown.

She pursed her full, glossy lips, a shimmering shade of peach, as she wrote something on a notepad. Her gaze returned to the man. Her lips garnered another look from Jake as she worried the bottom one a little, and he had the urge to coax her mouth into a smile with his, to take away the frown, to give her something positive to think about. Like *him*.

She glanced toward the door as a man walked into the restaurant. Wearing an expensive black suit, he was similar in build to the first: stocky and dark-haired, swarthy and all business as he glanced around the place with a wolf's wary manner. The woman quickly averted her eyes.

Surveillance. Jake bet she was working some kind of surveillance. But who were the men she was watching? And who did she work for?

The waitress returned to the table, delivered his steak and eggs, and asked, "Is there anything else you'd like?" She favored him again with a way-too-intimate pass, the connotation in her sugar-coated voice suggesting *she* could be on the menu if he was the least bit interested.

With a quick smile to indicate he'd gotten her message but just as quick a shake of his head to show he wasn't interested, Jake said, "No, thanks. I have everything I need, *right* here." He glanced back at the woman in the suit as if emphasizing he meant that included the woman who continued to be the object of his fascination.

The waitress's smile quickly faded. "Oh, you're interested in *her*." She paused as if she was thinking of saying something more about the woman. But then she shook her head and said, "I'll check back with you in a bit, then." She gave the woman in the suit a derisive look, but before the waitress could hurry off, Jake seized her scrawny wrist.

When she stopped and turned to face him, her pale-hazel eyes wide, he released her wrist and asked, "Do you know the woman?"

She gave a soft snort. "Oh yeah, she and her mother have been coming here for years. Skiing, ice-skating, hiking, you name it." Then the waitress leaned down lower and said conspiratorially, "She's mixed up with some bad types, and nobody but nobody wants to associate with them—or *her*. Let's just say it can lead to a *dead* end." She gave a little shrug.

"Bad types?"

The waitress rolled her eyes. "Mob ties."

"She's in with the Mob?" Jake asked, sounding incredulous. The guys she was observing looked like they might have connections, but...

"Her mother was dating one of them."

That put a totally new spin on the situation. "And the daughter?"

The waitress's lips curved up in a menacing grin. "Sure, like mother, like daughter. She gave up an honest-to-goodness decent sort to consort with a bunch of criminals."

He had the sneaking suspicion the daughter wasn't seeing someone like that. If anything, she was watching the two men in a way that made him think of a police sting operation, not as though she was friends with them. If she had been, she would have joined them.

But the waitress's words still gave him pause. "Thanks."

"Anytime." The waitress flipped around and hurried off, swaying her hips in an exaggerated fashion.

Jake sliced into his juicy steak, the aroma of the T-bone making his stomach rumble again, but the food still didn't interest him as much as the woman. Taking a bite of the tender meat, which was seasoned to perfection and melted in his mouth, he sat back and observed her further. She looked to be all work, no play, just like he was *normally*.

For some inconceivable reason, he wanted to gain her attention. Maybe because she'd hooked his to such a degree. On the other hand, he enjoyed watching her, studying her, and taking pleasure in her without her knowledge, without the anxiety-ridden pretension that often existed between two people meeting for the first time.

He looked again at her jacket. She could be an undercover cop. *Maybe*. A slight bulge under her jacket on one side could indicate she was packing a gun.

Jake raised his brows. She could be armed and deadly. Even more intriguing. Although the waitress's words still lingered in his thoughts: she could be dating a mobster like her mother was. She could be armed because she was one of the criminal element. Yet he couldn't help but feel she was working as an undercover cop. But if she was, he thought she was in way over her head on this case.

He glanced around the room. None of the other diners seemed to be watching the men *or* her. Why didn't she have backup if she was a cop?

Getting involved in human affairs that didn't pertain to the good citizens of Silver Town was not a good idea. Yet if she encountered any trouble, he'd be in the thick of it, rescuing her without thought of reward. Well, maybe a little reward. A heartfelt hug from that sweet body of hers would do for starters. A kiss from those lips would be welcome.

He sat back and finished his steak and eggs while she sipped more of her tea. She'd taken a bite of a cinnamon roll but nothing more. Was she as frugal as him? Or just not a big breakfast eater? Or was ordering the breakfast just as a ruse while she conducted her surveillance?

He wondered what it would be like to pull the pins from her hair, release it over her shoulders, and comb his fingers through the lush, silky strands. To disarm her—to see her wearing something softer, something that would reveal her womanly curves even more, or wearing nothing at all. And to taste her lips, sweetened by sugary cinnamon.

Turning his attention to the two men she was observing, he listened, trying to hear their exchange. The men spoke in low tones, but with the murmur of conversations in the busy restaurant and the distance Jake was from the men's table, he couldn't make out their words, even with his enhanced wolf's hearing. The men didn't seem to take any notice of the woman, either feigning ignorance or showing her that her effort to rattle them was in vain.

Jake glanced at one of the plate-glass windows and the pin-striped awning stretched over the top to shade customers when the sun rose in the sky. Two men sat out front in a darkened Mercedes—the one bearing the license plate that his mystery woman had photographed earlier. Bodyguard, driver, he assumed. And parked in front of that vehicle was another: similar make and model, same setup—two men.

Inside the restaurant, the two men under surveillance shook hands. One smiled, the look pure evil. The other nodded.

Jake glanced back at the woman to see her take on the matter, and his blood instantly heated with ire. A bruiser of a man wearing a dark-gray suit towered over her as he motioned for her to leave. When the hell had he entered the restaurant and approached her?

She remained seated, not budging, looking up at the man with loathing as he loomed over her. Jake could see that the man was wearing the hardware to back up his threatening posture, hidden under his jacket and pressed slightly into the fabric as a show of force. He had one hand inserted underneath the jacket, holding the gun.

Like a wolf ready to take down its prey, Jake rose from his booth with a cautious, predatory stalking motion. The man waved the gun underneath his suit jacket again in a sweeping motion toward the door. Defiantly, the woman continued to balk, glaring at him, not moving an inch, not saying a word. Jake admired her stalwart nerve. But he didn't believe she'd win this argument. Not without a little wolfish backup.

Wishing he had at least asked the waitress the woman's name before playing his cards, since the waitress seemed to know a good deal about her, Jake stalked across the floor to join her before the beast forced the issue. The woman's gaze shifted to Jake, eyes widening like pools of melted dark chocolate and drawing him in.

The bulky beast of a man turned to face Jake and narrowed his already beady eyes in confrontation. Just as a wolf would, Jake conveyed a real threat of his own in his posture, from his steely gaze to his taut muscles and rigid back. Even the hair on his arms was standing erect, just as his fur would be if he were wearing his wolf coat—another form of intimidation that made him appear bigger, more of a threat.

If anyone could deal with a tyrant like the armed guy in the suit, Jake was the man for the job, with or without a weapon. But fighting the man wasn't what he had in mind, unless there was no way around it.

Jake shifted his attention to the lady, offered a friendly smile, spread his hands a little as if in greeting, and said to her, "Julia Roberts!"

His smile broadened as he leaned down to give her a kiss on the cheek—the part of the plan he liked best—and her eyes were as round as twin full moons as she stared back at him. His hand moved to her back, gently caressing as if he'd known her forever and encouraging her to play along with him. His mouth lingered longer than was necessary on her cool, soft cheek, his free hand taking hers in much too possessive a manner for never having made her acquaintance before. If nothing else, Jake knew he needed to play his role well if he was going to convince the thug to back off.

"Why didn't you tell me you were going to be here today?" His voice had already changed from darkly interested to huskily enthralled, which wasn't part of the plan but more of that wolfish nature he had no control over.

His gaze moved to view her full, shimmering lips, now parted in surprise. He wanted to kiss her there, taste her, feel her, sample the sweetness of those lips.

"Tom Hanks," she said, quickly recovering, winking, and trying for lighthearted, but he saw the look of worry in her darkened eyes.

With his hand to his chest, he feigned being mortally wounded. "Last week, I was your Gerard Butler. Tom Hanks this week?" He shook his head, squeezed her hand reassuringly, and gave her one of his more wolfishly friendly smiles. Her hand was icy, and he held on tighter, hoping to show her she had nothing to fear. "Friend of yours, honey?"

"No, darlin'," she said with a drawl that didn't sound quite real. "He has mistaken me for someone else." She cast a brilliant smile at the man and then Jake, but the smile didn't reach her eyes. It was more of a we'll-show-you expression aimed at the thug.

Jake rewarded her with a slight tightening on her hand to say, "Well done."

He was in love. She was someone who could tease like he could on the spur of the moment, someone who could stand up to a man nearly twice her weight who towered over her and was a real threat. She would be perfect for Jake, *if* she were a wolf. And for the time being, he didn't give a damn about the ramifications of the problems *that* could create. All he cared about was getting to know the woman better.

"I asked the lady nicely if she'd come with me," the thug said, his voice thickly menacing. "Now I'm going to ask *not* so nicely." A telltale buzzing in the man's pocket shut him up. He pulled out a cell phone and gruffly said, "Hello?" His icy, slate-colored eyes stared Jake down, threatening him to back off or else.

Jake wasn't intimidated. The challenge suited him. Face-to-face wolfish confrontations were much easier to deal with than sneaky underhandedness.

He remained standing next to what he assumed was an armed damsel in distress, although he wanted to remove her from the powder keg of a situation. The men in the vehicles out front were most likely just as armed, so he was certain he'd be no match for all of them, even if the woman had a cannon underneath her jacket.

He might not be the pack leader in Silver Town, but Jake was just as alpha as his older brother and had no qualms about taking this man or anyone else down. But as a *lupus garou*, he was mindful of which battles to fight and which to leave alone. Going against a whole army of trigger-happy thugs wasn't in the plan.

The man nodded as if responding to the caller, then shoved his phone into his pocket. He scowled at Jake, then the woman, directing his comments at her. "Just so's you know, *next time*, you won't get off so easy."

Then he turned, nearly stumbled over the chair in his way, and cursed a string of swear words. After shoving the chair out of the way, he sauntered off like a disgruntled lumbering grizzly. Several customers looked up from their meals and glowered at him for disturbing the peace with such a vulgar commentary as he made his way out of the restaurant.

"I'd recommend we leave, but they've got more guns outside, so it would be prudent if we stay a little longer." Jake slid into the booth with her so they could talk more privately. Although she quickly scooted over to allow him room, his leg still touched hers, and the shock of it sent heat sliding through him.

But what made him even hotter was that she didn't pull away. Even though the intimation was that this was her booth, her table, and she wasn't going to be forced into the corner, the challenge in her posture only intrigued him more. But her eyes—which were now focused on his mouth—were what really got his attention.

His gaze strayed again to her lips. Upon closer inspection, he saw glittering speckles of cinnamon sugar just before her tongue slipped out and moistened her bottom lip, as if she was suddenly conscious of something on her lips that she needed to wipe away quickly. But she'd missed some at the corners and the top of her luscious lips, and he was dying to taste them and her.

Trying to get his mind off the reaction his body was having in close proximity to hers and the sensuous way she licked her lips as if preparing them for a kiss, and wanting to know just what this business was with the mobsters, he asked, "What's going on?"

CHAPTER 2

JAKE TILTED HIS HEAD TOWARD THE TABLE WHERE THE TWO men now ate their breakfast in silence, indicating that he knew the woman sitting beside him had been watching them with more than casual interest. He wanted to know just what was going on with the lady. Especially since he'd had to rescue her once already. And he suspected she might need his services again if she continued what she was doing.

He didn't expect her to tell him anything, since he suspected she was working undercover. But he was beginning to have his doubts about that because he was fairly sure she would have a partner. And the notion that her mother had Mob connections still lingered in his thoughts.

She shrugged. "You wouldn't believe me if I told you." Her eyes and lips hinted at a half smile that sparkled with feistiness.

"Try me."

"I'm a bounty hunter."

His mouth dropped open before he could hide his surprise better.

Her smile broadened. "Told you that you wouldn't believe me."

She took a sip of tea from a dainty teacup covered in tiny pink roses, and the way her lips touched the rim made him wish she was touching her mouth against his with the same pressure and with parted lips, drinking him in.

His eyes strayed to the slight bulge under her jacket where he assumed her gun was. "Bounty hunter." He sounded a little incredulous.

Here he'd thought she was an undercover cop and was most

likely better trained for the job. The thought crossed his mind that the waitress was mistaken or had lied about this woman's mother dating someone in the Mob. If the waitress's explanation held any truth, Jake wondered if the woman and her mother were involved with a rival family. But a bounty hunter?

She'd get herself killed. He didn't like the scenario in the least.

"Don't tell me you're after one of those men."

"The one on the right. Mario Constantino."

"Ah. And you're going to walk up to him, serve a warrant, and arrest him." His gaze shifted from the well-dressed thug to the delicate woman sitting beside him, her heady feminine fragrance—a mixture of woman and the hint of an exotic floral bouquet— stirring his interest. But she wasn't any competition for the bastard sitting at the table.

"Not yet. If he doesn't show up for his court date by tomorrow morning, I'll serve his warrant and rearrest him. But there's another one. Danny Massaro. He works for this guy. Danny is supposed to appear at court in Denver today, but according to my informant, he's meeting with Mario sometime soon in Breckenridge—and he has already missed his court appearance. Danny's not the man dining with Mario this morning, though. I want Danny too. And I *will* get them. Both."

Jake released an exasperated sigh. He imagined that issuing a warrant for one of them would be more than reckless. But trying to arrest the two of them?

"You're kidding, right?" She might be armed, but she was no match for a bunch of guys with Italian names who had Mafia connections.

"I told you that you wouldn't believe me. Want another cup of coffee?"

"How did you know I was drinking coffee?" He waved to the waitress for a fresh cup.

"I saw you sitting in that booth over there, watching me, before you looked to see what the men who I'd been observing were doing. Until you saw the big ape who was trying to force me to go outside with him." She paused for a heartbeat, judging Jake's response.

His lips parted for a fraction of a second. He was damned surprised. He'd thought she hadn't known he existed until he'd come to her aid.

She raised her brows just a hair, undoubtedly amused to see his reaction. She was good at this surreptitious stuff. Really good, he had to admit.

"But even before that, I observed you at the art gallery across the street, looking vexed because it was closed. I would guess you were on a schedule—self-imposed—and didn't like the proverbial wrench in your plans. You were trying to figure out what to do with your spare time until the gallery opened, saw the restaurant, and came in here."

"Saw *you* and came in here," he corrected.

If she was so observant, and he suspected from her analysis of the situation that she was—which reminded him of a wolf—he wondered why she'd left out the most important part. And he wondered why she'd taken such a keen interest in him. Maybe for the same reason he was intrigued by her. Or she might have thought he was trouble like these guys were and had just been keeping an eye on him.

"You were taking a picture of the Mercedes's license plate in a covert way. And that made me curious," he said.

She smiled, and this time it was a beautiful, heartwarming smile—her expression all-knowing—like she'd had him pegged from the beginning and wasn't clueless enough to believe his interest had everything to do with her taking a picture of a license plate instead of having more to do with the picture-taker herself. She might not be a wolf, but she sure seemed perceptive.

She lifted her cup of tea again. "This isn't the kind of place you usually frequent, I imagine."

He raised his brows, surprised *again* that she seemed so astute. He couldn't help but admire that quality in her—particularly when she could read him so well and was even interested in doing so.

"You're too…" she said, her gaze sweeping over him in an intimate way, and then she trailed her fingertips down his leather vest—and his body reacted, tightening with raw need. Her gaze slid lower to his stonewashed jeans, and then she lifted her eyes to meet his gaze. "Rugged, in a casual, cool sort of way," she finished. She brushed her fingers lightly over his cheek, tickling the short hairs of the couple of days' beard growth, her eyes considering his face. "Yep, too rugged for the likes of this place."

When she dropped her hand from his face, he asked, "So you *knew* I'd come in here looking for you?" His voice was a whole lot huskier than he'd intended. He wondered if after he'd kissed her and pretended a deeper friendship, she had played the role for Mario, the criminal she had under surveillance. In any event, Jake was game to deepen the role.

"Sure. That's why when you first came in, you couldn't find me. I ducked inside and found a spot to observe you while looking for where Constantino had perched, and then when I thought you looked fairly harmless…"

He couldn't believe it. She'd ditched him when she entered the restaurant so she could observe *him*, and he hadn't even been privy to the fact? The woman was a marvel. And definitely a wolf at heart.

But then her comment sank in. "I looked fairly harmless?"

"Oh, all right—handsomely, devilishly dangerous but more in an innocuous way. More of a lady-killer type, if anything."

"Innocuous?" He chuckled at that. He could be quite dangerous, and it didn't take much of a push to shove him in that direction. But the other part? "Lady-killer?" He really didn't see himself that way.

"The way the hostess and then the waitress were sizing you up…" She let the thought trail off and shrugged.

He wondered about the waitress. If she knew this woman so well, how well did his bounty hunter know her? He was more amused than anything, though, by her response that he was a lady-killer. He couldn't believe that as close as she'd come to real trouble, she could switch gears like this so completely. Nothing about her was timorous, and he liked that about her—to an extent. He still thought she should be a lot less confrontational with the bad guys.

"Do you know the waitress? She seemed to know you," he said, hoping to get to the heart of the matter.

The woman gave a little laugh, but her response was slightly bitter in tone. "Oh yeah, we go way back. Tami Lawson and I went to school together. I'm sure she had only *good* things to say about me." With a refilled cup of tea, she said, "I'm Alicia Greiston, by the way. I'd offer my hand, but I'm afraid that would look kind of strange since we're supposed to know each other already. Rather intimately even."

"I'd go for another kiss." He was only half joking. Except this time, he wanted to kiss her cinnamon-and-sugar-sweetened lips.

She chuckled. "Yeah, like I said, a real lady-killer."

Not in the least bit reluctant to feed into her fantasies of the kind of man he was, he reached over, took her hand, and brushed his lips against the back with a soft caress. He swore she melted a little on the seat next to him. "Jake Silver, *completely* at your disposal."

She raised her brows, her lips still imparting a small smile, and gently pulled her hand free of his. "Have a gun?"

"Nope." At least not on him.

She took a deep breath that seemed exaggerated and said, "That means I'll have to protect us *both* now."

Not in this lifetime. Although this matter wasn't any of his concern, he was ready to make it so if that kept her from getting herself killed. He couldn't help that her being a bounty hunter troubled him.

"Have you been a bounty hunter long?"

She shook her head. "I cashiered at a department store before this."

Hell, he hadn't expected that. "Sold merchandise?" he asked in disbelief.

"No. Cashed employee payroll checks, took payments on layaways and credit cards, sold fishing and hunting licenses, and gift-wrapped merchandise at Christmastime until we hired a professional wrapper for the season."

Wrapping up mobsters in Christmas ribbon and bows came to mind. Just what kind of training *did* she have? Trying to get his disbelief under control, Jake frowned, hoping that he wasn't jumping to conclusions and that she had been a bounty hunter for a number of years and was well prepared to arrest the most dangerous criminals. Maybe even that she'd served as a cop. Something that would make her seem better qualified and prepared.

"Exactly how long have you been a bounty hunter?" He kept his voice even, without a thread of emotion that might antagonize her. Or at least he tried to.

She raised her brows just a hint. "Since a few months ago."

At that revelation, he couldn't stifle a grunt of disbelief quickly enough and revealed his true feelings. The knowledge that she hadn't been doing this long filled him with incredulity. The woman had to have a death wish.

"Do you know how to use a gun?" He managed to cut off the "at least" part of his statement before he spoke the words, although they had been on the tip of his tongue.

At that point, the tension fairly sparked between them. Alicia's hackles rose as her whole body stiffened beside him, her gaze riveted to her teacup, her fingers tightening around it. Her family *must* have mentioned how dangerous and perilous her job could be and *warned* her not to take part in such foolhardiness. He couldn't imagine a woman whose appearance and training seemed so at odds with the kind of job she was determined to do actually accomplishing it.

But then she visibly relaxed. Her whole demeanor became coolly detached rather than reflecting her anger because he was prying into her business and questioning her ability to do her job. In that instant, he sensed a disconcerting vulnerability. With her jaw set and her eyes examining her teacup, she seemed determined to see this through.

He would bet the homestead that she was somehow being forced into this venture. And he intended to find out why and stop it before she got herself killed.

Jake Silver was the kind of dangerously exciting man Alicia had learned to avoid when she was growing up—and damn if she wasn't drawn to him like a spike of winsome, colorful foxglove seeking shade. His masculine touch made her fantasize about all kinds of carnal pleasures.

She loved how he had spied her, become intrigued with her, and ultimately come to her rescue, knowing if he hadn't, she might have been forced to call the local police. Which she didn't want to do. How would it look if she couldn't face these guys on her own?

And she didn't have a choice. It was her life or theirs. Simple as that.

But she didn't need any man questioning her abilities with regard to bounty hunting. She'd been fingerprinted and had her background checked. She had never committed a felony—she was one of the good guys—and she'd completed her bail-fugitive-apprehension training, which was necessary to become a bounty hunter.

Working for a licensed bail agent, she'd arrested several fugitives in the past few months, although none who were Mob-related. But the others had only been practice before she went after the ones who really counted.

Trying not to sound waspish, she said, "Sure I know how to use a gun. My first..." Alicia paused. She had *not* intended to talk about *that* mistake.

The look on Jake's face was one of rabid curiosity. She was about to tell a secret, and he was dying to know the truth. She sighed. She'd already let the proverbial cat partway out of the bag. "My first husband taught me how to shoot at a firing range. He was in the army—military police."

"Ah."

"I went hunting too," she said defensively, then was annoyed with herself for explaining her qualifications to him as if she owed that to him.

Jake's frown didn't fade. "What did you kill?"

She looked down at her hands, now strangling the linen napkin in her lap. "Nothing. Irvin was lousy at hunting. We never could find anything."

"So Irvin was your *first* husband?"

"Um, no." She hadn't planned to let on that she'd had two, but mentioning that the first was—she sighed—*first* indicated she'd had more than one, even though she'd meant to say *ex*-husband.

Jake raised his brows. She had not planned on telling him her whole blasted life story. "My second husband," she said in way too small a voice.

Jake's lips curved up just a hint. "Is that all of them?"

She gave him an annoyed look. "Yes."

"You can't be all that old."

"Twenty-seven."

"And what happened to the husbands?"

"Both of them were big mistakes. The last one was out of my life three years ago—after a year of marriage."

Jake sat back in his chair. "Sure there aren't any more of them?"

This time, she smiled. "No. I had an aunt who'd had eight of them, though."

He whistled softly.

She chuckled. "Luckily, no children, and only her death stopped her from having more husbands. I swear I'm not going down the same path as my aunt. I've strictly sworn off men. What about you? Been married before? Currently married or engaged? Your age?"

"Thirty. Never been married, engaged, or otherwise."

"You're kidding." She hadn't meant to sound so skeptical, but he seemed a trifle amused by her reaction.

"No."

She wondered how that could be, as good-looking as he was. But then the sinking realization he might be gay hit her, and she didn't say anything more.

Jake finished his coffee, set his cup down, and pointedly said, "You're wondering why I'm thirty and have never been married."

Hating to be put on the spot, she waffled. "Not everyone marries as many times as I did before the age of twenty-three." As soon as she said that, it sounded lame to her. He was thirty, not twenty-three.

"I like women, Alicia." He gave her a pleasantly amused smile. "I've just never found the right one to convince me to settle down."

Alicia's grim expression softened. "I never found the right guy either, but that didn't stop me from marrying two times. I'm cured of my impulsiveness now, though."

That was why, Jake thought ruefully, she had become a bounty hunter. Nothing impulsive about that. At least he managed to curb the urge to shake his head. He had imagined that she was a trained weapons expert, knowledgeable in the martial arts, maybe ex-military or an ex-cop. Not a former cashier in a department store.

Before he could ask her why she was a bounty hunter—figuring maybe for the excitement, for some sense of adventure, or because it paid better—she posed a question. "What were you doing at the art gallery?"

The notion she was in the business of asking questions and getting answers made him think she was like a police officer on a mission.

This got tricky, though. Only his pack members knew about his hobby of photographing flowers in the wild. If anyone thought it wasn't a macho thing to do, no one let on. At least not to his face. As no-nonsense as she seemed, he imagined she'd think his hobby was foolish. And as much as he told himself that shouldn't matter, he *did* care what she thought.

He shrugged.

She didn't miss a beat. "You have paintings you're leaving off, right? Nude women? Old girlfriends? New girlfriends?"

He laughed. The woman was precocious. "I'm afraid that if I told you, I'd ruin your image of me."

"*Ahh*," she said, drawing out the word. "I see."

"What do you *see*?"

"Landscapes, then."

He smiled and shook his head, but he was still thinking of where he wanted to go next with Alicia. In an instant, she had changed his mood from annoyed at having to hang around town until the gallery opened and then spending a fortune on a meal to being possessively chivalrous and wanting to just spend some time in town enjoying the day with a woman like her.

"So where do we go from here?" he asked, curbing the urge to pull her from the booth and escort her to the nearest bed-and-breakfast. But only if they served breakfast in bed.

CHAPTER 3

As much as Jake knew he had to get back to Silver Town, he was beginning to think he didn't need to return all that quickly. He was owed a vacation, and he couldn't remember a time when he'd taken one. Work and pleasure were all wrapped up in Silver Town and the pack. That was all that had ever mattered.

But now *she* mattered. Alicia Greiston, bounty hunter and bundle of sensuous woman, who was bound to get herself into real trouble. But the way she had played her role with him made him think she was also interested in furthering their relationship. He knew he should back off, knew that unless it would be a one-night stand with a human female, he shouldn't be encouraging this. Yet he had no desire to stop what was taking place. And he didn't believe a one-night stand would offer a fix for what he was feeling.

He could drop off the photographs and take in some sights with Alicia, if she could give up her surveillance for the time being and was interested in spending the day with him. Who knew what could happen with regard to the night?

She was about to say something when she glanced back at Mario as he walked past the table, not giving any indication he knew she existed. The other man remained seated, eating his breakfast.

As soon as Jake felt Alicia tense, as if she were a wolf ready to go after her quarry, he wrapped his arm around her shoulders and pulled her tight against his body, even though he already had her blocked from leaving the booth.

He shook his head and leaned over, his mouth brushing her ear as he whispered, "Too many of them."

Her expression shifted from hunting mode to resigned acqui-escence. That was until she spoke and he realized she wasn't as resigned to admitting she couldn't pursue the man as he had thought she was.

"You have to take your artwork to the gallery." She glanced at her watch. "Must be open by now." Her gaze met his in too busi-nesslike a fashion. "We could meet at a little Italian place up the street for lunch later today. If you're interested and you're hungry by then."

He was interested, but he was damned concerned that she intended to ditch him a second time, only in this instance so she could keep Mario under further surveillance.

"Italian?" Jake asked. The insinuation was that the Italian guys might eat at the Italian restaurant, and she had inside information that they'd be stopping for lunch there. Which didn't sit well with Jake. If he was to have a meaningful lunch with the lady, he wanted *all* her attention.

She shrugged, but the renewed sparkle in her eyes and the slight upward tilt of her mouth meant she had caught his meaning. She lifted her chin just a little. "Or anything else you're interested in."

His smile was sure to appear purely predatory. She had to know he was interested in *her*.

"To eat," she said, and she must have realized he was thinking like a man would.

His smile broadened as his gaze remained on hers. A faint blush colored her cheeks and creamy throat.

She quickly added, "They have steak houses, sandwich shops, seafood places, you name it."

"Will you go with me to the art gallery?"

"No. I've got some errands I need to run." Her tone was clipped and businesslike again. She wasn't going to be talked out of going it alone.

He didn't like it. He thought she was serious about lunch, but after she'd ticked off these men, he believed she'd be headed into real danger. And he was certain she was going after them further.

"So what will it be?" she asked.

"Steak house, but—"

"Okay, steak house it is. Main Street at 1:00 p.m." She rose to leave and straightened her skirt.

He wanted to change her mind, but she seemed determined. He stood to let her out of the booth and noticed that the suited man still seated at the table was watching them. Jake took her hands, leaned over, and slanted his mouth over hers, meaning to show the man that Alicia was his, and if anyone thought of harming her, there'd be hell to pay. Before he could do much more than press the merest of kisses against her soft mouth, she pulled her hands free.

Prepared to accept her rejection, Jake was about to separate from her, figuring she objected to going any further with this—at least here in the restaurant. Until she placed her arms securely around his neck, her breasts pressed against his chest in a tormentingly seductive way, and with an upturned face, offered her mouth to him.

Eagerness propelled him to take advantage, but he reined in his baser needs and licked her sugary-cinnamon-sweetened lips with a sensuous sweep of his tongue. His hands roamed down her back until they rested at the bottom edge of her jacket on the sensuous curve of her buttocks.

He said quietly, "Open your mouth to me."

The suggestion was like unlocking the bedroom door and letting him in. His tongue penetrated the small opening as she barely parted her lips to him, more in surprise than in agreement, he thought. But he breached any defenses she might have erected, one of his hands cupping the back of her head as he forged forward, the other keeping her body pressed against his hardness.

She responded like a woman caught up in lust, at first shyly kissing his tongue back, her body a little reserved. Then as if he'd overpowered her will to keep this at a standoff, he sensed her resolve falter. Felt her tongue play with his in a more aggressive manner, felt her arch against him, pressing her sexy, soft body against his. He nearly groaned when she deepened the kiss.

Sweet cinnamon and spicy woman greeted him in a way he'd never experienced with any other. Her soft body fit against his hard one, which was getting harder by the second. He wrapped his arms around her back and held on tighter until he finally felt the gun at her waist.

She murmured against his lips, "I thought you said you *didn't* have a gun."

"I didn't think you meant *that* one. Maybe we could have dinner later?" He was already hoping to spend the day and the night with her, keeping her safe while enjoying her companionship for a while longer.

She gave him a wistful smile back. For an instant, he thought he might be pushing her too fast. But this was the first time a woman had truly sparked his interest in eons, and he didn't want to let her go just yet. Her wit and wolfish intuition fascinated him.

A long-term commitment with a human female was fraught with difficulties and something his kind would frown on, but a tryst with one was perfectly acceptable if both were willing and agreeable. She seemed as interested as he was. Although a nagging concern told him that she wasn't someone he could get out of his system easily with an overnight venture.

"Your bill," Tami the waitress said, her face screwed up in hate as she openly glared at Alicia. She turned to Jake and gave him a small smile as she handed him the bill.

Alicia slipped it out of her hand before Jake could take it. "My treat," Alicia said to Jake, "for the rescue."

He fished out two twenties and tossed them on the table. "You can get the dessert later." He winked at Alicia and saw Tami's scowl deepen more. With his hand guiding the small of Alicia's back, he walked her outside. "What's up with your former schoolmate?"

"She wanted Harold. My first husband. I didn't know he'd been seeing her behind my back. He married me instead. If I'd known what they'd been up to, I would have given her my blessing and let her have him. But unfortunately, I didn't know about their affair until after we were married."

"The guy must've been crazy."

"No. I was, for not having my eyes wide open when I was dating him."

Not believing a human guy could be such a jerk, Jake shook his head and walked her to her car. "He still must have been crazy. I take it he didn't go back to her after you divorced."

"Nope. He was seeing other women while we were married. He liked them new and different. Once he'd been with a woman for a few weeks, the spark was gone, and he was ready to discard her for someone else. Much like he was with his expensive toys. When his motorcycle was nearly a year old, he ditched it for a new one. When his computer was six months old, he needed something newer that was just on the market. Cell phones, you name it. He was always in debt up to his hairline."

For an instant, Jake thought he saw sadness in her posture, her shoulders slightly slumped and her eyes averted from the mountain vista. She quickly shrugged as if it didn't matter and cast him a small smile. "I was lucky to be rid of him."

But her words and her actions gave her away. None of what Harold had done mattered as much as the fact that the jerk had lusted after other women when he had given his promise to Alicia to be her one and only.

Jake tried not to see anything more in his relationship with Alicia than serving as her protector until he could convince her to give up the nonsense of taking these men to jail. But he had the sneaking suspicion her past relationship with Harold had colored her perception of *all* men—that they were rats and couldn't be trusted—and she probably viewed Jake in the same way. It shouldn't have mattered, but the wolf side of him wanted to exclaim that his kind did not make light of relationships. Although since she was human, he couldn't admit how faithful his kind were when they made a commitment to their own.

Telling himself it was for the benefit of the Italian guy watching them to see how he and Alicia parted company, he gave her a see-you-soon kiss. He had hoped she would deepen the kiss, but she didn't encourage anything more than a quick meeting of the lips, as if she was already putting the brakes on their relationship. That again made him think she was playing her part for the mobster, and Jake worried she might still be planning on ditching him. But then he reconsidered. She seemed honest about wanting to meet him again for lunch.

He opened her car door for her. "I'll meet you at one then."

"Mm-hmm." She smiled, but her expression was strained.

If he'd acted on his wolf instincts, he wouldn't have let her run off on her own, and as soon as he shut the door, he had the resounding feeling that letting her go had been a grave mistake.

She pulled out of the parking space and headed down the street, then stopped at a floral shop. After making sure she got inside the shop all right and that no one was following her, Jake returned to his truck to leave his artwork off at the gallery. But he was plagued by the niggling worry that he should follow her and make sure she stayed safe.

Figuring he could drop off his photography quickly and then tail Alicia until their luncheon engagement, he rushed into the gallery and startled a woman, her blue eyes wide, who was wearing a conservative suit and had her hair cut short in a professional bob.

"Ma'am, I'm Jake Silver, with the photographs I called about displaying in your gallery." He spoke quickly and as if he was on edge.

He hoped his smile looked sincere and that he didn't sound as rushed as he felt as he stalked inside with his box-load of framed artwork. He was ready to drop the photographs on a table and head out again. But by the way the woman's mouth dropped open, he was sure she was wondering why they'd agreed to carry his photographs in the gallery in the first place.

He hurried to make his excuses as his thoughts remained on the florist shop and his next destination—tailing Alicia Greiston to keep her safe.

———————————

Totally rattled by Jake Silver, the most dangerously disarming hunk she'd ever caught the attention of, Alicia had missed her chance to follow Mario. She knew that had been Jake's intent, although she realized he had been right in warning her to use caution. But she didn't want Mario to get away with murder, and she was determined to make him pay. It had nothing to do with the bond money, although with a million-dollar bond on Mario's head, ten percent wasn't a bad day's wages. Even though she'd been tracking him for months to be ready in the event that he skipped his court date.

The opportunity lost for the moment, she'd have to pick up his trail later. After buying a wreath of pink, peach, cream, and lavender blossoms at the floral shop down the street, she drove to the hiking trail where her mother had been murdered, intending to pay her respects like she did once a week, no matter what else was going on with her life.

Although the conversation she was going to have with her mother today wasn't her usual kind.

She still felt angry that her mother had to die in the prime of her life and that she hadn't heeded Alicia's warnings. Alicia was driven with the need to avenge her mother's death and saddened by missing her so. But this time, a man she didn't even know had made her feel something different. More alive than she'd felt in years. Distracted from her mission.

Neither of her former husbands had made her feel the way Jake had with his heroics and sizzling kisses. Never had her body melted into a pool of ecstasy from the simple touch of a man's fingers at her back as he guided her outside or from the way he looked as though he wanted to eat her for dessert—her treat—after he'd so gallantly paid for her breakfast.

He was dangerous, all right. And armed!

She'd joked about it, but she'd really been flattered she could arouse him that much just by kissing him back. Of course, she told herself that she was only doing what she had to do to prove to Mario's breakfast companion that she truly did know Jake intimately and had backup if she needed it. But the way Jake had reacted showed he was playing the game for keeps—at least for an overnight tryst, she assumed. Even though she suspected he was not the kind of person who frittered away hours doing inconsequential things. Neither was she. Her mother had always said she was way too serious. But for Alicia, it had been a case of survival.

Still, after her two husbands and a number of no-account boyfriends, for the first time ever, Alicia was really feeling something for a man—just because of the kind and interested way Jake had treated her.

Alicia parked at the trailhead, changed out of her heels, and slipped on a pair of tennis shoes. Then, with the fragrant wreath in hand, she hiked along Spruce Creek Trail to where her mother had died, the summer breeze twisting tendrils of hair around Alicia's cheek and the sweet scent of pine drifting to her.

As she often did on the hike, Alicia thought about her mother, Missy Greiston, taking this very path as she started the trek to the Upper and Lower Mohawk Lakes to meet her lover at Continental Falls. Alicia had been there before and loved seeing the crystal water cascade in a foaming rush diagonally down a wildflower-blanketed hillside with alpine woods all around and abandoned mining cabins scattered over the area. But her mother had never made it that day. The macabre truth was that Tony Thomas, her mother's lover, had been left for dead long before Missy would have reached his location.

Alicia thought about the times she and her mother had gone skiing on the mountain together—intermediate blue trails, not black-diamond expert runs for them, unless they skied onto them by accident. And they had done that a few times. They had laughed as they tried to make their way down the steep trails, taking one difficult mogul at a time. Stopping, skiing to the next one, and hoping they'd make it to the bottom without breaking their necks. Vowing never again to get on another expert slope. Until they made the same mistake later on a different black-diamond expert slope.

Alicia swallowed hard, hating that she still missed her mother so much and wishing that her mother had listened to her, believed her when Alicia had told her she thought the man her mother had been dating might be a mobster and dangerous to associate with.

She soon stood in the thick-forested area where hikers had found Missy's body and notified police. Despite it having been months earlier, Alicia still felt as though the murder had taken place only yesterday. She took a deep breath, having to make a confession to her mother. One she really didn't want to make.

"Momma," she said in a hush, crouching to place the flowers beneath a tree, "I've tracked down the family that killed you. Mario Constantino was the one who ordered the hit. Danny Massaro was the man who pulled the trigger. The judge set them free while awaiting trial, so they can eat in fancy restaurants, drink their fancy drinks, and have their fancy women."

More strands of hair pulled loose from Alicia's bun, flipping across her eyes. She snagged them and then slipped them behind her ear.

"But the one, Danny Massaro? He's already skipped his trial, so as soon as I can manage, I'm turning him in to the police. Once Mario misses his trial date, I'll rearrest him too. I swore to you…" Alicia swallowed hard. "I swore to you I'd make them pay."

A tear and then another slid down her cheek, and she hastily brushed them away. "I've been…" She wiped away a couple more tears. "I've been missing you something awful. Everything reminds me of you—the little tea shop on Main Street that we used to eat at, even that Victorian restaurant, Victoriana, across the street from the art gallery." Her throat felt clogged with tears.

"I–I followed Mario into that restaurant this morning. *Our restaurant.* The *bastard*," she said softly. "But I met someone else there today. And…well, it made me think of something other than revenge for a change."

That made her feel guilty. How could she think about a man as beguiling as Jake Silver and how nice it would be to date someone like him when she had a promise to fulfill?

She didn't say anything for a while as she looked up at the wisp of clouds dotting the blue sky. She thought about how this was just like the kind of day she used to enjoy on nature walks with her mother and how her meeting with Jake would have been a godsend if not for what Mario and Danny had done to her mother.

"I'm not sure you'd approve of him." Alicia gave a sad little laugh. "You never really liked any of the guys I dated, and no wonder. They were all losers. But Jake, well, he seems different somehow. Dangerous in a good way." She stood and took a shaky breath. "You know what a mess I've always made of my life when it comes to guys." *Just* like her mother's relationships with men.

"I don't know what I'm trying to say. Only that Jake made me realize I wasn't totally dead like I thought I was. But it scares me. Not only because my past relationships were such disasters but also what if I fall for someone like Jake, and Mario or his thugs kill him too?"

Alicia knew they wouldn't hesitate to make her hurt even more than she did now. She folded her arms around herself and rubbed them, suddenly feeling a chill. She'd already lost her mother to these men. She didn't want them killing anyone else she felt something for.

As much as she wanted to have lunch with Jake later and see him further, she couldn't. For now, men and relationships were out of the question. Deep down, she knew that. Knew she couldn't keep their "date." That was why she'd had to slip away from him back in town. To get away from his enticing presence so she could think clearly again.

Car doors slammed near where she'd parked, and her whole body tensed with worry. Turning to look, she watched the path for some time until a dark-haired man and a blond woman—hand in hand and both wearing shorts and T-shirts—appeared, strolling along the hiking trail with their backpacks bulging. Alicia took a relieved breath.

They looked at her with odd expressions. The suit jacket and skirt and sneakers probably puzzled them until they saw the memorial wreath propped up by the tree and murmured greetings as they walked by her.

Unless they were out-of-towners, they'd probably heard about her mother's murder. Many people knew about the flowers she set out each week on the spot where her mother had been murdered. Someone always took away the spent flowers before she returned. At least, that was what she told herself. If someone was stealing her mother's flowers after Alicia left, she hoped they put them to good use.

The hiking couple had long since disappeared along the path and through the woods. Alicia was about to say her goodbyes to her mother so she could go back to town and try to catch up with Mario again when two more car doors slammed shut in the parking area. Hikers, more than likely. Still, she watched the path with apprehension, waiting for their appearance, unbuttoning her jacket in case she had to get to her gun, and hoping some of Mario's henchmen weren't coming to pay *their* last respects.

———————

Mary Clebourne identified herself as the gallery owner. She'd frowned at Jake's brusque greeting and jumped when he set the box of photographs on the desk a little too firmly.

He quickly said, "Price them however you see fit. I'd planned to meet with you earlier this morning when you were supposed to be open, but I've got another commitment right now."

She seemed to gather her wits and frowned even deeper. "We need you to sign some paperwork and—"

"I'll return later today," Jake said, heading for the door. It wasn't like him to let his imagination get away from him, but after the thug had threatened Alicia in the restaurant, Jake couldn't quit worrying about her.

"But…" the woman said.

Jake let the door swing shut on his departure as he rushed to his truck. He glanced up the street at the floral shop and noted that Alicia's car was no longer parked there. *Hell.*

With his truck in gear, he tore off down the street and jammed on his brakes in a parking spot at the floral shop. Barely shutting his vehicle's door, he stalked into the fragrant, refrigerated store where bouquets of flowers and pots of plants resting on terra-cotta tiles decorated four-tier circular shelves.

Dressed in a blouse and skirt covered in red roses, a gray-haired woman smiled in greeting, dimples appearing on her full cheeks. "May I help you, sir?"

"A woman came in here wearing a black suit, her hair dark brown, and…her name is Alicia Greiston. I need to track her down." He sounded as desperate as he felt.

The smile instantly fell from the florist's face, and a grave sadness marred her appearance. But she hesitated to say where she might think Alicia had gone.

"We met at the restaurant down the street for breakfast. Some guy was trying to strong-arm her out of the restaurant. I stopped him. Alicia and I are to meet later for lunch, but after I dropped off my photographs at the art gallery, I worried that the thug who had been bothering her might have followed her."

"A man? Oh." Her brows knit together in a deep frown. "You were at Cliffside Art Gallery?"

"Yes. You can ask Mary Clebourne. I dropped off some photographs of wildflowers just now."

The woman still hesitated, but her frown lessened some. He figured she was probably thinking that any man who photographed wildflowers couldn't be all bad.

"I need to make sure she's all right," he added.

The woman chewed on her upper lip and then said, "She bought flowers for her mother, Missy Greiston. The murder shocked everyone here in Breckenridge several months back."

"Murder?" Jake frowned, the bits and pieces he knew about Alicia and her mother swirling around in his thoughts. Why hadn't Alicia mentioned that her mother had been murdered locally? He supposed it wasn't the thing to talk about when just meeting someone. On the other hand, he suspected she hadn't wanted him to know.

"Oh my, yes. It was dreadfully awful. Mrs. Greiston had bought plants from me from time to time, whenever she and her daughter, Alicia, came to Breckenridge. They both really loved flowers." The woman cleared her throat and narrowed her eyes. "No one has pinned the crime on anyone yet."

Jake remembered what the waitress, Tami, had said. Alicia's mother had been dating a mobster. Like mother, like daughter. But had Alicia been dating a mobster? Or was that just a way for Tami to convince Jake not to get involved with Alicia?

"Alicia's at a cemetery?" he asked in a hurry.

"No. Alicia goes to the place where Missy Greiston died. It's the trailhead at Spruce Creek Trail, two miles south of town. And it has a well-marked parking area." She sketched him a map. "It's not far from here. And she just left. If you hurry, you should be able to catch her still there. Don't tell her, but...I always remove the spent flowers before she returns at the end of the week. I don't want her to see how sad the wilted wreaths look upon her return."

Jake nodded, said a quick "Thanks," and grabbed the map. He hurried out of the shop, the whole while wondering if Missy Greiston's murder had to do with Alicia following a bunch of mobsters. Hell, the woman had to have a death wish.

Maybe that wasn't so far from the truth.

Driving way over the speed limit and glad there weren't any cops or much traffic to delay him, Jake soon reached the site on the map. His thudding heart nearly quit when he saw not only Alicia's red car and a couple of others but one of the black Mercedes he was sure he'd seen parked at the restaurant. It was now sitting beside her car. And the occupant or occupants were already on the move.

Jake dashed out of his truck and sprinted up the heavily forested trail, hoping to hell he wasn't too late. Gunfire sounded, and another surge of adrenaline rushed through his veins. He had to shift. He didn't have any weapons on him, and he had no other way to protect Alicia against gun-wielding tyrants, if she was being targeted, except as a wolf. After dodging off the trail, he quickly jerked off his clothes and willed himself to shift.

With anger and frustration overwhelming him, he felt the heat already pouring into his veins grow even hotter with the shift as his body changed from a human form to his wolf body, complete with fur coat, raised hackles, and wickedly menacing teeth. He tore off after the men with a red rage filling his heart, ready to kill and praying that Alicia was still alive.

As he bounded forth, he saw one man ahead on the hiking trail, clasping his leg, writhing on the ground, and cursing a blue streak. Gun in hand, another man was trying to lift his companion. To Jake's astonishment, he noticed as a whiff of gun smoke drifted toward him that Alicia's gun was aimed at the crouching man. Her brows were furrowed and her eyes narrowed in contempt at the two men.

Jake stopped, momentarily stunned that she'd defended herself and come out on top, although the gunman could still shoot her. Jake growled low and deep, the urge to kill racing through his blood.

All three of them turned to look at him, the groaning man bleeding, eyes wide with fear, and the other gunman's eyes just as huge. The standing man was the one who had threatened Alicia in the restaurant, and his words came back to Jake: "*Just so's you know, next time, you won't get off so easy.*"

At least his *partner* didn't look like he was going to get off so easy.

Alicia's mouth had dropped open several degrees when she saw Jake in his wolf form, and her dark-chocolate eyes were now nearly black.

If she'd been in mortal danger, Jake wouldn't have hesitated to end the thugs' miserable lives. But if he did kill them, a hunt would ensue for a gray wolf who was a man-killer, and any gray wolf would be a prime suspect. Despite his noble intentions, he was sure Alicia would think he was an evil wolf from childhood tales.

The thug fired at Jake, but he had anticipated the move and dodged back into the woods. "Kill her," the injured man said through gritted teeth.

"Aim your gun in my direction, and I'll have to shoot you in a location that's a lot more fatal," Alicia warned the man threatening her with his weapon, her voice terse, her hands steady on the gun.

Jake watched from the cover of the woods, ready to come to

her rescue if she needed him, when the sound of a group of men talking and laughing and heading in Alicia's and the armed men's direction caught everyone's attention.

"Get up," the uninjured man said to the other. "Hurry, we gotta get out of here."

"Kill her," the injured man insisted.

"Another day," the other promised. He holstered his gun and then helped the wounded man to his feet as he cursed and groaned. Then they headed back the way they had come, the injured one walking with a pronounced limp as blood soaked his trouser leg.

Before the four men walking in Alicia's direction were in sight, Alicia had tucked her gun away, but she glanced warily toward the woods where Jake had taken off. He stayed hidden in the pines and continued to observe her until the hikers reached her.

When the four men saw her, they greeted her, looking her over and probably trying to figure out why two men and a woman were wearing business suits there, and one of the men appeared injured. The hikers glanced at the memorial wreath she'd laid at the foot of a tree, expressed condolences, and continued on their way, a couple of them looking over their shoulders in her direction. Her focus remained on the path in the direction of the parking area.

"She's the one whose mother was murdered in the woods," one said to the others in a low voice, but with his enhanced hearing, Jake heard.

"What about those two guys?" another asked.

"I told you I heard gunfire," the first said.

"Think she shot the guy?"

"It was hard to say, but the way he was limping and the other guy was trying to help him along the path, I'd say it was a good bet."

"Good for her."

Their conversation trailed off as they hiked on the path deeper into the woods.

Jake didn't like that Alicia was trying to put Mario Constantino and Danny Massaro behind bars on her own, that they'd gotten away with murder, and that she appeared to be all alone in the world. But getting into human affairs was one of the things his kind didn't do. That didn't stop him from wanting to do something, though, where she was concerned.

Satisfied she'd be all right until he could return to her, he raced through the woods to where he'd left his clothes, then shifted and dressed. When he was again on the hikers' trail, he stalked back with a hurried stride to Alicia's location to intercept her.

She was beautiful and sexy with the breeze tugging at her bun and more tendrils of her dark hair caressing her cheeks. Her jacket had been left open, and her silk blouse was now visible. She looked sensuously undone.

"Jake," Alicia said breathlessly as soon as she saw him. She was still standing in the same spot near the wreath of flowers, looking tense and anxious, and he assumed she was waiting until she presumed the thugs had left in their car. But as soon as she caught sight of Jake, she moved toward him, appearing glad to see him and a little shaken.

He quickened his pace, trying to keep his expression neutral. But he was angry—furious with the bastards who had threatened her and none too happy with Alicia for dismissing him when he *knew* something like this could happen. Not to mention annoyed with himself for not forcing the issue and staying with her.

His eyes trailed down her body, but she didn't appear to have been hurt. He took her hands and drew her into his arms. She trembled, and tears appeared in her eyes before she melted against him.

"Are you all right?" he asked, his voice a lot rougher than he'd intended as one arm curled around her waist and his free hand rubbed her back reassuringly.

She nodded, looked back at the wreath as if she was saying her

goodbyes to her mother, and then said with a shaky voice, "I've...
I've never shot a man before."

"He'll live," Jake said with sincere regret.

She walked with him in the direction of the parking lot. "How
did you know where to find me?"

"I watched you enter the florist shop before I dropped my work
off at the art gallery. I was worried that the man who hassled you at
the restaurant might try again." He took her hand and interlocked
his fingers with hers. Her fingers tightened over his in a welcoming
manner. "Do you live in Breckenridge?"

He didn't like the idea that she might be in danger if she lived
in the area and these thugs had easy access to her.

"No. I'm staying at a hotel for a few days. Just doing a job."

He stopped and looked down at her, his brow deeply furrowed.
"You aren't *just* doing a job."

Her chin lifted a little in defiance, her dark-brown eyes nar-
rowing. No argument there, which meant he was correct in his
assumption. He had to remind himself she wasn't a wolf. That she
didn't have a pack. That it shouldn't matter what a human female
had in mind to do.

But family took care of family. The thought kept nagging at
him—where was her family? A father? Siblings? Anyone else?
Why was she after these men all on her own? Why wasn't anyone
keeping tabs on her?

He assumed the judge had set a bail bond low enough that the
men had been able to post bail. If they had skipped their court
dates, as she assumed, she would be in danger while she trailed
them.

"Admit it. Mario and the other man you mentioned, Danny
Massaro, murdered your mother. It's a vendetta," he said quietly,
but the undercurrent of warning was there. What she was doing
was wrong, and it could get her killed.

"Not a vendetta," she said icily. "I don't plan to gun them

down like they did my mother. Just return them to jail where they belong. Permanently."

She tried to pull her hand free from his, but he wouldn't let go. With his free hand, he swept the back of his hand down her cheek with a tender caress. "All right, not a vendetta then." But he still couldn't see how she planned to safely take these men into custody.

He wasn't sure just what about her made his pulse race to such an extent, the way the heat of her hand penetrated his, the way he couldn't put her out of his mind, stirring a need to be with her and to protect her that he was having a hard time quelling. The expression on her face, though rebellious, appealed to him. Hell, everything about her did.

Her short-waisted suit jacket hung open as if she'd been ready to remove it to dress in a more casual manner. But he knew that had to do with her having easy access to her gun, although the holstered weapon was still hidden. His gaze drifted down to where the ice-white silken blouse revealed the faint outline of her bra and a hint of lace, baring the sexier side of her outfit. Round pearl-button fasteners on her blouse captured his attention, and briefly, he wanted to touch them, to poke one after another through the slivers of their buttonholes, to see the rest of her as nature had intended.

She cleared her throat, and he returned his gaze to her face. A small smile tugged at her lips, and her brows lifted in a way that said she knew exactly where his thoughts had roamed.

Although he wanted this issue between them resolved—wanted her to *promise* him she wasn't going any further with this futile effort to take down these men—when her hand rested on his shirt-covered chest, the vest now open and most of his shirt still unbuttoned because of hastily dressing, he thought she was going to push him away. Or at least try.

But her hand swept up his chest as if tentatively feeling the muscles beneath the shirt, memorizing the sensation of him, and judging his reaction, while her eyes focused on his chest as she continued to explore. Her touch left a trail of sizzling heat through the cotton shirt and a craving to touch her in the same way, except that he wanted to touch her skin to skin.

He lifted her chin and leaned down and kissed her. Potent need filled him as his mouth conquered hers, possessing and wanting, the worry that she could have come to harm still making his blood pulse hot and hard. His hands slid underneath the back of her jacket, gliding over the silky blouse while her head still tilted up to encourage his onslaught. Instantly responsive, she reacted as though she needed his comfort, his possessiveness, *him*, as she molded to his body, pressing harder against him, her hands exploring his back through the dress shirt with eagerness.

If they'd been back home in his own woods, away from civilization, free to do what they pleased, he would have liked to take her, conquer her, make love to her. It wasn't just sex that he was interested in having with Alicia either but something deeper. Although he knew he couldn't go there with her, not when she was human, and he had no intention of turning her.

With his thoughts shifting to his more primal needs, he barely registered that they were still standing on the path where hikers could come upon them at any moment. He wasn't familiar with these woods or how frequently visitors to the area might slip off the path and do some exploring on their own. Still, he wanted more, wanted her. And his baser, more primitive instinct told him she was just as willing as he was. To go with the moment, to find pleasure where they could.

But was Alicia truly as willing?

CHAPTER 4

JAKE PULLED ALICIA OFF THE HIKING TRAIL AND DEEPER INTO the woods, kissing her mouth and stroking her back while walking backward as she continued to press herself against him, pursuing him and getting caught up in the moment.

When she wrenched his shirt free from his jeans, he knew she was thinking along the same intimate lines he was. He broke free of the kiss, then slid his hand around hers and hauled her even deeper into the woods, far away from the beaten path. He was glad he'd moved her from the trail when the distant conversation of more hikers walking along it drifted to them.

Finally, he and Alicia reached a secluded enough spot in the forest, surrounded by tall, slender quaking aspens, their leaves twisting and bending in a fluttering dance to the tune of a warm, dry breeze and issuing a softly whispering rustle. He took a deep breath of the fragrance of the towering ponderosa pine trees, with their subtle vanilla-scented bark, although unless a human stood close to the tree bark, he or she probably couldn't smell it like a wolf could.

The trees creaked as a sturdy wind shook them. Pine needles rained down in a wistful shower to the forest floor, which was already coated with fallen leaves and pine needles of seasons past. The woods were dark and shady as birds flitted around on the nearby tree branches. Other than the sounds of the breeze in the trees and the twittering of the birds, the place was a perfect depiction of tranquility and beauty. Especially with Alicia in the picture.

Jake almost wished he had his camera to capture the timeless beauty. But this was all too private and personal, and he wanted to capture the image of her like this for his sake only.

He stopped and looked down at her. She gazed up at him with smoldering eyes, hot and sexy and dark with desire. He reached up, unfastened the copper clip confining her hair on top of her head, and watched with fascination as the dark-chocolate curls cascaded over her shoulders. Having imagined tons of pins confining her hair, he was glad that releasing it was this easy.

He tucked the clip into his shirt pocket, feeling as though he'd claimed one of the enchantress's treasures, forever binding her to him, as she smiled a little at the gesture. He combed his fingers through the luscious, heavy, satiny strands of hair as her fingers rested momentarily on his hips. She watched him as he luxuriated in the feel of her curls.

"Beautiful," he whispered, nuzzling his face in a handful of her curls. He breathed in the lightly perfumed scent and then leaned down to kiss her forehead with a lingering touch.

"Hmm, likewise," she murmured back, slipping her hands up the front of his shirt, her fingers brushing through his light chest hair, feeling his muscles, then sweeping across his nipples.

"Are you sure you want to—"

"Yes," she whispered, sounding nearly desperate to keep going.

He sucked in a breath, the heady feeling she created in him making him pause briefly to savor every whisper-soft touch of her roving fingertips, his body tight with anticipation. When she slipped her hands free of his shirt and began working on his buttons, he reached down and pulled her blouse free of her skirt. He'd just begun the arduous job of trying to push a round pearl button through the tiny slit of a buttonhole on her blouse when she finished unbuttoning his shirt.

She slowly peeled his shirt off his shoulders, taking the vest with it at the same time, sliding it lower until the shirt and vest rested midway down his biceps. He expected her to pull them both off, but instead, she held the shirt and vest in place, keeping him hostage as she leaned close and licked one nipple, then the other. The warm wind sweeping across his wet nipples created an arousing tingling he'd never experienced before, and he groaned with need at the sensation, wanting to do the same with Alicia. And much, much more.

More than the way her kissing and licking his nipples into ecstasy was affecting him, he was intrigued by the fact that she was controlling him, holding him hostage. No woman he had ever been with had done such a thing to him. After one last gentle pull on each nipple with her hot sensuous lips, she finally lifted her gaze to his and smiled, the skin beneath her dark, thick lashes crinkling slightly, her eyes sparkling with genuine delight. He cupped the back of her head and angled his mouth over hers, his shirt and vest still positioned in the middle of his biceps and keeping him from having a full range of motion. The confined sensation made him even harder and more desirous and Alicia more desirable.

He plunged his tongue into her mouth and tangled with her very willing tongue. Then she finally pulled his shirt and vest downward, forcing him to drop his hands away from cupping her head, their mouths still linked in a mating dance. After she yanked the shirt and vest free and deposited them on the ground, his hands went to her blouse buttons. But again, she thwarted him when she slipped her jacket off her shoulders and then tossed it on top of his shirt. His fingers returned to her buttons, finally managing to undo one, but then continued to struggle with the second one. Hell, at this rate, he'd take all day to get her out of the blouse, and he was ready to just yank a bunch of buttons off it instead.

"Here, let me do it," she said, sensing his frustration, her hands clasping his with a gentle, reassuring touch, her voice softly reaching his ears, although his lust-filled brain was having a hard time deciphering anything but the need to have her naked and in his arms.

He eagerly gave in to her suggestion and reached around her

back to locate the zipper on her skirt. But after running his hand around the back of her waistband, he couldn't locate the fastener.

"Side zipper," she said, indicating with her elbow which side as she continued to unfasten her blouse.

He noticed she was having a hard time with the buttons too. The thought occurred to him that if she were a wolf, the blouse would not have been part of her wardrobe as it would be too difficult to remove in a hurry if she needed to shift. But her skirt zipper easily parted for him, and she was soon wiggling a little as he pulled the skirt down her hips. Then she stepped out of the garment.

No slip, no hose. He stared at the pair of skimpy bikini panties she wore, the top edged in lace, and her bare shapely legs. He thought of the contrast between the business clothes she was wearing and the sensual silk and lace underneath. No matter what she wore from now on, he would always envision how sexy she was beneath the professional exterior.

She finally freed herself of the blouse and raised a brow, noticing that he was so distracted that he hadn't yet pulled off his trousers. Yeah, he was distracted all right, his gaze focused on her creamy skin, confined only in the scraps of lace—a white bra and panties—and a pair of trim leather walking shoes, also white.

Breaking free of his fascination, he quickly divested himself of most of the rest of his clothes. First went his boots, then the socks and jeans. Before he stripped out of his boxers, he crouched to untie her tennis shoes, giving her calves each a kiss while he was at it.

"Beautiful," he said again. The woman was all pleasing curves, silky skin, and alluring fragrance.

Her fingers combed through his hair while he pulled off her shoes, making his body react with ardent need. The bra and panties and his boxers were piled on top of the rest of their clothes, and he admired the fullness of her breasts and the dusky color of her aroused nipples. Dark curly hair covered her mons, and her long shapely legs caught his imagination as he considered how he would feel with them wrapped around his waist as he plunged deeply into her.

He looked up to see her taking her fill of him too. Her lingering perusal on his erection made him all the hotter for her, and he took her hands as he sat on the leafy forest floor, pulling her down on top of him in a sitting position to protect her delicate skin. Straddling him, she leaned forward to kiss him, her ripe womanly folds splayed to him, her breasts hanging down like tempting fruit.

He cupped her breasts as she kissed his mouth, her pelvis rubbing against his arousal, which was agonizingly ready for her. Slipping his fingers between them, he stroked the sweet spot between her thighs. She arched her back, her eyes closing, her lips parted as she panted with pleasure, her curls already dewy with expectation. She rested her hands on the ground as she leaned back a little more, barely breathing as he continued to stroke her.

She moved against him with urgency and desperation, soft moans of satisfaction escaping her lips. Seeing her in the dark pine shadows, opening herself to him with her knees spread wide, he thought only of giving her pleasure. When she gasped his name in a quiet, grateful manner, he slipped his fingers into her wetness, felt the climax hit, the pulsing deep inside her, and nudged himself at her entrance, waiting only long enough to see she was still agreeable.

Agreeable, hell. She took charge, centered herself over his erection, and rocked and squirmed on top of him until he was deeply entrenched inside her. He couldn't believe his fortune to have found a woman who could turn his furnace on high with just a lingering look in his direction, who could make him so completely entranced with her that he nearly forgot his wolf instincts for self-preservation at all costs.

His hands molded to her voluptuous breasts, her mouth on his, until he felt the world lift from his shoulders. Everything ceased to exist except Alicia: her body, her tongue teasing his, her fingernails flicking lightly over his nipples, and with his erection deep inside her, stroking him, tight and hot and wet, her body melding with him until they were as one.

Unable to hold off, he came into her with a burst of satisfaction. Climaxing had never felt this good. The overwhelming release sated him, making him experience a wolf's runner's high, a sense of being on top of the world, his body on fire with the feel of her snug internal muscles holding him tight. He didn't want the encounter to end ever.

He lay down on his back as she continued to sit on top of him, pushing her thick hair away from her face in a sexy way, her heartbeat rapid, her breathing quickened, every inch of her skin flushed with exertion. He could see in her eyes the question forming there. *What now? Where do we go from here?*

The thing of it was that he wanted her. *Permanently.* As a wolf shifter, the thought was lunacy. If he'd been strictly human, he would have done anything in his power to keep her, to enjoy the way she made him feel for hours, days, weeks, months. But he wasn't strictly human, and the situation was bound to get more complicated in a hurry.

She seemed to see the concern he had about them, and with as much grace as was possible as she sat astride him in all her nakedness, she climbed off him. Unable to move or to take his eyes off the wonder that she was, he watched as she slipped on her panties, hiding the dark patch of curly hair that protected her treasures, the enticing shadow still visible through the silky white fabric. White—he thought of innocence and sweetness and vulnerability. The way she'd made love to him, he thought of her wearing red—fiery and hot—rather than the innocence and sweetness of white.

She avoided looking at him now, making her the picture of vulnerability. She pulled on the lace bra, her aroused nipples straining against the cups as she reached behind her back to fasten the garment, the dusky areolas holding his gaze like two sensual beacons still visible against the white lace. She continued to avoid looking at him as if she was feeling self-conscious now that the adrenaline rush had subsided.

But she'd moved him like no one had ever done, and he couldn't think of anything else but being with her. Hell, he was already thinking about returning with her to her hotel room and having her all over again. And he knew it wouldn't be the last time he'd want her like that.

"I guess you'll be going home now." She still didn't look at him, even when speaking.

She lifted her blouse off the ground and shook off the pine needles clinging to it, her voice without inflection, as if the world hadn't rocked for her as much as it had for him, yet he knew she wasn't oblivious to what they'd just experienced. He also knew she was pulling away to avoid getting hurt.

He cursed himself for falling for a human female who intrigued him like no other. Something deeper stirred his interest. Something he couldn't pinpoint. He'd always known his mind, known the right thing to do as a *lupus garou*. Now, he was fighting any self-doubts he had that being with her was right—even though, deep down, he knew this was a big mistake.

He had never slept with a human woman after sex, often didn't have sex more than once with the same woman, and hadn't even had sex with one for the past six months. He never got involved with a human woman for more than the sexual act that mutually satisfied them both. Keeping relationships on that basis worked best for *lupus garous*.

But in Alicia's case, he wanted to take a hike with her to one of the lakes, see the falls, share her bed, wake up with her wrapped up in his arms in the morning, and make love to her all over again. He wanted to spend real quality time with her and get to know her in more than just a sexual way. And he didn't want to analyze why he was feeling that way.

Despite his better judgment, he ignored her comment, which had as much as said she thought he had just wanted her for the sex and now was leaving her behind. He tucked his arms behind his head. "I've only been to Breckenridge the one time. You might know the area better than I do. Anyplace you'd like to go? Hiking? Kayaking? Something else?"

Her eyes widened a bit as she pulled on her blouse and began buttoning it. "Are you serious?"

He thought from the tone of her voice that she might even be pleased. But her expression was still guarded. His gaze slid down her long bare legs, and again he envisioned her on her back and those shapely legs wrapped around his hips as he entered her again. He blinked, trying to get the image out of his mind.

"We could take in a movie. Drive-in preferred if they have any here in Breckenridge."

She smiled a little at the suggestion, and he swore he could see her thinking like he was—snuggling, kissing, getting hot and bothered in the back seat of his pickup, and forget whatever was playing on the silver screen.

"You *are* serious." Her expression brightened several degrees. "But the nearest drive-in is about three hours away."

In that moment, she looked innocent again, not at all as though she might imagine the lustful notions he was conjuring up. He took a deep breath. He had it bad.

It didn't seem fair to her that she didn't know what her sweet body was doing to his thoughts. Except that his body was already reacting to his lascivious ruminations.

"I had considered going back with you to your hotel and checking out your accommodations. To make sure they're safe." He suggestively waggled his brows, noting that she was having a hard time keeping her gaze focused on his, her eyes considering his physique as if she was amused he was having trouble keeping his bodily reactions under control.

And that was causing him further difficulty in keeping his mind on the idea of tackling other pursuits with her.

She smiled wryly at that. "Mm-hmm."

"I'm serious. I'm game for anything else you'd like to do. And we're still having lunch at the steak place later this afternoon—on me."

"All right," she said softly and tossed his boxers to him.

He caught them midair and grinned, the utterly wicked gleam in his eye saying he wanted her again. "You keep looking at me the way you do, and we'll be here all day *and* night." He gave her a lustful wink that said he was game.

Caught in the act of ogling him way too much, Alicia felt her face heat, and she smiled at Jake, although she hadn't thought he had noticed her studious appraisal of his sinful body since he was so busy admiring hers. She didn't recall either of her husbands caring anything about what she looked like after she'd been with them for a while, just as long as she removed her clothes quickly and was ready for them to sate their needs in record time. They had been drunk half the time when she was married to them and just wanted to get the deed done before they passed out.

But with Jake, it was so different. So right.

Trying to get her mind off his hunky body and her embarrassment at getting caught perusing him to such a degree, she leaned down to get her skirt. She figured that women were probably always taken in by his arresting looks and he was oblivious to it.

But she could kick herself for agreeing to do anything further with him when she should have been fighting this rabid attraction they had for each other all along. He was so hot. No one she had ever dated had been as sexy or funny or protective as Jake. She'd thought he wouldn't have been as good "in bed" as he was, that maybe having a fling would make her realize how he was just like her ex-husbands, neither of whom had made the effort to pleasure her.

She'd thought sex was about the man having all the fun. Not with Jake. Her needs, her arousal came before his own. For the first time ever, she'd really climaxed! She hadn't faked it. Hadn't needed to. She could still envision Jake's fingers entering her, as if he was ensuring she truly had reached the pinnacle before he found release in her. She couldn't believe he had done that and thought the world of him for it.

Yet something was holding him back now. A former relationship gone bad, maybe? A man who could have fun for a little while, but commitment wasn't part of his psyche?

It shouldn't have mattered. She shouldn't have even gone this far with him. But during the three years since her last divorce, she'd avoided men like the plague. Until she had seen Jake and been drawn to him, probably because he had been intrigued with her from the start and then definitely because of him coming to rescue her in the restaurant. And then coming for her here to protect her if she needed protecting. She'd never known any man to stick his neck out for her. Not her fly-by-night boyfriends or her two ex-husbands either.

She blamed her first marital misstep on her and her husband's youth and wanting to get away from her mother and the loser her mother had picked up at the time. The second marital mistake was one of those proverbial on-the-rebound blunders. Both marriages had been over in a flash since she'd married in Texas and they'd been army guys. Quickie divorces were the thing. Neither of the guys were hero types like she thought a man in uniform should be. Oh sure, many were. But with her luck with men, she'd picked up two who were anything but. Carousing, drinking, all-around losers. She'd attributed it to looking for love in all the wrong places.

She took a deep breath and zipped up her skirt. Before she could slip on her tennis shoes, Jake was standing before her, wearing only his jeans, his chest deliciously bare, his puckered nipples enticing her all over again. He had her tennis shoes in hand and a silly smirk on his face. He leaned over and kissed her cheek, then crouched in front of her. With her hands on his shoulders to steady herself, she treasured the sensation as he brushed off one of the soles of her feet with the soft dusting of his dress shirt, then slipped her shoe on. Then with equally tender reverence, he did the same with the other. She felt like Cinderella. And cherished.

Only in this case, she wouldn't turn into a penniless scullery maid who vied to go to the ball and meet the prince before midnight. Instead, she'd go back to being a bounty hunter who was bound to get her prince killed just by knowing him. That thought continued to nag at her as she tried to think of a way out of this. But she didn't want out. *Damn it.* She wanted him. Like she'd never wanted anyone in her life. She chastised herself again. This was insane.

After he tied her shoes, he rose and tilted her chin up to give her a light kiss on the lips, his eyes studying hers as if he was trying to see into her soul. Then he took a deep breath, slid his fingers down her cheek and her throat, swept them across a breast and the nipple, and then dropped his hand away.

He wanted her again, she thought. But not here. In her hotel room. And despite her misgivings, she felt the same way about him.

Then he left her to tug on his boots. She felt she should return the favor by brushing off his feet with tenderness, but he was already wearing his socks and quickly pulled on his boots. She reached for her gun in its holster and slipped it on, and then her suit jacket.

She considered what they could do together that might be fairly reasonable and keep them from interacting with the thugs for the time being. She needed a solution that would allow her to spend more time with Jake without putting him danger. Then at some point, she'd slip away from him and do what she'd come here to do in the first place. Locate Danny Massaro and arrest him, then turn him in for the bounty and forget her unreasonable interest in getting to know Jake better. Then if Mario didn't show up for trial, she'd arrest him too.

With that thought in mind, she watched Jake pull on his shirt, hiding his beautiful chest, and asked, "If you're truly game, how about ice-skating?"

"Ice-skating?" The arch in Jake's brows and in the tone of his voice made it sound as though ice-skating *wasn't* a choice he would have ever considered making.

Alicia didn't know what to think of him. One minute, he was acting like he couldn't get enough of her, and the next, she could feel him pulling away. Yet his words didn't fit his actions, as if he was fighting his own feelings.

Well, as she'd told her mother, men and relationships never worked out well for either of them. And certainly with Alicia's plans to return Mario and Danny to prison, starting a relationship could be a deadly business for the unsuspecting guy. She couldn't do that to Jake. She sighed and pushed her hair behind her ears.

After he tucked in his shirt, then tugged on his vest, he walked over and put his hands on her shoulders, his thumbs rubbing them and heating her body all over again. A small quiver of need started tingling in her breasts, making them swell, and then moved lower in her belly and even lower between her legs.

He kissed her lips gently but with real meaning. It was the kind of kiss that meant she wasn't getting rid of him anytime soon.

So much for ice-skating deterring him.

Although she still felt he was sending mixed messages. Either he was the master of deception, or he really was fighting with himself over making something more of their relationship. While he was pulling away from her, she was all set to keep this from going too far. But how could she push him away when he kissed her like he loved every inch of her and wanted her for keeps? And when she was afflicted with the same damn desire?

Some part of her told her she deserved a chance at real love, at real happiness. That she couldn't screw this up if it was meant to be. But the sensible part of her said she could lose him to violence, and there was no way in hell she was losing someone else she cared about like that.

"I've never ice-skated before. So you'll have to teach me how to do it. And I'll try not to embarrass you too much," Jake finally said, his thumbs still doing a sensual number on her shoulders.

Genuinely surprised he'd be game, she laughed a little. She thought of him as cool and collected, never ruffled. The notion of him falling on the ice had never crossed her mind. But again, she figured that ice-skating would be one activity where the bad guys wouldn't bother with them. So Jake would be safe, she was certain.

"I'll try to help you. But you can hold on to the railing if you need to. That's what many of the beginners do."

He shook his head. "Where you go, I go."

"Even if I'm doing figure eights?"

He grinned at that. "I think I'll opt for staying in the upright position and watching."

———————

By spreading their feet on ice and with the fur that protected their pads, wolves were very adept at maneuvering on ice. But as a human, Jake had never ice-skated, and if Alicia hadn't suggested it, he most likely never would have. They agreed to drop by her hotel room so she could change clothes. A business suit on ice wouldn't work out.

He hadn't planned on doing anything but waiting for her to

change clothes while he called his brother, Darien, to let him know he'd be a little later arriving home than expected. But the hotel room had one large bed and a bathroom, and Jake's eyes were riveted on that king-sized bed as if it were the most functionally beautiful piece of furniture in the world. Alicia had slipped out of her suit jacket and gun with holster, hanging them over the back of a desk chair, and pushed off her walking shoes. She entered the bathroom to clean up, shutting the door behind her.

The shower turned on, and he was still thinking about that bed and what he and Alicia could do in it together when his cell phone rang. He pulled it out of his pocket, saw the caller was his brother, and shook his head. Jake should have called him first.

"Yeah, Darien?"

"Lelandi wanted me to check on you since you said you'd be home right after you dropped off the photographs, and you're an hour late. Since you're never late, she was worried. If it were me, I wouldn't have been concerned. But you know how she's been recently, what with the babies coming so soon. Having any trouble?"

"The art gallery didn't open on time when I first arrived. But other than that, I'm staying longer to sightsee." He had no intention of telling his older brother he was smitten with a human woman and intended to stay with her through the night at least, hoping he could convince her to give up her quest and find some other scumbag to take down—one who was a lot less dangerous. And then he'd give her up before he got much more entangled with her. "I'll be home...tomorrow, sometime."

"Tomorrow," Darien said, sounding suspicious.

"Yeah, I'll call you when I'm on my way."

"Anything wrong?" Darien's tone was more worried now.

"No."

"You...don't...sightsee *ever*, Jake. What's up?"

That was the problem with having an older brother who was

the pack leader and who knew Jake too well. "Nothing's up. I needed a bit of a vacation."

"A vacation."

Jake supposed that sounded rather weird to his brother since vacations were not part of Jake's usual routine. "I'll be home soon. All right, Darien?" This time, his voice said he wasn't saying anything further, so give it a rest.

A significant pause followed, and Jake was fairly sure Darien was considering whether to pry further—and give some of his brotherly advice—or just leave it be. Then Darien said, "Is that a shower running in the background?"

Damn their wolf hearing. Jake looked back at the closed door to the bathroom, hearing the spray from the shower hitting the tub in a rush. He should have walked outside the room to take the call, but he hadn't been thinking. Not while he'd been staring at that inviting bed.

"Yeah." Jake didn't say anything more than that. Only one reason a shower would be running and he wasn't in it. Someone else was.

Another very long pause followed. Then Darien finally conceded. "All right." He tried to sound gruff, but Jake could hear the hint of a smile in his brother's voice. "Call us when you're on your way."

"Will do." Jake turned off his phone and shoved it into his pocket, annoyed with himself for getting caught in the act. Darien was sure to tell his mate, and Lelandi was sure to attempt her matchmaking with Jake again.

But with Alicia being human...that wasn't happening.

Jake shook his head, irritated with himself again, but then the shower shut off and his gaze flew to the bathroom door as he imagined a soaking-wet Alicia climbing out of the tub and into his arms.

CHAPTER 5

DARIEN PULLED LELANDI INTO HIS ARMS IN THE GREAT ROOM of his home, her belly seemingly getting bigger by the second the way the triplets were growing. He kissed her forehead and rubbed her back as she looked up at him.

"Jake's all right, isn't he?" Lelandi asked as Darien led her from the great room toward the stairs.

She was always worried about Darien, and she worried about his two brothers. He wondered how they had managed to survive before she came into their lives the previous fall. He smiled down at her. "He's staying through the night and will let us know when he's on his way home."

Her lips parted in surprise.

Darien shrugged. "He's taking some vacation time. Then he's going to do a little sightseeing."

Eyes huge, she stared at him. "*Jake?* Your brother Jake?"

Darien chuckled. "Yeah." He tugged on a red curl. "Do you want me to give you another back rub?"

"I don't want you to get tired of giving them to me."

He snorted and led her up the stairs to their bedroom. "You're carrying our future in there," he said, running his hand gently over her expanding belly. "Anything I can do to make you feel more comfortable until the babies come and beyond, I'll do. You're the one who's making all the sacrifices, after all."

When they reached the room, he shut the door, then helped her out of her stretchy shirt. She rested her hands on his shoulders as he removed her jeans and then her undergarments.

"Have I told you how beautiful you are?" he asked as he helped her lie down on her side, then tucked the pregnancy pillow under her belly and between her legs to take the pressure off her back.

He poured some cream onto his hands and warmed it between them before he began to massage her back.

"Hmm, Darien, you've said many times how beautiful I am, although I feel like a beached whale." She sighed. "What is Jake really doing? Hmm, oh, that feels so good, honey. A little lower if you don't mind. Yes, to the right… Wait, to the left… Yes, there."

He massaged her lower back and felt the tension ease in her muscles as she continued to purr.

"He was with a woman, I'd venture to guess."

Her eyes wide, Lelandi looked over her shoulder at Darien. "A woman? Are you sure?"

He chuckled. "Well, the shower was running, and he wasn't in it. The fact that he's sightseeing when he never does sure sounds to me like he's holed up in a hotel room with a woman."

Lelandi turned her head back to the pillow and didn't say anything as Darien continued to massage her back. Finally, she said, "He never sees a woman socially beyond a strictly mutual sexual encounter because of what we are. If he's sightseeing with her, does it mean she's one of us?"

"We won't know until he's ready to tell us. But if she's not one of us, I'm sure he just intends to stay with her tonight and return after that." He had no intention of second-guessing the situation.

Lelandi was quiet. Darien knew her matchmaking mind was at it again.

"What about that woman…the one you said called here looking for Jake, but he hadn't given her his number. Would it be her, do you think?"

"Sherry Slate, the lawyer? Jake told me if he had wanted her to have his number, he would have given her his private one. She must have done some research to come up with my name and number in an attempt to get ahold of him. He told me she was a nice woman but not his type."

"So who was she then?"

"She's a partner in a law firm in Denver. She met Jake at that art gallery in Denver where he dropped off some of his photographs. If you remember, he was late coming home that time too."

"No one told me that was the reason. I assumed he got hung up in Denver traffic or something."

Darien shrugged. "There was nothing to it, so no need to discuss it with anyone. She was a frequent purchaser at the art gallery. Modern art, though. Not the kind of work Jake does."

"Hmm," Lelandi said with speculation.

"I really doubt it's the lawyer. It may be just a fling with a human, Lelandi. I wouldn't make anything of it." He began rubbing her shoulders, kneading out the tension.

"He hasn't been with a woman in a very long time, you told me. And he never stays with one overnight. It sounds to me that she might be a *lupus garou*." Lelandi smiled and snuggled tighter against her pillow. "If he's found his mate, then I only have to work on Tom."

Smiling, Darien shook his head. "Tom's bound and determined to wait for his dream mate. After I found you, he said he wanted to find a woman like that."

"Well, if he doesn't find one that way, I'll have to help him along. Is Jake bringing the woman he's with home to us soon?"

"I don't know anything more than I've told you. And even that's circumstantial. He might have just been getting ready to take his own shower."

She frowned at Darien, looking as though she was annoyed he'd ruin her hopeful news. "But...?"

"Why would he be staying at a hotel in the first place? When I asked him about the shower running, he acknowledged it was but wouldn't say anything further. If he'd been getting ready to take a shower, he would have hurried to end the conversation. But he wasn't. As if he was waiting for someone to get out first."

He massaged some more as Lelandi took a deep breath. "Why wasn't he in the shower with her then?"

Darien chuckled. "How would I know?"

"Hmm, well, it sounds to me as if he's working his way up to things…which makes it sound like she's a *lupus garou*. If she were human, he'd just get on with business and be out of there."

"Maybe," Darien said.

She ignored him. "He didn't even want to go to Breckenridge. Guess he's changed his mind now. I wonder who she is."

Poor Jake. If Lelandi had anything to do with it, she'd have him mated to the woman before he knew what hit him.

The shower curtain slid aside and Jake's attention remained focused on the closed bathroom door. He envisioned Alicia's silky skin covered in water droplets and licking every one of them off.

Before he could give much more thought to the matter, she opened the door to the bathroom, letting the steam out. Dressed only in a skimpy bath towel, she stood in the doorway for a moment looking at him and seeming a little hesitant.

"Is something the matter?" he asked, frowning.

She twisted her mouth a little and shook her head. "I forgot to get a change of clothes." Her brows elevated a bit when his eyes shifted from her body to her face. But still she didn't move.

Wrapped in the towel, she was beautiful. Her dark hair was dry except for the ends that were dripping wet. The towel was so short that it was more like a big hand towel than a bath towel, unless it was for kid-sized individuals. The fabric had little body, and even less when it was damp.

Clutching the towel in front of her, she took a deep breath and moved toward him. He was frozen in place, wondering what she had in mind. Hoping she wanted to join him in the bed, which was way too big for just one person.

She paused in front of him and said, "My bag is behind you."

He didn't move. He couldn't. Stray water droplets clung to her breastbone, a couple cascading down her throat. He glanced lower and saw some trailing down her thighs. With a purely primal instinct, he rested his hands on her bare shoulders and licked the droplets off her throat. She sighed and acquiesced, tilting her head back and baring her throat to him.

If she'd been a wolf, it would have been the equivalent of showing how much she trusted him. She appeared to revel in the feel of his tongue on her skin, her free hand grasping his shoulder as if to keep her balance. Then he worked his way down to her breastbone, capturing all the sweet drops kissing her skin, and she released a soft moan, her fingers gripping him harder, as if she was about to sink into the carpeted floor.

But he hadn't finished and crouched at her legs, lapping up the sweet droplets clinging to her thighs. She chuckled, the sound throaty, sensual, aroused. "Tickles," she said with a hushed voice.

When he stood, he saw her nipples pressed against the thin, barely there towel and looking aroused and needy. He preferred thick and luxurious towels when he showered and dried, but on Alicia, thin and barely there was perfect.

His hand cupped a towel-covered breast as his mouth captured hers, moving her against the wall and pinning her there. As she moaned into his mouth, his desire for her ratcheted up several notches. He molded his hand to her breast, the terry cloth rough against her soft mound of flesh, the nipple pressing against the fabric. His thumb began stroking the taut nub through the terry cloth.

"Hmm, Alicia," he whispered against her lips, drugged by the feel of her, by the whisper of her heated breath against his mouth, by the sound of her heart pounding as hard as his. She clutched at the towel until he deepened the kiss, and then her hands went around his neck and the towel slid forgotten to the floor.

Scooping her up, he carried her to the bed, yanked away the cover, and deposited her. He shucked off his clothes as she watched him, her gaze lowering to his rigid arousal. She made him hard with a touch, a glance, a whisper of a kiss. No woman had ever affected him the way she did.

When he was naked, he joined her in bed, his hand caressing her breast, his eyes looking into hers—dark, rich chocolate and full of desire.

He bent his head and kissed her parted lips while her tongue touched his, teasing and penetrating his mouth, and he sucked on her tongue, smiling when she moaned in capitulation.

His hand massaged the supple mound of her breast, enjoying her softness compared to his hardness. He leaned over and licked her nipple, mouthed it, and tugged gently on it the way she had done his. But his fingers soon swept down her soft belly and lower until he found her wet curls and the place at the apex of her thighs already swollen and moist with eagerness. She parted her legs, combing her fingers through his hair as he plied her with strokes between her legs meant to bring her to joyful climax.

Her pelvis arched against his stroking fingers as she lightly moaned with pleasure, pushing him to deepen his movements while he watched the expression on her face—lost in bliss, her tongue moistening her lips, her eyes heavily lidded with lust. He loved the way she writhed under his ministrations. Loved bringing her to climax and seeing her expression of elation. Wanted to do it again and again.

———————————

Alicia hadn't meant to allow this to happen, hence the hesitation when she'd stepped out of the bathroom to get her skating skirt out of her bag but found Jake standing in front of it. Dressed as she was in the skimpy towel and the way he was eyeing her with interest, she was certain he wasn't going to let her get away with just pulling a handful of clothes from her suitcase. Not that she wanted to discourage him. That was part of the problem.

She didn't have an ounce of willpower when it came to wanting him. But she imagined that if she had managed to get dressed, he would have wanted to undress her once he saw her in the skimpy ice-skating outfit, and they'd be right where they were now.

His fingers stroking her caused a flare of white-hot heat to erupt deep inside her. With her nipples tingling with delicious feminine appeal and her freshly showered skin even more sensitive to his every touch, she arched against him like a feral animal, craving more and faster and harder and deeper. She'd never felt as wild or uninhibited as she did with him. She wasn't sure why, but at the moment, she didn't care. She just wanted to enjoy the fiercely intense sensations of pleasure that he made her feel.

Her bucking against him encouraged him to stroke and push his fingers deep inside her chasm, to explore and rub and send her hurtling to the edge of the earth and beyond. She was so close to climaxing, the sweet ecstasy just within reach, and then the explosion came, the rapture of his touch pushing her over the edge into a starry universe of pleasure. Her insides quaked with completion as she cried out softly, her hands clasping his waist, then moving over his hips and his buttocks, and sweeping up his back.

With that, he spread her knees farther apart and plunged deeply into her, hard and fully, with all control cast aside. He was thick and heavy and stretched her nicely, diving so deeply that she thought he reached places no one ever had been before. He felt so good with his muscular body working her, enjoying her as she thrilled in the feel of him, his lightly haired chest brushing against her nipples and making them even more sensitive to his softly abrasive touch.

He continued to thrust, his hands raking through her hair, kneading her breasts, and cupping her face, his mouth on hers, then her jaw, her throat, her breasts. Every inch of her felt cherished beneath Jake's sexy onslaught—from the way he licked her nipples, kissed them, and blew his hot breath on them, to how he smiled when she moaned and kissed her throat as his hand went back to massaging a breast.

Straddling him in the throes of passion in the woods had been an experience Alicia never would have thought she'd feel. And she hadn't thought she'd ever feel that way again. But with Jake, every time was different, exciting, and fulfilling, and she couldn't believe anyone would find her as appealing or as sexually stimulating as he seemed to find her. That made her feel special, although she had to remind herself their relationship was so new that, in a few days, it would surely be just like the way her ex-husbands had treated her. The newness worn off. The need to fulfill her desires secondary to fulfilling his own.

She shoved aside her silly self-doubt, reminding herself that this was all it would be, some really great sex with a really great man, and then he'd move on and she would, too, and that would be the end of anything between them.

But as soon as he thrust inside her, all her thoughts were swept aside as she explored every inch that her greedy fingers could reach, from sweeping them over his firm butt and fondling him to enjoying his hard-working muscles rippling under her touch and the silky feel of his skin. Taking in a deep breath, she savored his fragrance—musky male and pine breeze. She scraped her fingernails lightly over his buttocks and up his back, soliciting a low growl of ecstasy from him that made her smile.

He reached down and pulled her legs toward him so that her knees were bent, and he wrapped his arms around them, tightening them against his body as he deepened his thrusts. His pelvis rubbed against hers, her heart drumming with rapture as she arched against him, attempting to satisfy the need to soar all the way to the sun suspended in the late-morning sky.

And then she climaxed with much too loud a groan of complete blissfulness just as he came too. He kissed her mouth again before withdrawing and moving off to lie beside her. His fingers captured a handful of her hair that he brought to his lips and kissed, his eyes and lips smiling at her with a sense of smug satisfaction. She shook her head. She had known that if she got anywhere near her suitcase wearing that skimpy towel, this was exactly where she'd end up.

His arm captured her and rested there, his face nuzzled against her cheek as he closed his eyes. She realized that, at least for now, they weren't going ice-skating or anywhere else. She rolled onto her side like she was used to sleeping, although taking midday naps wasn't her usual thing. But having conducted surveillance on Mario late into the night and then early this morning and having made love to Jake twice today, she felt blissfully tired.

She thought Jake had fallen asleep, but he pulled her into his arms, spooning her with his thighs and chest and with his arms around her body in a possessive way, claiming her as his own for the moment, his face nuzzled against the back of her head. His heated breath caressed her ear, and she sighed. He was sexy and hot...very hot and, for the moment, all hers.

She didn't even want to think about saying goodbye. Yet all along, she knew that was where this was headed.

———

"You said you didn't want the bitch dead," Danny Massaro, Mario Constantino's cousin, muttered to him as Mario sat on his leather couch reading the morning paper, irritated as hell with the two buffoons who'd botched the job. "We wouldn't have bothered trying to bring her in alive if you hadn't ordered us not to kill her. But she shot Carino on the trail," Danny insisted.

"You've told me three times already," Mario said darkly, flicking a hard look at Danny. "You both knew she was armed. That she's nothing like her mother. You should have handled it better."

Mario had two cousins. *Two.* Danny and Ferdinand Massaro. And although Danny, the younger of the two brothers, was loyal as could be, Ferdinand was the one who could be counted on to get a job done right. Too bad Mario had pissed him off. But the damned woman Ferdinand had been seeing had stolen a hell of a lot of money from Mario's Vegas casino. And no one got away with that without paying for it big-time. He had a reputation to maintain, after all. He just hadn't realized how hard Ferdinand would take it. Hell, family loyalty was supposed to take priority over some damned broad.

"Alicia's a bounty hunter now. If she catches sight of me, she can arrest me and turn me in for the reward," Danny said.

As if some woman could get the jump on Danny. When Mario didn't respond, Danny shoved his hands in his pockets, his action whenever he was stumped about what to do next. "What about the guy? Can't we kill him?"

"The artist?" Mario snorted. "Lover boy?" He shook his head. "The woman has something I want. Don't kill her. As for the guy, he'll disappear soon enough. One way or another. If he's smart, he'll leave and live another day. If he's not..." Mario shrugged and looked back at the paper, reading an article about a drunk driver who had ripped out forty feet of fence on a local ranch.

Nothing noteworthy in the area. Not since killing the Greiston woman six months ago. Or the shooting at the same location today, if anyone had been aware of it.

He really should have killed Danny and Carino after they'd botched the job of murdering Alicia's mother. Killing her right next to the trail, where hikers could find her, was more than stupid. And murdering her lover at the falls? Double the stupidity. Yeah, he'd wanted it done, but *discreetly*. Idiots.

He sighed, opened the paper to the crossword puzzle, and laid the paper down on the coffee table, then pulled a pen out of his pocket. "Has Carino gone home?"

"Tucker took him back to Denver so Doc can patch him up without the authorities getting any word of it."

Mario nodded and read: *One Across: Lupus, four letters.* He wrote: *wolf.*

"What now?" Danny asked.

Mario looked up at him. "You said the artist met with her in the woods."

Danny balled his fists in his pockets. "Yeah, she must have planned to rendezvous with him there. I saw his truck parked near her car in the lot, but I didn't see any sign of him when I brought Carino in. Later, I found both Alicia's and her lover's vehicles parked at her hotel. They were still there when you told me to meet you here."

"All right. Well, she's not going anywhere. Not when she thinks she's going to take me down for the murder of her mother. She'll come after me again. And she'll do it alone. You can leave a message from me to her ensuring that's the case." He grabbed a scrap of paper he'd been using for his daily crossword puzzles and wrote a note: *You want me, come and get me. But if lover boy is with you, consider him dead.*

He folded the note in half, wrote *Alicia Greiston, Room 101* on the top of it, and handed it to Danny. "Go buy an envelope, stick this inside with her name and room number written on the envelope, seal it, and drop it off at the front desk—but only leave it when it's busy enough that no one will notice you. Can you do that? It'd be easy enough to do when a clerk is busy with a customer. Just leave it on the counter and walk away. All right?"

"Yeah. I can do that." Danny acted annoyed that Mario had to spell it out for him as though Mario thought Danny wasn't bright enough to do the job right.

But hell, Mario had made the mistake of trusting him before. The problem was that he needed someone damn loyal, and Danny was it.

Mario glanced back at his crossword puzzle. "Go. As soon as she's following me again, grab her, and she and I will have a little talk."

He smiled darkly. This time, he'd learn what her mother might have passed along about his operation, and then—he wasn't sure. He glanced out the window at the ski slopes and felt the waxing moon stirring his blood. The mother wouldn't succumb to his needs. Maybe the daughter would do.

But he still had another problem. Danny's brother, Ferdinand, was a loose cannon. Mario needed to get rid of him as soon as he could get ahold of him. The last time Mario had attempted to have Ferdinand murdered had only made him madder...and more willing to get Mario back.

In a tangle of legs at the ice-skating rink, Alicia laughed out loud as she found herself on her butt on the ice again with Jake. His eyes were bright with laughter as he pushed her hair out of her face and grinned at her. She hadn't laughed this much in forever.

"I haven't fallen this many times in an hour on the ice since I was a little girl. And I was a *lot* lower to the ground then. But then again, I haven't had this much fun in years."

And she meant it. She had applauded every wobbly bit of success Jake had accomplished. And when they'd fallen, she'd laughed and enjoyed his good-humored responses. She wasn't the only one who was interested in Jake, though. From older teens to college-aged women, he had their undivided attention. She was certain they wished they were entangled with the hunk on the ice instead of her and laughing their heads off. She had to admit, they looked fairly risqué at times with his leg wedged between hers and her short flare skirt thrown back, exposing the panties of her leotard.

If Jake hadn't had such a difficult time staying on his feet and keeping from tripping Alicia up, she figured he would have been more hot and bothered in an intimate way by their close proximity. But he hadn't let on, and for that, she was grateful.

Two of the women watching him with hungry, desirous gazes had been bold enough to come to speak with him when he told Alicia he wanted her to demonstrate how she did the figure eight and other ice-skating maneuvers. She hadn't wanted to leave him for a second, and now she knew for certain what a mistake that could be.

Even though she had wanted to chase off the voluptuous blond and striking brunette, she concentrated on her performance and gave Jake the show of her life as if she were trying out for the Olympics while he stood propped against the railing, smiling at her with admiration. She loved him for it because no one had ever cared how she skated except for her mother and her grandmother. But this was different, seeing the look in his eyes as she skated for him—a sexual attraction, a feral, desirous look in his gaze—and his lips curving upward as if he was thinking sinful thoughts about some of her sexier moves.

When she was through with the last jump, she skated back to Jake. He pulled her into his arms, holding her tight, and gave her a kiss that could have melted the ice. It certainly warmed her from the tip of her cold nose to her cold toes, and he made her feel special all over again.

"You're beautiful, you know?" he murmured against her ear.

His two new fans gave her simpering smiles, but their smiles were designed to get his attention. He ignored them, thankfully.

Alicia smiled up at him. *He* was beautiful and fun and the best thing that had ever happened to her. "You make me feel beautiful." She leaned against him, loving the heat and hardness of his tall body but knowing they needed to skate or leave. Before they got kicked out of the rink for too much sexy cuddling. "Do you want to ice-skate some more?"

"I need to drop by the art gallery and sign some consent forms. And it's past time for lunch, if you've had enough fun and are ready to go. I'm afraid watching you skate is getting harder and harder for me." He cast her a wickedly salacious grin.

She chuckled, wanting to check out his package, but...what the heck. She glanced down at his crotch, saw the rigid bulge in his stonewashed jeans, and was ready to ease his discomfiture any way that she could.

"All right." She gave the women a smile that said, "He's mine, so hands off," and then skated slowly to the exit with him so that he could keep up with her. "You were gathering quite a fan club."

"I was the only male on the ice, and I looked a bit needy," he explained.

"You looked anything but that. I think the idea of you getting tangled up with one of them was more what they had in mind."

He laughed. "I wasn't interested in getting tangled up with anyone else, believe me."

When they reached the sitting area, she helped him off with his skates first. His hands reached up to cup her face as she crouched in front of him. "You're lovely, Alicia. A free spirit, unpretentious, charming."

Her face warming, she smiled a little shyly, not used to any man complimenting her like that. She hoped he didn't feel obligated to say such things to her. She didn't expect them, and she was a little suspicious of his motives for doing so.

"You're not used to anyone complimenting you, are you?" he asked, tilting her face up to look at him. His eyes challenged her to respond, but she couldn't. "Are you?" he asked again.

She gave a small exhalation of breath and said, "No. Once when I was in high school, some guy said he liked the way I smelled.

I had spritzed on one of my mother's perfumes before I left for school that morning. Anyway, he asked me out to have pizza, and on the way over to the pizza place, he pulled into a park and said how much he wanted me. How beautiful I was. That was right before he copped a feel and was suddenly all over me, tugging at my blouse with his other hand under my skirt. I demanded he take me home before I screamed rape."

Jake's expression hardened. "The guy was lucky I wasn't around."

She smiled at Jake. "I'm afraid a lot more would have gone on at the park if I'd been with you instead. You're sort of…addictive and hard to say no to."

He pulled her to the seat and switched places and removed her skates. "I would have meant everything I said, if it had been me with you in the car." He looked up at her. "I just hope you're not wearing a ton of bruises after all the falls that I caused." His hand caressed her calves.

His caress was gentle but oh so provocative. She shook her head. "A couple, but they'll soon fade to nothing."

He helped her from her seat, then escorted her outside, his fingers interlocked with hers as if they were a boyfriend and girlfriend on a date. She liked the sensation and would have wanted more if only her mother hadn't gotten mixed up with Mario and his thugs. Alicia was destined to play the scenario with the mobsters out to the end, no matter what.

Jake unlocked the truck doors with the push of a button. "I have to admit, seeing you do some of those spins, jumps, and landings and thinking of the figure skaters who dance together made me wish I could glide across the ice with you in my arms like ballroom dancing, only, to my way of thinking, a hell of a lot sexier."

"Hmm," she said, climbing into his truck. "That's because the women's tiny skate skirts, or the formfitting skating dresses that barely cover anything, are so revealing. And then tights or tan pantyhose look pretty—"

"Sexy." He reached over from the driver's side and stroked her thigh. "Good thing no other men were there watching you perform. I would have had to fight them off."

She laughed. "My ex-husbands thought my skating was boring. After watching me the first time, neither of them would bother. They were into ice hockey—guys beating up guys on the ice."

"They were crazy. I'd much rather watch you dancing solo as eloquently as you do or be the one making the moves with you on the ice."

Alicia gave him an appreciative smile as he started the engine. Where had Jake been when she could have used him years earlier in her life? Her life was way too messed up now.

She peered out the window on the drive back to the hotel. She kept watching for any sign of a black Mercedes, but she didn't see one. With the way Jake was glancing up at his rearview mirror or out his windows, she thought he was watching for anyone following them too.

"Late lunch next after I sign the papers at the gallery, all right?" he asked.

"Sure. I'll just change while you're gone." She looked over at him to see him glancing down at her short skirt, and she had the sneaking suspicion he wanted to do something else first. "Don't tell me you need to work up an appetite first."

He chuckled, and the sound was deep and dark and aroused. But he shook his head and ran his hand over her thigh with a gently caressing touch. She got the distinct impression it wouldn't take much for him to change his mind.

When they arrived at her hotel, Jake escorted her to her room, his hand in hers, but he seemed to be in a real hurry. As if he was afraid he'd stay and forget his business, he smiled broadly and framed her head with his hands against the outer wall beside her door instead of entering the room. "If I don't run over to the gallery now, I'm likely to get awfully distracted and wait too late, and then they'll be closed."

She smiled, brows raised, hands sliding up his chest. "Then you'd better run over there, because I think you might just be right."

And with that, he gave her one of his searing kisses that promised much more later. Desire curled in her belly, making her feel that if she hadn't been leaning against the wall, she would have melted into a puddle at his feet.

"I'll be right back. Twenty minutes, max."

She smiled and tugged at his buttons. "By the time you drive back into town, sign the papers, and return, it'll be more like forty-five. But that's fine. I'll change and lie down for a few minutes."

"If you fall asleep before I return, I'll be happy to wake you." He kissed her again and strode off before she could tug him into the room and give up on napping or anything else.

The women at the rink didn't know how really good he could be. And she liked him way too much already.

But as soon as he disappeared down the hall, she shuddered, feeling the first real inkling of fear. For as long as she could remember, she'd been the survivor of one disaster or another. And her anger after her mother's killing had kept her blood hot for revenge, so she hadn't really felt anything but a compelling urge to take her mother's murderers into custody. On the darker side, she hadn't cared whether she made it or not, as long as they paid for their crime.

Now, for the first time since her mother's death, she did care. Because of a man named Jake Silver. Because of the joy of living he'd awakened in her. Because for once in her life, she felt worthy.

And that scared her.

CHAPTER 6

ALICIA ENTERED HER HOTEL ROOM, AND HER HEART SKIPPED A beat when she saw an envelope on the blue-gray carpet where it must have been shoved underneath the door. Before she picked up the note, she considered that it might be from her informant. What if Mario and Danny were again on the move?

Her breathing suspended, she tore the envelope open and pulled out the folded note. *Alicia Greiston, Room 101* was repeated on the piece of paper, but in another man's hard-bitten scrawl. She swallowed hard and opened the piece of paper and read: *You want me, come and get me. But if lover boy is with you, consider him dead.*

Her heart felt as though its motion had been suspended midbeat.

Jake would die.

No matter how much she wanted to be with him, to live again, to enjoy life to the fullest, she'd known her meeting him had been too good to be true. He'd leave her anyway. She reminded herself of the way he'd reacted after they'd made love in the woods, as if this was a mistake.

It *was*. A grave mistake. If Jake died, it would be as though she had pulled the trigger herself. All she'd been thinking of was herself, *damn it*.

No more. She had a job to do. And Jake had to stay out of the picture.

As fast as she could, she changed into jeans and a T-shirt, tossed the rest of her clothes and cosmetics into her bags, and hurried to the lobby. There, with her heart racing, worried Jake would discover her leaving before she could disappear and guessing he wouldn't allow it, she stood at the checkout counter, trying not to tap her fingers on the polished surface as she waited for the clerk to get off the phone.

As soon as he did and she got her bill, he said, "Miss Alicia Greiston, you had a message." He passed an envelope to her, eerily like the first, with her name and room number written on top. But she thought she recognized her informant's handwriting, although she couldn't be certain because the scrawl was often disguised. With a quick thanks, she stalked toward the back door where her car was parked outside. As soon as she stowed her bags in the trunk, she drove away from Breckenridge and opened the envelope.

> *I want to take Mario down too. But if you get to him first, I'm all for it. He'll be in Denver at a condo in Cherry Creek North, listed under John Smith.*

It was the same type of encouraging, cryptic note that she'd received before, telling her that Mario and Danny were now in Breckenridge. Whoever her informant was, he had been right. She was still concerned that he might be one of Mario's men, but gut instinct told her she could trust he was not working for Mario. She also assumed he was not one of the strictly good guys or he'd identify himself. More than likely he was someone who had a vendetta of his own.

Turning the car around, she drove in the direction of Denver, two hours away, and hoped Jake wouldn't hate her too much as a damnable tear slid down her cheek. She had to draw on her anger if she was going to take Mario and Danny down. Remorse and regret would get her killed before she could accomplish her mission otherwise, and she definitely would get Jake killed if she had anything more to do with him.

Impatiently, Jake signed the paperwork at the art gallery, agreed on the pricing of the photographs, and after leaving all his contact information, headed back to Alicia's inn. He was thinking he should be noble and take her to a late lunch first, although he already wanted to make love to her again. He'd never felt that way about a woman—that being separated from her for even an hour would make him crave her all the more. He was thinking of a hike on a trail, although probably not the one where he'd found her earlier today, facing off against two more thugs. Maybe he could take her to a movie at the local theater later tonight. Or even better, find something on pay TV and order room service. Ice up a bottle of champagne. Anything she wanted to do was fine with him.

Before he'd even reached the lot where her car was parked in the back of the inn, though, he began to have a bad feeling. He wasn't sure why he was feeling so uneasy until he realized that Alicia's red car was gone.

He parked, and with his heart beating furiously, he headed for her room. He didn't have a key card and just pounded on the door. When there was no answer, he wasn't surprised. She had to have run into town for something. Even though he knew she had to be all right and was just running an errand, he couldn't help the foreboding that said something more was wrong. If he'd thought about it and not been in such a rush to get to the gallery, he would have given her his cell number. He considered using the lockpicks that he carried like most *lupus garous*, but because of the gnawing worry that something more had happened, he went to the front desk instead. There, he broke in on a conversation the clerk was having on the phone.

"Excuse me, did Alicia Greiston leave a message for me, Jake Silver?" he asked the scrawny suited man with slightly balding temples.

The clerk shot an annoyed look at him, shook his head, and then continued to talk to the person on the phone.

"Are you certain?" Jake persisted, leaning against the counter, ready to climb over it and force the clerk to answer him immediately.

The clerk said to the person on the phone, "Excuse me for a second." With his hand over the mouthpiece of the phone and a peeved look on his face, he turned his full attention to Jake. "She had a couple of messages, one delivered to her room and the other here at the counter."

"Who delivered them?"

"I wouldn't know."

Jake ground his teeth. "She could be in danger."

The man raised his brows as if he thought Jake was giving him a line.

"She's a bounty hunter tracking some real criminals. They've threatened her once already, and I had to intervene to protect her earlier in the day. I have to make sure she's not heading into danger."

The clerk looked unmoved by the comment and said nothing.

"Can I see her room? Make sure it doesn't show signs that she was coerced into leaving?"

"I'm sorry, sir. Our policy is—"

"Have someone go with me. If there's been any sign of force, you'll have to call the police. If foul play has occurred and you don't do your part to see that she was safe in a timely manner, your job could very well be on the line."

The man's steely gaze narrowed even more. But he took an annoyed breath and said to the person on the phone, "Let me have your number, and we'll get back to you." Then he scribbled the number down, said goodbye, and spoke to another clerk in an office. "I'm checking out a guest's room. I'll be right back."

"All right," a woman said.

Then the clerk escorted Jake to Alicia's room. "I waited on her when she was checking out, and she seemed in a rush. She was looking over her shoulder, but it didn't seem that anyone was with her."

"She looked anxious, though?"

"Yes. She was in a real hurry. I was on the phone at the time, but I could see she was really apprehensive. She kept looking over her shoulder as if someone might arrive at any moment and stop her." He glanced at Jake, implying he might have been the one she was trying to avoid.

The clerk opened the door to her room and led the way. Nothing was amiss. The bed was still unmade, but her bags were gone. Jake glanced around the room, looking for anything else that might give him a clue as to why she left so abruptly. While the clerk checked out the bathroom, Jake noticed a note on the dresser, saw her name and room number on it, and opened it. Someone had warned Alicia not to stay with Jake or he would die, damn the perpetrator's soul who had written the note.

"Was that something important?" the clerk asked, pointing to the paper in Jake's hand as he rejoined him.

"Yeah, the perp threatened that if she took me with her, I'd be dead. I told you this was serious."

The man's eyes widened. "Shouldn't we call the police?"

"Yeah. That's what you need to do. Tell them she's a bounty hunter trying to catch Mario Constantino and Danny Massaro, who are bail-bond jumpers. And they've made a death threat against me." He handed the clerk the slip of paper. "I'm going to look for her and see if I can catch sight of her car anywhere. It's a red Neon. Not sure of the license plate number, but you probably already have it from when she signed in."

The clerk pulled at his tie as if it was suddenly strangling him. "We would. Shouldn't you wait here until the police arrive?"

"Not if I'm going to try to locate her before she comes to harm. Here's my cell phone number. The name is Jake Silver," he reminded the clerk. "I can't wait until it's too late."

His heart beating a million miles a minute, Jake left the clerk standing in the middle of the hotel room and stalked back out of the building into the parking lot. Within seconds, Jake was driving his truck back into town. As much as he hated that Alicia had left without word for him, he figured she'd been misguided into thinking she could keep him safe. He couldn't help but admire her for worrying about him, if that was the case. But the thought of her tangling with these men on her own nearly gave him heart palpitations.

For an hour, he scoped out Breckenridge. Not finding any sign of Alicia's vehicle, he went back to the street where he was supposed to eat lunch with her. Three restaurants offered steak platters on Main Street, but none of the places was specifically called a steak restaurant, and he cursed himself for not learning the actual name. After repeatedly checking all three restaurants while looking for her, Jake finally stood in the middle of the sidewalk, hoping she'd still make their engagement but knowing in his gut she wouldn't.

After another hour of waiting and fuming with himself for not having kept her with him when he went to the gallery, he couldn't quit worrying that she had followed the men she was tailing and was going to get herself killed, if she hadn't already.

He drove all over Breckenridge, looking for her car into the night, searching through lodges, rental-condo parking lots, and B and Bs. Anywhere that she might have stayed so she could continue to trail Mario.

He remained vigilant, searching all the next morning, returning to the inn and then the restaurant where he'd met her, and continuing to look for her until late that afternoon. Not finding any sign of her, he left word at the art gallery to call him if she dropped by looking to reconnect. Then hating to leave Breckenridge, dejected and miserable, fearing for her safety but not knowing what else to do, he headed for home.

He kept thinking about the trouble she might have gotten into with the men on whom she'd been conducting surveillance.

And how he could have protected her—and hadn't.

Alicia had checked into a hotel in Denver and then searched for Mario's trail, finally finding it but not where her informant had said he was. The bloodred moon dominated the black night like the harbinger of death as Alicia stalked her prey. Mario Constantino was headed for the front steps of a redbrick town house. Just as she'd suspected, he hadn't bothered to show up for his court date.

She'd lost track of Danny Massaro, so Mario was the first one she planned to arrest. And she was ready with the arrest warrant and firepower—pepper spray, a stun gun, and her pistol. She hadn't told Jake that she had earned a black belt in jujitsu, but he probably would have dismissed that training as not enough either. And leaving the scene promptly was better than tangling with an armed assailant. But she was confident she could do this.

Every minute she'd been driving to Denver from Breckenridge, she'd thought about Jake Silver and felt bad about giving him, her hero, the slip. About him worrying about her. She should have left word that she had to leave to let him know she was all right.

But having no boyfriend meant having no *dead* boyfriend. And no matter how much she wanted to see more of him, no matter how much she had wanted what she was sure he would have continued to offer her, she couldn't with a clear conscious allow him to get involved. Not after what had happened to her mother. These men meant business. They were ruthless.

She kept waffling about sending Jake word she was all right, but she knew that would involve lying to him, telling him she didn't want to see him further. She thought he might not believe her, considering it was a lie, and might want to protect her and stop her from doing this. But she had to finish the job. It was the right thing to do—not only for her mother's memory but for those Mario and his gang might hurt in the future.

Alicia took a deep breath of the cool night air, trying to fortify her ragged nerves as she walked silently toward the town house.

On the other hand, she consoled herself with the notion that Jake was probably glad to be rid of her. Or even might have someone else in his life back home. The thought was a sour reminder that they had no future.

For now, this was her life. And as a loner, she was fine with it. She had no intention of risking anyone else's life, but she owed it to her mom to keep her promise and put Mario and Danny behind bars for good.

Leaves crunched softly underfoot as she kept her distance, certain Mario didn't hear her following him, as far away as she was, hidden in the shadows and guided by the mellow brass streetlamps lighting the way. But she should have known it was too easy tracking down the bastard, who had a rap sheet as long as she was tall. Why the judge had set bail for him, she still couldn't fathom. Unless he had bribed the judge.

Maybe this was a wake-up call. She was used to getting her man, or woman, with the least amount of collateral damage—mainly because they usually weren't all that intelligent and often were way too predictable. The job often depended on wit over brawn to subdue a perp. A little psychology could go a long way.

But this time, it felt wrong. This was just too easy, as if she had been led into a trap.

The hair at the nape of her neck and on her arms stood on end as she watched Mario knock on the door of a brick town house. It silently opened to him. She couldn't see anyone inside, as if it were one of those nightmarish haunted houses with automatically opening ghostly doors that drew the unwilling victim inside. He entered, then the door shut with a clunk.

Damn, he was supposed to have been alone.

The lamplight nearest her sputtered ominously and then flickered out, plunging her into darkness. Immediately, the setting seemed perfect for a blood-seeking vampire moving silently through the night beneath the hunter's moon. Again, her thoughts shifted to her mother and how she'd introduced Alicia to her love of vampires when Alicia had been a teen and they'd watched handsome and sexy Count Dracula sweep the heroine off her feet in a college stage play. Alicia had wished she was the heroine the count intended to seduce.

Snapping herself out of her memories, she saw something move in her peripheral vision. A shadow glided quickly toward her from a drive-through alley between that town house and the next. A vampire, her brain registered; only of course it wasn't. He was a man and a genuine threat.

Pepper spray already in hand, she whirled to spray him in the face, but footfalls raced directly behind her before she realized two of them were coming at her from different locations. Before she could whip around and protect herself, a sharp pain to the back of her head registered.

She felt herself falling, the can of spray slipping from nerveless fingers, heard the can clunk as it struck the stone walk, felt her body hit the unforgiving walk, and saw the red, red moon watching her as if saying it had warned her about the night. And she should have taken heed. The last thought she had was maybe it was time to bury her pain and find a new occupation.

Then the red moon faded to black.

———

"Alicia Greiston," a husky male voice said, penetrating the darkness, but the pain in her head splintered every thought she tried to conjure up.

A hand roughly shook her shoulder. She wanted to open her eyes and see where she was, instantly remembering her mission—take Mario Constantino into custody—and her failure to do so. She'd been attacked from behind.

Was this man one of his henchmen? This really wasn't good.

"I know you're awake." His voice hinted at dark amusement. The smell of cigarette smoke wafted in the air, and a sickly sweet cologne penetrated her airspace.

Then he drew closer, and she realized she was lying on a soft mattress, and he was pressing his body against her side as he leaned over her. His fingers worked clumsily on the buttons on her jacket. Oh God, what did he plan to do to her? Rape her? Torture her? Kill her? Maybe all three. But her head hurt so badly she couldn't gather the wits to respond in any way.

He jerked the sleeves down her arms, then removed her gun holster, the gun still in it. Her head was pounding so hard that she only had a tenuous grip on remaining conscious. Her mind was slipping away into grayness until his fingers began working on her blouse buttons, which instantly gave her more clarity.

Intent on fighting him despite the way her head was splintering with pain, she opened her eyes and saw only blackness. How could he tell what he was doing in the dark? She couldn't even see his face.

She grabbed his wrists—big, rawboned, powerful. He laughed, the sound husky and eerie.

"I knew you were awake." He easily shook free of her hold, seized her wrists, and held them above her head. "We can do this easily or we can do this the hard way. Either suits me."

All the moisture in her mouth evaporated. She had to fight him, but not yet. When she could, she would knee him in the groin, find her gun, and—

"I admire you, Alicia. Not just anyone could have tracked Mario down like you did with the scant clues I was able to give you. He would have killed you if you'd approached him, though. You have me to thank for saving your life." The man's tone was disquieting, as if she owed him and he meant for her to pay big-time.

"Who are you? What do you want?"

"I like that. To the point. No pussyfooting around. I'm Ferdinand Massaro, your knight in shining armor. The one who has been giving you clues as to where Mario is staying. They were only roundabout clues since I never could get a real handle on where he was at any one time, but you did it. Used your investigative skills to find him. Now I'll show you what I want. Just be patient. But *don't* fight me on this. I'd just as soon knock you out and take you that way. Your decision. A word of warning, though. If my brother, Danny, gets ahold of you or me, we're *both* dead."

Trying to get her rapid heartbeat under control, Alicia attempted to stall him, realizing that the man who had pulled the trigger and killed her mother was this man's brother. "Are you a friend of Mario's?"

"A friend?" Ferdinand laughed bitterly. "No. His friends don't live long. We're cousins, if you didn't know. He sent one of his men to kill me. Only I got the upper hand and killed Mario's henchman first. But the assassin gave me a *present* before I ended his miserable life." Ferdinand let go of her hands and went to work on her belt, but she couldn't let him rape her or whatever he planned on doing.

With a superhuman effort, she tried to sit up, intending to hit him or kick him or something, but the pain streaked across her skull with a vengeance, and she collapsed back against the bed in a near faint.

"Hell, I figured you wouldn't go easy. Just know this. You're mine. The bastard who turned me is dead, but I'm not about to live alone like *this*. And since Mario killed Candy, you're it, doll-face. Mine." He slammed his iron fist into the side of her head, creating an eruption of pain so profound that she cried out, and the darkness swiftly closed in on her again.

The sound of gruff angry male voices brought Alicia to semi-consciousness as she lay naked on a soft mattress, presumably in Ferdinand's bedroom. Her head pounded, her arm throbbed and stung, and she couldn't figure out why it hurt when only her head should have. The room was black as night, but a thin strip of light appeared beneath a closed door.

"You been following Mario," a brusque man said in another room. "And Jimmy's been following him too. Only Jimmy's paid for his...*mistake.* He said it was your idea to trail Mario. So what the hell for?"

"You're wrong," Ferdinand said, his voice just as dark. "My cousin's damned paranoid."

"You know Mario's already pissed off at you."

"Because his thug didn't kill me last time." Ferdinand sounded defiant, as though he still had the upper hand. "He shouldn't have murdered Candy."

"Candy shouldn't have stolen from Mario's casino. Not only that, but Mario said you got in his way with Missy Greiston."

Her mother? Alicia swallowed hard.

"She was dating a loser. How did I know Mario wanted a piece of the action?"

"You wanted her because Tony was working for Mario and knew his business. You wanted to muscle in on Mario's territory. And you figured you'd get the goods on Mario through Missy. The straw that broke the camel's back? Candy's gambling scheme that made Mario lose some big bucks. He doesn't like to lose. Not to a woman. And not when you'd been porking her on top of it. He figured you had something to do with Candy going after his money. Admit it."

Something hit something with a dull thud and a crunching noise, and a loud grunt of pain sounded. Cursing followed, mixed with moans, and then the words spoken were suddenly silenced. No one said anything further for what seemed like an eternity. The sound of Alicia's blood pounding in her ears was the only thing she heard as she strained to hear what else was happening in the other room.

"He doesn't know anything," another man said, his voice quieter, much more sinister.

The silence that followed was more frightening than the harsh words. Because with the silence, she couldn't tell whether the men were still a long way off or coming for her.

"Was Ferdinand alone?" the sinister-sounding man finally asked, his words spoken in the direction of the bedroom as if he was suddenly looking that way, suddenly aware Ferdinand might not have been alone.

"When I grabbed him in the living room getting a whiskey at the bar, he was the only one who made a sound. If anyone else was in the place, she would have checked to see what was happening."

"Hell, he was naked. I thought you would have already checked to see if he had a woman stashed back there before I arrived. Jimmy said Ferdinand had grabbed a woman and taken her away with him. Maybe's he's got her tied up and gagged in the bedroom."

The nightmare was only going to get worse. Alicia knew they'd look for anyone else in the place, and she figured she didn't stand a chance if they found her.

She swung her legs over the bed, felt dizzy and sick at the same time, and forced her vision to clear. Then she swept her hands over the mattress, snagging articles of clothing: bra, panties, slacks, stockings, shirt, jacket. Everything but her shoes. She meant to stand, but as soon as her bare feet hit the carpeted floor, she crumpled. She couldn't walk. Couldn't do much but slide under the bed. With pain shrieking through her head and her arm throbbing as if it had been cut badly, she managed to slip underneath the bed, knocking her shoes under there with her.

Dust floated upward underneath the bed, and she stifled a sneeze, holding her nose and gritting her teeth.

The door opened; a light flipped on. Footfalls walked around the room, black leather dress shoes squeaking. Heels toward her, the shoes paused at the edge of the bed. She froze. She smelled a man's pungent cologne and the thick odor of smoke. The leather shoes walked away, and the footfalls headed back down the hallway. "No one else here. Kill the bastard."

Ferdinand didn't object. Why didn't he say anything? Had they knocked him out? Taped his mouth shut?

She shivered with fear. If they found her, they'd kill her too.

No one said anything further. She heard no other sounds until a door in another room opened and closed.

Then eerie silence prevailed. Too frightened to leave her safe spot underneath the bed, she lay there waiting, her head and arm hurting so much that she didn't think anything could get any worse.

She was wrong.

CHAPTER 7

ALICIA MUST HAVE SLEPT FOR SOME TIME, SHE THOUGHT, AS SHE found herself pinned under the framework of a bed, but she felt strange, lying on her side and unable to move to her back. Her arms weren't right. Her legs either. She shifted her head, and it didn't seem right any more than the rest of her did.

As if…as if she was living in an alien body. She struggled to turn onto her back, but her strange legs wouldn't allow it. She was experiencing another nighttime paralysis. *Had to be.* The way she struggled to move and couldn't, her heart racing, her mouth opening to cry out in frustration. But then she recalled Ferdinand and the men with him and worried they might be in the other room, so she grew very still.

After a few minutes, she couldn't stand the suspense any longer and again tried to roll onto her back, but she couldn't in the confined space beneath the bed. And she couldn't use her arms to crawl out from under the bed either. What was wrong with her?

Somehow, squirming and clawing at the carpeted floor, she finally managed to extract herself from under the bed and stared at herself in a floor-length mirror in disbelief.

She was a wolf.

Pointed ears, beige fur under her chin, darker markings around her ears and framing her face, light-gray legs, and attractive darker markings on her torso, with a big, bushy tail swishing from side to side—a beautiful wolf, but not real. This *couldn't* be real.

It had to be sleep paralysis. Except that the only time she'd experienced it, she hadn't been able to move at all or to yell. She had just whimpered, unable to free herself from sleep. Yet she'd been aware she was trying to escape the sleep paralysis. And when she awoke, she remembered the terror of being paralyzed and unable to break free.

But in this case, everything she smelled and touched with her wet nose, felt under her paw pads, and tasted with her tongue was too real to be a dream.

She meant to laugh at herself for thinking she was a wolf, but a *woof* erupted from deep within her throat. For a moment, she was too stunned to react.

She struggled to remember what Ferdinand had said to her.

But the assassin gave me a present before I ended his miserable life.

Ferdinand had gotten the best of him and killed him. But the man had given him a present first. A present? A virus? That made Ferdinand capable of biting someone else and infecting that person with the virus? That person being Alicia? Who now was a wolf?

She closed her eyes and tried to think of what else Ferdinand had said that might give her a clue.

The bastard who turned me is dead, but I'm not about to live alone.

The assassin had turned Ferdinand. *Turned* him. As in…had bitten him and…

She glanced down at her foreleg, which was matted with blood. Had Ferdinand bitten her arm? As a wolf? It had hurt like the devil before when she was lying naked on the bed. Naked. He'd stripped her of her clothes and then bitten her to…to turn her?

She paced across the floor, panting, so confused, so upset that her thoughts were scattered a million miles wide. She had to be dreaming, *no*, experiencing a night terror.

She swallowed hard and focused her attention on the doorway to the bedroom.

When Ferdinand had undressed her, the room had been pitch-black. She couldn't see him, couldn't understand how he could see her. If he…if he was…

She shook her head and began to pace again. The room was dark, the curtains drawn, the lights all off. Yet *she* could now see in the dark.

And wolves had nocturnal vision for hunting. Which meant? Ferdinand had...

She wanted to laugh out loud, but the sound came out like a garbled *woof*. Ferdinand had been a werewolf. That was too weird to believe.

She paused and glanced back at the doorway. What had become of him?

Her heart was in her throat, and fear cloaked her with the worry that she still could be discovered. But the need to learn what had happened to Ferdinand overwhelmed her need for self-preservation. She loped out of the bedroom and down the hall, smelling the shampooed carpet, the cologne worn by three different men, whiskey, and lemon wax cleaner. Her ears twisted back and forth, listening to the sounds outside—cars driving by, a siren way off in the distance, the hum of an air-conditioning unit, but otherwise an eerie silence prevailed.

As much as she wanted to see what had happened to Ferdinand, dread bunched in the pit of her stomach. The hall opened into a living room, spacious with high ceilings, richly carved dark wood furniture, and two couches and four chairs—all covered in brown brushed leather. She stopped dead.

Sitting on one of the couches, head lolled back against the top of the cushion, Ferdinand Massaro, her former informant, was staring lifelessly at the ceiling with cold, black eyes. She barely breathed, felt her furry legs wobble beneath her, and sat before she collapsed.

Silver duct tape covering his mouth and with his head tilted at an odd angle, Ferdinand looked as though his neck had been broken. She blinked away tears. The room was dark, no lights on in the recessed fixtures, yet she could see the man's hefty size, over six feet tall and meaty, with matted black hair covering his chest, and hairy legs. He was naked. Had he raped her before he was murdered?

She didn't think so. Her front leg still pained her where she'd been bitten, and she wondered if he'd… The notion was too unreal to believe, but what if he'd shifted into a wolf, then bitten her and, after that, shifted back into a human form? Then the men had come for him before he could do anything more to her.

Her mouth still agape, she felt chilled all over despite her warm wolf's fur coat, her brain fuzzy from the knowledge she might have been infected with some weird virus, and the man who undoubtedly had done it to Ferdinand had been murdered. Then Ferdinand himself had met his fate.

I'm not about to live alone like this, Ferdinand had said. *Like this*, like some cursed being? She had to wake up from this nightmare. She wasn't a wolf. She couldn't be.

Trying to get her rapid breathing under control and attempting to banish the light-headedness she was experiencing so she could think more clearly, she finally realized she had to get out of here—*now*. The realization didn't mesh well with the notion she was fighting that she was a wolf, consciously sitting in Ferdinand's living room and staring at his dead body. Smelling his dead body.

What if someone called the cops or one of Ferdinand's murderers returned to tidy up the place?

She had to get out of there.

Hours passed before Alicia finally managed to shift back to her human self and dress. She left Ferdinand's town house and walked forever until she could call a taxi far from the town house where he had lived. Then after picking up her car near the town house where Mario had been meeting someone and where Ferdinand had grabbed her, she returned to her hotel on the outskirts of Denver. She intended to get some sleep and leave before dawn and get as far away from there as she possibly could. She couldn't quit thinking of what she had become, of what that meant for her if she had the horrible urge to shift again—especially if she wasn't hidden from the eyes of the world *if* it happened once more.

Scared, exhausted, and unsure of what to do, she stripped off her clothes, showered, and pulled on a slinky black nightgown covered in pink and yellow flowers. She collapsed in the hotel-room bed, intending to push all the worries out of her brain until she could think more clearly in the morning. And make some sound decisions about what she would do next.

Lying in the hotel bed, Alicia finally closed her eyes, unsure whether she would wake again in the form of a wolf or as herself. She gave a soft snort of disbelief and halfway wondered if Ferdinand's blows to her head twice in one night were making her loopy. Or if he might have drugged her with something that was making her imagine stuff. Something like LSD. Maybe in the morning everything would again be clear and she would realize it had all been a really bizarre nightmare. A total figment of her imagination. Except that it had seemed *so* real.

One thing was certain: Ferdinand was dead.

With all those thoughts running through her tired mind, she finally succumbed to sleep and dreamed like she'd never dreamed before.

With the hotel curtains shut tight, the bed covered in an orange floral spread, and prints on the walls of floral bouquets, Alicia dressed in a satiny black nightgown touching her ankles, with a slit up the side and spaghetti straps that bared her shoulders as she headed from the bathroom to the bed. But her attention was drawn to the sitting room as a flicker of movement caught her eye.

She turned. To her astonishment, Jake Silver stalked toward her, naked, his lean, muscled body gorgeous in the low light of the room, his eyes and lips smiling in a lustful, greedy way. She knew as soon as she saw him that he desired her as much as she craved being with him. But somewhere in the back of her mind, she knew this was a big mistake.

Yet she couldn't remember why. Why was seeing him not a safe thing to do?

And she vaguely wondered why he was here. How he had found her. And why he had no clothes.

She didn't care and stretched her arms up to take hold of him. To embrace him. To make love to him. She wanted him with a passion that she couldn't quell.

His kiss on her mouth started a low, slow burn growing in the small of her belly, the heat spreading outward as his hands cupped her face, holding her just the way he wanted her. The pressure on her lips increased until she openly invited him in. And he leaped at the invitation, plunging his tongue into her mouth, his hands shifting to her shoulders, gripping her as if he'd lost her forever and had once again found her. He pulled her into his hard embrace, holding her tight as his mouth kissed the top of her head and his arms encircled her back as if they were two lovers reunited.

The familiarity felt phenomenal. As if they belonged together. As if they were bound to each other in some mysterious way.

Yet something was terribly amiss. She felt it in her bones. Something was wrong with her. She couldn't...be with Jake. Because...because...

No matter how hard she tried to think, she couldn't come up with the reason. His hands brushed down her naked back, his mouth sweeping across her jaw, lower, his tongue on her throat, and then his lips took in a nipple, licking and sucking, and she squeezed his broad back and moaned.

Hot, hot, she was burning up with heat. Delicious, sexy heat. And the realization dawned that he wasn't upset with her for leaving him without a word.

All that seemed to matter to him was that they were together again. She cherished him for it, wanted to meld with him, be one with him, and never let go.

Forever, he touched her and kissed her, as if he couldn't get enough of stroking her. Then he looked into her eyes, his gaze filled with the smoky haze of lust and something more—a yearning to be with her almost as if this wasn't enough. And then he swept her up into his arms and carried her to the bed and collapsed in it with her in a purely fun-hearted way.

The kisses began anew as he fondled her breasts, his mouth on hers, on her cheeks, on her eyes. She kissed him back rabidly, her fingers stroking his shoulders, his back, his waist, hips, and buttocks, wanting to feel every hard inch of him.

And then his fingers began stroking her, capturing her in a web of exultation, the feeling uplifting, tantalizing, wanting, until the world split in two.

———————

Jake couldn't wait a second longer when he felt Alicia shudder with climax, and he plunged deep between her spread thighs—into the woman of his dreams. He thought he'd lost her for good. The worry that had plagued him for days was thrust aside as he wrapped himself in her heat and loved her like no other woman he'd ever been with. He wanted her, body and soul. He swore this was only the beginning.

Jake jerked awake, stared at the empty mattress next to him, and wondered what the hell had happened. She was real. Alicia Greiston had been with him, loving him as he'd loved her back.

He raked his hands through his tousled hair, staring into the dark. He had barely thought of anything but Alicia since he'd lost her—wondering if she'd planned her disappearance or if the men she'd been after had planned it for her. And he couldn't quit berating himself for not having stayed with her.

But the dream had been so real, like she had truly been with him. He wasn't a dreamer. Had never recalled anything that he dreamed. The experience left him longing for her touch, to know she was safe, and when she was gone, he felt bereft. He couldn't quit thinking of her, sharing a kiss, a smile, heart pounding, bare bodies pressed together, breath intermingled, hands clutching each other, tongues touching, her lips parting for him, offering herself to him fully.

In that brief nocturnal moment, she was his. He prayed she was alive and well, that his dream of her was a manifestation of the real Alicia Greiston, and he wondered if it represented a need to make everything real between them again. He vowed to find her and keep her safe, no matter how long that took.

Tomorrow, he was searching for her again.

CHAPTER 8

FOR SEVEN WEEKS, JAKE HAD VISITED ALICIA IN HER DREAMS while she was kept on the run, sure Mario's men were searching for her. But her dreams were so real, as if Jake was coming to her in the middle of the night and overwhelming her with deeply pleasurable emotions as she ravished him back.

She couldn't put it off any longer. Having remained human for a whole week without one inkling of an urge to shift, the second time she'd had such a shift-free week, Alicia had made up her mind. She'd finally tracked down Mario Constantino and Danny Massaro once more, and forgoing her bounty hunter's fee, she had called the police and told them where to find the bail-skippers. Tackling them alone would be too dangerous. And with the shape-shifting problems she was having, her situation was even more precarious.

With her life turned upside down by this strange being that she'd become, nothing mattered but trying to get her untenable condition under control. Although she thought maybe the condition had gone away since she hadn't had another episode of changing into the wolf for a whole glorious week, twice now. She hoped that maybe it truly was some weird virus that had finally run its course. Still, the worry lurked in her bones that at any moment she might once again become a wolf through no choice of her own.

But she had to take care of one more thing before she disappeared for good.

She drove to Breckenridge, intending to go to the art gallery to see if anyone could give her information on where Jake lived or just send word to him to let him know she was all right. She couldn't see him any further. Not now that she was whatever she was. She had to vanish from Colorado altogether. Yet the dreams wouldn't allow her to let him go.

Nursing a cold cup of brewed tea that had been hot at first, she sat in the restaurant across the street from the art gallery, waiting until a tourist busload of visitors filed out of the gallery, her thoughts centered on Jake's first kiss at this very table after he had rescued her from one of Mario's men. Gentle and unassuming, his kiss had sparked a desire for him that she couldn't have quashed even if she'd wanted to. She thought back on ice-skating with him, making love with him in the woods. She'd never been so adventurous or uninhibited with a man. Nor enjoyed being with one as much as she had with him.

Her nighttime dreams of Jake had made her believe she was being punished for running away without a word and not telling him she was all right. She was safe, at least as safe as she could be, with this wolf business that plagued her now…and Mario's men tailing her from time to time. At least that was who she *thought* had been following her. Although having found "bugs" on her car four times in the early days while she tried to track down Mario, she thought maybe someone *else* was on her trail.

But Mario had said Jake would be dead if he continued to tag along with her, and she knew that hadn't been idle bullying. Mario's kind didn't make pointless threats. Hopefully, he was behind bars again. She'd had the notion that she might get in touch with Jake after Mario and Danny were again incarcerated, but that didn't matter now. Not with what she'd become.

She clutched her teacup tighter, then released it and sighed. With nerves steeled, she paid for her tea, left the restaurant, and headed across the street to the gallery before the shop closed for the evening. Chimes rang when she opened the door and stepped inside.

A woman in a flouncy floral skirt and pink shell was talking to a man wearing a ponytail and dressed in black as if he was a goth. The man's chin rested on his fist while he nodded and stared at a blob of orange splashed against a sea of purple. Alicia raised her brows. If only she could get thousands of dollars for "artwork" like that while staying hidden at home. She hadn't attempted any more bounty hunting, what with the unpredictability of her new condition. She wasn't sure how she was going to earn a living in the future.

Another woman dressed in a business suit was speaking to a small group of what looked to be college students and a slightly older woman who might have been their art teacher.

A suited man was busy talking to a woman who seemed more intrigued by him than the painting they were standing in front of.

Alicia frowned. She needed to question the staff pronto and return to her hotel room, then leave the area forever. That made her sad as she thought about how she wouldn't be able to visit her mother where she'd died any longer, although she'd made one last trip there before she'd stopped at the restaurant.

The art gallery staff continued to court those they had been speaking to when she'd arrived. Not being able to question them about Jake, Alicia searched for the photography he had done. A group of paintings of naked women caught her eye, and she smiled a little, thinking of her conversation with him about painting his old girlfriends in the nude and the sexy smile he'd given in return. But the name signed at the bottom wasn't Jake Silver.

She checked on landscapes next, mostly featuring the Rockies, but none of them had his signature either. Lots more blob pictures were featured all over the place, not his unless he was too embarrassed to sign what he painted and used a different name to disguise his own.

But then she came across a display of photographs. And became engrossed in them. Wildflowers of Colorado. Wild, exotic, in colors so vivid that they looked unreal. The details so defined that she felt she could reach out and touch them and feel the soft velvety petals. Deep-orange paintbrush and red fairy-trumpet flowers, cinnabar-red alpine wallflowers and rosy pussytoes, fuchsia fairy-slipper orchids, bright-pink primrose, and spotted tangerine wood lilies.

Her mother had taught Alicia the beauty of wildflowers in their natural habitats when she was younger. Her mother had loved to hike and observe the great blue sky, wisps of clouds, majestic mountains, and towering trees. Even though her mother had been an extrovert and fed off the hustle and bustle of being around tons of people as she waitressed in a busy cafeteria, she still liked to soak in the beauty of nature, and Alicia had shared her mother's love of the wilderness.

Alicia tried to rein in her sadness when she thought of her mother dying alone in that wilderness with no one to protect her. She took a deep shuddering breath, reminding herself why she'd become a bounty hunter, which had ultimately led her to the unfortunate condition she was in now. Who would have ever thought?

But for the moment, seeing the photographs brought back the happier memories of Alicia and her mother on nature walks, and tears formed in her eyes.

"May I help you?" the woman in the flowery skirt asked. Ponytail Man had left, apparently without buying the orange blob, as it was still hanging on the wall.

"Yes, I wonder if you could tell me about Jake Silver. He was leaving something off at the art gallery a few weeks back. I need to get in touch with him. It's important."

"J. S." The woman smiled brightly. "Oh yes, he's…" She sighed and didn't have to say what was on her mind. The guy was a virile, hunky stud. The woman motioned to the photos. "The photographs you're admiring are his."

"J. S.?" Alicia looked down at the extremely small print. Modest, or embarrassed to proclaim they were his? They were beautiful.

"Yes. That's his autograph. We just started carrying his work. I hope we sell a lot and he makes more trips up here."

"Up here?"

"Yes, he's not from around here. I don't recall where he's from exactly, but it's not Breckenridge. He did come in a few times in the past several weeks, looking for a dark-haired woman, who—" The woman's eyes widened. "Who looked like you, from his description. Are you Alicia Greiston?"

"Yes, I am." Hope stirred anew that Jake had left contact information for her, yet the knowledge he was looking for her saddened her too. He had to have been angry with her for running out on him the way she had. She wanted so badly to see him, but...

She swallowed hard. How could she see him, knowing what she'd now become?

The woman's mouth pursed a little. "Oh. Well, he left something for you." The woman didn't look pleased and stalked off to a desk near the entrance.

So it wasn't Alicia's imagination that the woman was interested in Jake. Feeling bone-deep sadness that she couldn't see Jake further and that she had to cut any ties with him, Alicia watched as the woman pulled an envelope out of a desk drawer, then returned. But a streak of jealousy raced through Alicia's veins, too, as she considered how the woman would most likely ply her feminine wiles on Jake every time he chanced to visit the gallery when Alicia wished she could be with him instead.

Alicia's hand trembled as she took the envelope, dying to see what he had said to her. Afraid also.

She tucked it into her purse and said, "Thank you."

She glanced back at the photographs. Although she knew she shouldn't buy one, that taking one with her would remind her of the time they had spent together and what she had lost, she reasoned that her mother would have loved having one of them. With that thought firmly in mind, Alicia decided on the tangerine spotted wood lilies. Although she wanted the fuchsia fairy-slipper orchids, the picture was too big and cost too much. "I'll take that one."

Alicia handed her a credit card, and the woman feigned a polite smile. "I'll just wrap this up for you."

As soon as the woman had taken the photo down and walked off, Alicia pulled the envelope out of her purse and ripped it open. In bold strokes, Jake had written: *Call me!* And left his phone number where she could reach him.

Her stomach tightened. She sensed from his note that he was angry and frustrated with her for having taken off without a word. And she didn't blame him. He seemed the kind of man who wouldn't have given in to threats by Constantino or his men. If Jake had known why she had left him, he would have been furious, wanting to deal with them in his own way. But he didn't know what the men were capable of. And his wonderfully macho nature wouldn't have kept him from being murdered. On the contrary, his protectiveness for her would have gotten him killed faster.

She pulled out her phone and opened it. The battery was dead. She'd have to call Jake when she got to her hotel room.

Then she noticed the suited man moving his hands down the arms of the woman he'd been talking to in a solicitous manner while she adoringly looked up at him. He glanced back at the other two employees, saw they were occupied, and then with a smile, he motioned to a little room, led the woman inside, and shut the door.

At the same instant, Alicia felt sudden heat penetrate every inch of her body. The heat. *Oh God, no*.

The urge to shift hit her fast and furious. Heat shimmered through every cell, through every tissue. She glanced around the gallery, looking for a way out of this nightmare.

The woman with Alicia's photo had disappeared into a back room. She had Alicia's credit card, and Alicia *had* to have it to survive. The other saleswoman was walking outside with the art students and their teacher, blocking the doorway.

Looking for the restroom, Alicia spied a sign directing her down a hall and rushed to make her way there before she had an "accident."

As soon as she entered the ladies' restroom and found no one in there, she hurried into the handicapped stall. Normally, she avoided using the handicapped stall if another stall was available, leaving it to women who truly needed it, but tonight she was as handicapped as anyone.

Slipping out of the short-sleeved dress she wore, she hung it on the hook on the door, then kicked off her pumps. Barely free of her bra and panties, she shifted, the heat fusing every inch of her body until her bones felt as if they were liquefying and remolding, but in a flash. The next thing she knew, she was dropping down on all four feet—furry, long legged, with a long bushy tail—a small gray *wolf*.

Once again, she cursed Ferdinand Massaro for having bitten her and leaving her to face this dilemma on her own. Although she wouldn't have wanted to see what he'd had in mind to do with her if he'd lived. And she would have been in a lot more danger if she'd remained with him because of his connections.

As if she wasn't in danger now.

Pacing, she stalked back and forth in the stall—still too small for a highly agitated wolf. It was nearly closing time. She wasn't sure how long she'd been in the restroom, trying to will herself back into her human form, when someone knocked on the restroom door and opened it.

She froze in place inside the stall. Could they see her wolf legs beneath the door of the stall? She backed up against the tile wall. Her heart was pumping even more rapidly, if that were possible, as she barely breathed.

"Closing in two minutes," a woman said, sounding impatient. It was the woman who'd been talking to the students.

Instinctively, Alicia knew she couldn't be caught in a wolf's form. She'd discarded her bra, panties, and heels on the restroom floor. With the shift hitting her so quickly, she couldn't do anything else but drop them. What would people think? That she'd eaten Little Red Riding Hood? Or that she *was* Little Red Riding Hood and the Big Bad Wolf all wrapped up in one?

Oh God, what was she going to do? Since being turned, she'd never been in this bad a fix. As her grandfather used to say, *This will learn her.* She could never, *ever* be out in public again during the phase of any moon—waxing, waning, or full. So much for not having to shift all last week. She was making up for it now. It seemed she'd never get rid of this condition or learn to control it.

At least she hadn't wanted to rip out people's throats, like the old werewolf tales portrayed. And she had her human conscience, so she wasn't totally a feral animal. And she was a beautiful wolf, not some hideous beastly creature. Not that any of it mattered while she was stuck in a restroom stall as a wolf with women's garments strewn about her paws.

Concentrate! She tried again to will herself to shift.

Another minute went by, and knocking sounded on the door. Yes, all right. She knew. It was nearly closing time. She'd worked on the clock before. She knew how employees wanted to go home when it was time to go and how rude customers were to expect employees to stay until all hours at their convenience.

"Ma'am?" a woman said, then heels clicked across the floor toward the stall.

Wolves couldn't sweat, or Alicia would have been perspiring up a storm. They panted when they were overheated, but she didn't want to even do that, afraid the woman would hear her. Instead, she stood frozen like a furry wolf statue in the corner of the stall, as far away from the door as she could get, her mouth shut tight, her ears focused on the woman's approaching footfalls. The slight tremor in the floor reverberated through Alicia's paws as she kept her eyes riveted on the door.

Two choices. She instinctually knew she had only two choices. Bite the woman and turn her into what Alicia was. Heaven forbid. She wouldn't want to wish this condition on anyone ever! But then the woman would scream bloody murder. The other two employees would come running or call the cops, or both. Then she'd have to bite all of them too. Or kill the woman. Which would be the same scenario. In the end, they'd put her down like a vicious wild animal.

A rough knocking on the stall door nearly gave Alicia a heart attack.

"Ma'am? Are you all right?"

No, no she wasn't all right. *Please... don't... come... in!*

"Ma'am?"

When Alicia still didn't respond, the woman hurried out of the restroom.

She was going for the authorities. Probably worried a dead body was in the stall. Would be, too, if they caught Alicia like this—and killed her.

She paced some more. *Shift, damn it! Change! Turn!* What were the magic words?

"A woman's in the stall. She was the one who bought Mr. Silver's photograph. She looked to be late twenties or so, not all that old, but I think she's died or something. She's not responding," the woman said frantically to someone outside the restroom door.

"Did you look under the stall?" a man asked, his voice darkly controlled.

Alicia glanced at the bottom of the stall door. If anyone peered underneath, they'd see her. And that would be the beginning of the end. Shrieks would ensue. Her heart would fail.

"No. I–I didn't." The woman sounded a bit shaken.

The door opened, and heavier footfalls approached. A man's footfalls. *Oh God, oh God, please, please help me.*

She felt the heat race through her bones and muscles, her

nerves and blood. And prayed it was the change. And not caused by the frantic panic filling her blood. That she would once again be her normal self. *Normal self.* She laughed at herself over that. This proved she'd never be her normal self again.

Just as the footfalls ended abruptly at the stall door, the shift swiftly overtook her. She stood naked on the tile floor, the cool air-conditioning sweeping across her bare skin, and she quickly squeaked out, "Sorry, I fainted. I'm pregnant. I'm sorry. I'll be right out."

It had been the only thing she could think of in her haste, remembering the time her mother had said she'd passed out when she was pregnant with Alicia.

As quickly as Alicia could, she jerked her panties off the floor and yanked them on. She fumbled with her bra after that, realizing the man was still standing outside the stall door, waiting for her to open up—probably in case she "fainted" once more. Heat again shimmered through her, but it was more of a skin-deep heat from embarrassment. If he opened the door now while she was half-naked, what in the world would he think she'd been up to?

She tugged the dress over her head and decided she didn't look pregnant in the least, but she was extremely flushed and now perspiring. She was sure she looked overcome. Just like she felt.

After slipping her bare feet into her pumps, she wrenched open the stall door and smiled a diminutive, weary smile—at least that was how she tried to make her expression look. Although she knew she had to look overwrought in any event.

"I'm sorry. I must have fainted again. Not enough electrolytes. My mother had warned me." She rattled off the words, feeling truly light-headed and still worried her furry wolf half might try to take over again.

Then she headed for the sink and washed her hands, just like she would have done after using the facilities, if she'd used them.

The man still watched her warily, but she wasn't sure whether he thought she was lying—he did look at her flat belly beneath the dress—or worried she'd faint again. She couldn't look at him, couldn't look to see his expression. But then a horrible thought occurred to her. What if he'd thought she was doing drugs?

She took a couple of steps forward, then grabbed his arm as if she might pass out again, and this time, the expression on his face was one of pure horror. Not that she was faking much of anything. Her head wouldn't quit spinning.

He grabbed her around the waist and sputtered, "D-do you need an ambulance?"

"No, thank you. I haven't been eating enough. Or drinking enough fluids. I'll…I'll be all right."

Still, he didn't let her go, and for the first time in her life, she really wished she had a hero type like him—like Jake, rather—in her life. Practical, no nonsense, she'd never really felt she'd needed anyone. But now?

"Get her something to drink," the man said quickly to the woman hovering near the door.

Alicia sighed. She really needed help. Then she felt a wave of depression hit suddenly. How could she see Jake or *anyone* when she was a damn werewolf? Wouldn't she want to do to him what Ferdinand did to her? Bite him? Change him? Make him live like she had to live? Her heart sinking into a pit of despair, she knew she couldn't get in touch with Jake directly. Not now, not ever.

"Are you sure we can't call someone for you?" the man asked as he helped her toward the restroom door.

"No, *thanks.*"

The woman who had sold her the photograph had stepped into the restroom now, too, with the picture wrapped in paper cradled in her arms. She pointedly looked at the envelope half-sticking out of Alicia's purse.

"What about him?" the woman asked quietly, as if she thought Jake was the father of Alicia's baby and they'd had a falling-out. The other woman must have told her what had happened.

Poor Jake. He was now thought to be the father of a nonexistent baby, and he was truly the dream lover of a woman who was part wolf.

"No," Alicia said again, almost sounding desperate.

The man and women shared concerned, knowing looks.

The man continued to help Alicia out of the restroom, and she did really feel shaky from nearly being caught in the altogether as a wolf. He must have sensed her unsteadiness and held on tighter. When they left the restroom, the other female employee had a cell phone in one hand and a chilled bottle of water in the other, ready to call 911 probably, and everyone was looking a lot more worried than irritated about leaving work late.

That still bothered Alicia. She hated that she really had inconvenienced them. But Ferdinand was the one to blame for all this. Damn his black soul.

"Mary said you were trying to locate Jake Silver," the man remarked.

"I gave her the envelope he left for her." Mary pointed at the incriminating evidence in Alicia's purse pocket, halfway exposed.

"Does it have an address?" The man sounded really annoyed with Jake, so Alicia figured he thought Jake was the father of her faux baby too. How could things get into such a mess?

"A phone number," Alicia said. "I'm to call him." She tried to sound as enthusiastic as she could under the circumstances.

The man and the two women exchanged glances. They thought Jake was a villain.

"He has a home in Silver Town, Colorado," Mary blurted out, as if she wanted Alicia to know the truth in case Jake had steered her wrong.

"Thanks," Alicia said very sweetly.

Maybe she could call Silver Town and leave a message with someone else to get word to him that she was all right, and that would be it. She didn't dare call Jake directly because she was afraid he'd try to locate her—and what a disaster that would be!

The man helped her to a chair, and the woman gave her the water. Alicia only wanted to leave as quickly as she could before she had another damnable urge to shift. Politely, she drank a little of the water, never being one who could drink a glass of anything in a hurry. But she was trying her damnedest while everyone watched her expectantly.

They didn't seem interested in leaving either, instead being more concerned about her welfare. God, what a fraud she was. She was three-quarters of the way through the bottle of water when she had to go to the bathroom. She could make it to her hotel if she hurried.

"Thanks so much, and I'm so sorry I've made you late for closing." Rising from the chair, she cradled her purse and the nearly finished bottle of water in her arms.

They all looked at the bottle as if it held magic water and if she didn't drink all of it, she'd pass out again.

"Are you sure you'll be all right?" the man asked, his hand outstretched in rescue mode.

"Oh, yes. I'm feeling so much better." She started to move toward the door.

"Could one of us drive you home?" the man asked. "One of us could follow behind."

"No, no, I'll be fine."

"Do you need one of us to follow you home?" Mary asked, clutching the framed photograph in her arms.

"No, really. I'm all right now."

"All right. Well, I'll walk with you out to your car," Mary said.

The man and other woman did, too, and when Alicia had settled herself behind the steering wheel, Mary handed her the wrapped, framed photograph of the wood lilies, casting her another look of sympathy while the man and woman watched her gravely.

The other woman quickly handed her credit card to her.

Alicia thanked them all profusely.

When she drove out of the parking space, Alicia noted in her rearview mirror that they were still watching her. Mary shook her head.

Poor Jake when he returned to the gallery. What if they made him remove his photographs? They wouldn't do that to him. They *couldn't* do that. Alicia let out her breath. She could write and tell them how much she loved their gallery and that when she had more money, she'd buy another one of his photos. That would work, wouldn't it?

Either that, or they'd think she was in love with Jake and pining over him but he was trying to call it quits with her. She felt bad all over again. She hoped she hadn't ruined his reputation with the art gallery.

A car's headlights followed her through town, and she had the creepy feeling the vehicle was following her. Call it woman's intuition, a sixth sense, wolf wariness. She'd considered leaving without her bags, but she couldn't. Besides, she was dying to go to the bathroom.

She pulled into the hotel parking lot, hurried out of the car, used the bathroom, and then grabbed her bags to leave the room she'd already paid for. With every intention of leaving Breckenridge for good, she returned to the car, dumped her bags in the trunk, and headed out of town.

Again, she felt as though she was being followed, but when she left town, the car turned off down a rural road. Relieved, she figured she'd stay in the next town of Crestview. But the concern lingered. What if Mario could still pull strings and send men after her even from prison? Or what if the men who'd killed Ferdinand Massaro in his town house had somehow learned she'd witnessed his death? Although she couldn't know who they were, they wouldn't know that. And she would be a loose end easily tied up.

CHAPTER 9

SHE WAS HIS OBSESSION. AN APHRODISIAC JAKE SILVER HAD little control over. The dark-haired siren of his dreams. *Alicia Greiston.*

And just as with last night and every night for the past seven weeks since she'd first appeared to him in his dreams, seducing him with her mouth, her eyes, her touch, he sought her out. In his nighttime fantasies. Because, as real as she was, he knew the visions of her were only dreams. But she had been real, and he wanted the real woman again. He'd hoped and prayed she'd go to the art gallery and get the envelope he'd left for her, then call. But she hadn't yet.

As much as he hated to admit it, he was ready to turn in for the night just to be with her. But as soon as it was light out, he was returning to Breckenridge to search for her again. She hadn't even returned to the florist shop to leave wreaths in memory of her mother. That would have worried him more if he didn't keep dreaming of her. She had to still be alive.

Tired and out of sorts, Jake was ready to skip dinner. The questioning sidelong glances his younger triplet brother, Tom, gave him, plus the more openly concerned looks his older brother, Darien, cast at him were enough to curb his appetite. As pack leader of Silver Town, Darien was always concerned about the pack members' well-being. And since he was Jake's brother, Darien's concern about him was heightened. Added to that, Darien's mate, Lelandi, was analyzing Jake's behavior based on the psychology courses she was taking. Jake felt as if he was a proverbial open book for everyone to read.

Except he would *not* let them know why he wasn't sleeping well. Hell, at the very least, if he died from lack of sleep, it would be with a smile on his face.

What gnawed at him most was that Darien had said the dream mating that had occurred between him and Lelandi before they had met was fate and that their family had a history of such occurrences. Which Jake couldn't believe in.

Yet the truth of the matter was that he felt as though he was linked with Alicia through his nighttime fantasies, which couldn't be. She was human. The lack of sleep was driving him slowly mad.

Except for the clinking of forks as Tom and Darien scooped up their mashed potatoes and gravy, the dining room was silent. Then Lelandi spoke up. "Everything's fine at the leather-goods factory, right?" She had asked Darien, but her gaze again slid to Jake, as if she thought something was bothering him about some trouble with the factory.

"Everything's fine," Darien said. "Everywhere. No pack problems at present, no problems with the mine. The town is running without any difficulties, and the factory's doing well. Just as everything should be."

Lelandi set her half-eaten slice of bread on her plate and rubbed her belly. She was due this fall; another month and she would have the triplets. That was making Jake antsy. And he felt guilty about it. All pack members revered the pack leaders' offspring. They took care of them and provided for them, just as they did other pack members' children. Yet as much as he hated himself for it, he felt twinges of jealousy for his older brother when he'd never felt that way before.

Normally, Lelandi was beautiful and glowed with motherhood, her red hair spilling over her shoulders, her green eyes bright with laughter. But now, she seemed just as concerned as his brothers. They wouldn't prod him too hard. But Lelandi? She was bound to ask him before long what was wrong. And he didn't want to lie. But he wasn't telling her the truth either.

He respected her for bringing Darien out of the deep pit of despair he'd been wallowing in. And with the impending birth of their children, she certainly didn't need to be worrying about Jake.

But then she smiled a little as if she'd figured out what was bothering him. Maybe she'd been able to work out the mystery intuitively, or maybe he'd given himself away. Or maybe it was something altogether different. He still couldn't read her like he could his brothers and they, him. Although he was certain they couldn't figure out his behavior right now.

Lelandi turned her attention to Tom and lifted her bread from her plate again. "Woman trouble?"

Tom immediately glanced at Jake. Hell, Jake didn't have woman problems, except in the form of a damned beguiling woman who continued to appear to him in his dreams and who in the worst-case scenario had gotten into trouble with the Mob. Lesser worst-case scenario, she'd just stood him up. Jake scowled further.

Tom gave a small smile. "Can't have any woman trouble if there's no one around to give me difficulty."

Lelandi looked at Jake, but she didn't repeat the question, although it lingered in the air as if it hung invisibly between them, begging to be answered. He imagined his expression said she'd better not pose the question.

But damned if both of his brothers didn't look to him to answer her query as if she'd blatantly asked him. He finished his meal, not intending to be drawn into this, took the plate to the kitchen, rinsed it off, put it in the dishwasher, and then returned to the dining room.

All three watched him.

He paused, thinking to ask them about dream mating—could it involve a human woman? But not wanting to get into a discussion about this when he was dog-tired, he said instead, "I'll see you in the morning."

The looks they all gave him showed surprise. If they'd worn

watches, which as *lupus garous* they didn't, he figured they'd all be glancing at them now to determine just how late it was. And see that it was way too early for him to retire when he normally didn't hit the sack until midnight. Unless he went for a midnight run as a wolf in the woods. Then it was even later.

Darien cleared his throat. "Do you want to talk to me privately about something?"

"No. And there's no sense in putting this off any longer," Jake remarked, not intending to mention it again, but it was time. He'd been renovating their grandfather's home, which was situated farther from town than Darien's house. The renovations were complete, and it was past time to settle in there.

Tom cast a glance at Lelandi. She'd been the one attempting all along to convince him to change his mind. Darien and Tom knew better than to try.

"I told you and Tom, *both*, you don't need to leave. Just because the babies are coming, I don't want you feeling like they're pushing you out of your own home," Lelandi said softly, her eyes welling up with tears, her throat choked with emotion.

Hell. She wasn't often emotional, but with being pregnant, she'd had unnatural bouts of weepiness, which was another reason he couldn't stay. He hated to see her cry—especially when he had anything to do with it.

Darien reached over and took her hand and squeezed.

"The cabin is so…isolated. It has electricity and running water, but no television or telephone service. It's so primitive. What if you run into trouble out there?" she asked, quickly dabbing with a napkin at tears trailing down her cheeks.

He knew her well enough to realize she didn't use the tears to make him feel guilty, even though they still had that effect. No matter how many times she cajoled him to stay, he couldn't. He thought Tom was waffling, though. That was fine with Jake. He didn't mind living at the house alone since he'd only be there at night. He'd spend his days working with the family, with the pack, and still have dinner with them unless he just had to get away. He was a family kind of guy, and that wouldn't ever change. He'd told Lelandi that, and he wasn't going to repeat himself.

But something deeper was bothering him. The need to have a mate. He was seeing Darien and Lelandi together with the babies coming, and now the damnable dreams of Alicia were making him crazy. He had to get away.

"You'll need more room," he said and headed out of the dining room before anyone could say anything further to him.

He knew they'd all be giving each other looks, trying to figure out what was wrong with him, staying silent until he was well beyond earshot, and then discussing his actions in private.

He heard Darien's phone ring and hoped there wasn't trouble he had to take care of with the pack or town tonight, considering how much he wanted to sleep—*dream*, rather.

Why was he going to bed this early? Depression, Lelandi might surmise from her psychology classes. Never in a millennium would she or anyone else guess that he couldn't sleep because of his desire for a woman's silken touch.

"You need to speak with *Jake*?" Darien said in the dining room to whoever was on the phone, his voice sounding surprised.

Jake paused in the great room before he reached the stairs.

"*Yeah*, he's *here*. Let me let you talk to him." Normally, Darien would have hollered to him that the call was for him, although why anyone would be calling him on Darien's line was a mystery. But instead, Darien left the dining room to join Jake in the great room, and *that* didn't bode well.

Already he was thinking that something bad had happened to Alicia. Although how anyone knew their connection, he couldn't be sure. Unless she'd been hurt and the gallery staff had made the correlation.

Darien held his hand over the mouthpiece on the phone. "Sheriff got a call from Breckenridge."

Already apprehensive, Jake could feel his legs turning to rubber, and he was sure his face had drained of all color, as light-headed as he felt. As observant as he always was, Darien noticed and frowned. "Hell, what's going on?"

"What's happened?"

Darien raised his brows, then shook his head. "You've got some talking to do. An Alicia Greiston passed out in the art gallery's ladies' restroom after she bought one of your photographs. Apparently, she's pregnant. But they said you'd left your number for her to get in touch. Your cell phone must be off, so they called our sheriff, trying to locate another number for you, and Peter gave them mine. What's this all about?"

Pregnant?

Darien didn't wait for Jake's answer but handed him the phone and remained watching him like a wary wolf.

His heart in his throat and worried as hell about Alicia, Jake said, "Hello, this is Jake Silver."

"I'm Mary Clebourne from the art gallery in Breckenridge. I'm the one who gave you the contract on your work. I just wanted to let you know I gave your girlfriend your phone number like you asked me to, and she said she'd call you. Has she called you? We've been worried about her. She passed out in the ladies' restroom. Said she was pregnant and apologized all over the place. We wanted to follow her home, but she said she'd be all right. Did she call you?" Mary repeated.

Girlfriend? Pregnant? "No. She didn't. When did this happen?"

"Tonight. A couple of hours ago. I wanted to give her time to reach you, but then I worried she might not, so I thought I'd get in touch with you just in case. Then I couldn't get ahold of you and called the sheriff of Silver Town, figuring he'd know your family and someone would pass the word along. But since I couldn't get ahold of you, I assumed she only had the number I couldn't reach either."

Hell, the phone was charging in his bedroom. "Did she mention where she was staying? Leave a phone number or anything?"

"No. Nothing. She said that she hadn't been drinking enough fluids. We gave her a bottle of water, and she seemed better but still awfully pale. Before the episode, she bought your tangerine wood lily photograph."

Pregnant. Damn guy probably had left her. Hell, that was why she had been reluctant to see Jake further. But then why in the Sam Hill was she chasing down bad guys in her condition? She hadn't been showing when Jake had been with her. Maybe she hadn't known that she was pregnant right away.

The part about her buying his photograph finally registered. And he was concerned all over again. It was as if she wanted to reach out to him but was afraid to.

"All right. I'll be there in the morning." But he'd leave after a few hours' sleep, arrive way before dawn, and search for Alicia's car at hotels all over Breckenridge. Hopefully he'd locate her before she had a chance to vanish again.

"I just thought you should know."

"Thanks, Mary. I really appreciate this."

"You ought to marry her, you know. I didn't see that she had a wedding ring."

Jake glanced at Darien, knowing that with their enhanced hearing, his brother could hear what was being said through the mouthpiece.

Darien raised his brows again.

How could he tell Mary that, in werewolf fashion, they didn't marry but mated for a lifetime? And since Alicia was human, that meant turning her. But with her carrying a baby, no way in hell could he or any other wolf risk the consequences. Turning a human was chancy at best and rarely done on purpose.

"Thanks, Mary. I'll stop by tomorrow."

They ended the call, and he handed Darien his phone.

"My office," Darien suggested, although it was more of an order.

Jake knew Darien would tell Lelandi what was going on because she jointly led the pack and she had a need to know. But he didn't have to like it.

As soon as Jake shut the door to Darien's office, Darien took a seat in the sitting area instead of behind his desk.

"What's going on, Jake? She has a gray wolf name."

"But she's not one of us. She has a wolf's name, but you and I both know that the names we've chosen are *not* exclusive to our species."

"All right." Darien leaned back in his tall leather chair. "So what's this all about?"

"She's human and got into trouble at a restaurant where I had eaten breakfast while waiting for the gallery to open. The opening had been delayed. Anyway, she's a bounty hunter and—"

"*Bounty hunter*?" Darien looked surprised as hell.

"Yeah, and she's after a couple of mobster types."

Darien didn't say anything for a minute, then shook his head. "She's *pregnant*?"

He didn't voice any opinion about why Jake would have been having sex with a human woman who was pregnant. He had to figure that Jake had sense enough to know better.

"She didn't look pregnant when I saw her. She had a man under surveillance, and he'd sent one of his thugs to remove her from the restaurant where I was having breakfast. So I came to her rescue. We were supposed to have a late lunch together, but she left before we could do so. That's why I stayed overnight. I thought either some harm had come to her after all, or she was trying to ditch me."

"You were at a motel together, though."

The shower incident came back to Jake in a vivid recollection. He frowned at his brother. Normally, that should have been his own business. He let out his breath in exasperation. "She *didn't* look pregnant. All right? Give me credit for having better sense than that."

Darien tapped his fingers on the arm of his chair. "Maybe she broke the engagement because she wasn't showing and she was too embarrassed to tell you. Or maybe she's still married. Or separated from a husband."

Jake sighed darkly. "I assume it's something like that now, yes. But I'm glad she's not in danger."

"That doesn't explain why you're returning to Breckenridge."

When Darien's probing look changed to one of concern, Jake sat taller and ground his teeth. "It's just something I have to do."

"Why, Jake? What the hell is going on between the two of you?"

Jake raked his fingers through his hair and stared at the floor before he again held Darien's gaze. "Tell me about this dream mating that happened between you and Lelandi."

Darien's mouth parted. Then he clamped his lips tight and didn't say anything for a moment. "You've never believed in it."

"Hell, Darien, I dreamed of her last night. And every night for the past seven weeks. Ever since the day she disappeared."

"The human woman?" Disbelief coated Darien's words.

"Yeah, damn it. She's so real, I swear I made love to her last night. *Again.*"

Darien looked at him thoughtfully, then shook his head. "Can't be happening. Must be just that you're so fascinated by her, you're dreaming about her. We can't dream mate with humans."

Jake let out his breath in exasperation. "Maybe it's an anomaly. Maybe it's just a really rare occurrence. But from what you've told me about you and Lelandi, this is the same thing that happened between the two of you."

"If this woman's not a wolf, she's carrying a human child. You *can't* change a woman and her child. A woman, if the situation is dire enough, but not her unborn child."

"All right, all right. I hadn't planned to turn her. I just want to know she's safe."

Darien frowned at him. "I'm *serious* about this, Jake."

"Your *concern* is duly noted. Is that all?"

"Jake..." Darien's tone was consoling.

Jake didn't need consolation. He needed to see Alicia again, craved seeing her, and had to find out what had happened to her over the past seven weeks. He had to be sure she was truly safe and well.

Jake nodded. "I know my place, Darien. I know what I can and can't do. See you in the morning."

His heart warring with his mind, he left Darien's office and headed for the stairs. He was past ready to move out.

He hated that a dream could make him crave someone so badly. Hated that he couldn't have her in the flesh the way he wanted.

She was pregnant. He just couldn't believe it.

In his bedroom, he jerked off his clothes and dropped them on the floor. He glanced at the polished top of his dresser, at the copper hair clip that had bound Alicia's satiny curls when he had made love to her in the forest in Breckenridge that one day—the only physical evidence he had connecting him to her.

He yanked his bedcovers aside. No matter how much he told himself it was insane, he climbed into bed and waited for her— with wretched eagerness and abject desperation.

———————————

She had it bad, Alicia thought, as she pulled off her clothes in the scroungy room—in the only motel she could find in the tiny town of Crestview—and laid her things neatly over a chair. If it hadn't already been so late and she hadn't been afraid she wouldn't find another hotel with a vacancy in another town, she'd have driven on.

Right now, all she wanted was to be with the man of her dreams, but she had a job to do—relocate and start her life over.

She couldn't risk any of Constantino's cronies catching up to her if he thought to get revenge for her turning him in. In the future, until she could figure out another way to make a living, she'd go after only bail-bond jumpers with non-Italian names, to stay on the safe side. And only work during the day, although she'd shifted some during the day as well, so that wasn't a guarantee of anything. But she hadn't realized that the moon was nearly full, and she suspected that was why she'd felt a sudden need to shift.

Hating that she would be driving right past Silver Town tomorrow and beyond without a word to Jake, she wondered if there was another route she could take.

Jake! She meant to at least call someone in Silver Town and leave a message that she was alive and well. But when she pulled her cell phone out of her purse, she flipped the phone open and recalled that the battery was dead. She had to charge it. She started the charge and glanced at the room phone. If she couldn't call him on her phone after taking her shower, and it would have been charging for an hour or so, she'd make a long-distance room call instead.

Then with her lavender shampoo and tangerine body wash in hand, she walked into the grungy bathroom. The grout in the floor was no longer white but a dirty gray, rust stains lined the sink from a perpetually dripping faucet, and the shower curtain was covered with a light sheen of soap scum, but the floor of the porcelain tub seemed clean enough. She turned on the water, waited for it to get hot, then slipped inside to shower.

She soaped up her hair with the shampoo, wanting to wash away the past few weeks' events, going back to when she'd been doing damn well. Her hands stilled in the suds on top of her head where she'd piled her soapy hair. When the men had come to kill Ferdinand at his town house, she'd smelled the cologne of the man who'd entered the bedroom where she'd hidden under the bed. Ferdinand had already bitten her by that time. And her sense of smell had been highly attuned. A wolf's sense of smell. Would she recognize the man's odor again?

She groaned. If he did come to get her, she'd most likely recognize him because of her enhanced sense of smell and know she was a dead woman before the deed was done. Some help that would be.

She rinsed out her hair, grabbed her bottle of body wash and poured some on her hands, then slathered her whole body with the silky, fragrant wash. It helped disguise the unfamiliar, unwanted odors in the bathroom and hotel room.

After towel drying her hair and body, she stalked back into the bedroom, unzipped her bag, and drew out a silky blue nightie. She pulled it on, then climbed into bed and slipped between the harsh sheets. She was glad they smelled of bleach and not the last occupant's odor. Sometimes to save money and to avoid the work, the hotel staff didn't bother to change the sheets between customers. Not that she'd let them get away with it.

Woe to those who didn't have a wolf's senses and couldn't detect such a thing. On the other hand, there was something to be said about the old adage—*Ignorance is bliss*.

She closed her eyes, wanting to welcome her dream lover into her arms, and waited. Breathless with anticipation.

The first time he had come to her, she had known it was just a dream. Very, very real, but just a dream. And she loved conjuring him up, loved making him come to her. He was every bit as much an addiction as chocolate—the really rich, dark kind.

She breathed in the stale air, the smell of bleached sheets, the faint odor of cigarette smoke in what was supposed to be a nonsmoking room, the dustiness. Felt the scratchy sheets against her bare skin and the equally scratchy comforter decorated in brown palm trees that probably had never been washed, noted the picture of palm trees nailed to the wall—and wondered if the Colorado motel owner fantasized about having a resort in Florida. She hated not being in her own bedroom on her comfortable saggy mattress, the sheets supersoft, and having her pillow too.

But she was afraid if she returned there for very long, they'd catch up to her. If she could, she'd clean out her bank account, give notice, take as much from her apartment as she could fit in her car, and leave the rest behind with no forwarding address. Although she'd worked hard to afford her furniture, and she hated having to abandon it.

Sometime during the night, as the heat of the day subsided and a dry coolness filled the room, she began to slip off to the world of sleep.

Vaguely, she became aware of another presence in her room.

At first, a peculiar sense of recognition washed over her, reassuring her that she was safe, that whoever or whatever she was sensing wouldn't harm her.

Then she saw him, materializing in the darkness like a shadowed lover. Distractedly, she remembered the phone call she hadn't made. Damn. Tomorrow, first thing.

Jake approached, and she forgot everything else but him.

Advancing, his hair the color of rich, dark-brown earth after a summer rain, his eyes of the same shade and darkly intense, his masculine lips curved up faintly in the hint of a smile, he moved toward her in a slow, methodical, predatory way. In the past few weeks since she'd been turned, when her world seemed to be spiraling downhill faster, only Jake had made her life bearable. She wanted him at night, every night, for as long as she lived, which might not be very long the way things were going.

Naked, he flexed his muscles, stood a little taller, and saw her and only her. Still covered in the comforter up to her neck because of the chill in the air, she gave him a subdued smile back. It was always the same. An acknowledgment that they were here in concert for this, but no wild throwing themselves together in the heat of the moment. Deep down, she felt it was because she feared that if she did leap from the bed and jump into his waiting arms, he'd just vanish. Poof. And never come again.

So she waited for him, waited for his large, capable fingers to pull back the comforter, to feel his hands lifting her gown off her. He always started with his gentle, then urgent strokes, his lips and tongue teasing her, his mouth on her breast.

But this time, he seemed hesitant. She frowned a little. He couldn't leave her now. Not when he was the only bright spot in her life. A too-real figment of her imagination.

He raked his fingers through his hair. She parted her lips as if to speak. She never had spoken to him before. Had never needed to. Didn't think she really could. But he seemed so unsure, as if he was reevaluating why he was here.

He couldn't. He was here because she made him come. She pulled her arms free from the comforter and was about to stretch them out to him, to encourage him to join her. How could he come to her and then decide he couldn't do this?

And then he sighed, although she never could hear sounds in her dreams, except for the blood rushing in her ears, her own panting breath when he stroked her into submission, her heart beating wildly. Her smile widened.

But he didn't smile back. Still reserved, she thought. Still bothered by something. Yet he approached her with an aggressive stride, yanked the covers aside, and stared at her belly, the pale-blue gown she wore having risen to her thighs. Her naked legs didn't hold his attention, and his gaze focused on her waist. He slid the silky fabric up her thighs, past her hips, higher until her belly was exposed, then kissed her there. She wasn't sure how to read his actions, but then she reached for him, spread her legs willingly, opened herself to him, and encouraged him to join her.

He climbed onto the bed, situating himself between her legs, but kept his weight off her as he tackled her mouth with his. His kiss was hard and fierce, his jaw lightly whiskered and rough. If she didn't know *better, she'd swear she'd have whisker burns on her cheeks after they made love. His tongue dove into her mouth, impatient, impassioned, and she met his craving move for move. God, he was beautiful, and she desired him with all her heart.*

"You're the only good thing in my life," she mouthed against his lips, wishing there could be more to their relationship than this.

He paused, staring at her with such intensity that it was as if he'd truly heard her words and felt her sentiment, and then he kissed her hard again. His hand encompassed a breast, fondled and stroked, caressed her nipple with the pad of his thumb, teasing the tip, which was tingling and aching with need. Her breasts were slightly tender, fuller, more sensitive to his touch. Then his mouth moved down her throat, and he brushed his lips across her sensitive skin, licking her there. He seemed desperate with wanting her, just as much as she felt about him. His hand stroked her deeply between her legs, where she was already hot and wet and swollen for him, her core aching with such an intensity that she could barely last.

She envisioned she was still at home in her own bed with the man in her dreams making wild passionate love with her. His fingers dipped in between her legs, caressing her into climax while she gripped his waist and never wanted to let go.

She felt the earth shift, the bed, the room, the whole world as she reached the peak and shattered with the most riveting ecstasy. Vaguely, she felt his fingers withdraw before he filled her with his arousal, hard and hot and very much ready for action.

But this time, he raised her legs over his shoulders for maximum penetration and dove into her with hard, deep, satisfying thrusts, his face dipping to kiss her breast, to lick the nipple, her hands running through his hair as she moaned with satisfaction. He knew how to give her pleasure like she'd never felt before. His lusty gaze shifted to hers. His expression was still dark, and she couldn't read it now. Before, he'd always been so pleased with her, to see her, to be with her, but now... something was amiss. As if he was tired of playing this game. But he was hers, her dream. He had to be here for her whenever she drifted off to her fantasy world of dreams.

She moaned as he stole her thoughts, brought her rising again on another tidal wave of pleasure, had her grasping for his sinewy arms, and he groaned, pumping into her until he was spent, then collapsed and didn't move. He was heavy and sweaty and felt protective and manly and wonderful.

He lay there for some time, and at first she thought her dream lover had fallen asleep, but then he lifted his head, sighed, and rolled off her, then pulled her into his arms and held her tight. He kissed the top of her head, caressing her arm with a soft touch. He'd kiss her and caress her and nap and take her again and again all night long, and by morning, he'd be gone, and she'd still miss him. Until the night returned.

But a vaguely ominous worry crept into the dream. She couldn't shake loose of the feeling that Jake was in danger—and all because of her.

But then something else seized her attention. A sound. Not a key, but...*something*...like...the sound of a plastic card being slipped between the doorjamb and the door with a hard whooshing, sliding sound.

Like someone was trying to break into her room.

CHAPTER 10

ALICIA WAS CLOAKED IN THE WARMTH OF HER DREAM STATE, STILL wrapped in Jake's arms when he turned to look at the rickety motel-room door that could easily have been shattered with a swift booted kick. His hand froze in midcaress along Alicia's arm, as if he could recognize that someone was trying to break into her room. Then he set Alicia aside, climbed out of bed, and stalked toward the door like her knight without his armor.

For a second, she didn't know what to do. Get dressed, her mind shouted at her. Get your gun, do something—before Jake is killed.

Her heart rate had picked up into flight-or-fight mode, and the adrenaline was already pouring through her veins. But she couldn't move. She was frozen in place, only able to stare at Jake and at the door.

Then she felt her mind awakening. She was still in a dream. Jake wasn't really here!

Still half-asleep, she tried to break free of the dreamy fog that shrouded her mind. If she didn't fully wake from the dream, who-ever was trying to break into the scuzzy room would be in soon, and she could be in real danger.

Unless... she sighed deeply...that was only part of the dream.

The card scraping between the door and frame sounded louder, more urgent, and she opened her eyes in disbelief. She sat up in bed, pulling completely free of the dream, and found herself alone, but the plastic card continued to jerk up and down in the doorjamb in an attempt to disengage the lock.

Heart pounding as if she were running a race, she quickly con-sidered her options as she thrust her covers aside and got out of bed.

If she turned into the wolf, she could face the would-be intruder with a set of frighteningly wicked canines. He'd most likely believe she was someone's guard dog. And run like hell. Or she could get her gun, which she was still licensed to carry. But it was in her bag on the other side of the room. She might not be able to shift. She'd never tried to force herself to shift into the wolf, only to shift back into her human form. That knowledge sent a prickle of worry skittering over her skin.

Naked, she sprinted across the room, only to reach her bag when the lock clicked open on the door. Thoroughly immobilized, she shifted her gaze to the doorknob. And prayed her ability to shift would kick in.

To her profound relief, she felt the shift coming on. With heat suffusing every cell, her bones and skin and muscles painlessly melted into what felt like heated taffy—like her grandmother, God rest her soul, had made when she lived with Alicia and her mother.

In the next instant, Alicia was standing as a gray wolf next to a small dresser, her fur fluffed in offensive mode to make her appear larger and more threatening, her ears twitching back and forth, listening for every sound the intruder made, her tail straight out, her eyes focused on the door, her mouth still closed. She backed even farther into the dark corner.

A human couldn't see her in the lightless room. Not unless light reflected off her eyes. And then? Her eyes could appear to glow yellow, green, or even red, she'd noticed when she'd glanced in a mirror one night and thought, "How cool."

But she'd never bitten a human before, or a wolf for that matter, and the only notion she had was that she'd snarl and growl and look threatening. If he had a gun, though, would he be all that scared?

Getting shot didn't appeal. They'd broken Ferdinand's neck, so she knew she could die in more ways than just by a silver bullet.

She laughed at herself over that. Would a silver bullet really kill, or was that strictly fantasy?

She remained quiet and watched, seething that this creep would break into her room. Yet it reminded her of the thugs who'd come to Ferdinand's apartment, threatened him, and then killed him. Killed the other man he knew too. If they had known she was there in his apartment, hiding under the bed, she was certain she would have faced the same death.

The door remained closed while her heart pounded pell-mell. What was he waiting for? Was he afraid? Waiting to see if she responded with a phone call to 911?

She glanced at her phone. Still charging. But if it had a partial charge, she could still use it.

The door opened just a hair, then farther, with no squeaking, no sound, except heavy breathing and hearts pounding, both hers and his. He was scared. As much as she hated to admit it, so was she.

The door opened a little wider. A pinprick of illumination poked into the blackness from a flashlight. The lamp on the outside wall appeared to be out. It hadn't been when she'd checked into her room, so the intruder must have knocked it out and was working virtually blind.

The flashlight's faint beam was pointed in the direction of the bed, but it didn't stretch farther than a few inches and so didn't reach beyond the door, which still shielded her view of the intruder.

With what appeared to be fresh resolve, he moved quickly beyond the door, headed for the bed with flashlight and gun poised. *Shit.* He was armed and looked like he wanted to play really rough.

Despite the black hoodie hiding his hair and some of his profile, she saw his large hooked nose, and he looked damn familiar. She narrowed her eyes.

The creep that had tried to force her out of the restaurant in Breckenridge before Jake came to her aid. The same one who had been with the man she'd shot on the trail where she'd laid her mother's memorial wreath. His light flicked over the empty bed, the covers tossed aside. His flashlight swept over the chair where her clothes now lay. *Hell.* He would know she was still in the room. That she hadn't gone out to party. Party, right. The town boasted one rickety motel, and the whole place looked to have rolled up the sidewalks hours before sunset.

His gaze shifted to the bathroom. She barely breathed. Not once looking in her direction, he headed slowly for the bathroom.

Had he followed her all the way here from Breckenridge? She wondered if he'd watched her when she arrived at the motel and then waited until she'd taken her shower, turned out the lights, and climbed into bed. Maybe waited until sufficient time had passed for her to fall asleep. Or had he just located her car and was working blind?

She didn't think she had enough time to shape-shift and then dress and bolt from the room, start the car, and leave. *No*, she knew she didn't have time for all that.

The thought of running out of here in her wolf form terrified her. She wasn't equipped to deal with the wolf angle in the wild. She didn't want to leave her car behind or her other possessions. And if she bolted out of here, the thug would discover that Alicia, the woman, wasn't here and most likely would wait for her to return.

He slid the shower curtain aside with a swift jerk, the metal rings sliding across the metal pole with a scratching sound.

Now he knew for certain she wasn't in there, and he'd come out, maybe try looking under the bed, or maybe glance in her direction and see her standing here as a wolf, staring him down in the dark.

He'd shoot her, and no one would ever know she'd disappeared, and no one would even care.

She changed her mind and was able to summon the shift again—to her astonishment and guarded relief—before he left the bathroom. Maybe having been a werewolf for seven weeks with a couple of weeklong breaks and then the trouble she'd had with it earlier, like she'd just had to get used to it again, had finally enabled her to get some control over this shape-shifting business.

She grabbed the gun from her purse.

As soon as the pinprick of light headed out of the bathroom and he followed, she wondered if she had made another mistake and should have stayed in her wolf form. Standing naked with only a gun in her hand for defense made her feel horribly vulnerable.

But then again, she could see well in the dark while he couldn't.

That was when he must have caught a glimpse of her, and he aimed his weapon with cold-bloodedness. She'd already anticipated his action and moved right before he fired a shot. The round hit the wall behind her, and she fired three times, all three slugs hitting something solid. His only response was a grunt, then he slid down the wall, leaving a trail of blood.

Oh God. She stared at him in disbelief as the acrid odor of gun smoke wafted through the air. How could this thug do this to her? The past few weeks had already been bad enough!

Then she shifted her attention to the open door. What if there were more of them? What if he wasn't acting alone? They never acted alone. At least she didn't think so.

Her hands shaking, she quickly shoved her gun in her purse, sprinted across the floor, and closed the door, locking it—although that hadn't done a lot of good before. She rushed to the man and checked his wrist and then his neck for a pulse. None.

She returned to her suitcase, pulled out black jeans and a black sweatshirt, and hurriedly jerked them on.

She looked back at the man, his mouth open, his eyes staring lifelessly at her, his head leaning against the wall.

Dead. He was dead.

Perspiration trickled down her breasts despite the cool air, and she rubbed her arms as her heart continued to beat at a racer's pace. God, what was she to do now?

She had to call this in to the police, as much as she didn't want to. If any of this guy's buddies were about and she hung around to meet with the police, she'd be dead meat. And no number of police in this rinky-dink little town could protect her. If they even had any police here.

But she was one of the good guys, she had to remind herself. She couldn't kill a man and leave the scene of the crime without just cause.

She paced.

Hell, if she didn't call it in, someone else in the motel was sure to have heard the gunshots and would dial 911, and then the police would question her as to why *she* hadn't called it in. She would sound guiltier than she already felt. Even though *he* had broken into her room and tried to kill her first.

She jerked the phone off the hook next to the bed and punched in the number, then lifted the receiver to her ear. An eerie silence met her ear. The line was dead. Another spiral of fear cascaded down her spine. He'd cut the phone lines. This was *so* not good.

Then she heard two car doors open and shut just outside her room. Either a couple of legitimate hotel guests were arriving late for the night...or they were cohorts of the dead guy. She was certain she wasn't hearing the police because it would be too soon for them to arrive and no police lights were flashing outside the window.

She stood frozen with indecision and went back to her earlier plan. Change into the wolf, or hope that, fortified with only a gun, she could be as lucky against two armed men, if that was what she faced, as she had been against one. With the way her luck was going, she was sure it had just completely run out. She raced across the floor, grabbed her cell phone, and flipped it open. Thank God, it had a little bit of a charge.

After punching in 911, she watched the door, waiting for someone to answer the phone, waiting for anyone to touch the doorknob. Then in her panic, she couldn't remember. Had she locked the door?

The doorknob twisted. Her heart thundered.

Someone spoke into her ear. "Sheriff's department. What is the nature of your emergency?"

Alicia nearly dropped the phone in surprise at hearing the woman's deeply brusque voice.

The doorknob didn't twist any farther. It was locked. Alicia didn't say anything into the phone, afraid that if she did, whoever was trying to gain entrance into her room would hear her. Which was probably crazy. He had to have figured she'd killed the other thug already.

Startling her, the woman repeated the question, more insistent this time. "This is the *sheriff's department*. What is the nature of your emergency?"

Alicia licked her lips and said in a whisper, "Someone broke into my motel. Crest—"

But the minuscule relief Alicia felt that the person at the door couldn't open it without unlocking it didn't last long. A strong kick at the door broke a lower section of the paneling away, the crash making Alicia jump back.

"They're trying to kill me! Crestview Motel. They're breaking in!" she shouted, the need for secrecy a moot point, as she hoped the sheriff's department was close by. But she hadn't seen any sign of one when she had stopped there for the night.

She dropped the phone, still open, still charging, on the dresser, but she didn't have any more time to speak to the operator.

The woman was trying to get her attention. "Miss, stay on the line. What's happening? Police are being dispatched to your location. Your name?"

So they could identify her in the event these men killed her and stole her identity? Or took off with her and left her for dead in some deserted place? What would it matter then?

Alicia decided that, for better or worse, she'd shift—if she could. She thought she was really getting the hang of this, and she figured it was her only chance.

She tugged out of her clothes and dropped them on the floor. The woman on the phone kept talking to her, although Alicia's attention was riveted to the door, where the man kept kicking at the splintering wood, while she tried to force herself to shape-shift again. She couldn't make out the woman's words over her own.

"*Shift, damn it,*" Alicia ordered herself. "*Now. Shift.*"

Fresh fear rippled through her. What if she could only shift so many times in so many hours?

Yet it was her only chance. If she could startle the intruder enough when he saw her as a wolf, she might manage to flee past him and run into the woods surrounding the small town.

And then? She didn't know what to do, just get away from here as far as possible, find a way to steal some clothes, shift, and then keep moving on to somewhere new and different and far, far away from the life she had known.

―――――――――――

Jake was already pacing as he dressed. He knew the woman in his dreams was real, if Darien's dreaming of Lelandi was any indication. And Jake knew Alicia was in trouble, damn it. Yet he couldn't reach out to her, couldn't learn where she was or what had happened to her. She wasn't in the usual places, the nicer hotel rooms with large beds and mirrors and pictures and dressers.

In his dream, she'd been in a dirty, run-down motel, he guessed. The bed had been covered with a comforter of brown palm trees, hideous and garish, along with the picture of palm trees on the wall. Yet…he didn't sense it was Florida. Why not Florida?

Because Mary from the art gallery hadn't called him that long ago. He didn't believe Alicia would have had time to reach an airport by car, then fly to Florida and get a room.

The phone book. Sitting on the bedside table in Alicia's room, it had "Crestview" printed on the front. That was a town one hour southeast of Silver Town.

And someone had been about to break in.

He called Silver Town's sheriff, waking him from a dead sleep. "Peter, call the sheriff who oversees Crestview. See if a woman has called in a 911. Get back with me ASAP."

He clicked off the phone and headed into the hall. Everyone in the family was still asleep. He didn't intend to wake them if it was all a wild goose chase. How in the hell could he explain he was attempting the rescue of a woman from his dreams? Darien didn't even believe Jake could be dreaming of her for real. Not as his dream mate. Not when she was human.

But how else could he explain the motel room and the phone book, when he'd only passed through the nearly nonexistent town a few times during his life? He was climbing into his truck when Peter called him back.

"There was a 911 call from the Crestview Motel, just like you said. The caller was a woman who said men were breaking in and were going to kill her. The operator said loud bangs could be heard in the background, and she figured a man was trying to break down the door. But she couldn't get anything more from the woman. Then shots were fired."

Hell. "And?" Jake was already barreling down the highway toward Silver Town and would go south on the road toward Crestview from there.

"Her name was Alicia Greiston, with an *e-i* rather than an *a-y.*"

Jake felt sick to his stomach. "Was?"

"Well, I'm not sure. She's gone. By the time the sheriff got there, he found one dead male, his torso riddled with three bullets, and a bullet wedged in the wall across the room. Her purse, clothes, gun, pepper spray, and stun gun were there, and her still-active cell phone was charging on top of one of the dressers, but there was no sign of the woman. And her car is still locked and parked at the motel, driver's side window bashed in. The car battery was gone, so she wouldn't have been going anywhere in the car anyway if she'd tried. Either the man who was dead had broken into the room, and she ran off, or there were others and they've taken her."

He cursed under his breath, not liking any of the scenarios. "Alicia." Jake frowned.

Peter hurriedly said, "What did you want me to do?"

"For now, nothing. I'm heading out there."

"Had she called you?"

Jake didn't say anything.

Peter cleared his throat. "The woman who called from that art gallery in Breckenridge said she gave Alicia Greiston your number."

"Yeah, but Alicia didn't call."

"The phone line was cut to the room, and the cell phone was being charged, so she might not have been able to earlier. But how did you know she needed help if she didn't call?"

"Family thing," Jake said vaguely.

"Oh, okay."

"Thanks, Peter. If I need backup, I'll give you and Darien a ring." He wanted to tell Peter not to inform his brother, but Darien was the pack leader, and if Peter thought Darien needed to know about this, he'd fill him in. And Jake knew Peter would. Darien would most likely be pissed that Jake was continuing to leave him out of the loop.

Sure enough, Jake wasn't more than five minutes down the road when his cell phone's familiar jingle alerted him. He yanked the phone from his pocket and said, "Yeah."

"What the hell is going on?" Darien said hotly.

"She's in trouble. The woman I keep dreaming about. She's not pregnant. Or at least she sure as hell doesn't look that way."

"Then why would she say…" Darien didn't say anything for a moment, then he grunted. "You said she's not a gray wolf. Are you *certain*?"

For a split second, Jake mulled that over. Then he frowned. "Of course I'm certain. I was with her in Breckenridge that first day."

"What if she was bitten *after* you saw her?"

Jake considered that scenario, his hackles instantly rising. "Hell. If she's been bitten recently, she most likely has very little control over the shift." But that would explain why he was dream mating with her. She needed him desperately.

"She could have shifted at the gallery and didn't know what else to do about being stuck in the ladies' room."

"It makes sense." Jake let out his breath. It changed everything between them. "Then who turned her?"

"Someone who's after her possibly, or someone who's dead. That may be the reason she's never tried to hook up with you. Without knowing you're also a wolf, she wouldn't want to risk discovery."

"Hell. Alicia has to be frantic." He only hoped to hell she was still alive so he could rescue her once again. And then they'd deal with all the issues she had to face—these men, a possible pack, her wolf genetics, her need for a mate—*him*.

Silence met Jake's ears, then Darien finally said, "All right. Well, Peter said she's in a hell of a lot of trouble. You can't go it alone."

"I'm going to track her down, locate her scent, see what I can come up with."

"Fine. But I'm sending Peter and Tom for backup. And next time you have the urge to rescue some damsel in distress, let me know first, will you?" Darien hung up on Jake.

Jake let out his breath in an exasperated huff. Yes, they worked together as a pack. And Jake was obligated to let his pack leader know what he was up to when there was trouble in the wind.

But that was under normal circumstances. This was way beyond normal. And he wasn't about to wait for everyone to get a move on when he was well on his way to locating his dream mate, with or without his pack's help.

Jake was doing this *his* way.

CHAPTER 11

As a gray wolf, Alicia bolted out of the hotel and ran at a gallop, tearing through the woods and keeping close to the road that would take her to Silver Town. At this point, she figured she had *nowhere* else to turn. Although in the back of her mind, she kept telling herself she shouldn't try to locate Jake. That seeing him again would cause more problems than she was willing to face. He'd want to see more of her, to protect her. And she knew she'd end up having to bite him. Turn him. Just like Ferdinand had done to her. So that Ferdinand—in his own words—wouldn't be alone. If she turned Jake, *she* wouldn't be alone.

But she couldn't do that to Jake.

So why was she still running toward Silver Town? Because for the first time in her life, she *really* didn't know what else to do. And she realized then just how isolated she'd become. No real friends, not after her mother had been murdered by the Mob, and no family left.

Running through the pines and spruce and ash trees, she just hoped no one would shoot her.

She'd have given anything to see those bastards' faces after she'd bitten the one in the arm who'd swung around to shoot her, once he'd broken into the room and seen his buddy sitting dead against the wall. His jaw had sagged, his eyes had widened, and he'd lowered his gun in surprise. She'd lunged at him as if it was instinctual and bitten as hard as she could, afraid anything less wouldn't have gotten the message across.

And the other big, burly, black-haired man had squeaked like a girl when she'd swung her head to bite him. *Danny Massaro.* The guy she was supposed to serve a warrant on. Ferdinand's brother, whom Ferdinand said would kill Alicia and him if Danny had the opportunity. She recognized his cologne. He'd been at Ferdinand's condo and had come looking for her when she had hidden under the bed. He was partly responsible for Ferdinand's death. Maybe even the one who had ultimately killed him or given the order.

Danny had fired off three shots at the night sky as he fell on his butt, trying to avoid the snap of her jaws and her wicked teeth.

For a damned instant, she'd wanted to arrest him! As if he'd have given her time to shift, dress, grab the arrest warrant and gun, and rearrest him. But then she'd regained her senses, and too concerned he might aim the gun at her the next time, she hadn't stayed around to find out if he was aiming at her for sure.

She thought she might have bitten the other guy a little too hard, though. She wasn't certain, but he'd lost the gun, which was her whole reason for biting him, and her jaws were so powerful that she hadn't realized her own strength. It felt as though she'd crushed the bones. He had cried out in the most guttural pain, then dropped to his knees and collapsed on his face. He couldn't have died, unless she'd given him a heart attack. Right now, she didn't care. She was alive and wanted to stay that way. And the truth of the matter was, if he *had* died, that meant one less killer on Mario's payroll who'd be after her.

She'd run across the street and headed for the woods, only looking back to see Danny still sitting on his butt, staring after her as if he had seen a ghost. Then he scrambled to his feet and ran into the room, ignoring his partner in crime. She was fairly sure he was looking to take care of her—as Alicia the woman, and not in a pleasant way—not realizing Alicia was the wolf that had just escaped them.

Her werewolf condition was wrought with mixed blessings. She didn't like the lack of control she had with shifting. Especially when she couldn't always shift at will or fight the shift during the full moon. But this biting business could come in handy. At least she was a lot more frightening as a wolf than she'd been as a woman with a gun. And to an extent, she liked her enhanced hearing, although trying to focus on one conversation at a time had proved difficult sometimes. The sense of smell was something else. She smelled way too many odors that she didn't want to.

For the first time as a wolf, she'd run good and long and hard, and she wasn't even tired. As a human, she couldn't have run half as fast or long without having gotten stitches in her side and leg cramps. She would have been doubled over, trying to catch her breath. In that sense, she loved the freedom that being a wolf gave her. Until she saw a pickup truck on the road beside the woods headed toward her.

Before she could dodge deeper into the forest, the truck applied its brakes and screamed to a halt. She nearly had heart failure and dove deeper into the woods.

A man hurried out of the truck yelling, "Alicia Greiston! Wait!"

She stumbled in surprise to hear the man calling her name, and the odd familiarity in his voice made her pause for a second.

The door slammed and the sound of crashing through the underbrush forced another healthy shot of adrenaline surging through her veins, and she bolted again.

He couldn't think he could chase her down. And how the hell did he know her name? That she was the woman who was now a wolf? Had Ferdinand told someone that he'd turned her before he died?

That was the only reasonable explanation she could come up with. But even so, how would he know she was in these woods?

"Alicia! It's me!"

The man's voice sounded like Jake Silver's. The truck, now that she thought about it further, did look like Jake's. But it couldn't be him. That had to be wishful thinking on her part. Wishing he'd come to her rescue. A *wolf's* rescue, rather.

Whoever it was would never catch up to her. Then just as abruptly, she didn't hear the sound of his crashing through the underbrush any longer, and she slowed to a trot. She didn't want to get too far away from the road and lose her way.

But then she heard something else. Something quieter approaching her at a run. She whipped around and nearly had a heart attack. A *big* gray wolf was running toward her, and her heart skipped beats all over the place. She turned to run away, but he leaped and tackled her. Her heart stuttered.

With his heavier weight, she fell beneath him, and he pinned her down, his mouth at her throat, forcing her to hold still. He didn't hurt her, but she knew that those wicked teeth clamped around her throat could kill her instantly.

Oh God, she'd managed to save herself from a bunch of thugs only to be killed in the wild by a real wolf.

She whimpered, scared out of her wits, wanting to thrash at him with her teeth but afraid he'd crush her throat. He was panting and so was she. His chest heaved, but hers even more so since she'd been running for so long. Forever, it seemed, he just held her there, not letting her up, pinning her to the forest floor, in charge, in control. Wouldn't he be surprised if she just shifted into a woman? Yeah, and then he'd kill her for sure.

He couldn't be thinking of mating with her, could he?

Oh God, what a horrible thought.

She struggled a little, testing him to see his reaction. He squeezed tighter on her throat, still not hurting but showing her he was in charge.

She might not have grown up around wolves, but she got the distinct impression his actions meant hold still, don't move, or else. She held still. She was a quick learner.

She closed her eyes, tired from running and being up late with her dream lover and fighting the bad guys. The wolf relaxed his grip on her throat, but as soon as she moved just a hair, he clamped down again—not injuring her, just keeping her where he wanted her. She'd already gotten the point, but they couldn't stay like this forever. What did he want with her?

The roar of an engine, braking of a vehicle, and slamming of two doors up at the road forced a fresh wave of panic to swallow her whole. She struggled to get up; the wolf forced her to lie still. He couldn't be crazy enough to want to keep her here. What if those who were coming were Mario's men? More than that, no wolf in its right mind would want to remain here when humans were approaching.

"Jake?" a man called out. His voice sounded eerily like the first man who had yelled after her, calling her by name.

But what had happened to that man? The wolf couldn't have torn into him. She swallowed convulsively.

Then she reconsidered. The only one she knew by the name of Jake was Jake Silver. And the voice. The voice sounded like his. Yet he couldn't have known she was out here. And if he'd had any inkling that she was, why had he stopped his truck by the roadside and chased after her—a wolf—calling her by name?

No way in hell could he know she was the wolf. Unless…unless *Ferdinand Massaro* had told him. A cold chill ran through her. She shuddered.

What if Jake was in on this with Ferdinand? What if Jake also had a vendetta against Mario? And that was why Jake had come after her at the restaurant once he'd spied her, then made friends with her in Breckenridge, *trying to keep her safe*. Maybe it all had been a ploy. Keep Alicia safe from Mario's men so that he and Ferdinand and whoever else was in their little gang could use her to do their bidding. Maybe Jake knew Ferdinand wanted Alicia for his own. Maybe Jake had also wanted her.

Because he was a werewolf too.

She swallowed hard, her throat as parched as a dry Colorado summer. She couldn't believe any more werewolves existed. How could she have been so naive about Jake? Thinking that he'd really cherished her like the way he'd behaved? She should have known the way he'd acted toward her wasn't genuine. No one had ever treated her the way he had, as though he had really cared. The notion would have upset her more if she'd had time to reflect and wasn't so desperate to get away.

As soon as she could, she had to escape the whole lot of them and disappear for good. How in the world could her life have turned so inside out?

She twitched her ears, listening to the approaching men as they ran through the woods. What if the two men headed into the forest toward Alicia and this wolf holding her hostage were all werewolves too?

A shiver stole up her spine.

As the two people grew closer, she again instinctively struggled to free herself. And the wolf again forced her to stay still. If he'd been a normal wild wolf, he would have run off to protect himself. Even if he'd been someone's pet, she didn't think he could be trained to pin down another wolf until his "master" arrived.

The only saving grace? They didn't seem to want to kill her. But she was still one of the good guys, and being the lover of anyone who would call Ferdinand Massaro friend wasn't in the plans.

"Jake?" the man called out again and sounded worried.

The other person running with the one who was speaking remained quiet.

And then they drew close. Really close, their feet tromping through the underbrush only a few feet away. Then she saw them.

Alicia's mouth gaped as she stared at the one man, who looked a hell of a lot like Jake Silver. His brother. Had to be.

This man was tall and broad-shouldered with brown hair a little lighter than the man who had stolen her heart. This one had a more jovial expression, and his eyes were lighter. He looked so much like Jake that the similarities were uncanny, though.

"Hey, Jake, is this Alicia Greiston?" the man asked, crouching near her head, his gaze focusing on hers, but she thought he was addressing the male wolf pinning her down.

As much as she couldn't believe it, the wolf had to be Jake Silver, her dream lover.

She took a deep breath and smelled the new man. A wolf. A sexy, virile wolf. She couldn't believe he was one too.

The other man joined him, his hair nearly black and his eyes just as dark. But what impressed her most was the police uniform he was wearing. And for the first time since her nightmare with the Mafia guys, she relaxed. But then she recalled Mario had a fair number of cops in his pocket. And a judge or two.

She stiffened.

"Is it her, Tom?" the police officer asked.

"If the way Jake's holding her still is any indication, it sure looks to be," Tom said. "What do you want me to do with her, Jake?" He dropped a bundle of clothes down next to the wolf that was pinning her down.

Without a doubt, Jake was the wolf, which meant *he* had to be a werewolf. Newly turned like her? Had Ferdinand turned him too?

No, no, Ferdinand had said he was all alone. That he didn't want to be alone. She was sure that was why he had turned her.

She stared at Jake in disbelief. She'd never get used to any of this. How many were there really?

Jake slowly released her, but she didn't move. His eyes told her to stay still. Dark concerned eyes. He sat up, but he was still way too close. She was certain that if she tried to bolt, he'd pin her right back down.

Tom put his hands on his hips. "Two of the men who went after her got away. They could be looking for her now. Should we take her home with us?"

But she hadn't seen Jake since she'd been turned. He couldn't have known unless Ferdinand had told him. None of it made any sense. Maybe Ferdinand hadn't been making any sense to her that night.

And maybe all of these men were in with Ferdinand Massaro. Or maybe only Jake. The others might be clueless about what Jake had been doing in Breckenridge.

The wolf stood and kept a wary eye on her. She finally moved to a sitting position, figuring she didn't have much choice about where she was going. Surely, these men meant to protect her for now, which had to be a good thing. Until she could shift, grab some clothes, and run.

Tom motioned back to the road. "We'll take you with us. Don't run, Alicia. Jake will chase you down if you try, and we'll have to resort to other measures. We'll give you protection at our home. You won't get a better offer."

Offer. The kind that no one could refuse. Jake had no intention of letting her go. Just like Ferdinand, if he hadn't been murdered, had planned to keep her for his own.

She would probably shift again before long, and then without clothes to wear, what was she to do?

Alicia stood, more shakily than she wanted to let on, then trotted back toward the road. Jake kept pace beside her, brushing her shoulder and hip with his as if to remind her he wasn't going to permit her to deviate from her path. But his touching her was also a reminder of the intimacy they'd shared and which seemed odd now that they were both wolves. She wouldn't have thought she could feel that way about him in this form. Yet the deep feelings of longing for him stirred in her blood just like they always did when he was with her, either for real or in her dream state.

She didn't try to move away from him, too aware of the way his heated body felt touching hers, making her desire him something fierce. She craved that closeness and wanted to renew their friendship, to make love to him in the flesh again and rekindle the bond that came of the sexual contact. And that made her hate herself for allowing herself to be taken in by his dark, seductive ways. For wanting a wolf. But he wasn't just a wolf. He was Jake. The man of her dreams. The man who had swept her off her feet the minute she'd laid eyes on him in Breckenridge that first day.

She glanced at him and couldn't help but admire the beautiful way his dark-brown fur masked the hairs between his eyes and ears, the fur dark red down his nose, and the same dark red coloring the curves of his ears, while he had beige fur underneath his chin and on his throat and chest. Dark-brown fur covered his back like a saddle. He looked…distinguished, intelligent, his darkened brown eyes looking back at her, watching her expression as if he was trying to read what she thought of him. And in an instant, she *remembered* him from before. Remembered the way the wolf had growled at the two men who had accosted her on the trail where she'd left the wreath for her mother. *This* wolf. Jake.

She barely breathed as she thought about it further. About how the wolf had run off, then Jake appeared shortly afterward on the path. It had been Jake, coming to her protection.

That again tied him in with Ferdinand Massaro, didn't it? He was a werewolf like Ferdinand, so they had to have a connection. That he and Ferdinand both were gunning for Mario. But when the men had come after her, definitely Mario's men, Jake had once again stepped in to ensure her safety. She didn't want to think of Jake like that. She didn't want to believe he'd just been using her.

Breaking into her dark thoughts, Jake nuzzled her face, and the feeling was akin to the caress of a soft cheek against a soft cheek, only in this case, fur against fur. But her whiskers were extremely sensitive, and his touching hers was pure delight, no matter how much she attempted to rally against the feelings he stirred in her.

He licked her face, then continued to run beside her, sticking close, touching, endearing, reassuring. Like when he'd held her cold hand in the restaurant, letting her know he was there for her when the menacing thug was ordering her from the place, Jake was here for her now. But it seemed unreal to feel these things for him as a wolf when he was also one.

Maybe he did truly care for her, but the fact that he had been with Ferdinand ruined any chance she and Jake would have ever had.

"Peter can drive if you don't want to shift back," Tom said to Jake. "Or I can. I'll let Darien know we're headed back to Silver Town." He pulled a cell phone off his belt and flipped it open, then punched a button. "Hey, Darien, we've found Alicia Greiston. The little lady's a pretty gray wolf. We're headed back to town now." He paused and looked at Jake. "Yeah, Jake's a wolf right now too. All right. See you in about an hour," Tom said into his cell phone, then snapped it shut and shoved it back in its pouch.

Peter pulled open the door to his Suburban, and Tom tossed Jake's clothes in the back seat.

"I'll drive Jake and Alicia. You can drive Jake's truck back to the house," Tom said.

"Will do." Peter loped ahead to Jake's truck.

"Too bad I didn't know you were one of us, or I could have brought a change of clothes for you," Tom said to Alicia. "Wait!" he called out to Peter. "Why don't you drop by the motel in Crestview and see if you can get Alicia's suitcases released to you?"

The police officer shook his head. "They'll confiscate everything at the crime scene. The sheriff will need to get Alicia's statement, too, once she shifts back."

Great. In a way, she'd thought she was off the hook with the police. How in the world was she to explain what had happened at the motel? One minute she was human and the next a wolf?

"All right," Tom agreed, then let Alicia into the back seat of the vehicle. "I'm Tom Silver. The big gray wolf behind you is Jake, my older brother by five minutes. And from what Darien said, the two of you are already well acquainted. Darien is our eldest brother and our pack leader and runs Silver Town. Jake and I are subleaders, and Peter Jorgenson is the sheriff for the town." Tom gave her a broad smile, his eyes sparkling with humor. "Welcome to the pack."

———————

Jake sat next to Alicia in the back seat of Peter's vehicle, his feelings raw and mixed. He was relieved as hell she was safe and in his custody. And he was glad to know the woman he'd been sharing nocturnal pleasures with was a gray *lupus garou* and that if his family history was correct, she was meant to be his mate.

But this business about the thugs she'd gotten involved with could be a real problem. And the fact that she had to be newly turned was also a dilemma. Who had turned her, and where was he now? Had he mated with her, and if so, was he still alive? Because if he was, Jake could not claim her for his own. That made him wonder if the wolf who had turned her had taught her what she needed to know as one of their kind.

And had the wolf turned her against her will?

He was certain that if he hadn't pinned her down and kept her that way, she would have run off. Until she realized who he was. But she was newly turned, and he was sure the whole wolf business was too unreal for her to swallow yet. She was probably just as stunned to learn he was a wolf, as were his brother and Peter.

At least for now, she seemed resigned to her fate. Jake had half a notion of shifting to reassure her that it was truly him. To speak with her. To learn all he could about her.

She sat staring out the window, avoiding looking at him, he thought. Or maybe she just wanted to see where they were going. But he assumed she was upset.

He couldn't quit watching her, the way she sat so rigidly, so tense, her ears twitching back and forth as she took deep breaths to sample the air. She was smelling the smells, memorizing them, cataloging them. Just as he had memorized her fragrance as a wolf.

He would know her scent anywhere now and even the paw-pad trail she'd left behind as they'd made their way to the vehicle. If she ever ran as a wolf, he'd find her without any difficulty.

Tom said to Alicia, "Either Lelandi can loan you some of her clothes, or one of the other women can."

Hell, Jake wanted to talk to her, and he couldn't do it as a wolf. He shifted, and as soon as he did, she whipped her head around, eyes large and brown and endearing. He gave her a dark smile and pulled on his jeans.

She glanced at Tom. Jake frowned. She hadn't thought her dream lover had been Tom, had she? They did look a hell of a lot alike, except Jake's face had rougher angles, and his hair and eyes were darker.

She looked back at Jake, her gaze taking all of him in, and she swallowed hard.

"Tom, when we get to town, stop at the lingerie store." Jake smiled at Alicia. He had every intention of taking care of her every need.

"Silk and Lace Delights?" Tom's voice sounded surprised. "She won't be open this late."

"I'll call ahead. And we can drop by the all-night discount store after that."

"Do you know her size? As a wolf, she appears taller than Lelandi. But she's not as big as some of our female wolves. Maybe Silva's height?" Tom asked.

From what he'd seen of Alicia, and that was every inch of her delectable body, he figured her to be Silva's height when Silva wasn't wearing high heels to make herself appear taller like the other grays while she waitressed at the Silver Town Tavern. Silva was just as buxom but taller than Lelandi, since Lelandi was a red wolf and Silva a gray. Yeah, he imagined Alicia and Silva were about the same build.

Jake thought about the logistics of the situation further. He wanted to get to know his soon-to-be mate unaccompanied. His grandfather's house would be the ideal setting. Isolated. Away from family so they could really be alone.

"After we shop, you can drop us off at Granddad's old place."

"Darien expects me to bring her back to his house," Tom said, again sounding surprised.

Jake didn't care for that scenario in the least. Everyone would get involved in his business with Alicia when he needed the time alone with her.

"Want me to call and—"

"No." Jake jerked on his shirt. Then he grabbed his cell phone from his pants pocket and called Darien. When his older brother answered, Jake said, "We're making a couple of clothing stops because Alicia has no clothes to change into. After that, we're staying out at the old homestead."

Silence. Jake knew Darien didn't approve.

Darien finally said quietly, "She's unmated?"

"She's not mated." He sure as hell hoped not anyway.

Tom looked up at the rearview mirror. At least Jake didn't think she could be, considering the way she'd made love to him in the dreams.

"Not pregnant either?" Darien asked.

Jake glanced at Alicia. "No, she's not pregnant." At least he guessed she wasn't.

"Bring her to the house," Darien said finally.

Not once had Jake ever gone against Darien's rulings. He might disagree and tell his brother what he felt in private or just with his immediate family present, but not once had Jake openly gone against Darien's decisions. This time, he had to clamp down on his words before he spoke them.

Darien waited for Jake to acknowledge his order, knowing that with every second of delay, Jake was showing how displeased he was.

"We're dream mated," Jake finally said, reminding his brother that Alicia and he were meant to be together and nothing would stop that from happening.

Tom's gaze shot over the back of the front seat from Alicia to Jake, then to the road again.

Darien laughed over the phone. Alicia's ears perked up.

Hell, Jake didn't need this. He would have hung up on his older brother if Darien hadn't finally said, "Bring her home, Jake. We need to learn what's going on with her."

That was when Jake came to his senses, *somewhat*. Thugs had tried to kill her. If they attempted to follow her here, the pack would need to know so they could deal with the threat effectively.

"We'll welcome her to the pack right," Darien added.

The pack. She wouldn't just be Jake's mate but an important member of the pack. And Darien sounded serious. As if he believed Jake had found his mate. But why laugh about it initially? Because Jake had been so obstinate about not believing in such a thing.

He settled back against the seat. "All right. We'll come home."

But he was not resigned to making this a family affair.

***

Feeling a ton of emotions—frazzled, relieved that she was safe for the moment, unsure of herself—Alicia lay down on the seat, having heard Jake's brother tell him to bring her to his home. And Jake was fighting the order. But she could tell by the way Jake's body had lost some of its tension that he was giving in. Reluctantly, but nonetheless, he had capitulated. In a way, she wished she and Jake could have been alone. She'd have a better chance at stealing away from them then.

She hadn't a clue about what would happen when she met the others in the pack, having never been around other werewolves.

And she'd never even considered that werewolves lived in packs. Loners, yes. Like Ferdinand and whoever bit him first. Or just some abnormal aberration—a rabid wolf that had bitten a human and infected him, and no others existed.

But her thoughts kept straying to what Jake had looked like after he'd shifted—in the flesh, totally naked. No longer a dream but the very hard, virile muscled man she'd felt and stroked and loved when they'd first been together. And then she reminded herself how he'd known she was a werewolf. Ferdinand *had* to have told him.

Then she wondered why Jake's brother asked if she was pregnant. Mary. At the gallery. Oh God, poor Jake. Mary must have called him and told him Alicia had fainted at the gallery. And he thought...

She glanced back at him. He was watching her. Then he took a deep breath and ran his hand over her back in a loving caress. It felt good. He felt good. She wanted so badly to share their nighttime fantasies for real again. Damn her soul for falling for him.

She laid her head down on the seat and closed her eyes as he continued to stroke her back. The wickedly sexual part of her wanted to go with him to his grandfather's house and make wild passionate love to him.

But she considered what Jake and his brother had discussed. The mate issue didn't make any sense. Must be a werewolf term for sex with another of their kind. So why did he assume she hadn't been with anyone else? That she hadn't mated? If Ferdinand had lived long enough, she was certain he would have had sex with her—against her will. But thankfully, he hadn't.

Then she saw a sign announcing they'd arrived in Silver Town, and she felt self-conscious. Up until now, she'd been living on her own, putting up with this werewolf stuff the best she could in secret, until she'd bitten one thug's arm and momentarily scared the other witless. But now to be around a whole pack of werewolves when she was so clueless made her feel vulnerable and anxious.

When Tom parked, she quickly sat up and stared at the store's large glass windows. A gold-and-pink-lettered sign perched on top proclaimed the store to be *Silk and Lace Delights*.

Her eyes widened. She'd envisioned a plain, old shop full of the usual—flannel nightgowns for winter, long satin nightgowns for summer, shorter versions, and pajamas. Instead, fiery red corsets, fringed hot-pink bras and thongs, fishnet camisoles and G-string panties, and an iridescent sequin-draped camisole were displayed on headless mannequins in the big windows.

Jake couldn't be serious. Not that she planned to wear other women's undergarments or that she wished to go without—even though sometimes it seemed she might have to when she was in one of her panic-stricken states and needed to strip before she shifted—but what was he thinking?

She looked at another mannequin and read the sign: *peekaboo camisole*. The slits in the bust fitted neatly over the nipples. Her mouth dropped open.

"Stay here with her," Jake said, and when she swung her head around to look at him, he grinned at her. "Be right back."

No thongs, she wanted to tell him. No way was she wearing a piece of silk wedged between her legs. Or a camisole that left her nipples exposed.

But then he was gone, and Tom turned to observe her with a look of wonderment on his face. The sheriff parked beside them and waited, watching Jake enter the lingerie shop, a smile tugging at the corners of his mouth.

Mortified was how she felt. If she hadn't been wearing a coat of fur, she was sure she'd be blushing furiously.

She just hoped Jake didn't get her what *he* thought she should wear to seduce him rather than what *she* would wear for comfort. But when he spoke to a clerk and lightly touched a royal blue corset pushing up the bust situated in the window, Alicia was ready to bolt out of the vehicle and tell him that if he bought it, *he* could wear it.

CHAPTER 12

NORMALLY, JAKE WOULDN'T HAVE BEEN CAUGHT DEAD IN A lingerie store. Certainly not that one. The women loved to get the corsets for the annual Victorian Days for some fun after the celebration, although without a mate, Jake hadn't thought he'd ever get to partake in that part of the fun. The difficult part for the ladies seemed to be trying to pick just one.

Lisa Grae, the thirty-year-old owner, was dressed in a conservative pale-blue dress. She raised her brows to see him come into the shop.

"Hi, Jake. You didn't say why you had to come here tonight." She sounded more than surprised.

"I need some things for a woman who's staying with us."

"Oh. Can she visit and—"

"No."

"But her size. Did she tell you what—"

"She's in the car in her wolf form and has no clothes."

Lisa glanced out the window and frowned. "Oh. Is Sheriff Peter posing as a bodyguard?"

"Yeah."

She sighed. "All right. So you're not looking for anything fun. Just functional."

No, he wasn't looking just for functional. But he let Lisa lead him to the racks of bras anyway. He ran his fingers over the lacy cups, then the satin ones. He picked up red ones, one lace, one satin, the one without any padding, the other with padding beneath the breasts. He didn't know which Alicia would prefer so he would get both.

"Are you certain that's her cup size?"

He put his hand around the cup and nodded. "Appears right."

"Hmm," Lisa said, smiling, and the sound she made was one of speculation. Then she took him to a rack of panties. He selected three pairs of bikini panties in red.

"Maybe a pair of white?"

He shook his head. Red suited her.

Then he looked back at the royal blue corset.

"What about nightwear? A robe or something?"

But now he couldn't tear his gaze away from the body hose that a couple of mannequins were wearing. One was a seductive fishnet, long-sleeved body stocking with an open crotch, and the other, a spaghetti-strapped sheer fishnet body stocking, also with an open crotch. Envisioning Alicia wearing any of it made him hard and wanting.

"A robe?" Lisa repeated, drawing his attention reluctantly from the body stockings.

He fingered a sheer, red-lace short robe.

Lisa smiled and folded her arms. "Does she wear a lot of red?"

He glanced at Alicia watching him through the Suburban window and thought about it, but he didn't remember her wearing anything but white.

"I'll take this," he said, picking out a red shirt-like baby doll that reached just below the crotch, sheer enough to be revealing but opaque enough to entice. He hastily paid for the garments, thanked Lisa, and headed for the door.

Alicia might not wear red normally, but he knew she'd look hot in all of it.

With sack in hand, Jake returned to the vehicle. He smiled at Alicia as Tom drove them to the casual-clothes shop where Jake figured he'd get her a pair of jeans and a T-shirt and sweatshirt. "I'll bring you back to town to shop once you're ready so you can pick up whatever else you might need until we can get your suitcases," he said as she eyed the sack.

When she poked at his hand still grasping the sack, he reached in and pulled out the red lace bra. She looked up at him. "Red would look good on you," he said.

Tom glanced in the rearview mirror.

Jake pulled out a pair of panties. "To match the bra." He slid the robe out and put his hand underneath the fabric, smiling when he could see his skin through the sheer material. He could just imagine what she would look like in the robe. "Do you like it?"

She shook her head. He couldn't tell if she was smiling or shaking her head in disbelief. But he didn't think she was unhappy with his selection. Tom pulled into the parking area of the casual-clothes shop, and Jake didn't take long to pick out two T-shirts, a sweatshirt, and a pair of jeans. He got her some flip-flops, too, not knowing her shoe size but guessing.

Then Tom drove them to Darien's home out in the country. Trying not to show how apprehensive he felt about her shifting when they got there and learning everything about her in front of his family, Jake caressed her back, which helped both of them to relax.

He just hoped to hell he'd learn she wasn't already mated.

As soon as they arrived at Darien's home, Lelandi and Darien greeted Alicia as if she were a long-lost pack member. She remained glued to Jake's side, however, and he recognized that she was feeling anxious.

"Come with me," Lelandi coaxed, "and I'll show you the guest room." She smiled brightly. Jake didn't think he'd seen Lelandi this excited in weeks. She fairly glowed, and he was glad she was so thrilled to see Alicia. That would make it easier for her to fit into the pack. Although Alicia didn't seem any less anxious.

The last newly turned wolf they'd had, Carol, had been from the town, had had psychic visions of what werewolves were beforehand, had been resigned to the fact that she'd be turned, and had had a pack to teach her the ways once she'd been turned. Alicia didn't know anyone here and might not know a lot about being a wolf if a pack hadn't been watching over her. And he didn't think one had.

Alicia glanced up at Jake, and his heart went out to her. If he didn't think it would upset Lelandi, and if he didn't think Alicia might still feel unsure of herself as far as shifting into a naked woman in front of him, he would have insisted on going with her instead.

What the hell. He crouched in front of her and stroked her underneath the chin. "Alicia, did you want me to go with you?"

Her large brown eyes studied him for what seemed an eternity. Tom and Peter were standing behind them, waiting for her response. Darien and Lelandi were just as quiet. Alicia shook her head.

Jake smiled. "All right." Then he handed the two sacks of clothes to Lelandi and rubbed Alicia's head between her ears. "Go with Lelandi then. I'll wait for you down here."

She nudged his thigh in an intimate agreement, then went with Lelandi. He knew Lelandi would be good for Alicia, no matter how apprehensive she might be feeling right now.

When she'd disappeared up the stairs with Lelandi, Darien said to Jake, "We have to talk."

Tom looked halfway glad he wasn't needed for the lecture Jake was sure his brother planned to give him. When Jake and Darien entered his office, Darien took his seat on the couch rather than behind the desk. It was a way of saying, *This isn't pack business as much as it is family business.*

Jake sat on a chair nearby and waited for what Darien had to say, already feeling defensive.

"All right, you don't know for sure if she's mated, do you, Jake?"

"She came to me in my dreams."

"Jake."

"No, not for sure."

"And you don't know if she's pregnant or not."

As much as he hated to admit he truly wasn't one hundred percent sure, Jake shook his head.

"Why are these men after her?"

Jake leaned back in the chair and explained as much as he knew from the time he'd met her to what Peter was sure to have passed along to Darien from the sheriff who oversaw Crestview.

Then women's laughter drifted to them all the way from the upstairs guest bedroom.

Darien raised his brows, questioning Jake as if *he* had a clue what the women thought was so funny.

―――――――――

"Oh, you poor thing," Lelandi said, holding her belly, tears in her eyes because she was laughing so hard as Alicia chuckled again in the guest room where she would be staying. Lelandi's red curls clashed with her red cheeks as Lelandi ran her finger over the "barely there" crotch of one of the red thongs. "I never liked wearing anything this skimpy. Jake must really have it bad for you."

Alicia smiled. "I should buy him one and see how much he likes wearing it."

Lelandi laughed, her green eyes smiling. "He might just like one. You never know. As soon as it's feasible for you to go shopping, I'll take you. Lisa, who owns the lingerie shop, must have been shocked to pieces to see Jake buying for a wolf no one knows."

"Does she know what we are?" Alicia asked, incredulous. She couldn't believe she was in a house full of wolves—Darien, Jake, Lelandi, Tom, and Peter, but that there could be more in the town seemed surreal.

Somehow she had to ask Lelandi about Jake's ties to Ferdinand Massaro, though. She wondered if maybe he alone was tied in with them. That maybe the rest of Jake's family was clueless about his association with the criminals.

"Oh yes. Of course." Lelandi reached out and squeezed Alicia's hand. "We run the town."

"Run the town? Jake said Darien did. But—"

"Our *pack* does. As far as I know, it's pretty rare for a pack to run a whole town. Most packs just infiltrate towns, work at jobs among the humans, live among them, and have their getaway spots when they have to take a run on the wild side. But they don't decide who works in all the key positions. We only allow wolves to run the hospital, in case we have an emergency. And the vet clinic is wolf run too. So are the bank, the bed-and-breakfast, the florist shop, and other businesses. But we'll explain all that later." Lelandi lifted the nearly sheer robe and raised her brows. "This barely covers anything lengthwise, and it's practically see-through. I've got an extra robe if you need one. Do you like red?"

Alicia frowned at the push-up bra. "It's all right. I would never have worn red lingerie, though, if Jake hadn't bought it for me." She pulled on the T-shirt and jeans.

"I have to ask you," Lelandi said, growing serious. "Are you mated?"

Lelandi seemed so concerned that Alicia paused at zipping up the jeans. "I heard Jake talking about it to Darien. Does it mean having had sex with a man?"

Lelandi's eyes widened marginally. "Only if he was a wolf."

"No. Not with a man either, since I was turned." Except for her dreams with Jake, and she didn't figure that counted.

"Good. And you're not pregnant?"

"Oh. No. I'm so sorry about that. I'm afraid I got poor Jake into a lot of trouble over that. I didn't know what else to say when I shape-shifted so all of a sudden at the art gallery. No one saw me, but I had to give a reason for not answering them when it was closing time and I wouldn't leave the restroom stall."

"That must have been horrible for you, Alicia. You're too newly turned to be out in public. I don't want you to worry about it. But the pack is your family, and we take care of our own."

Alicia was so overcome that she gave a hug to Lelandi, who returned the gesture with heartfelt sincerity. Alicia had been so worried about how others would view her that she couldn't believe how welcoming they were. But she had to know if any of them were connected to Massaro and his cohorts. "When are you due?" Alicia asked.

"A month. Triplets are on the way."

"Triplets? Oh my. And…" Alicia's eyes widened. "Jake is a triplet?"

Lelandi smiled. "Mm-hmm."

"Oh." The idea was finally sinking in that if she'd ever had a child with Jake, it could very well be three at once. The worrisome thought suddenly struck her—would they be werewolves too?

"Where's your family?" Lelandi asked, quickly changing the subject, and Alicia wondered if Lelandi could read the worry in her expression.

"I don't have any." Alicia thought Lelandi gave a slight sigh of relief. "My dad ran off when I was two, and my mother and grandmother raised me. But they're both dead now."

"I'm sorry to hear this," Lelandi said with genuine feeling. "But in a way, it makes it easier, because keeping your *lupus garou* genetics secret from them could be a trial." She shifted on the chair and rubbed her lower back. "Darien said you are a bounty hunter. But until you're sure you've got the shifting under control, you'll have to put your job on hold."

Alicia relaxed a little. "I was rethinking whether I should stay in that job anyway after what had happened this last time. Although I often go after women so that we don't have cases of some woman screaming that there was sexual misconduct."

"Something we can talk about later." Lelandi took a deep breath. "Where's the man who turned you?"

Good. The opening Alicia needed. "Dead. And the man who turned him is dead also. Ferdinand Massaro was the name of the one who turned me." Lelandi showed no recognition of the name whatsoever. Alicia tried again. "I thought you might know him since he was one of you."

"Oh my goodness, no," Lelandi said thoughtfully. "Given our uniqueness, our secret is well guarded. Certainly we run into each other in communities beyond our own, but that's the only way we learn others exist."

Alicia sighed with relief. At least Lelandi didn't seem to know this man. "But Jake must have known him then."

A faint look of wariness appeared in Lelandi's eyes, but she quickly changed her expression and gave Alicia a faked smile. "You'll have to ask Jake. Although I have to tell you that when we locate other wolves in other locations, or when they stray into our own territory, we share that knowledge with our pack. It's instinctive. As co–pack leader with Darien, I would have been made aware of this discovery. In that light, I don't believe Jake knew the man who bit you."

Alicia didn't know what to think. On the one hand, she got the distinct impression Lelandi was defending Jake—that the coolness or hint of condemnation Alicia had tried to keep out of her voice when she mentioned Jake knowing Ferdinand had put Lelandi on the defensive. Alicia had to remember she was dealing with a family—one that seemed cohesive and all supporting. And *she* was the outsider, no matter how happy they seemed to be that she was now among them.

"Then if none of you knew Ferdinand Massaro, the knowledge he is dead is of no great importance to you," Alicia said coolly, watching for a reaction.

"We would only be concerned if he had done something to gather the attention of humans, revealing what he truly was either in life or death." Lelandi rubbed her belly and frowned at Alicia. "Was he…" She hesitated.

"Was he what?" Alicia had the impression Lelandi was about to ask if the creep had been her lover. But how could Lelandi think that when she could see how much Jake wanted Alicia and how she felt about him?

"I'm sorry. I meant to ask… Did he force himself on you? Did he turn you against your will?" Lelandi's questions were spoken in a manner that showed concern mixed with controlled anger.

Her reaction took Alicia by surprise. She hadn't thought anyone would ask her the question, let alone be upset about it. Except maybe Jake. She suspected if he'd known Ferdinand had planned to do this to her, he would have killed him. Yet wouldn't Jake have wanted to do the same thing to her? Turn her so they would live together as werewolves and have…werewolf kids?

"Alicia?"

Alicia looked up from her hands, not even realizing she'd been wringing them. Tears filled her eyes as she recalled what had happened to her that night. Thinking about Ferdinand stripping her of her clothes. Fearing that he intended to rape her, torture her, and kill her. Recalling the bite on her arm and the men who had come to murder him and who had searched for her while she'd hidden from them in abject terror. How she'd turned into the wolf and felt she'd become some alien being—all alone to face her uncertainties.

Lelandi took her hand and squeezed. "It's all right. You can talk to me about it later when you feel more like it. I'm sure the men are waiting for us to return to them downstairs. There are tons of things we'll need to discuss with you so you'll understand what we're all about. But I don't want to overwhelm you."

Alicia sighed, having to get this off her chest. "Ferdinand declared I would be his, knocked me out, and when I came to, I'd already been bitten. Men were with him in another room. They murdered him, and I must have passed out from the earlier blows to the head. Anyway, when I came to, I found I was a wolf. I couldn't shift back for some time, but I left his place as soon as I was able."

"Where were you when they killed him?"

More than idle curiosity was backing Lelandi's question, Alicia thought. Did she wonder if Alicia had watched the murder take place and then walked out of there on her own? That she was in on this whole mess? One of the bad guys?

"I was half-groggy from being knocked unconscious the two times," Alicia said quietly. "Somehow, I managed to pull my clothes off the bed and slide underneath it."

"You were naked?" Lelandi's brows were arched in surprise.

Alicia swallowed. "Yes. I–I assumed after what had happened—as far as I could piece together, I should say—that Ferdinand meant to bite me and..." She shrugged, figuring Lelandi could fill in the blanks. "I was terrified the men would find me. I still remember the odor of the cologne worn by the man who came to look in the bedroom. His method of searching for anyone in the condo reminded me of one of my..."

Alicia had done it again. She hadn't meant to mention her ex-husbands. Her face feeling warm, she clenched her fingers together. "My ex-husband would look for something but if it wasn't lying out in plain sight, he'd ask me to find it. He never thought to look under anything. In this case..." She shuddered. "It was a good thing the murderer didn't look beneath the bed."

Lelandi let out a breath as if she'd been holding it in. She'd probably never lived half as dangerously as Alicia, not with a caring pack to watch over her. And the notion anyone would have wanted Lelandi dead would be alien to her.

"This Ferdinand Massaro just grabbed you off the street?" Lelandi asked.

"He was my informant, although I'd never met him before in person. But yes, he grabbed me when I was about to issue the warrant for his brother's arrest."

Lelandi's eyes grew big. "I see."

"No, I don't think you do. Ferdinand told me where to find

his brother to make the arrest. Turning me was only part of his agenda."

"So what about the men who came after you at the motel in Crestview?"

"They were part of Mario Constantino's family. One of them, the only one who got away unscathed, was Danny Massaro. The man who shot and killed my mother. He also was Ferdinand Massaro's brother."

Lelandi's lips parted, then she closed them and didn't say anything.

Alicia got the distinct impression that Lelandi and her pack wouldn't like having a troublemaker like Alicia in their midst. "I don't want to bring any danger to your family," Alicia reasoned. "Maybe Darien could help me return to my car in Crestview, and I'll be on my way."

Lelandi didn't say anything right away, and Alicia thought she was considering her request favorably. Then she said, "You'll stay with us, dear Alicia. We won't let any harm come to you. As I've said, because of our uniqueness, we must keep what we are a secret. Newly turned, you can't possibly get along on your own without a pack to..." Lelandi hesitated. "We'll guide you. But I don't mean that in a controlling way. It's just that living among us, you'll learn how to cope with your abilities. Besides, Jake said the two of you are dream mated. And if you haven't figured it out yet, he's not about to let you get out of his sight again."

"I don't understand what dream mating means," Alicia said, not about to get into a discussion of what Jake wanted or didn't want.

"It seems to run in the Silver genetics. We were all confused, though. It only happens between wolves, and Jake swore you were strictly human."

"Having...dreams of him didn't happen until after I was turned. And then it was as if Jake was coming to comfort me after what had happened to me. As though it didn't matter what I'd become. Of course, I kept thinking that being a werewolf was like some kind of weird virus and that it would go away. But when we were together, at least in the dreams, I knew he didn't care what I was. Which in retrospect was crazy, because how would he have known I was a part-time wolf? In my dreams, though, I felt as though he knew because I did."

Lelandi ran her hand over her arm. "You don't know how worried I was—well, all of us were—when Jake seemed so depressed. He kept retiring to his bedroom earlier and earlier, and we couldn't figure out what was wrong."

Alicia smiled at that. She knew the feeling.

"At first, he'd been so reluctant to drop his pictures off at the art gallery in Breckenridge. Then he didn't come home until the next night. Darien and I figured he'd met a woman and hung around a while longer. But when he was so disconsolate upon returning and said he was going back to Breckenridge, we didn't know what to think. Darien was sure Jake was planning on turning a human woman. Not something we do lightly."

Alicia's jaw dropped in astonishment. "You weren't turned?"

"I was born as a *lupus garou*. Same with most of our people. A few were turned a very long time ago. Every once in a while, the choice has to be made to turn someone who has seen what we are."

"Or kill them?"

Lelandi nodded. "Not something we want to do, but sometimes it's our only choice."

Alicia swallowed hard. "When the woman came to the restroom at the gallery and I had shifted, I was so afraid I'd have to bite her. And then the others. And once the police were summoned, I knew I'd be dead. They'd figure I was a rabid wolf."

"Until you died," Lelandi said softly, squeezing Alicia's hand. "Then you would have turned into a human. And, well, that would have taken some explaining."

Alicia's mouth dropped open again. "Ohmigod."

"Yes. That's why until you get your shifting abilities under control, you need to stay with only our kind."

Then Alicia had another horrible thought. "One of the men who planned to kill me… I bit him. What if I turned him?"

CHAPTER 13

Danny stood before Mario in his Breckenridge condo as Mario forked up another sausage link, trying to keep his temper under control. "What I want to know is why you failed to bring the woman back with you and how two of my men died. Hell, it took seven weeks just to locate her."

Mario's voice was low and cold, and he was ready to kill Danny with his bare hands. He hadn't murdered anyone like that since he was in his teens. For years, he'd had his henchmen doing his dirty work. Looked like he was going to have to get this job done himself if he wanted it done right.

He still couldn't believe the woman had given up her chance to earn the bounty on him just to turn him in. He smiled evilly at the thought. Too bad she'd had her information wrong and the police had arrived at his old residence only hours after he and Danny had split.

He shoved his clean plate aside, grabbed his pen, and pulled the newspaper crossword puzzle closer.

Ten across, nine letters: Extremely unpleasant experience.

Danny looked peeved, not at all like a man whose head would be on the chopping block next. "I told you, Boss. She shot Smithie and escaped. A vicious dog was in the room, and when me and Cicero tried to storm the place, the dog attacked. I got Cicero to the car and he died. I didn't know he had a heart condition. But that's what Doc said. The damned dog crushed Cicero's arm, and it triggered the heart attack."

Mario wrote in the word *purgatory* on the crossword. "Describe this *dog* to me again." He lifted his eyes from the newspaper.

"It looked like a German shepherd. The same kind of head. But...not *exactly* the same kind of colors."

"Could it have been a wolf?"

Danny stared at Mario as if he was crazy.

"Could it have been?" Mario demanded.

"I guess so. I never seen a wolf up close." Danny's face looked drained of all color, the notion that a wolf might have gotten the best of him probably crossing his mind. "Yeah, it could've been."

Mario looked back at his puzzle. *Two down, six letters: Vibration.*

"When you killed your brother, there wasn't any sign of a dog in his place, was there?"

Danny stared thoughtfully at the floor. "*No.* I didn't see any water dishes, dog-food dishes, nothing."

Mario shook his head. "Just a dog."

"No. Ferdinand was alone. He wouldn't have had a dog. He didn't like kids or animals."

"Before you killed Jimmy, he said Ferdinand had grabbed a woman. That she'd been following me. Jimmy didn't know her name, but it had to be Alicia Greiston. So where was she when you located Ferdinand at his place?"

"I swear I looked through the place. She wasn't there."

Mario just bet she had been. Damn, if only the henchman he'd sent to murder Ferdinand in the first place hadn't gotten himself killed instead! And he wondered now if the man had bitten Ferdinand somehow in the process and turned him.

Mario pondered that as he stared at the crossword puzzle, not really seeing it. If the idiot had attacked Ferdinand as a wolf but Ferdinand had managed to kill the assassin instead, Ferdinand had to have turned into a wolf later too. No wonder he'd been so good at tracking Mario.

Mario had turned some of his men himself, thinking they might become better assassins, but the experiment had proved fruitless. Three turned gunmen on his payroll were now dead; all three had had problems with shape-shifting at the most inconvenient times. He'd considered changing his cousin, but Mario didn't think Danny could handle it any better than his other men had. He thought about Cicero too. If the man had survived the heart attack, he probably would have been turned when the wolf bit him.

But if Mario's men had trailed Alicia to her hotel in Crestview and she'd been alone, where had the "dog" come from? Mario allowed himself a small smile as the crossword puzzle came back into focus and he wrote *tremor*. Crossword puzzles were his daily regimen—an attempt to keep Alzheimer's at bay, as working the puzzles was supposed to do, since the insidious curse had affected both his parents.

His thoughts shifted back to Alicia Greiston. He assumed she was a wolf now. Ferdinand must have shape-shifted, then bit her and turned her, wanting her for a mate. Maybe even realizing Mario wanted Alicia. Since Mario had murdered Ferdinand's girlfriend, Candy, turning Alicia would be a way of getting back at Mario.

With Ferdinand dead, Alicia was Mario's. He'd been a wolf for five years, since one of his adversaries had bitten him. He'd been angrier than hell at the time, but he'd soon realized how beneficial his newfound traits were. Except for the need to have a mate. The gorgeous bubbleheads he'd turned all had ended up being liabilities. Until he'd had them eliminated.

"What do you want me to do, Boss?"

Alicia had to be running as a wolf. Newly turned, she might not be able to control her shape-shifting ability. Until the new moon appeared. Then she wouldn't be able to keep her wolf form. Danny wouldn't be able to locate her as well as Mario could. Not without wolf instincts. This was one job Mario had to take care of on his own. Although he'd send his men out looking for her just the same. Didn't hurt to be sure. But in the end, he had to do this alone.

One thing was certain: he had no other competition in the

area. The she-wolf would be his, especially after all the trouble she'd caused him.

———————

Jake had had a devil of a time forcing himself not to pace while Lelandi was still upstairs with Alicia. He wanted Alicia alone, but Darien insisted on speaking with her. As much as Jake hated to admit it, Darien was right. The pack leader always had to know what trouble his pack might be up against. Jake knew that, yet he was having a hard time letting go of his need to be with Alicia after their forced separation and her near-death experience.

When he heard two pairs of footfalls on the stairs, he turned to watch for the women.

Darien rose from his chair, and Tom joined them from the kitchen. Sheriff Peter had solicited some of their men for outdoor guard duty so he had already left the house.

As soon as the two women appeared, Jake had eyes only for Alicia. Her eyes were dark and shadowed, her skin pale despite the red T-shirt reflecting off it. Her brown curls swept her shoulders, but his gaze quickly took in her clothes. The T-shirt fit her nicely, showing off her perky breasts, and the jeans fit snugly. She wasn't wearing the flip-flops, though. Her bare feet made her appear even sexier, like she was ready to shuck the rest of her clothes to be with him.

His gaze lifted to her face, and she gave him a tremulous smile. He crossed the room at a quickened pace, drew her into his arms, and when she tilted her face up to his, he kissed her.

Nothing gentle about it—his need to see her safe and protected was warring with his craving to make her his own. He didn't care that his brothers or Lelandi were undoubtedly watching him unabashed. His kiss was just as greedy as Alicia's was, yet tender in the way they pressed and nuzzled and opened up to each other, exploring and loving all over again.

"Guess we don't need a Gathering," Tom said, his tone amused.

Jake ignored him. No way in hell were they having a Gathering to give any other eligible bachelors in the pack the chance to court her. She had been Jake's the moment he'd laid eyes on her, and she had shown her interest in him right back.

He finally broke free from the kiss, saw the tears in her eyes, and gave her another heartfelt embrace.

In pack-leader mode, Darien said, "I know it's late, but we need to talk."

Jake slipped his hand around Alicia's with a firm, possessive grip and led her to the love seat where they sat down together, thighs touching. But it wasn't enough. Jake wrapped his arm around Alicia and pulled her against him, wanting to feel her warmth and breathe in her heady fragrance, to enjoy the softness of her body against his, to know she was truly all right and wouldn't leave him again.

He wanted to tell his brother to hurry up with the questions because Alicia would be his mate tonight, but he held his tongue. She needed to see the workings of a viable pack, and Jake butting heads with his brother wouldn't help her cope.

Darien took Lelandi's hand and sat with her on one of the couches while Tom sat on a wide-winged chair. Darien kept his hand on Lelandi's, resting it on her thigh. For the first time since Jake had lost Alicia, he felt comfortable seeing the intimacy Lelandi and his brother shared. But it was only because Alicia was with him again. He wondered how Tom felt being the odd man out, but his expression remained neutral.

"So what are we up against?" Darien asked Alicia.

———————

Alicia honestly didn't know what to think. After all the questions Darien had asked her and all the questions she'd asked of him, no one in Jake's pack, nor Jake himself, seemed to have known of Ferdinand Massaro or his brother, Danny, or Mario and his thugs.

Which meant? Jake truly had been interested in her for herself when he first caught sight of her in Breckenridge.

Lelandi patted Darien's thigh. "It's very late, and I'm exhausted. Let's go to bed. If you have any more questions, you can ask them tomorrow."

Darien looked from her to Alicia, then to Jake. Alicia wasn't certain, but she thought some unspoken communication was going on between the two brothers. She and her mother had been capable of giving each other a look, a subtle raise of an eyebrow, or slight gestures to send each other some secretive message or another. She hadn't realized how much she'd missed that special connection until she saw the nonverbal communication pass between Darien and Jake. If she ventured a guess, Darien was warning his brother against her.

Darien had nothing to worry about there. She'd already had two failed marriages. She wasn't about to embark on a third with Jake—or anyone else, for that matter. So Big Brother didn't have to worry about her blemishing the family tree when they were all born *lupus garous* and her werewolf abilities had come about because she'd been forcibly bitten.

Lelandi said, "Jake's always an early riser and makes a delightful breakfast." She suddenly flushed a brilliant red, quickly said good night, and hurried off with Darien, his arm wrapped around her waist. He chuckled low next to her ear and kissed her there.

Tom gave Alicia and Jake a nod, then headed up the stairs after them.

As soon as they were all out of sight, Alicia said, "Your brother seemed concerned about me."

But Jake didn't seem interested in any further conversation. He cupped the swell of her breast in an unassuming manner and captured her mouth with his in a totally assuming way. His tongue demanded entrance as his hand hovered near the tip of a breast that was already swelling and tingling in anticipation.

His eyes were closed as if he was memorizing the feel of her, the taste of her, the scent of her, just as she was of him. Her tongue flirted with his, and he took charge and dove deeper, the pad of his thumb barely touching the tip of her breast. When she moved into his mouth as his tongue caressed hers, the erotic sensation set off a firestorm in her belly. He groaned with need.

"Alicia," he said, sounding damned desperate.

She threaded her fingers through his hair, wanting him as she'd never wanted any man before he'd come into her life, but—

She pulled her mouth from his, saw his eyes glazed with lust, and worried that she'd shift in the middle of making love to him. She was burning up, just like when she'd shift. His hands cupped her face, and he leaned down to kiss her again as he trapped her against the soft cushions of the sofa.

She put her hands on his chest and said, "No," against his mouth. "We can't." Her voice was breathy and barely there.

His actions seemed to be on auto drive as he again tried to kiss her.

"No," she said louder and kept her hands planted against his chest.

She seemed to break through his lust-filled gaze as he looked down at her inquiringly. "Alicia?" His voice was thick with need.

"We can't."

His hands dropped from her face to her shoulders, and he rubbed them lightly. "What's wrong?"

"Your brother doesn't like it that I'm newly turned and would become part of the family like this."

"Nonsense." He leaned down to kiss her, but she held him at bay again.

"He gave you a look," she insisted.

Jake frowned at her, appearing puzzled.

She said in exasperation, "He gave you a frown, telling you to watch yourself with me."

A slow predatory smile curved Jake's mouth. "He wanted me to take it easy with you because you're newly turned. He doesn't know anything about our nighttime fantasies." He lightly pinched one of her nipples through the T-shirt and bra. "Which bra are you wearing?"

"What if I shift in the middle of making love?" she asked, frowning.

"You won't." He drew her T-shirt partway up her tummy and slid his hand underneath the fabric, feeling first the underside of the lace bra, then higher to the swell of her exposed breast, his touch making her blood heat and her skin tingle with an aroused sensation.

He smiled in a way that looked inherently smug and immeasurably pleased. "You're wearing the push-up bra."

———————

Jake kissed Alicia then—melting away the pent-up frustration of not finding her for so long, the unwavering need to know she was all right, that she was with him again. Holding her, touching her, overpowered any sense of renewing their acquaintance at a more leisurely pace. Hell, from the beginning, he hadn't been able to restrain that need to have her *now* and fully.

Her mouth was instantly pliant when his lips pressed gently against hers as he tried his utmost to coax a willing response instead of battering down the defenses she had initiated.

His tongue briefly licked hers, his fingers threading through her thick hair, cupping the back of her head, pressing her body against the couch. "I've dreamed about you like this ever since you vanished from my life." He kissed her again, this time conquering and possessing, her lips and tongue drugging him.

She responded in a way that proved she craved his touch as much as he wanted hers. Her fingers clutched at his back, pulling him against her, and her insistent, frantic touch was just as needy.

Dragging his mouth away from hers with the utmost willpower, he huskily said, "Let's take this upstairs."

"They'll hear us."

"They won't." He took her hand and pulled her from the couch. "I thought I'd lost you for good until you came to me in the dreams."

"I wanted to be with you so badly," she admitted, and Jake swept her up in his arms and carried her up the stairs to a bedroom of dark, rich burgundy.

He caught her astonished look at seeing the photographs of predominantly purple wildflowers on the walls.

"I love it," she whispered.

He pulled away the bedcover. "If it wasn't so late and I didn't think you were a bit tired, I'd take you to the lake where we could do some skinny-dipping."

She laughed, the first true expression of happiness she'd made since they'd found each other again.

Fully clothed, he laid her down on the mattress, then pressed his body against hers onto the soft bedding. He fanned his fingers over her nipples in that delicious way that made them tighten with need.

He smelled so good, like the pines that they'd run through as wolves, when he renewed his probing of her willing mouth with his insistent tongue. His arousal pressed hard against her parted legs, and she stirred against him, rubbing him, inviting him in.

"Alicia," he mouthed against her lips, his hand sliding up her T-shirt and pushing down the lace cups of the push-up bra. His hands swept over her breasts gently, almost reverently. Her fingers slid up his T-shirt and combed through the dark hair on his chest, more desperate than anything as she felt the muscles flex beneath her fingertips. His warm breath tickled her breasts, caressing the flesh, his hot tongue teasing a highly aroused nipple. He rubbed his erection against her thigh as if showing her just how turned on she'd made him.

Fire consumed her as she tugged at his shirt to get it off. And when he yanked it over his head, he was again kissing her throat, his hand pressed gently down her belly, slipping under the waist-band of her jeans and lower until he was stroking her through the red satin panties.

She writhed under his fingers' skillful touch, tugged at his belt, which he quickly jerked free, then pulled her hand across his rigid length and pressed hard. She caressed him through the soft jeans, and he quickly yanked off her T-shirt as if he'd lost any restraint he'd managed to have until now. Until he saw the red lace push-up bra beneath her breasts, which were now reddened from his lightly abrasive two-day growth of beard and all the kissing he'd been giving them. He unfastened her jeans and pulled them off. Then he removed his own jeans in haste.

She tsked as she saw his nakedness.

He smiled. "I was in a hurry to rescue you."

"I nearly died when you came for me as a wolf," she whispered.

"It was the only way I could catch you."

But then he feasted his eyes on the red bra and the red silk panties, groaned in needy approval, and slipped her panties off.

She felt irresistibly beautiful to him, loved and desired, just as much as she felt about him.

His fingers found her wet and willing, and his strokes made her wild. The feel of his touch was so much more pleasurable than in the dreams, so much more real and exquisite, reminding her of their love bouts before she'd left him. Without being able to cling to the moment, the climax crashed over her with ecstatic fervor, and she felt that elusive high she always had with him. Before she could cry out, his mouth was on hers, and he was pressing his erection inside her, thrusting, savagely claiming her as much as she was taking him in deeper, holding him, wanting him, claiming him back.

Her senses were revved, she realized with blissful shock. Because of the wolf in her, every sense she possessed was stronger, more alert, more attuned. The musky male scent of him, the sound of his heart beating rapidly, of his breath coming hard, the feel of the hairs on his chest and his chin brushing against her sensitive skin—and she felt the earth-shattering climax hit her once again. She moaned with pure pleasure as he thrust one last time and sank against her, spent only for the moment. Because with Jake, once was never enough.

———————

Late the next morning, Alicia woke to the aroma of freshly brewed coffee and eggs and ham cooking in the kitchen. She looked up at Jake, whose arms and legs were wrapped around her, but she wasn't sure if he was being protective or purely possessive.

She loved being with him like this, yet she felt an odd sense of disquiet. She thought it might be because she still worried about Mario and his men causing trouble for Jake and his people.

Jake smiled sleepily down at her and kissed the top of her head. "I think they finally gave up on waiting for me to cook breakfast for them this morning. You were sleeping so soundly that I wouldn't have disturbed you for the world."

She sighed. "They'll be annoyed with me then."

He chuckled. "No. We all love to cook. I just tend to get up earlier than anyone else."

She slid her hand between them and touched his rigid erection. "I know," she said coyly.

He grinned at her. "Waking up to you has been my fondest desire."

She stroked his chest with her fingernail and looked up at him. "I didn't dream last night about you. The first time in seven weeks. Did you dream about me?"

He shook his head. "I didn't need to." He kissed her cheek.

"What time is it?"

"Late morning. Everyone will be heading to work—should have been already—all except Lelandi. She's working on a psychology degree through an online college program, so she can study at home. Sheriff Peter and some other men are hanging around outside in the event Mario or his men learn you're here."

"I didn't want to cause trouble for you and your family," she said with regret.

He held her tighter. "I wouldn't have allowed any harm to come to you. You shouldn't have left your hotel like you did. I saw Mario's note to you in your hotel room, Alicia. I know you thought Mario would have me killed. But it couldn't have happened."

"I couldn't know that," she said quietly. "You said you didn't even have a gun."

"Not on me. I realize you were afraid for my life. I realize, too, how hard it must have been for you to leave me. And I know you couldn't quit thinking of me."

She chuckled and tweaked his nipple. "You think so, do you?"

"I know so." He gave her a smart-ass smirk. "That's why," he said, brushing his thumb softly against her cheek, "you've been dream mating with me. And that's why you went to the art gallery to find out where I was living. Then when they were after you, that's why you headed toward Silver Town to find me."

She took a deep breath and snuggled against his chest, her breasts feeling heavier than normal and the tingling renewed again. She'd missed her period, thinking at first that it had to do with her werewolf changes. But with every passing day, she feared that might not be the reason at all.

She couldn't deal with this right now and tried to pull away from Jake. But he wouldn't let her go.

"Can you get my bags from the police in Crestview today?"

"They'll need to talk to you about what happened first, most likely."

"I will. But I need my bags."

"I told you I'd take you shopping as soon as you can manage. When the new moon appears, you won't change at all."

"I won't?" She relaxed a little. Was that why she hadn't shifted for two of the weeks out of the past seven? There was hope for her to live a seminormal life yet.

He caressed her shoulder with his fingertips in a slow, lazy pattern. "No. Only royals, so called because they have so few human links in their past, can change at will during any phase of the moon. The rest of us can't. So it'll be a good time for you to enjoy seeing the area, circulate a bit, and get to meet the pack."

"That's why for about a week, on two different occasions, I thought the virus had passed. That I was cured."

He raised his brows.

"I guessed I wasn't cured of the condition when I shape-shifted at the art gallery. I'm so sorry Mary thought you had gotten me pregnant."

"I *will* get you that way," he said, smiling, rubbing his hand over her belly. "Just a little later than she would believe."

For a minute, Alicia barely breathed under Jake's skillful caresses. She took a deep, steadying breath. "I swore after my first two disastrous marriages that I'd never get married again. That was before I ran into you, or I should say, you began to follow me. I kept bemoaning the fact that I'd met you too late—after I'd gotten myself into this mess with the Mob—and I was afraid they'd kill you."

His fingers stilled on her belly, and he finally really looked at her. "It's not happening. Trust me in this. From the moment I met you, we were in this together."

She sighed. "Then I was a werewolf. And if I came to see you in Silver Town, even though that's exactly where I was headed because I had no other alternative, I *knew* I'd bite you and turn you."

He smiled. "So see, that proves you wanted me."

"Yeah, in the worst way. But I couldn't do that to you."

"No worries there."

She looked anxious, but he couldn't figure out what was still bothering her. Before he could ask, she blurted out, "I don't want to have a child out of wedlock."

"We couldn't have had a child before you were turned. Well, except in rare instances. Lelandi's brother, Leidolf, was telling us about a case he learned of on the Oregon coast. But it's so rare that there's nothing to be concerned about. If you conceived wolf babies, they wouldn't be considered born out of wedlock anyway. Not once you're mated."

She stared at him, then pulled free and sat up in bed. "Don't tell me the rules for marriage are different for werewolves."

Jake frowned at her. Then he slowly rose to a sitting position. "We're dream mated, which means we were meant to be together. We consummated the relationship last night—several times, I might add. We're mated, Alicia, for life. That's how *lupus garous* do it. Just like our wolf counterparts do. We don't have a wedding per se. No divorces either. I thought you knew that."

She closed her eyes and groaned, then opened them and tried to leave the bed, but he grabbed her wrist and pulled her close. "I thought you understood."

"How could I?" She pulled her hand free, and this time, he let her go. She grabbed her clothes and headed for Jake's bathroom and shut the door behind her.

Jake stared after her in disbelief. She was his. He was hers. Had to be, according to the dream-mating scenario. Hell. He would never have taken her without her first agreeing to the conditions.

Although he would have worked damn hard early on at convincing her to agree. They were meant to be together, but he would have waited until she realized the truth.

He cursed himself for not better understanding her newness at being a wolf. And vowed to make it up to her. But there was no taking back what they had done.

For life, that was how wolves mated, just like their wolf cousins. He wanted to join her in the shower and convince her how right they were for each other. But the shower turned off, and he waited instead.

She finally emerged from the bathroom. He caught sight of her reddened eyes, and he felt his whole world deflate.

"Alicia," he said, moving to take her into his arms, "we're meant to be together."

"I think I might be pregnant," she sobbed, her tear-streaked cheek planted against his bare chest, her fingers curled into fists at her sides, her whole body language showing defeat. "I should have let you know before we were…mated. Now from what you say your kind practices, you're stuck with me." She gritted her teeth and looked at him with such a woeful expression, he quickly moved in close to her.

Being *stuck* with her forever was just how he wanted to be. He gathered her in his arms and tried to console her, but his thoughts were swirling as he tried to sort out the possibility of her being pregnant. "I wanted you from the first time I saw you. This changes nothing between us. But you said you only think you're pregnant? You don't know for certain?" he asked cautiously.

"Yeah. I don't know for certain, but…it's possible."

"I couldn't have made you pregnant," he said glumly.

"So you already said."

That was what was eating at her. Only one person could have made her pregnant, he thought, if she was right in her assumption. The bastard who bit her.

"Ferdinand Massaro?" He tried to keep his tone consoling, but if the bastard had made her pregnant, he had raped her.

She let out a ragged sigh. "I didn't think he'd done anything to me. Except bitten me. But I've been feeling...*different*. And my...period is...late. But I thought maybe it was all this stress with the werewolf shifting that was making me feel strange and had thrown me off my regular cycle."

Jake hugged her tight. "No matter what happens, I love you, Alicia. If you're pregnant, the child will be ours." She sniffled but wouldn't look at him. He tilted her chin up and looked into her red eyes. "It doesn't matter. Do you hear me? I'll love our child as much as I love you. All right?"

She nodded, but she didn't look like she believed him. He sighed and kissed her lips, then gently caressed her face with his thumbs to brush away the tears trailing down her cheeks. "Do you want to get breakfast?"

She hesitated.

"I can bring something up here to you." He hated to suggest it, feeling that she needed to be with the family, but he realized how difficult this might be for her.

"I don't want to say anything about this to anyone," she said. "Not until I know for sure one way or another."

"About the baby?" he questioned. He wasn't hiding the fact that they were mated.

Her lips parted, then she nodded.

"Certainly." But that didn't mean he wasn't checking into Massaro's background. And deep down, Jake was disturbed about this whole matter. Not only about the fact that she might be carrying Massaro's child, although he'd love the child as his own, and because of the way Massaro would have gotten her with child. But also because she was reticent about being mated to Jake. He felt bad that he hadn't given her a choice about that. Although ultimately, there would have been only one choice to make.

"You might want to dress before we go downstairs." She gave his nude body an assessing look, then gave him a small smile.

He laughed. "Sure you don't want to stay up here, and I'll make us a special breakfast after everyone's left for the day?" He waggled his brows.

"It's tempting," she said with a sigh.

He took a deep breath. "You're really not upset about our mating?"

She gave him a watery smile. "When all I've wanted is to be with you, night after night? I could think of hardly anything else, and now I'm with you for real."

"You're worrying about being pregnant then?"

She gave a shallow nod.

He took her hand and kissed it. "Everything will be all right, Alicia. You've got me, and you have a whole pack to be your family now. You're not alone in this. You'll never be again. I'll grab a quick shower, and we can head downstairs. I'll show you my grandfather's home where we'll live once we resolve some other issues. We'll have lunch and an afternoon nap after that. How's that sound?"

"You don't have to work?" She sounded as though she was afraid he'd leave her alone.

"Not anytime soon. Darien won't need me for a few days, time enough for you to get acclimated to the pack and to our ways. Besides, until we know that Mario and his men aren't coming after you, I'm staying with you."

She shook her head, a small smile appearing that cheered him, and gave a breathy little laugh. "You must have thought it was funny when I said I'd protect us both because I had a gun."

He chuckled and ran his hand through her thick curls, then held a handful with reverence. "I was thinking, 'If you only knew.'"

CHAPTER 14

WHEN JAKE AND ALICIA FINALLY WENT DOWN TO BREAKFAST, Tom and Darien both looked up at them as Jake steeled his expression and guided Alicia into the dining room. A large picture window faced out onto the woods, Jake's photos of woodland flowers hanging on the walls, and the long oval table was covered in golden sunflower place mats. Alicia's attention was riveted on his floral photographs, and he saw real admiration in her eyes. But his brothers exchanged looks, and Jake knew that despite trying to keep his expression neutral, he'd conveyed strife in paradise.

Both observed Alicia, and he imagined they could tell she'd been crying.

"Good morning," Darien said to Alicia, and Tom echoed his words, although Darien gave Jake a harsh look as if he'd been to blame for Alicia's upset.

"Good morning," Alicia said quietly, avoiding looking at them, while Jake only nodded.

Lelandi came out of the kitchen appearing tired. Jake imagined that the babies kicking in her belly were keeping her awake, although her expression brightened when she saw Alicia. A flicker of concern fluttered across Lelandi's face when she noticed Alicia's red eyes, but she quickly smiled and motioned to the table— where the yellow ceramic serving dishes were filled with eggs and ham, biscuits, and cantaloupe, watermelon, and honeydew melon.

"Have your pick," Lelandi said cheerfully.

After Jake pulled out a chair for Alicia, she took her seat, and he sat beside her.

"I'm dying to hear about your chosen profession as a bounty

hunter," Lelandi said, her enthusiasm contagious as she took her seat next to Darien.

Jake thought Lelandi was the perfect person to help get Alicia's mind off her troubles. Maybe the psychology courses were part of Lelandi's need to analyze and try to help anyone in need, although he suspected those traits had more to do with her nurturing personality.

"You would not believe the kinds of cases I've been involved in." Alicia forked some fruit onto her plate, and for the first time, she seemed at ease.

"Coffee? Tea?" Jake asked her.

"No, neither."

That surprised Jake because she'd had tea when she'd eaten breakfast before.

"Juice? Milk?" Lelandi asked.

"Milk, thanks."

Lelandi returned to the kitchen and soon popped back into the dining room with a glass of milk. She handed it to Alicia, then sat across the table from her. "Okay, tell us about this bounty-hunting business of yours. It sounds like it could be fascinating."

Alicia's choice of beverages made Jake wonder if maybe there was something more to her being pregnant. He again glanced down at her waist, but she wasn't showing yet. Too soon, he suspected. He wondered how he could get her in to see Doc Weber. Surely Doc could tell whether she was or not. Especially since seven weeks had passed since Ferdinand Massaro had turned her.

Alicia held up a finger as she finished chewing a sausage link.

Jake's brothers had finished their breakfast, and it was past time for them to be on their way. Although as efficient as the pack was at running the town and the Silver businesses, they didn't need the pack leader and his subleaders micromanaging any of it. Still, Jake had hoped they'd leave so he'd have more alone time with Alicia.

But they didn't appear to be in any hurry to depart. He

suspected that since Alicia was newly a member of the family, they wanted to know everything about her.

"Once," Alicia said, "I was supposed to arrest a woman who'd stolen a good deal of money from the department store where she clerked. She would give a refund to a customer, then pocket a refund herself. It was a one-for-you, one-for-me kind of affair. She was addicted to gambling and was a habitual lottery-ticket purchaser. But besides the obvious shortages in her register at the close of her shifts and the camera's catching her pocketing the money, she skipped her trial. I had the job of serving the warrant, but her family was hiding her. So I put out the word that she had won a lottery ticket." Alicia smiled. "That did it. I delivered the search warrant in place of the winner's fees and escorted her to jail."

"Goes to show gambling doesn't pay," Lelandi said, smiling.

"Yeah. Most of the cases I've dealt with were petty criminal cases. One was a car thief who failed to see his parole officer and was ordered back to jail. I found him hiding underneath a mattress. Really brilliant since the one side of the mattress was elevated so high that any fool could have seen someone was wedged between the mattress and the box springs even though he was fairly scrawny.

"Another time, I found a woman hiding underneath a flipped-over swimming pool in the backyard, while the dog stood wagging its tail at me right beside the plastic blue pool. Another time, a guy hid in the attic. In his panic, he stepped through the ceiling. By the time I had him in plastic ties, he was a mess and covered in itchy insulation. I was lucky that I never had to arrest anyone really dangerous, though."

Jake raised his brows at her. Her gaze shifted to him, knowing he would have something to say about that.

Looking a little flushed, she buttered a biscuit. "Until now. The bondsman I work with liked to give me cases where he needed a woman rearrested, so that there could be no threat of someone screaming about sexual misconduct. Or cases where the perp was not a member of a gang or anything. One of the other bounty hunters I knew had gotten into a real bind trying to take down an individual who was a drug dealer and had ended up in a house full of meth, money, drugged-out wackos, and guns."

"But this time?" Lelandi probed.

Jake bit his tongue to keep from saying anything about this time being personal. But he was having a damn hard time not voicing his opinion. He sighed. He and his brothers would have reacted the same way as Alicia did, truth be told. Even Lelandi had responded the same way concerning her sister, which had gotten her into a world of danger. So he couldn't really blame Alicia. Although in their cases, they were wolves, and the thought of a female human going it alone didn't sit well with him.

"The man I worked for did me a favor. He let me go after Danny Massaro and Mario Constantino on my own," Alicia said.

Lelandi rubbed her lower back. Evidently the babies were giving her spine trouble again, which prompted Darien to move his chair closer to hers and to begin rubbing the area she was attempting to soothe. She smiled at him. "Thanks, honey." Then she frowned at Alicia. "It seems to me that these men are awfully dangerous sorts. I would think the man you worked for would have worried about your safety as well as your success."

"I…" Alicia wouldn't look at Jake, her head slightly bowed. Then she raised her chin in defiance. "I had inside knowledge. My informant wouldn't deal with anyone else. So the bondsman had to let me do it if he wanted any assurance that the men would be taken into custody."

"Hell, the informant was that bastard Ferdinand Massaro. And he was the one who changed you," Jake growled. "Why did he have designs on you in the first place?"

He couldn't help the way he felt about it. Not only was he

pissed off that the man had turned her, still hating himself for not having been there to protect her, but the possibility that the man had raped her rested heavily on Jake's mind. The vehemence in his voice had all eyes engaged on him. All except Alicia's. She was wringing her hands in her lap, staring at the table.

Taking a deep breath to settle his irritation, Jake swept a curl away from her cheek and pressed a kiss to her temple. "We'll take care of them." His words were spoken quietly now but with dark resolution.

"But you don't have a bounty hunter's training. You can't turn them in without it," Alicia said, looking up at him.

"If they're wolves, Alicia," he said, taking her hand in his and caressing the palm with his thumb, "they can't go to jail."

Her eyes were wide, filled with a fresh shimmer of tears. "But they can't be allowed to get away with murdering my mother. They can't!"

When she tried to pull her hand away from his, he held on even tighter, unwilling to let go of the tentative connection they had. He realized then she probably didn't even know about wolves' longevity.

"We live long lives. *Very* long lives. If you've read any werewolf lore, you probably know it's not easy to kill us. But what you might not know is one of the reasons werewolf legends have persisted from ancient times is that we live so many years."

"You...told me you...were thirty," Alicia said cautiously.

He cleared his throat and glanced at his brothers, then at Lelandi. Their faces were expectant, almost pitying. He had never expected to fall in love with a woman who would be newly turned. He wasn't sure how to acclimate her to their ways without upsetting her. Then he squeezed her hand as her eyes filled with worry and questioning.

"Thirty in human years. In werewolf? We have a very slow aging process. Once we turn eighteen, the aging process slows down. Many humans look youthful for years—and it's hard to tell exactly what age they are, but for us, the length of time is even longer. Charles II was crowned the King of Scots at Scone the year I was born. The same year that the English forbade the transportation of goods produced in the colonies to England on non-English ships."

Alicia glanced at Lelandi. She smiled. "I'm not quite that old. But any man who would ask a woman's age is *not* a gentleman."

Jake raised his brows at Lelandi, then turned to Alicia. "That's part of the reason we can't go to jail. Let's say the men did get life in prison and they're wolves. They would outlive everyone. And appear to age way too slowly. If they're not one of those who have very few human influences in their family roots, like Lelandi, a royal, they would have to shift sometime during the phases of the moon. Except for the new moon."

He paused and stroked her hand again. "Can you imagine what the prison guards would say if they caught their prisoners pacing in their cells as wolves? Orange prison jumpsuits lying on the floor? The two men gone? If we determine they're not wolves, they can go to prison. You can turn them in for the bounty money even. But *we'll* take them down."

Alicia took a deep breath. "What if they are wolves?"

"We take care of ours in our own way. They won't get away with murder, Alicia."

She nodded and slid her free hand over his thigh. He smiled at her, sure that the look was as hungry as what he felt for her.

"What did you plan to do today?" Darien asked Jake. "A couple of police detectives investigating the break-in at the motel in Crestview called earlier this morning and said they wanted to get Alicia's statement. I said they could speak with her in an hour or so. Hopefully, she won't have the urge to shift. Beyond that, what do you intend to do?"

"I wanted to take Alicia to see Grandfather's old homestead.

But I need to locate Mario Constantino and Danny Massaro. And find out what happened to the other thug who vanished from the motel. The one she bit and the other who got away without injury. I need to learn if any of them were wolves."

"I'll have Tom and Peter check out the motel she was staying at. See if they can pick up any wolf scents. You stay here with Alicia," Darien said.

"I can't hide from him," Alicia said. "I worry about your family." She pointedly looked at Lelandi and her pregnant condition. "These men are ruthless."

"You're staying with us. You're not going to act as bait," Jake said pointedly.

"What do you think we're truly up against, Jake?" Darien asked. "You've seen some of these men."

"The one who tried to force Alicia out of the restaurant was human. The two men who threatened her on the hiking trail were human. I don't know about Mario. The air conditioner was blowing in the wrong direction for me to get a whiff of him. I never even considered he might be a wolf." He paused and looked at Alicia. "You're perfectly sure Ferdinand was the one who bit you and no one else?"

"He was the only one with me. When I came to, I'd been bitten. The two men who were interrogating him before they murdered him didn't know I was there. I doubt another man—werewolf—was there, then conveniently disappeared after he had bitten me. Come to think of it, I did smell that a wolf had been in the room. At first, I thought it was just me. But all wolves give off a slightly different odor. I only got a whiff of the odor of decay from Ferdinand's body since he'd been dead several hours before I could leave his apartment."

"All right." Jake considered the situation a moment more before speaking. "If Ferdinand Massaro was a wolf, then what about his brother, Danny?"

"They're cousins to Mario," Alicia explained.

"Then I'd say it's very likely they could also be, but their hench-men are not," Darien said. "I'll make some inquiries into this Mario Constantino."

Jake's jaw tightened. Darien was the pack leader, and it was his job to go after Mario, who was like the pack leader of a gang of thugs, whether he was a wolf or not. But Jake wanted to take Mario down. Call it the instinct to prove to his mate that he loved her, that he had the mettle and the intelligence necessary to take down the bastard who had threatened her, but he wanted to take more of a role in this.

Alicia's gaze met his, and recognition dawned that he was feel-ing antsy about this whole situation. She said softly, "If you want to go and chase after the bad guys, I'll understand."

Then it hit him. He didn't need to go after anyone. He needed to be right here—with her, for her. He wasn't leaving her alone again.

He smiled evilly at her. "Last time you sent me away, you tore off without a word. That's not happening again. Besides, like I said, I'm sticking by your side."

She squeezed his hand in a way that said she was happy with his decision.

When the police from Crestview arrived to get Alicia's story about the men breaking into her motel room and the one man's death, they brought her purse and suitcase, for which she was grateful. They'd kept her gun, though, because she'd shot and killed one of the men who'd broken into her room.

She was more than nervous as Jake sat beside her in the great room filled with soft sofas and chairs enough for a big crowd. The room's high, vaulted ceilings made it appear even more spacious, while more of Jake's beautiful photographs adorned the walls. She wondered if he'd taken some of his photographs to the art gallery in Breckenridge because he'd run out of room in the house to hang any more.

Jake held her hand while Lelandi sat on the couch nearby, and Sheriff Peter, Darien, and Tom remained standing as they listened in.

Before the police detectives arrived, Jake had explained to Alicia how important it was to tell as much of the truth as she could to match the details of what the police might have uncovered without letting the werewolf tale out of the bag. She couldn't help but be nervous as Jake's family watched her, well aware that if she screwed this up and the police determined what really had happened, Jake and his brothers would most likely have to turn these detectives.

But she knew she must look as guilty as she felt about having to lie. Just as guilty as the people looked when she came for them as a bounty hunter with warrants for their arrest in hand.

Notebook and shining silver pen in hand, dark-haired, mustached Detective Simpson now sat in a chair, leaning forward, intimidating, while his blond-haired, blue-eyed partner whose tie was just as blue, Detective Tandy, was standing nearby. Tandy had his hands shoved in his pockets, his appearance solemn, trying for relaxed, but he was studying Alicia's every body movement, every hint of facial expression, waiting for her to give herself away before she even spoke.

Garnering her attention again, Detective Simpson said, "Tell us in your own words what happened exactly." His voice was calm, but his posture denoted something else. He appeared ready to pounce if she said one thing that wasn't in line with his view of the crime scene.

Alicia swallowed hard, her hand clammy in Jake's. He squeezed her hand lightly to reassure her. And instantly both men's gazes refocused on Alicia and Jake's clasped hands. She feared she would get nothing past them but the God's honest truth. And *that* she couldn't give.

"I–I was asleep when I heard someone trying to break into my room at the Crestview Motel. At first, I thought it was just a dream. I recalled someone was trying to unlock the door with a plastic card. I wasn't sure what to do at first. But then I realized my gun was in my bag on the other side of the room. I rushed over to get it. When the man entered, using a flashlight to find his way, I was standing in a dark corner of the room. He saw the bed was empty and went into the bathroom. I heard him jerk the shower curtain aside."

"Did you recognize him?" the detective asked.

"Yes, he was the man who tried to force me to leave the Victoriana Restaurant in Breckenridge. I assumed he worked for Mario Constantino, the man I was tailing. I had information that Mario was meeting Danny Massaro, the man I intended to serve a warrant on."

Alicia took a deep breath. So far, so good. Everything she'd said was the absolute truth.

Detective Simpson scribbled some notes, then looked up at her. "How could you see him so clearly? The room was dark. He couldn't see you. He only had a flashlight. How did you know him?"

She'd seen him because she was a wolf. She would have sworn, if she didn't know any better, that her heart had stopped beating. But with her silence, her trying to come up with an explanation, the way her body heated with panicked concern, she worried she was signing the Silvers' death warrants or fates as werewolves if she didn't come up with something fast that sounded plausible.

She gave a little nonchalant shrug, never taking her eyes off the detective, not wanting to see how Darien and the others were reacting or what the other detective was doing. Watching her? Watching them? She knew that if she saw their expressions, she'd fall apart more than she felt she was doing now.

"I assumed it was him from his build and the way he walked. When he was at the restaurant, he reminded me of a big, disgruntled bear. I suppose, in retrospect, I didn't really know for sure who he was until I felt his pulse after I shot him. Once I'd seen him up close, I realized it was him. He must have followed me to Crestview." She frowned in feigned annoyance. "I forgot where I left off."

She wondered if that had been a ploy on the detective's part to disconcert her. Or if he was used to asking questions when they popped into his mind. He was right in asking her the question. She just wished she hadn't made the slip. Then again, she supposed that made her appear more human.

The detective flipped back a page in his notebook and said, "You said you heard him jerk the shower curtain aside in the bathroom."

"Oh. Yes. When he realized I wasn't in the bathroom, he returned to the bedroom. That's when he saw me in the corner of the room. He raised his gun and fired. I responded by firing three times in return. Because he was holding the flashlight, I was able to pinpoint him better. He dropped his gun and sank to the floor. I worried others might be with him because the men usually travel in pairs, so I ran to lock the door, then checked his pulse to see if he was still alive. He wasn't.

"I dressed." She'd been naked. She couldn't tell the detective that. Wouldn't he wonder why? She faltered. "I mean, I changed out of my nightgown and into jeans and a sweatshirt."

Now she sounded damned suspicious. He could have assumed she'd been dressed in her nightgown already. She was getting rattled. *Calm down*, she told herself. She swallowed hard, her throat dry as a drought in summer. Now she wished she'd had some water to drink. But if she asked for any, she'd sound like she was getting nervous because she *was* guilty of a crime.

Tom slipped out of the room, catching her eye and everyone else's. She wished she was free to go also.

"Go on, Miss Greiston," the detective prompted.

"I went to call the police, but when I punched in the number and held the receiver to my ear, I discovered the phone line was dead. My cell-phone battery had run down so I was charging it and hoped it would work. I was able to use it to call 911. But then another man tried to get in. He tried the doorknob, found it locked, and then began kicking the door in."

This was the hard part. How had she gotten past two armed men without getting herself killed? But she hadn't had her gun with her. Not when she'd been tearing out of there as a wolf. And she'd left the gun behind, along with her cell phone and purse and everything. How could she have managed to escape them as a woman without any weapons?

"So only one other man was there?" the detective asked, pen and brows raised.

If there was only one other, the detective might have figured she had slipped past him and then he fired at her but missed. But how could she have avoided two gun-toting men? But what if there had been eyewitnesses? Oh my God, what if someone had seen a wolf run across the parking lot?

"Miss Greiston?"

She jerked her head up to look at him. "Two of them. I was hiding in the dark. The one went to check on the guy I'd…killed, while the other hurried into the bathroom, looking for me. At least I presume. I dashed outside. Someone fired three shots, but I kept running and never looked back."

Tom returned to the great room with a glass of water and handed it to her.

"Thank you," she murmured, her eyes meeting his, his expression telling her she was doing fine. "Thank you," she said again and took a swallow of the cold water.

"Did you have a dog with you in the room?" Detective Tandy asked in a consoling manner, his blue eyes fixed on her gaze.

She knew his ploy. Pretend to understand the perp's situation, then throw the book at him or her. Just as she'd often done. Only in the case of the men and women she arrested, they were the bad guys.

"A dog?" she asked, her voice barely audible.

"Yes. Well, in truth, *a wolf.*"

Jake's hand tightened fractionally on Alicia's. Her teeth were clenched together, and she didn't know what to say. She was innocent, but if these men pushed her too hard, Jake and his family would be forced to turn them. She didn't think the pack could kill them. That scenario would be too difficult to explain. But if they turned them, they'd have to take them into the pack, and Darien had already said he didn't want two more newly turned pack members—male types, who probably had families of their own. And that would cause an even greater ripple effect of trouble.

The detective flipped through his notebook as if he needed to refresh his memory on the details of his investigation. She was certain this time it was a ploy to make her squirm. She didn't squirm, although she felt light-headed and was afraid her face had drained of all color. She was barely breathing, and Jake looked anxiously at her. She scolded herself for not hiding her feelings better, but she couldn't help it. They knew something. About the wolf.

And she was feeling damn guilty. How could she not? She'd bitten one of the two men. She *was* guilty! Nothing in her bounty-hunter training said she could bite a perp into submission. Not that she had been after these guys, but still…

The detective tapped his pen at the open page. "Says here two men in the room next to yours saw a dog run out of your room. A big dog. Like a German shepherd. They never saw any sign of a woman leaving. One of the men had fired into the air, scared by the size of the wolf."

Wolf. Twice he'd referred to it as a wolf. But if the eyewitnesses thought it was a dog, why did the detective think it was a wolf?

The detective flipped through some more pages of his

notebook, while the other one continued to watch her expression. Her blood ran cold. She didn't want to say the wrong thing and force Darien's hand. But she didn't know what to say that wouldn't cause trouble for their kind.

"Blood was found on the rug near the door. A man's blood. But not the same as the blood from the one who died. Wolf saliva was mixed in with the second man's blood." The detective looked up from his notes. "So what about the wolf?"

Her stomach bunched tightly into a knot, Alicia licked her suddenly very dry lips. Yet she thought the detective was feeding her a story. No one would look to see if saliva was a wolf's or a dog's, would they?

"Wolf saliva?" she asked. "You mean canine saliva, right? Is there a difference between a dog's and a wolf's?"

"Believe me," the detective said with a smug expression. "The saliva sampled from the blood was wolf DNA. They can determine that to rule out that it wasn't some other animal's bites."

She took a shallow breath and said, "I—"

"It's not illegal to own a wolf," Jake interjected, his voice quietly firm, as if he was a lawyer who knew her rights when it came to pet wolf ownership.

She supposed that to protect themselves, Jake and the rest of the pack would know about such a thing for self-preservation.

The detective switched his attention to Jake. She thought Detective Simpson was fighting a smile. Jake to the rescue. But it was more than that. It was as if the detective had caught them in a falsehood. But she wasn't rolling over and playing dead yet.

"*No*, you're right, Mr. Silver," the detective said with emphasis, "not unless the wolf owner takes the wolf within the city limits of some cities, which *is* illegal. Crestview is not one of those cities. But the wolves have to be fenced in with at least eight-foot-tall fencing. Every access has to be locked to prevent the wolves from escaping.

"Taking a wolf into a motel room *isn't* legal, nor a safe thing to do. If Miss Greiston was afraid for her life and was using the wolf for protection, it wasn't really a smart idea. Nor was it legal. The wolf could have injured anyone. Since it has bitten someone now, we'll have to hunt it down and make sure it wasn't rabid." He sat taller and turned to Alicia. "So what about this wolf, Miss Greiston?"

"He wasn't mine," she said stubbornly, head held high, voice confident.

The detective raised his brows.

She shrugged. "I don't own any pets. Never have. I don't know where the animal came from or where he went. You can check with my apartment manager. I've never had any pets at the place. They're not allowed."

At least the part about not owning any pets was true. But what if they checked out the hotel rooms where she'd stayed over the past month? What if they found wolf hairs on the carpet where she'd restlessly paced, trying to shift back into her human body?

"The wolf ran off into the woods, the eyewitnesses said." The detective studied her for a moment more, then asked, "But where did *you* go? Why did you run away?"

"Jake came for me."

"You'd left your phone charging on the dresser. Only one phone call had been made. To 911. The sound of the men breaking into the room was captured on tape. They heard the one man cursing up a blue streak as he said, 'Come on, Cicero, damn it. We've gotta get out of here before the police arrive. She's run off. Holy crap.' Then there was a lot of grunting and groaning and moaning. We assume that was when he helped the injured man outside. After several minutes, doors were opened and slammed shut. Then a car engine roared to life, and the vehicle tore off down the road. Detective Tandy and I arrived shortly after that."

"They had guns, Detective. I wasn't about to hang around to get shot at again. If they could have, they would have come after me, I'm sure."

"So how did Mr. Silver know to meet you?"

"We had prearranged a meeting." She patted Jake's hand with her free hand. "We've been seeing each other. We planned to get together last night. Only instead of finding me at the motel, he found me on the road heading for Silver Town."

The detective's brows arched heavenward. "Long hike."

"I didn't know where else to go, and I was sure Jake was already headed to Crestview. I couldn't hang around to get shot at again," she repeated. Then she had to explain her connection to Danny Massaro, who had also murdered her mother, and the other, Cicero, who she hadn't seen before.

After two long, exhausting hours, the detectives finally left and Alicia felt drained. "They didn't believe me about the wolf," she said to the family as Darien walked back into the great room after seeing the detectives out.

"You did fine," Darien said, his tone reassuring, and she believed he really meant it. "They won't find a wolf, and Peter has learned that the man you bit never went to any hospital or clinic in the area to get the wound taken care of."

"It had to have been awful," Alicia whispered, still feeling bad about what she'd done. "I didn't mean to bite so hard, but I–I think I crushed the bone. I didn't know my own strength."

"I believe he died," Darien said matter-of-factly. "Peter had already talked to the eyewitnesses, and they said the one man was practically carrying the other out to the car. The injured man slumped in the seat, his face ice white. If Danny Massaro had to take him someplace any distance from the motel, the man probably died. We know for sure he didn't take him to any area medical facilities. Peter's already checked. We still want to confirm the man died, but it appears that way."

She narrowed her eyes at Darien. "If you already knew that the men had seen a dog, *why* didn't you tell me before the detectives arrived?"

"The witnesses hadn't mentioned a dog," Peter said, speaking up in Darien's defense. "I had asked them about the men who had broken into your room, trying to get a description so we could locate them before the police did. The witnesses said the parking lot was dark. And so was the walk in front of the motel because the men had knocked out the lights.

"But when the car's interior lights came on, the injured man looked pale as death, and the other man was shaking him and hollering at him. The wounded man was unresponsive. The other was cursing as he backed out of the parking lot and roared off. I assumed you'd shot the other man too. I didn't realize you had bitten him." Peter looked contrite. "It was my fault that I didn't think to ask the witnesses if they'd seen anything else near your room."

"I have a question for you though, Alicia," Darien said, his look stern. "Why did Danny Massaro and Mario Constantino kill your mother?"

CHAPTER 15

ALICIA WAS ALREADY UPSET BY ALL OF THE POLICE-DETECTIVE questioning she'd had to endure, so Jake wondered why in the hell Darien had to bring up the motive for her mother's murder on top of all that. Jake knew Darien had good reasons for anything he did, but the timing seemed piss-poor.

But Alicia didn't seem upset by the query. Instead, her lips parted, and she seemed surprised.

She cleared her throat and held herself stiffly on the couch. "Mario had my mother murdered because she was seeing a man named Tony Thomas. Mario had him murdered as well. Why? I don't know. I speculated it was because Tony was either making a deal with the feds, incriminating Mario in his sordid operations, or trying to go into business for himself."

She sounded as if the notion didn't make any difference. Only the end results mattered, maybe because that was all she dealt with in her line of work. The reason *why* the perp didn't show up for trial or see his or her parole officer wasn't important. Nor was the reason he had committed the crime. All that mattered was that the person was returned to jail.

Suspecting he already knew the answer, Jake ran his hand over hers in an attempt to put her at ease. "Why would Mario want you dead too?"

"I planned to put him behind bars. Then I turned him in to the cops."

That was what he'd thought. "Since Danny came after you, the police must not have incarcerated Danny and possibly not Mario either." That thought gave Jake major heartburn. These men seemed intent on getting to Alicia, and she wouldn't be safe until they were stopped.

Alicia dropped her gaze to their locked hands. "Maybe my mother knew something about Tony's business or Mario's. Maybe something was going on." She didn't say anything for several minutes. Then in a voice that was hollow with defeat, she said, "Then again, I hadn't wanted to know. I reasoned that the less I knew, the better. But now…"

She took a deep, shaky breath and met his gaze, her eyes swimming in tears. "Maybe if I had known more of what was going on in my mother's life, I could have put Mario and Danny in prison. Maybe I could have stopped Danny from murdering her." She looked weary and overcome.

Jake wanted Darien to drop the subject, to give her time to deal with the changes in her life, but they had to know if something her mother had in her possession might further incriminate Mario. If the man was only human, they could turn the evidence over to the police. If he was one of the wolf kind, that could be a different story. But Darien seemed to want to know if there was more of a connection between Alicia and Mario and that was why Mario continued to target her.

"What kind of relationship did you have with Tony? Your mother's boyfriend who was murdered. How well did you know him?"

Alicia's jaw tightened as she stared at the coffee table. Jake wondered if there was more to the story than she had let on.

"Sometimes…sometimes I thought he was trying to be the father I never had. I thought maybe he was planning on marrying my mother." She shrugged. "I didn't need a father. Hadn't had one all those years. And at my age, why now? But at other times"—she looked up at Jake—"he would distance himself as if he was afraid to know me. Like he was afraid for me to know him. Which was probably because he was tied to the Mob."

"Was Tony ever jealous of your relationship with your mother?" Jake thought that could very well be the case.

Alicia shook her head with conviction. "No. That was the oddest thing. He seemed to appreciate my close relationship with Mom. As if I was good for her. I often wondered why he wouldn't resent that she and I were such good friends. Instead, he seemed to admire our relationship. I don't know. Maybe he'd never had a mother or father who was there for him growing up. Or maybe he'd been close to his mom and understood.

"He wasn't exactly like the other men she dated. They were... never intimate with her like Tony was. He tried to hide his affection for my mother when he was with her around me. But even so, I'd catch a shared kiss. Him holding her hand. A warm embrace. The other men were just...there. Accompanying her. I never saw any sign of affection or intimacy."

That seemed strange to Jake. "Where are your mother's things? Did you go through them?"

"In my apartment. She'd had a furnished apartment in Dillon. She didn't have many personal effects. And mostly at the end, she'd been living with Tony in his condo. I gave away all her clothes to the women's abuse center. There wasn't much left. I didn't really take time to look through her things. I never thought she might have anything incriminating against Mario. I–I haven't returned to my place for the past month, afraid these men would know I'd lived there, and one of them would be waiting for me to show up. So I've just paid the bills and stayed clear of the place."

That was why Jake dreamed that Alicia was in different beds when they made love in their dream states every night. He looked over at Darien to get his okay for what he was about to do next. Darien nodded, giving him his consent.

"I'll take you back to your apartment," Jake said. "We'll see if we can find anything, evidence, something that will clue us in if there was more of a connection to you than you believe. I have a sneaking hunch that Mario coming after you has more to do with you than your attempt at putting him behind bars. And I halfway suspect when we arrive at your place, it'll look like a tornado hit it."

The drive to Alicia's apartment seemed to take forever as Jake chauffeured her in his truck, while Peter and Tom rode in Peter's Suburban as their backup guard. Pete wore his sheriff's uniform, although he'd be out of his jurisdiction.

Their presence was more than comforting, especially since Alicia couldn't take her gun with her since the police still had it. But she was armed with a can of pepper spray.

She'd been alone for so long that she enjoyed the sense of belonging that Jake's pack members had offered her. She still hadn't come to complete terms with being mated to Jake forever or all the strange things she was learning about her werewolfism and pack-member politics. She could only swallow the news in little bites.

But the worry of what she might find at her apartment was over-shadowed by the concern she might be pregnant. She clenched and unclenched her hands, then finally said, "Can we stop at a drugstore? There's one in the strip mall on the corner before we reach my apartment."

She figured if she had to shop at a drugstore in Silver Town, the whole pack might know what she purchased. That was one bad thing about the closeness of a pack, she was learning. And Lelandi had said the businesses were werewolf-run. Alicia imagined even Lisa, the manager of the lingerie shop, might have told everyone what Jake had bought for her there. Lelandi wouldn't have, though. Alicia felt Lelandi was one person who wouldn't give her secrets away. Unless keeping them might harm the pack.

Jake was silent for so long that Alicia thought she'd spoken so softly he hadn't heard. But with their wolf hearing, she decided that wasn't it. She assumed he was trying to figure out why she needed to stop at the drugstore.

He finally nodded and grabbed his phone from his pocket and punched a button. "Tom? We're making a stop at a corner drugstore."

"They don't need to come inside with us," Alicia quickly said. She didn't need the whole world to know what she was up to.

He glanced at her, then said to his brother, "You can wait outside for us. It'll only take us a minute. Right." Then he put his phone away. He didn't say anything for a moment, but she could tell by his furrowed brow that he was bothered by her request. Then he said, "What is it that you need?"

She raised her brows at him. "Is nothing sacred?"

He gave her the wolfish grin that melted her insides to mush. "Not between us. Not now that we're mates."

"Ah, so if I wanted to probe into your deepest, most private fantasies or past history, you'd freely tell me about all of it?" she asked.

He reached over with his big hand and squeezed her thigh in a way that made her shiver with interest. "You only have to ask."

"All right. Well, I want to get a pregnancy kit, and I don't want anyone else in your pack—"

"*Our* pack."

"*Our* pack knowing about it. They might get the wrong notion." Like it was Jake's child, if she were pregnant. She swallowed hard, hating that she'd have to admit if she was pregnant that it was Ferdinand Massaro's child.

Jake ran his hand over her thigh in a tender caress meant to console. Then his mouth curved up and his hand slid to her belly. "When Mary called from the gallery with the news you were pregnant, I was angry. I thought you had another man in your life and hadn't told me. But I couldn't be more pleased if you're having a baby."

"Most men wouldn't like it if it was some other man's baby," she said, trying not to sound so disconsolate.

He drove into the parking lot of the strip mall and parked, then rested his hand beneath her chin and lifted and turned her to face him, his eyes pinning hers with resolve. "I love you. And if you're pregnant, the baby's ours. I'll raise her as my own."

"Her?"

"Wolves in our pack statistically have fewer females. So we're always hopeful we'll have a few more females—keeps the males from getting too rambunctious."

She chuckled. "I never thought I'd hear a man say he'd rather have a little girl than a boy."

"Having two brothers probably has something to do with it." He cut the engine.

She knew he was teasing. By the way he spoke to his brothers, she could tell he was really close to them. She had barely opened the truck's door when Jake hurried around the front of the vehicle to help her down.

"I'll have to add running boards," he said as he held her hips and helped her hop down to the pavement. "If you are pregnant, you'll never be able to climb up into the cab."

"Not without a forklift," she teased, trying to feel better about it.

He smiled down at her but then said, "Would you agree to see Doc Weber? He'd be discreet."

"And what would people think who saw me join the pack, then immediately see the doctor?" She shook her head.

Peter drove up beside them and parked, and Alicia suddenly was aware that he and Tom were watching them both. She hoped the guys couldn't read lips or hear their conversation through the Suburban windows.

"Be just a minute," Jake said to Tom as he rolled the window down.

"Sure you don't want us to watch your backs?" Tom asked, his expression concerned.

Alicia was touched by the way he genuinely seemed worried about her, but she quickly shook her head. "We'll be right out."

Tom gave Jake a look, and she couldn't tell if it was because she was making the decisions without allowing Jake to have a say or because Tom suspected something else was going on. But it made her even more self-conscious, and she hurried Jake into the drugstore before her whole heated body gave her away.

━━━━━━━━

Tom watched Jake and Alicia head into the drugstore as Peter leaned back against the driver's seat of his Suburban and said, "Wonder what *that's* all about that she didn't want us to see what she had to purchase."

Tom didn't want to speculate, but he couldn't help it. Alicia was definitely anxious about something. He'd never seen a more expressive woman, unable to hide her feelings like his kind normally could do. He supposed it was because they'd been born as wolves.

After seeing how much Alicia had gotten under Jake's skin, how much he really cared for her, Tom was damned worried she was going to get herself killed over this situation with Constantino and his thugs, though.

He couldn't help worrying about both Alicia and Jake and how Jake would deal with losing her again, if it came to that. He'd been unable to focus on work or anything in the pack during the last several weeks after he'd lost Alicia. But Tom assumed Jake had continued to believe she was all right. Then there was that damnable business of chasing after her without any pack backup when she was in trouble in Crestview. Hell, Darien had curbed his anger, wanting everything to turn out for the best, but he'd been furious with Jake for not waiting for Tom and Peter to catch up to him. Jake wanted her to be safe, sure, but Darien didn't want to lose his brother in the process.

If anything happened to her now, Jake would be devastated. And Tom couldn't let him down.

"I've never seen Jake allow a woman to order him around," Peter said, his tone solemn. "I've never seen him fall so hard for a woman. She's something special."

Those were Tom's sentiments as well.

Peter glanced at him. "You seem awfully quiet, Tom. What are you thinking?"

That the woman had gotten under Tom's skin too. How could she not when Jake had fallen in love with her? And Lelandi had found a new friend in her. Alicia's sadness concerned Tom, and he wondered whether she'd be happy with their pack. It didn't even matter that Alicia was new to being a wolf. They'd make sure she felt as if she'd been with them forever. But something was the matter, and he suspected there was more to the story than just the trouble with Mario and his gang.

Tom cleared his throat when he realized Peter was watching him, waiting for a response. "Maybe Jake felt we didn't need to go in. He might have thought we'd be more protection if we watched the front door while they went inside."

But Tom knew that wasn't the case. Sure, Jake had to have felt it was safe enough for Alicia since he hadn't insisted that Tom and Peter come inside even if she objected. But Tom couldn't for the life of him think of what had her so bothered that she would be afraid for others in the pack to know. Maybe it was a female thing.

Peter rubbed his chin and stared at the door, then dropped his hand away and shook his head. "I heard her vehemently say we didn't need to come inside. So that made me wonder what she didn't want us to see that she was buying."

"Probably a woman's thing, Peter," Tom said.

"Oh."

But Tom still wondered what was going on with Alicia. He couldn't help thinking about that morning and how red her eyes had been when she'd first come down for breakfast. Jake had been tense, ready to defend her, from the way he had hovered over her. Something was wrong. Not that Tom had thought it had anything to do with the trip to the drugstore. Then again, maybe it did.

A few minutes later when Alicia walked out with Jake, his arm around her waist and escorting her to his truck, Tom eyed the small package she carried. Her expression was glum. Jake's wasn't any more cheerful than hers. If it hadn't been for the trip to the drugstore, Tom might have thought they were just concerned about what they might find at the apartment, and further, what they might discover among Alicia's mother's things. But the small package made him think something else was the matter.

"Condoms?" Peter asked as he started the engine, then pulled in behind Jake as the truck headed back onto the street.

"Jake would have told her we don't wear condoms when we have a mate. Hell, we don't ever wear condoms. No need."

Peter didn't say anything right away, but then he cast Tom a sly smile. "Maybe she's afraid of having triplets since they run in your family."

Poor Jake, if that was the case. No wonder he looked so glum.

Normally, Jake and Tom could talk about anything and often did, even about Darien when he had been in such a black mood before Lelandi came into his life. But Jake had refused to tell Tom what had been bothering him while he'd been frantically trying to locate Alicia. Tom and Darien had talked at length about what could have been upsetting Jake, assuming it had to do with the woman who'd been in the shower running in the background that Darien had heard over the phone.

Tom sighed. No matter what, when he found the right woman to mate, *he* wouldn't be anything but bowled over with joy.

The most noticeable things about Alicia's two-story redbrick building were the gardens in front of each of the town houses. Alicia's was overflowing with vibrant red roses and golden sunflowers and yellow daisies.

Jake pulled a gun from his glove box, and Alicia's eyes widened. He patted her leg. "I said I didn't have a gun *with* me when I first saw you in Breckenridge. But it seems prudent that I take a gun with me anytime I go out with you now." He pulled out a lockpick set and helped her out of the truck.

She frowned at him. "Lockpicks? I've got my keys." She patted her purse. "Why do you have lockpicks?"

He was so accustomed to using lockpicks to get into places that weren't family-owned that he hadn't even thought about her keys. "Most of us carry these in case we have an urgent need to get inside a building and hide ourselves. If there's a wolf on the premises, I'll have to shift quickly and deal with it."

"Oh," she said, sounding surprised.

Her response reminded him how newly turned she was and how difficult it had to be for her to think in terms of being a wolf or that others might also be wolves and had to be dealt with differently.

Peter and Tom joined them at Alicia's apartment door and hovered close as Jake said quietly, "Tom, I want you to stay with Alicia until Peter and I make sure the place is all clear."

Using her key, Jake unlocked the door, and with guns drawn, he and Peter stepped inside the house. The place was quiet, and Tom and Alicia remained in the entryway watching their progress.

Jake lifted his nose and took a good strong whiff, just like the others did. He smelled the telltale scents of several men who had been here recently. Pungent colognes, primarily. The odor of male testosterone and sweat. And the faint odor of wolf. Male wolf.

He and Peter quickly scanned the small living room, which was filled with a blue floral couch and two solid-blue love seats, a light-oak coffee table and a couple of end tables, leaving nowhere for anyone to hide. A cheerful yellow kitchen was just beyond the living area, and in an open dining room were a glass table and wrought-iron chairs but nothing else. The bar divided the kitchen from the living room, however, and anyone could be crouching behind it.

Jake motioned for Peter to follow him, and they quietly strode to the kitchen, but he shook his head at Alicia and Tom when they found no one there.

A creaking noise in the bedroom floor upstairs caught everyone's attention. No one said a word as Jake and Peter quietly stalked up the carpeted stairs, Jake leading the way. He wasn't sure what he would face—a wolf or a man. But he smelled the scent of a wolf and a man on the way up the stairs. If the man was in his human form, he'd be armed and dangerous. If he was a wolf, Jake would take care of the problem once and for all.

When they reached the landing, a short wall half protected a suited man with his gun aimed for a kill, but Jake saw the man before he could fire the shots. Jake ducked into a crouch behind the wall. Three pops rang in the air. Three bullets slammed into the wall behind Jake with a *thunk, thunk, thunk*.

Peter whipped around the low wall at a crouch and fired, hitting the man twice in the arm and making him drop his weapon. The man collapsed on the floor and passed out. Jake cursed under his breath and then rushed forward to feel the injured man's pulse. His pulse was thready, but the man was alive.

"He's alive," Jake called out, loud enough for Alicia and Tom to know that everyone was all right.

The injured man wasn't a wolf. Someone else had been here, though, who *was* a male wolf.

Jake kicked the gun away from the gunman and then rummaged

through his pockets, looking for any ID. None. Not that he'd expected to find any.

Peter stalked into the bathroom. "No one in the laundry room or bathroom," he said.

"Call the local police, Peter. We'll have him hauled off and then take care of our business here."

Surprisingly, nothing seemed to be out of place. Jake assumed that was an attempt by Mario's man to give the appearance that no one had been there. Then if Alicia had arrived, she would have felt safe as she entered her apartment. The man would have waited like a venomous snake until she reached the bedroom and then would have pounced on her.

The bedcovers were tousled where the gunman appeared to have been lying down, waiting for Alicia to show up. He must have heard them downstairs, thinking Alicia had come home. Jake wondered just how long the man had been here waiting for her. Maybe only since the night before because the men seemed to have been tailing her before they lost her at the Crestview Motel.

Mario might have thought she'd finally return here with no place else to go.

Jake headed back down the stairs as Peter watched the man while calling the shooting in to the police. "This is Sheriff Peter Jorgenson of Silver Town, calling about a shooting incident at 452 Sunnybrook Apartments."

Jake caught Alicia's pale features as he hurried to join her at the front door. "The man's passed out but just wounded. He won't be firing another gun for a good long while." He took her in his arms and gave her a heartfelt embrace. "If you're up to it, do you want to look at him and see if he's anyone you recognize?"

"Yes, of…course." Even though her speech was hesitant, she seemed resolute about getting this over and done with.

He rubbed her back. "The police will be here soon. They'll have more questions to ask you, I'm afraid. But at least Peter shot the man, who had fired his weapon first. Although I am licensed to carry a gun. All of us are, just in case we need to be. He's human, Alicia. But a wolf has been on the premises."

"I smelled the wolf, but I wouldn't know who he is." She looked toward the stairs. "My mother's things are upstairs in a linen closet."

He took her cold hand and led her up the stairs. She took a steadying breath at the top of the stairs and moved closer to the man, who was stirring now as Peter stood over him. Peter shoved his cell phone into his pocket. "Police are on their way."

The man's eyes suddenly popped opened. He groaned and grabbed his bloodied arm. He saw Peter first, wearing the forest-green shirt and khaki trousers and the gold seven-point star badge identifying him as a sheriff. At that sight, the man grew very still, his dark eyes round.

"Why did Mario send you?" Jake asked, his voice low and cold, which had the man jerking his head around to see Jake standing with Alicia, his hand at her stiff spine.

His gaze quickly shot to Alicia's. She said, "This man was a friend of the guy my mother was seeing. So much for being any-one's friend in their organization."

The man narrowed his eyes at Alicia. "Friends take care of friends. If they turn traitorous, you stick with the guy with the most firepower."

"So why *did* Mario have your friend killed? Was Tony trying to take over the business?" Jake asked.

Sirens sounded in the distance, and when the man wouldn't answer, Jake urged again, "What about Alicia? Why does Mario want her dead?"

The gunman's gaze again swung to her. "He doesn't want her dead."

She was barely breathing now. Jake rubbed her back. "Then what?"

The guy gave a half shrug with his good arm and groaned again.

"Hell, he wants her. I dunno why. But despite her killing one of our guys and shooting another, Mario wants her. *Alive.* Frankly, none of us gets it." He cast an evil half smirk at Alicia, as if to say Mario would get his way, then she'd pay.

Tom shouted up the stairs, "Police and paramedics are here."

The sirens cut out in the parking lot.

"Send them up, Tom." Then Jake growled at the injured man, "If you see Mario, tell him Alicia's off-limits."

"And who should I say said so?" The guy gritted his teeth and squeezed his bloodied arm tighter as they heard the front door open and Tom telling them the man was upstairs, wounded but disarmed.

"Jake Silver," Jake said. "Of Silver Town."

Might as well give Mario an invitation to visit the pack. See if he had the fortitude to try to grab Alicia there. If he was a wolf, and Jake was beginning to think so, they'd have to take him down in their own territory where they could handle the matter much more discreetly.

The man's eyes narrowed. "If I see him, I'll pass along the word. He likes dealing with a guy with steel balls. More of a challenge that way."

Men rushed up the stairs, four officers and two paramedics. The place was swarming with people, and with the crowd in her small bedroom, Alicia went back downstairs since she hadn't witnessed the shooting. Jake and Peter stayed to explain what had happened. Jake only hoped she wouldn't falter when the police interrogated her about the connection between this incident and the one the night before. He would have given anything to keep her from having to deal with this again.

As soon as he could return to her, Jake headed back downstairs to see her sitting on the blue floral couch, her hands clasped tightly together in her lap as Tom stood beside the couch in protective mode. This time, she was armed with a glass of water.

Jake joined her on the couch and held her hand to fortify her before two of the officers came downstairs to take her statement.

He felt her tense, her heart beating rapidly, as she barely breathed. He squeezed her hand to reassure her, hoping to hell this would be the last case of anything like this happening.

Tom looked just as tense, and Jake knew his brother was in protective wolf mode in the event anything went wrong with the police questioning.

———

Alicia swallowed hard and tried to settle her raw nerves. She was afraid she'd be in for even more of the third degree, considering her connection with the incident the night before. What were her ties to a mobster? She couldn't let them know about her mother's possessions in case she and Jake could uncover anything about what was going on.

One of the police detectives, a redhead with bright-green eyes and a stern look, said, "I'm Detective Hanover, and this is my partner, Detective Brumley." Then they both showed their badges. Detective Hanover sat down on Alicia's wide-winged armchair and opened a notebook. "Okay, first can I see some ID from everyone?"

Alicia dug around in her purse and swore she needed to clean it out as her fingers searched for her wallet and instead ran into a tube of lipstick, a package of tissues, a ton of receipts for motel bills, a brush, a comb, keys, and nail scissors that she managed to stab herself with in her frantic search. Finally, she grasped her leather wallet and pulled it out. Searching each of the pockets, she found: credit card, library card, car insurance card, health insurance card, dental insurance card, store-points cards...

She frowned as she went through every pocket of the wallet. Where was her driver's license? She looked up to see the detective handing driver's licenses back to Jake, Tom, and Peter. Then the detective focused his attention on her.

"Miss Greiston, your driver's license?"

CHAPTER 16

ALICIA FELT HOT WITH EMBARRASSMENT MIXED WITH CONCERN as she faced the policemen grilling her while Jake and his brother and their own sheriff gave her moral support. Where in the world had her driver's license gone? And when had she lost it?

She couldn't remember the last time she'd noticed it. "I seem to have misplaced it."

Detective Hanover nodded as if that wasn't important, that he already knew who she was. "Can you tell me in your own words why you returned to your apartment with three armed men from Silver Town, one being a sheriff of the same town, and what your relationship is to everyone, Miss Greiston?"

How did Alicia tell the detective she was "married" to Jake when she wasn't? Not really. She had no paper proof. And not even his name to call her own. For the first time, she realized just how much that part bothered her. The rest of the pack must have grown up with the notion, and it seemed perfectly fine to them, but being tied to someone as his life mate and yet unmarried seemed unthinkable to her. And despite thinking she never wanted to marry again, considering the way she felt about Jake and her need to be with him ever since they'd parted, she realized her only reason to swear off men was that she'd always picked the wrong sort.

She couldn't have asked for a man who was more concerned for her, more protective, and wanted to make her happy in the worst way. She'd never had anyone care for her like that. How could she not want to be married to a man like that?

But what was she to say to humans in a situation like this?

She squeezed Jake's hand. "Jake and I are engaged to be married."

She focused on the detective's eyes but sensed the tension in the room among Jake, Tom, and Peter. Worse, just as the words spilled from her lips, another two police officers escorted Mario's henchman down the stairs, and she was sure he'd heard what she'd said. If he had a chance to speak to Mario, he'd tell him what she'd said. Then Mario would have even more of a reason to eliminate Jake: to hurt her.

She didn't speak any further until the policemen had taken the man outside, followed by the paramedics, and then shut the door.

The officer glanced down at her hand, but Jake's hand was covering hers and hiding any ring she might be wearing.

"Recent engagement?" the detective asked.

"Yes. We met a couple of months ago."

His brows raised and he shifted his attention to Jake, who gave him a slight smile. She was sure the detective was thinking Jake had either been suckered into the relationship or was a really fast mover.

"Love at first sight," she clarified, just in case the policeman needed the clarification.

He seemed slightly amused and probably unconvinced about such a thing.

"Tom is Jake's brother, as I'm sure you already know." She motioned to him. "And Peter is the sheriff of Silver Town," she said coolly.

"So you take a bunch of armed men to your apartment for protection, anticipating trouble. One of my partners talked to your apartment manager, and she says you have been paying the rent but haven't been here in some weeks. Why come here now?"

"I came home for some personal things. Because of the trouble I had with Mario Constantino's men last night in Crestview—I overhead Jake already apprise you of the situation—I've moved in with Jake and his family until we get married. But we knew I might not be safe if I came here alone or with just Jake accompanying me, after Mario's men lost me last night."

The detective leaned back in the chair, putting welcome distance between them. "You could have called us and let us check out the place first."

"Would you have spared any men to investigate on an unfounded assumption?" she asked.

He didn't say anything for a moment, then asked, "Did you know the man upstairs?"

This got really tricky. She tried not to reveal any emotion concerning her mother's connection, but her damned voice broke when she said, "My mother…" She paused and looked down at the coffee table, trying to keep the tears flooding her eyes from spilling down her cheeks. But she couldn't control her feelings where her mother was concerned yet. "She was seeing Tony Thomas, one of the men who worked for Mario. I don't have any idea what Tony did for Mario. But my mother's association with Tony got her killed. And the guy upstairs? He was friends with Tony, who also was murdered."

"And"—the detective leaned forward again, and his steely look pinned her with the question before he even asked it—"what about you? What was your association with this man who was dating your mother before they were both murdered?"

"None. Only that I had warned her I thought he might be a member of the Mob. I worried for her safety." Her voice hardened to fight the tears. "She wouldn't listen to me. She said she loved him. It got her killed."

"Are you sure there wasn't something more to this whole case? Seems odd that Constantino would come after you when only your mother was involved with a member of the Mob."

"I've been trying to put him back in jail where he belongs," Alicia said coldly.

"As a bounty hunter," the detective said. "We ran a check on your background. You've successfully brought in a number of cases, but no one that dangerous. It seems to me you're a little out of your league on this one. When it becomes a vendetta…"

"I'm not trying to kill him, just put him back in jail!" She swallowed her anger. This was not helping, but Jake had said the same thing when he first met her and had triggered the response.

The detective continued in the same tranquil manner. She wished she sounded a lot more coolheaded, but she guessed that with Jake and Peter finding Mario's man in her apartment and hearing the shots fired, and then worrying that Jake or Peter had been hit, she'd been unnerved more than she thought.

"Did you think Constantino would be here waiting for you today?" the detective asked.

"No. I wouldn't be that naive. He sends his henchmen to do his dirty work."

"Even in the event of your mother's murder?"

Alicia took a steadying breath as she thought of how her mother must have been terrified in the final moments, facing Danny Massaro, his gun held out to shoot her. "He ordered the hit. But Danny Massaro did the killing."

"And you knew this how?"

She felt Jake tense a hair. He hadn't asked her himself, and she hadn't thought to tell him. "Danny's brother, Ferdinand Massaro, told me."

The detective quickly began taking notes, then looked up at her. "Where can he be reached?"

In that moment, she knew she was doomed. The police hadn't known she knew anything about Ferdinand's untimely death. Or that she even knew him. How could she explain she'd been at his place, had managed to run away without being killed by his murderers, and had never told the police she had been there?

Every time there was a murder of one of the Mob in Mario's

employ or related to him of late, *she* was involved! The word would leak to Mario and his henchmen that she might be a possible witness to the murder. And then they'd want her eliminated even more than before.

She shook her head. "Ferdinand always left me messages."

"Left you messages?"

"He was my informant, telling me where Mario could be reached, hoping I'd take him down because I was a bounty hunter."

"Why was he informing on Mario for you? If his brother worked for Constantino, seems to me it was a good way to get his brother killed."

"I don't know. I suspected Ferdinand had his own vendetta."

The detective motioned to his partner and said, "We need to locate this Ferdinand Massaro, ASAP."

"Right." The other detective left the apartment and began talking on his phone.

Alicia swallowed a lump in her throat. She didn't have any idea if Mario had disposed of Ferdinand's body or just left him dead in his condo. What if the police could tie her to the crime scene?

"The place looks clean, unless you tidied it up," Detective Hanover said to Alicia.

For a moment, she thought the detective was referring to Ferdinand's condo, but then she realized he was talking about her apartment. *Get a grip, Alicia!*

"It was like this when we arrived," she offered.

"Then it appears Mario's henchman was only waiting here for you and wasn't searching for anything incriminating you might have had here. Or he was very neat when he went about his business."

She didn't say anything, thinking the same thing, but why say one way or another when she truly didn't have an answer? Besides, she didn't want to give away the fact that she had her mother's belongings, which she'd be going through if the police would ever leave her alone.

Detective Hanover watched her for a long time before he finally said, "All right. Well, one other thing."

Something in the way he said "one other thing" made her think it was significant, although he tried to make it sound like an off-hand last-minute question. She tried to not tense up while she waited for him to say what that one other thing was.

He tapped his pen on his notepad like Detective Simpson had done at Darien's house, and for an instant, she felt it was a training technique they all had learned in police detective school. A way to fluster the interviewee in a crime-scene investigation.

"Two 911 calls were made in Breckenridge, both about you," he finally said.

She stared at him in disbelief.

He paused, observed her reaction, and then forged ahead. "The first was nearly two months ago, coinciding with when you said you met Mr. Jake Silver." The detective read from his notebook, "A handwritten death threat was left at the room of one Miss Alicia Greiston. Myron Baker, assistant manager of the Mountainview Inn, called to report that Alicia Greiston had hastily paid for her hotel room and left without sending word to Mr. Silver although they'd had a prearranged engagement later that day.

"Now," Detective Hanover said, "my father happens to be the police chief in Breckenridge and led the investigation."

Police Chief Winston Hanover. Of course. She'd met him when he was trying to solve her mother's murder several months earlier. Who would have thought his son would now be interrogating her in another incident?

"My father was unsuccessful in locating the missing woman, you, Miss Greiston. He assumed you had gone missing, not wanting to see Mr. Silver any further. Although my father was still concerned about your interest in Constantino, that the mobster has been spending time in the area, and that you believed there was a connection between the man and your mother's death, not to mention her lover's murder as well. None of which my father has been able to corroborate to date."

Alicia barely breathed.

"So what happened, Miss Greiston? Why did you suddenly disappear from your hotel that day?"

"The note containing the death threat explains it all. I feared for Jake's life and left before Mario killed him for hanging around me."

"And now?"

"Jake assures me that Mario has no chance at doing him any harm."

"Hmm," the detective said. Then he flipped to another page in his notebook. "Then a day or so ago, a 911 call was made from the Cliffside Art Gallery, and the woman frantically tells the operator that a woman is in trouble. Her name is, *surprisingly*… Alicia Greiston. But the woman quickly tells the operator it's a false alarm and the woman had passed out due to being pregnant. Since no real medical emergency existed, the operator concluded the conversation. But when my father heard of the call, his interest was instantly piqued. Now he knows the woman is still around, still alive, but he's disconcerted that he hadn't had a chance to talk to her…you.

"But it doesn't end there. That night, another 911 call is made. A high-school buddy of mine gets the call about the shooting at Crestview Motel, and guess who's at the heart of the shooting? Why, our elusive Miss Greiston. Of course, Detective Simpson didn't know you'd gone missing in Breckenridge or been the subject of the call about a pregnancy mishap…" The detective hesitated, and his gaze dropped to her waist.

She felt her face burn with embarrassment as she could imagine both Peter and Tom looking her over again, trying to figure if that was what all this was about. Had she'd gotten pregnant with Jake's baby? But the timing wasn't right, as far as her having been turned, if a werewolf couldn't impregnate a human.

"And now this. It seems as though no matter where you are, trouble follows you. My boss says we need to put you in protective custody, considering who you're dealing with and how much my father would like to take Constantino down. But I wasn't sure which one of you he was concerned more about protecting, considering all these shooting incidents that have occurred. You or the men who hassle you and keep ending up shot or dead."

And he didn't even know about the man she'd shot on the trail where her mother had died.

"I'll be fine with Jake and his family."

"In truth, you're bound to put his whole family at risk. There's a good chance somebody's going to do something rash and someone you love is going to get blamed for it when they've never done anything criminal in their life." Detective Hanover looked at Jake, as if to say he was the one the detective was talking about.

Jake shook his head. "We'll be careful. We're just picking up some of Alicia's things from her apartment and giving notice. She's permanently moving in with me."

"I'll need your address," Detective Hanover said. "But think about it. If you change your mind..." He handed Alicia his business card. "Just call me."

The other detective opened the front door of the apartment, and from the grim look on his face, he probably had learned Ferdinand Massaro was dead. "Can I talk to you for a moment out here?" he said to Detective Hanover, his gaze shifting to Alicia, then back to his partner.

They couldn't know she was involved in that murder, too, could they?

"Sure." The detective looked at Alicia as if he *knew* she had something to do with the latest report, which had her on edge all over again.

The two men left the apartment and shut the door, and the detective's partner began talking.

Alicia slumped against the couch, realizing just how tense she'd been up until now. Jake wrapped his arm around her shoulders and gave her a comforting hug. But none of them spoke while she and the others all listened, trying to hear what was being said outside the apartment.

Because of the large glass window and their enhanced wolf hearing, Alicia and the others heard the man say, "I learned Ferdinand Massaro is dead. Found in his condo by his cleaning lady the next morning. He'd been murdered the night before. A couple returning from a late-night movie saw a woman fitting Miss Alicia Greiston's description leaving the condo, frazzled and upset, sometime in the middle of the night. Several blocks from the condo, a cab driver gave a woman fitting Miss Greiston's description a ride to her car parked in a suburb on the other side of the city."

"Hell. Now why did I guess she might have been involved in another shooting incident that was connected with Mario's gang?" Detective Hanover asked.

"Not a shooting this time. Massaro's neck was broken. The coroner said it had to have been a man who killed him because of the trauma to his neck. But it only figures, Hanover. The little lady gets around. She sure has a hell of a lot more gumption than she appears to."

"She's good at staying alive, I'll give her that. Anything else you can give me before I go in and question her some more?"

Alicia closed her eyes against the pounding headache developing in her temple.

Jake kissed her cheek. "Are you okay?"

"No," she whispered. "What do I say now?"

CHAPTER 17

ROUND TWO, JAKE GLUMLY THOUGHT AS HE PULLED AWAY FROM Alicia and held her hand so she didn't look ready to collapse under pressure before Detective Hanover came back into her apartment to grill her further. When the detective and his partner returned to the interrogation, Detective Brumley looked almost smug as he watched the proceedings. Alicia hadn't had time to prepare what she'd say, nor had Jake had time to counsel her.

Tom and Peter attempted to look unconcerned, but Jake could tell both were worried. She'd been at a murder scene and hadn't reported it. What was she going to say now? Jake was tempted to get one of their lawyers involved before this went any further, but the problem was that the murder had taken place in Denver. They needed a wolf lawyer there to defend her, if that was what it took. But they didn't know any wolf packs in the city, since the packs usually avoided most bigger cities and stayed closer to home. Except for Sherry Slate. Jake didn't figure she'd like it that he hadn't been interested in her beyond a couple of dates but now he'd taken up with Alicia and wanted Sherry to defend her.

"So, Miss Greiston, do you want to tell me what happened on the night of July 15 when you visited Ferdinand Massaro at his condo?"

"He told me to meet him at his place. That he had information about where to locate Mario. He left the message underneath my hotel-room door. When I went to his place, no one answered the door. I rang the doorbell several times, but still no answer. I didn't have his phone number, so I couldn't give him a call. I figured he'd left. Or maybe I had the time or location wrong. Or he might have."

"But you say he had left a message under your door. So you must have had the right information."

"I thought so. But then I thought maybe I didn't. I hadn't brought the piece of paper with me."

"Do you still have it?"

She shook her head. "I tossed it out."

"So you left the place in the middle of the night and...?"

"Finally got a taxi and returned to where I'd parked my car. Then I drove to my hotel."

"Why get a taxi to get to your car?"

"I was being cautious in case any of Mario's men might be following me."

"Hmm," Detective Hanover said.

Jake knew she hadn't parked her car and taken a taxi from there, not when Massaro had grabbed her at the other location, but he couldn't tell if the detective knew that or not. He assumed the detective would make a note to check out the cab records to verify her claim and find nothing of the sort.

"And then?" The detective looked up from his note-taking.

"I moved from place to place, trying again to track down Constantino and Danny Massaro. When I finally found where they were, I notified the police, and they picked them up."

Detective Hanover studied her for a moment, then quietly said, "But they didn't. Pick them up."

Her mouth dropped open, then she snapped it shut.

"They're still free?" Jake asked, rubbing her hand and having assumed that was the case.

"Yes. The police arrived too late. But if you're a bounty hunter who's supposed to be bringing them in, why turn their location over to the police?" Detective Hanover asked Alicia.

"I figured they were too dangerous for me to try and arrest."

"Because you had witnessed Ferdinand Massaro's murder."

Jake could hear Alicia's rapid heartbeat. He felt her clammy hand in his and knew she was trying to make the best of this situation. He wished he could get her the hell out of this nightmare legally, without causing further stress or trouble for her.

"Murdered?" she asked, her voice hollow, and despite knowing Ferdinand had been murdered already, she sounded convincing enough that she hadn't already had a clue. "The…the night I went to see him?"

Genuine tears filled her eyes. Jake knew they weren't faked. She must have been terrified to see what she had in the condo, further horrified that she could have ended up like Ferdinand.

"It fits you were there after he was murdered."

Not before, good. Or maybe the detective was giving her an out to see if she'd let anything slip. If anyone had seen Ferdinand take Alicia into the condo after he'd knocked her out, wouldn't they have reported it to the police? Maybe not, thinking she was dead drunk.

Hanover's partner got a call and said into his phone, "This is Brumley. Yeah?" He looked up at Alicia. "All right. I'll tell Hanover. Yeah, we're still questioning her. Thanks." He hung up his phone. "Want me to ask?" he questioned Hanover.

"Don't tell me it's about another shooting," Hanover said dryly.

Brumley said, "Yeah, it is. Seems some hikers thought they'd heard a shot fired and then saw two men in suits coming off a hiking trail near Breckenridge, one with a bloodied trouser leg. The hikers said a woman was standing by a wreath of flowers near the trail."

"For Missy Greiston," Hanover guessed, looking directly at Alicia. "So who shot the man, Brumley?"

"My guess?" his partner asked.

"Take your best shot," Hanover said, never taking his eyes off Alicia.

She remained ramrod stiff.

"Mario's men came after her on the trail and met up with Alicia

Greiston when she was visiting the spot where her mother had died. Mario's men threatened her. Miss Greiston defended herself. The men left but, in their usual fashion, didn't report the gunshot wound. Because of that, there was no crime to report. No real witnessing of a crime. Only circumstantial evidence."

"Gun casings? Bullet fragments?"

"None."

"All right." Detective Hanover slapped his hands on his thighs, rose from the chair, and said, "That about wraps it up. If you think you might have seen someone or something in connection with Ferdinand Massaro's murder, you'll let us know, won't you, Miss Greiston?"

"Of course," Alicia said softly.

———

Detective Hanover gave his head a little shake and followed Brumley out the door. Once it was locked, Alicia let out a shaky breath, then looked at Tom's and Peter's grave expressions.

"I didn't witness any *other* shootings or killings. I swear it," she said with a frown, her voice sharp.

They both chuckled darkly.

"Let's go through my mother's things, then we can pack up some of my stuff and go. I did want to keep my furniture, though." She looked at the new couch and love seats she'd bought the previous year and that she'd saved hard-earned money to purchase. And she longed to sleep in her own bed too.

"No problem. My grandparents' place has old furniture that needs replacing. We'll get a moving van and move your things there." Jake said to Tom and Peter, "You can wait here and make sure no one comes that shouldn't be here."

"Do you want me to rent a moving van? It shouldn't take anything very big to haul Alicia's furniture and personal effects back to Silver Town," Tom said.

Rising from the couch, Jake looked to Alicia for a decision. She nodded. She might as well get this over and done with. No sense in paying rent on a place when she wasn't going to be living there. "I'll have to give notice, and I'll lose my deposit for not giving a month's notice."

"It won't matter. I make enough money for the two of us." He took her hand and helped her up from the couch.

She gave him an easy smile and looped her finger through one of his belt loops. "I should have asked that right away."

"I didn't realize that was the only thing holding you back from saying yes."

She gave him an annoyed look and a tug on his belt loop as she headed for the stairs. "I don't recall being asked anything that remotely required me to say yes."

"Do you want me to call Darien and give him the heads-up concerning our progress?" Tom asked, cell phone in hand.

"Yeah, tell him we're getting a moving van so it might take a little longer to return home. And you can let him know that we had the shooting incident here at her apartment and gave police statements again. Tell him there's a little trouble about Alicia's being sighted at the condo where Ferdinand Massaro died, in case we need to find a lawyer in Denver, and that we're about ready to go through Alicia's mother's things."

"Will do."

A little trouble? Witnessing a murder was bound to get her into a whole lot more trouble. Why had she ever mentioned knowing Ferdinand Massaro?

When they reached the bedroom, Jake moved into the closet to pull out the boxes of stuff belonging to Alicia's mother.

"Just dump the contents on the floor, and we'll sort through them that way," she said, her heart in her throat. She'd thrown everything in the boxes without really going through any of it, so she hadn't a clue if any of it needed to be discarded or not. But smelling her mother's perfume on her personal effects and seeing the jewelry and trinkets she'd collected since her mother had been a young woman was still hard for Alicia to deal with.

After searching through two of the boxes of knickknacks that Alicia decided she couldn't part with, while she randomly wiped away her errant tears, Jake paused and asked, "Where do you keep your tissues?"

"Bedside table."

He returned to her side with the box, crouched in front of her, and wiped away her tears himself. "Alicia, if this is too difficult for you…"

She shook her head. "I might see something that would mean something to me but that wouldn't to you." She smiled through her tears at him and swept her hand down his arm until she was holding his strong but gentle hand, and she squeezed lightly in thanks. "Thanks, Jake. Have I told you I love you?"

He gave her a quirky smile. "Not in so many words, but I knew it anyway."

She gave him a watery smile, and he tilted her chin up and kissed her lips. But he quickly broke off the kiss, gave her a light hug, and then went back to searching through a sheaf of papers. She knew he wanted to get this over with, the sooner the better, and be on their way. She wished she could look through everything as clinically as he could.

She was leaning forward to move aside more papers when her hand brushed against something oddly familiar—a small, sturdy red envelope that was big enough only for a key. She recognized the bank key at once, and her heart began beating faster. She lifted the envelope, shook out the key, and held it up to show Jake. "The key to my mother's safe-deposit box."

Jake paused from reading through various papers he'd found and looked up at her. "Where is the box?"

"A bank in Breckenridge. She…didn't want to keep it in Dillon."

"Why?" His dark brows were slightly furrowed.

"I don't know. I never asked, and she never said." Alicia had never given it much thought, but as intensely as Jake was looking at her, she suspected he thought the key could be vital to discovering clues.

"Do you know what it contains?" he asked.

"Personal papers, I guess. She had me sign the signature card so I could have access if I ever needed to. I never did, and I have no idea what she kept in it. I always thought it was kind of odd that she'd have it there instead of where she lived permanently. After her death, I didn't give it any thought. She never had anything of real value. Just fake jewels that she kept with her at home. So I figured she kept her birth certificate, Grandmother's death certificate, her social security card, stuff like that in there."

Alicia tried not to sound as anxious as he was making her feel, but she wanted to check out the bank vault that day. She knew they wouldn't have time. Not when they had to move all the furniture and her other household goods to Silver Town. The bank would be closed by the time they got to Breckenridge.

"We'll have to check it out first thing tomorrow," he said.

"Yes, of course." She'd known that the minute she discovered the key in her mother's possessions. She tucked the key into her jeans pocket and then spied another key. This one looked like a house key, she thought. She sniffed it and frowned. "This wasn't my mother's. It smells faintly of cologne. The same smell I got a whiff of in Ferdinand's apartment when one of Mario's henchmen came looking for me. Danny Massaro."

"You're sure?" Jake asked, taking the key from her. He gave it a good whiff, memorizing the smell of it.

"Yes. Would a wolf's nose lie?"

He squeezed her hand. "No. So it's Danny's key. Why would your mother have it?"

"I don't know. What if Tony had stolen it and given it to Mom to keep hidden in her stuff? Maybe it's Danny's house key, and Tony was trying to get some goods on the guy or something."

"Hmm," Jake said noncommittally, still looking through more of the stuff on the floor. "I don't see anything in these boxes." He looked up at her. "Do you?"

She shook her head.

"All right. Well, I'll put everything away if you want to take your clothes out of the drawers and pack up your items in the bathroom."

"Okay," she said and looked around at her apartment. She had truly thought she'd return to it someday. She had never expected to be a werewolf mated to another and leaving her apartment to live with him in another town.

She was still sitting on the floor when she noticed Jake wasn't putting things back into the boxes any longer. She turned to see what he was doing. He was watching her. "Are you all right, Alicia?"

She nodded. "Yes. I'll need some boxes for my clothes, though."

Before she could stand, he pulled her to her feet, and then he gave her a warm hug. "I plan to settle into my grandfather's house tonight. Darien might say no, but if we can get a bodyguard detail together, that's where I'd like to be with you tonight. In our own place."

"I'd like that." Although she didn't have a clue what his place looked like. What if she didn't like it?

She'd love it, she decided. If Jake was with her and she could help him decorate, she'd love it. "Are your photographs hanging on the walls?" she asked as she headed for her chest of drawers.

"No. I'll leave the walls for you to decorate to your heart's content." He continued to reverently put her mother's things back in the boxes.

"I want that photograph of the fuchsia flowers at the gallery, unless you have another like that. Oh." She put an armload of sweaters on the bed. "What about my car? Your photograph of the wood lilies is in the car."

"You can have any photograph you want, Alicia. You didn't need to buy any of them." He chuckled. "You might be my only buyer." Then he grew serious. "But your car will have been towed to a service station in Breckenridge. The window will be replaced and everything will be set right."

"Good. I would have hated to lose that picture."

He was so quiet that Alicia looked over from unloading another drawer of her underwear. He was reading a note.

"Anything important?"

"An address." He looked up at her. "Danny Massaro's address."

"So my mother had Danny's key and"—she read the address—"an address I don't recognize."

"The key could be to any place. But it really wouldn't matter. I have lockpicks, remember?"

Four hours later, they were finished unloading the furniture at Jake's grandfather's place, a spacious brick ranch-style home. Alicia wandered around the three-bedroom house, finally standing in the living room and turning to look at Jake as she watched men she hadn't met help settle her furniture in the place. The same men had already moved out his grandfather's old furniture and even cleaned up the house. Jake said he and Tom and some others had worked on renovating the place for months in preparation for moving in. She was already really warming up to being part of a pack.

"Is the house to your liking?" he asked, studying her response.

She smiled. "It's lovely, Jake. All the beautiful stained-wood trim, the moldings, the rustic stone fireplace. I can't wait for winter to come when we can sit before the fireplace, sipping hot chocolate and watching the flames flicker." She looked out the expansive window at the forest surrounding them. "All my life, I've lived on top of people, crunched up beside people in apartments. Heard all the noise of neighbors walking on my ceiling or banging against walls when hanging pictures or moving furniture. Or hearing angry words when fights occurred. I love it here with the peace and quiet, the wide-open space, yet the surrounding forest makes it comforting."

He joined her and wrapped his arms around her. "You don't feel isolated out here? Scared? Frightened of the woods? You've lived all your life in town. You won't feel you've been dumped in the wilderness, will you?"

She nestled against his body. "No. I love it here. I used to love going on nature walks with my mother, wishing I had been a pioneer and could have lived out away from people."

"Truthfully, in a pack, we're never very isolated. We might have our own homes or apartments, but we're never really alone."

"I can see that," she said, smiling up at him as she listened to the men moving the master-bedroom furniture around as Tom directed the placement of the dresser.

"Lelandi wants us to come home for dinner. If that's all right with you."

"Of course."

"But…" He leaned down and slanted his mouth over hers and then, with an openmouthed kiss, stroked her lips with his. When she parted her lips for him, he tongued hers. Their hearts were already beating faster, his body hardening, her nipples spearing him. "We'll set things up a bit before we return to their house."

She knew what he had in mind. "Will it be safe?"

Already his eyes had darkened with desire. "Guards will be posted outside the house. You'll be safe. I'll just talk to them. If you want to"—he waved at the hallway that led to the bedroom—"start making the bed. I'll help you finish up in a minute."

The only thing bad about being with a pack was the knowledge they all knew exactly what she and Jake would be doing after he cleared the house out. As soon as the men finished with the bedroom, she slipped into the room and dug around in a box, then found a set of fresh sheets as she listened to hear what Jake was telling the men. Not a word. Just a shuffling of boots, and the front door opened and everyone marched outside.

A few minutes later, Jake was stalking into the bedroom. "I set a detail around the house. We'll be safe enough."

"They don't mind?" she asked, searching for the pillows.

"No, of course not. We'd all do the same for each other. Why did you have such a big bed when you're such a little thing?"

"Didn't I tell you? I'm a kangaroo in bed. You'll probably decide to sleep in one of the other bedrooms once we furnish them. Or on the couch."

With only the bottom sheet on the bed, he maneuvered her over to the mattress and began pulling up her shirt. "The couch."

"Yes, in case I fight you too much at night."

His fingers pushed through her hair, and he cupped her head as he leaned down to kiss her mouth. "You won't move an inch when we're together, and we won't need but half that bed to sleep on."

A promise was a promise, and making love with Jake was only the beginning of fulfilling that promise. No matter how tender or rough or rushed or slow and measured his moves were, he was the perfect lover.

The bedroom was cluttered with packing boxes and the newly painted walls were bare. The bed had no other covering but the one fitted bottom sheet—silky cotton, no pillows, just her and Jake and their bared bodies as he pulled off her clothes and then his. She loved the way he wanted her, as if he couldn't get enough of being with her. That she was beautiful and desirable, and she prayed he'd always feel that way about her. As she prayed she'd always feel that way about him.

He took his time pleasuring her, stroking her, making her wet and aching with need, only stopping to suckle a breast or kiss her mouth or slip his tongue between her parted lips, stirring her desire to have him deep inside her, thrusting and taking pleasure in her.

She slid her hands over his hard muscles, loving the feel of his smooth skin, the rough hair on his chest, his puckered, aroused nipples, his rigid sex rubbing against her in urgent desperation.

She wanted him. Needed him. Craved him.

He kissed her throat, trailing a hot, wet tongue down her breast, stopping briefly to lick her nipple, then down to her navel. He kissed and licked her there, sending her senses reeling in a whirling pool of desire. Her fingers combed through his thick hair, her body arching as the ache between her legs intensified.

And then he was stroking her most intimate spot, wringing her senses in the most erotic way. She fought crying out as her heated body rose, the wave building pleasure higher and higher. Like the rising crescendo from a well-orchestrated piece of heaven, she felt uplifted until the climax hit, pulsing through her and staggering in its pleasurable sensation. He was in her before she barely had begun to sink into that dreamy state of complete satisfaction, thrusting, massaging her breasts with loving tenderness, and kissing her lips with sizzling passion.

God, he was beautiful. She hadn't believed women could have orgasms. Jake proved she was wrong. Over and over again. Just his tongue simulating sex, the way he thrust it into her mouth, could give her a near orgasm. His body rubbing hers, his finger stroking her, his mouth teasing her nipples into submission. The way he moved into her brought her again to that higher plane of existence—to that other world of blissful sexual fulfillment.

And when he came, she felt the trembling sweet exhilaration in joining with him again.

"Hmm, Alicia," Jake mouthed against her breast and then licked a nipple, lifting his head to study her with a contented smile on his face. "If you don't mind, I'll call Darien and Lelandi and tell them we won't be going over there for dinner tonight."

Alicia smiled and caressed his whiskery chin. "I'm sure they'll understand."

"But," he said, running his hand over her belly in a loving way. "It doesn't mean you'll go without supper."

Supper consisted of homemade beef stroganoff and a glass of milk. And Alicia realized what a bargain she'd gotten in Jake when she'd mated with a wolf who could cook gourmet-style meals. Then it was back to bed, and sleep would come next as Jake fulfilled the first of his promises. They'd only use half the bed as he tucked her into his arms and held on tight, and he wasn't sleeping on any couch ever.

Early the next morning, they left for Breckenridge to check out her mother's safe-deposit box. Alicia hadn't thought they would need all that much firepower, but Darien wasn't taking any chances, and several of the men in his pack had volunteered.

Darien was staying close to Lelandi at home in case she had the triplets early, but Jake and his brother Tom accompanied Alicia, along with Peter and a half-dozen other men from the pack.

At least she felt safe. She was nervous about what might be in her mother's safe-deposit box, though. As she rode up to the bank in a black Suburban, with another leading the way, she felt like she was a member of an FBI team on a SWAT mission. That was much different from driving around in her little red Neon when she was about to serve a warrant.

Going to the bank should have been a private affair, with Jake at her side and her bodyguard force tagging along. But after all the incidents in the past—her mother's murder, the shooting on the trail, her own planned disappearance, and her false-pregnancy faux-fainting episode at the art gallery—she feared that Detective Hanover's father, the chief of police of Breckenridge, might get wind of her reappearance and send a patrolman to question her. What if the word had gone out to be on the lookout for her?

That was the way she felt as she entered the bank. The three tellers turned to look at her, smiles disappearing to be replaced by looks of surprise. And two of the loan officers' expressions mirrored theirs. But then again, maybe it was because of the handsome men Alicia had accompanying her. Not often did one enter a bank with an entourage of wolfish-looking guys.

In that instant, Alicia felt incredibly lucky. The other men made sure she was safe inside, then headed back outside to guard the entrance. Jake stuck by her side, while Tom and Peter stood by the door watching them.

She hoped that from the concerned looks on the staff's faces, they didn't think she and the men intended to rob the bank. She and Jake approached the woman in charge of the vault. The woman led the way, then unlocked and pulled the safe-deposit box out for them. After asking Alicia to sign the register, she left them alone.

Alicia lifted the lid of the steel box with trepidation, while Jake looked on as if she were opening a treasure box or a booby-trapped mine. On top of a stack of papers was her mother's lease agreement to her apartment, but off to one corner, a ring glittered, catching Alicia's eye. She pulled it out from under the papers and stared at the carat diamond surrounded by smaller diamonds. Had her father given this to her mother? If he'd cared enough to give her this nice of a ring, why had he left her?

Jake watched but didn't say anything.

She moved aside more papers and found a little black book. Inside were tons of dates and figures and initials, but none of it made any sense.

"Looks like some kind of code," Jake said.

"But what would my mother be doing with something like this?"

"Maybe it wasn't hers."

Alicia looked up at Jake. "Tony's?"

"Might have been his."

Alicia glanced back at the ring, wondering about her father, wondering if what her mother had told her had really been true. She opened an official-looking envelope. Inside was her mother's birth certificate. She slipped it back in the envelope and opened another. Alicia's birth certificate. She wasn't going to look at it closely, figuring it was a copy of the one she had at home, until her hand brushed over the embossed seal.

She opened it, wondering why her mother would have had two original embossed copies, and scanned the information. Birth date, time of birth, Alicia's name, her mother's...all correct. But when she looked at the father's name—Antonio Frasero—she realized it wasn't a name she'd ever seen before. She felt incredibly light-headed all at once.

"Is something wrong?" Jake asked, seeing her distress.

"This isn't my birth certificate." She ran her finger over the embossed seal. "Either that, or the one I had at my apartment was forged."

"Let's take it with us, and we'll check it out. What's different about it?"

"My father's name."

Jake looked troubled. "What do you know about your father?"

"Nothing. Just that he left us when I was two. No reason. Just left. That's what my mother always told me. When I asked her, she didn't want to talk about him. She would just wave away my question, but she'd become teary-eyed, and no matter how long it had been, I could tell she still loved him."

"But to your knowledge, he never returned?"

She stared at Jake, then closed her gaping mouth and shook her head. She sifted through more of the papers. Nothing. She'd half expected to find divorce papers, a custody agreement for visitation rights, parental financial support, sole support, something, but no sign of...

She paused when she unfolded the last document and quit breathing.

Her mother's marriage certificate to one Antonio Frasero.

The same name as on Alicia's birth certificate in the safe-deposit box. Antonio…Tony? The man who'd been her mother's lover? And subsequently had been murdered near Continental Falls by Danny Massaro? Had Tony been her father? But he had to have had an alias then. Tony Thomas. Not Antonio Frasero. And he'd been murdered. Like her mother.

"Alicia!" Jake called as her face turned as white as the tile floor, and she crumpled in his arms. If he hadn't seen the stricken look on her face, he probably wouldn't have caught her in time.

Hearing his shout, the bank clerk hurried into the cage, along with Tom and Peter. "What's wrong with her?" the bank clerk asked horrified.

"Overcome with grief," Jake said, not knowing what else to say.

"Oh, of course." The clerk's cheeks grew pink with embarrassment.

"Alicia," Jake said, "honey…"

That was when a police officer poked his head into the room. "Can I help… What's going on?"

"She fainted," Jake said, exasperated that everyone was crowding him in the small bank vault.

"She's pregnant," the police officer said, nodding. "That's what the 911 call was about from Cliffside Art Gallery. The chief is on his way. Does she need medical assistance?"

"The chief?" Jake asked. What the hell was *that* all about?

"Yes, the police chief. He's been wanting to ask the young lady some questions."

"Bring her to our staff lounge, if you would, sir. We have a couch she can lie down on until she feels better," the clerk said.

"What's wrong?" Tom asked for Jake's ears only.

"She'll be all right," Jake assured him, not wanting to discuss what was the matter in front of all the others.

But Tom looked as though he didn't believe Alicia would be all right. And Jake wasn't sure he believed it either. Now he wondered if she had actually fainted in the restroom at the art gallery and had only said she'd turned into the wolf.

"Is she pregnant?" Tom asked quietly.

"I think she had some disturbing news." Jake gave Tom a quelling look as the police officer followed them into the lounge, talking to someone on his phone. Jake didn't want any of this to become common knowledge until they could sort out the details.

"Yeah, she's at the bank, just like Suzie said she was. But she's fainted again," the police officer said.

Jake laid Alicia down on the couch as she stirred and opened her eyes, her lips parting in surprise. Not only were Jake and his brother and Peter watching her as Jake crouched next to her, pushing her hair from her face, but three clerks, the police officer, and a couple of suited men were also hovering nearby.

Jake squeezed her hand. "Let's get you home."

Forget the over-the-counter pregnancy test. As soon as they returned to Silver Town, he was having Doc Weber examine her in the event she was pregnant and that could be what had affected her. He wanted to make sure she was truly all right.

The police chief strode into the room, brows raised to see Alicia sitting up on the sofa, despite Jake wanting her to lie still longer. "I'm fine. Really," she said, her eyes growing big as she looked beyond him at the police chief and police officer in attendance.

But she didn't look like she was fine at all. Her face was still deathly pale.

"The Denver police want to speak with you, Miss Greiston," the police chief said as he drew closer and peered down at her through silver-rimmed glasses. He looked similar to his son,

Detective Hanover, who had questioned her the day before at her apartment, but he was about sixty, with graying hair, and had an aged appearance that made him appear like a kindly grandfather. At least toward Alicia.

Jake suspected the chief's demeanor had to do with his worry that Alicia was pregnant and was sick because of it. Chief Hanover looked like he could be as tough as granite if he wanted to be.

"The police," she parroted wearily.

At this rate, she was going to be talking to police all over the state of Colorado.

"Yes, Miss Greiston. My son told me you were at the scene of Ferdinand Massaro's murder. The Denver police will want the details. But I have a couple of questions for you also. Since you're looking a little peaked, if you don't mind, I'll just ask you here. If everyone will clear out." He directed the comment to the bank staff.

The men and women agreeably and quickly filed out of the staff lounge.

The chief glanced at Tom and Peter, but Alicia said, "I'd prefer to have Jake and his brother Tom and Peter, our sheriff at Silver Town, stay, if it's all right with you."

"Certainly." The chief sat down in a chair and said, "My son tells me he talked to you about the shooting on Spruce Creek Trail. Can you tell me what happened exactly?"

"I really don't have anything else to say. I left a wreath of flowers for my mother like I do once a week. I assumed the two men who approached me were Mario's men, and they asked me to go with them. I refused. Then they left."

"They left," the chief said, "after you shot one of the men."

She said nothing, her jaw and fingers clenching, but waited for him to speak further.

He cleared his throat and continued. "Witnesses said they heard gunfire and saw one of the men with a bloody leg limping back to his car, cursing up a storm."

She didn't say anything for a minute, and Jake was glad she didn't offer any other explanation for what might have occurred. Finally, she said, "Did the man seek medical attention?"

"No, not that we could learn of. But if they were who we think they were, they would have seen someone who would doctor him without reporting the shooting incident to the police."

Alicia didn't say anything further, but her unspoken expression said volumes as she lifted her eyebrows slightly in a way that meant the chief could prove nothing.

"We're on your side in this," the chief finally said, sounding resigned. "If I could put Mario away for life, I'd do it. But I don't want you getting yourself killed in the process, young lady. Nor do I want you to get into trouble for doing something illegal." He shoved his hands in his pockets and looked down at the floor as if he were trying to decide whether to say anything further, but he hesitated.

He finally let out his breath, fixed her with his gaze, and said, "I shouldn't be saying this, but the police in Denver have evidence you were in Massaro's apartment. Just a heads-up, when you speak with them."

Her lower lip dropped, then she quickly clamped her mouth shut and swallowed hard.

Hell.

"What evidence?" she finally asked, sounding more timid than Jake liked to hear.

"Your driver's license was found inside Massaro's apartment."

Her lips parted.

Jake stifled a curse. He was dying to know where they had found her driver's license. He wondered if Detective Hanover, the chief's son, had known this when he had asked her for her driver's license, testing her to see if she knew it was missing. If so, what had he concluded? She wasn't guilty of a crime? Massaro had stolen it from her? Or she'd left it there by accident when she was fleeing the crime scene?

But then Jake was certain the detective would have been asking himself why Massaro would have taken her driver's license and nothing else. However, just because her driver's license was found in the condo, that didn't confirm she'd been there. He could have stolen it. Although why that and nothing else?

"When did he get it from you, Miss Greiston?" the chief asked.

So that was the crux of the matter. If she hadn't actually seen him, hadn't been able to enter the condo to speak with him because he was already dead, how did he manage to get ahold of her driver's license?

"Where did the police find it?" she asked, her voice dry.

The chief tapped one boot on the tile floor. "The Denver police wouldn't say."

"If you're done with Alicia…" Jake let his words trail off, not wanting her to be subjected to any more of an interrogation when the chief had no business asking her questions concerning the crime scene in Denver.

The chief straightened a bit and looked sympathetic. "They found blood on the sheets, Miss Greiston. And in a couple of other unspecified locations. I'm sure the Denver police will want to take a sample of your blood. Did he hurt you?"

Alicia had to have bled when the bastard Massaro bit her, Jake suspected. Hell. The only good thing in the whole matter was that forensics couldn't determine her wolf changes. But poor Alicia. Her face took on a whole new shade of white.

"Do you mind?" Jake asked the chief as he leaned in to help Alicia up from the couch. "We'll be headed back to Silver Town. If you have any further questions…"

"They found your fingerprints on the inside front doorknob, so they know you'd been in the condo," the chief said to Alicia and added with a nod to Jake, "My son gave me the information of where she'll be staying. Thanks. And good luck, Miss Greiston. We want to solve your mother's murder as quickly as you do. Let us know if you learn anything further, won't you?"

She half-heartedly nodded.

"Good. Then we'll be seeing you."

Jake wrapped his arm around Alicia's waist and helped her out of the bank and to the vehicle while Tom and Peter followed, and their guard detail reloaded into the SUVs.

"Drive, will you, Tom?" Jake asked, his voice terse as he pondered what they were going to do about the Denver police.

CHAPTER 18

JAKE HELPED ALICIA INTO THE BACK SEAT AND WENT AROUND the vehicle to join her while Tom settled into the driver's seat and Peter rode in the passenger's seat. Their guard force led the way again. Jake hoped to assuage Alicia's concerns at once. Although the problem of her connection to Massaro's murder wasn't going to be easy to explain to the police.

"Oh, Jake," Alicia said on a moan as soon as he shut his door, "the Denver police will learn what I am as soon as they analyze the bloodstains."

"No, don't concern yourself." He took her in his arms as Tom drove back to Silver Town. "Our wolf genetics are such that as humans, we have only human DNA. As wolves, only wolf DNA. Now, if they found both, blood from when you were a wolf and from when you were human, it'd make them believe a wolf and a human were in the room."

She melted against his chest and sighed heavily. "Then if they do discover wolf's blood in the condo, they'll assume I lied about having a wolf at the Crestview Motel. I'm just getting myself deeper and deeper into this. And dragging your family into the whole mess. Before long, don't you think they'll get a warrant to search your place to see if I'm hiding a wolf there?"

"They won't find any."

"But what if I shift? I thought I was controlling it, but anytime now, I could just, *poof*, turn into a wolf. And if I do it in front of a bunch of police officers—"

"We'll deal with it, Alicia. You're one of us, part of a pack. We'll take care of this in any way that we have to."

Tom said, "You want me to take her home." But the tone of his voice was more of a question—did Jake want to take her to see Doc Weber instead?

Of course the doc made house calls when necessary, but in Alicia's case, Jake assumed he'd need blood work, a urine sample, and a proper physical exam to tell if she was pregnant and make sure she and the baby would be all right. At least he thought that was what was needed. He was certain that if he proposed it in front of Alicia with Tom and Peter listening in, she'd be upset with him. On the other hand, he didn't want to take her to the hospital under false pretenses.

"The hospital, Tom."

Alicia tried to pull away from Jake, her spine stiff, her whole body posture saying she was mad at him for even suggesting such a thing, but he held on tight, forcing her to remain in his arms until he felt the tension drain from her. She relaxed again, but not of her own accord, he felt. Rather, she just wasn't feeling up to fighting him.

He kissed the top of her head and enjoyed the feel of her soft supple curves, her feminine fragrance, and her thick, silky hair beneath his cheek. He wanted to give her a life free of worry by sequestering her from the interrogations, taking care of Mario and his bastards, and showing Alicia the way of their people until she felt comfortable being one of them.

But now they had a new dilemma. Who was Alicia's father?

Jake expected Alicia to say something about the visit to the hospital, but she didn't voice a word. He felt guilty for forcing this on her, but they had to know. If she was pregnant, she needed to be seeing the doctor anyway.

"Call ahead to the hospital, will you, Peter, and make an appointment?" Jake said to the sheriff. He didn't want to let go of Alicia for a second to try to fish his phone out when she seemed content enough to relax in his arms.

Peter opened his cell phone and said, "Bethany, we need an appointment with Doc Weber scheduled for"—he glanced at the clock in the car—"two hours and fifteen minutes from now. Yeah, it's important. For Jake's mate, Alicia Greiston." He paused, cleared his throat, and then said, "Possible pregnancy." He spoke as softly as he could so that Bethany could still hear him but not softly enough that Jake and Alicia couldn't, what with their wolf's hearing. Although Jake gave him credit for making the effort. "Thanks. We'll be there then," Peter said and put his phone away.

"We'll have to get married," Alicia grumbled against Jake's chest. "I'm not going to keep telling people I'm engaged to you. I didn't think I'd ever say I'd want to again, not until you walked into my life and became my knight."

"We don't wear jewelry. So wedding rings are out." Jake tried his damnedest to be consoling, but this was probably one of the hardest things for newbie *lupus garous* to get a handle on. "We don't need rings to stay faithful. But even so, it would be especially difficult for you to wear any jewelry because you don't have the shifting under control. Trying to remove rings or necklaces and bracelets in the process of a shift could prove disastrous. As for marriage, we're mated. That means more than a marriage certificate. It means we commit to one another for life."

She frowned up at him. "If I am *pregnant*, I want to be *officially* married. With the paper to prove it. Blame it on my human upbringing."

He looked down into her dark-chocolate eyes and thought of how addicted he was to looking at her, to feeling her close, to being with her. He would be with her always. He wished she could understand that. "We don't marry because we make a commitment—"

"*I...want...to...be...married.* I understand, or at least think I understand, how you commit for life without the need for a witnessed document. But I never knew who my father was and never knew if my parents had really been married. I want our baby to have the security of knowing we're formally committed."

He really wished they could have this discussion in private. He could just imagine what his brother and Peter were thinking. They were probably glad neither of them was trying to deal with an unreasonable newly turned wolf. He realized then her feelings might have something to do with her father, though—the fake birth certificate and not knowing what was going on with him. Her father's abandonment of her and her mother without letting Alicia know. Maybe, beyond all that, she was concerned Jake wouldn't live up to his promise to be the baby's father if she was pregnant.

"Any baby you have will be mine and yours, Alicia. And he or she will be raised as a wolf, knowing how we live our lives and that a formal marriage isn't part of the equation. You don't have to worry about that."

She let out her breath in an exasperated manner. "You're a man," she said sourly.

He wanted to tell her he wouldn't be like her father had been to her mother. But he didn't think she would believe him, even if he tried to convince her. All he could do was prove he'd stick by her side forever.

He kissed her cheek and stroked her shoulder. "You wouldn't want me to be anything but." He let out a heavy sigh. Hell, he was an alpha male and his mate was already dictating to him. If word got out, he'd never live it down. But he wanted her to be happy. Whatever it took. "All right. The judge can marry us."

"All right," she said grumpily, then gave him a smidgen of a smile.

He tightened his hold on her, giving her a somber smile back and loving her all the more. She hadn't had a family to call her own. He and his family would be there for her in any way that she needed, even if they had to bend or break a few golden wolf rules in the process. "All right."

Never in a million years would he have thought he'd be the

only one in the family or the pack ever forced to get a marriage license. Then again, he could just get the judge to sign off on one. No need to go through any kind of ceremony, even if he knew it would just be in the judge's chambers. All she had to want was the paper proving they were husband and wife.

The whole notion grated on him, no matter that he tried to think of it as important to her and meaningless to him. He squeezed her tighter against his body. Well, not so meaningless to him because it meant so much to Alicia. And her happiness was paramount to him.

When they arrived at the hospital in Silver Town, everyone on staff looked Alicia over curiously, and she avoided their inquisitive gazes. Doc Weber dismissed Jake, even though he wanted to be with her in the room. Instead, he was left to pace in the staff lounge.

Peter and Tom stayed with him while Tom broached the subject of Alicia's fainting at the bank. "You said she got some upsetting news?"

"We need to learn everything we can about an Antonio Frasero."

"I'll get on it," Peter said. "How does she know him?"

"He's her father."

"I'll let you know what I find out." Peter hurried out of the lounge, looking like a man with a mission.

Tom studied Jake. "The name Antonio Frasero sounds Italian."

"Yes, it sounds that way." Jake glanced back at the doorway to the lounge, wondering what was taking Doc so long in determining if Alicia was pregnant or not.

"If she's pregnant, is it Massaro's baby?" Tom asked.

"Most likely," Jake said, trying to keep his voice even.

Tom nodded.

Then Doc poked his head in through the doorway. "Looks like the *lupus garou* population of Silver Town is going to increase by another three early next year. I understand Silva's struggling to knit a pair of booties for the first of Lelandi's triplets. She's going to have a lot of practice in the next few months."

Jake couldn't say anything. The first thought he had was that Alicia's babies were his. He was a triplet. Darien was having triplets, although Lelandi had been a triplet also, while Alicia had been an only child. But still, what were the chances that they were Massaro's?

Tom looked just as stunned.

"Thanks, Doc. Thanks," Jake finally managed to get out.

Doc smiled. "She's worried they're not yours. But I have the sneaking suspicion they are. If I were you, I'd check out the guy who turned her. She said he had been murdered. The police would have done an autopsy, and if he'd had sex with a woman sometime before he was murdered—which would have been the case if he'd raped her from the timeline she gave me—the doctor who examined the body would have learned of it. Alicia said he's the only one who could have made her pregnant. But we all know there are exceptions to every rule."

"They'll be mine, no matter what, Doc," Jake said firmly.

"I understand. I've prescribed some vitamin pills for her. Just make sure she gets plenty of rest and plenty of nutritious foods to eat. Otherwise, she's healthy and the babies will be fine. I've got other patients to see, but…" Doc uncharacteristically slapped Jake on the shoulder, smiling broadly. "You've got your hands full." Then he headed out of the lounge.

Tom looked like he was dying to leave the staff lounge. He wasn't the town gossip, like Silva was, so Jake wasn't sure what was eating at him. Tom finally said, "I'm looking into this Ferdinand Massaro."

Jake took a deep breath. His brother wanted to know the truth of the matter as much as he did. "Peter can probably get further with questioning the police than we can since he's a member of law enforcement. Have him check to see if in the autopsy that was done on—" Jake paused when he heard footfalls approach the room.

Alicia peered into the lounge, then seeing Jake and Tom alone, she joined them. "I heard your voice," she said as if she was afraid they'd think she'd been eavesdropping.

Jake hurried to take her arm, alarmed that she still appeared pale and unwell. "You still look peaked, Alicia."

"Deep down, I expected to be pregnant. But I *never* thought I'd have a whole family in one fell swoop." Her teary eyes studied his. "Doc said because they're triplets, they're probably yours."

"That's what he told me too."

She took a deep, steadying breath. "But if they're not…"

He pulled her into his embrace. "We'll have three lovely girls to adore."

Tom gave a small smile as if to say that was wishful thinking and headed out of the room. He hoped Tom would tell Peter to see if an autopsy on Massaro revealed he'd had sex with a woman before he died.

If Massaro hadn't, Jake would rethink the story Lelandi's brother, Leidolf, had told them about the woman who was the product of her human grandmother and a wolf's intimate liaison.

"Let's go to Darien's place," Jake said, but more than ever, he wanted a whole lot of answers to lots of new questions.

———————————

Standing in his living room and staring out his window at the brick wall surrounding his back courtyard, Mario listened on the phone as Danny ranted, "Someone was here…in my place. Looking through stuff."

"How do you know?"

"I know, all right? I leave things around, just in case. But the house wasn't broken into. Nothing taken as far as I can tell. But things aren't…*the same*."

Mario shook his head. Danny was becoming obsessed with

being watched. "How aren't they the same?" he asked, trying to hide his exasperation with his cousin.

"I–I leave pieces of hair glued with saliva across my desk drawers. The hairs were broken or no longer there."

Hair? Saliva?

Mario shook his head. "Are you sure they didn't just drop on the floor? Fall off? That *you* opened the drawers and forgot to replace the hairs?"

"No. I check them every time I get home."

"Did you have anything important in the drawers?"

"No."

Mario let out his breath. "Then no problem." He figured Danny was just being paranoid. That nothing had truly happened.

"I found a bug in my phone."

His face heating, Mario said slowly, "Which phone?" It had better not be the one Danny was talking on now. Or if it was, he'd better have gotten rid of the bug.

"It's gone," Danny said, reassuring him. "But the feds have been here."

"How did they find out about your place?"

Danny didn't speak for a while, then said, "Hell, I don't know. Cicero said something about Tony getting my key and making a copy of it. But I didn't believe it. And anyway, even if Tony did get a copy of my house key, he wouldn't have known where my house was."

"Why didn't you tell me Tony had gotten a copy of your key?"

"I changed the locks. The key wouldn't have worked even if he had found the house."

"You should have told me Tony got a copy of the key to your house, Danny. What were you thinking?" Mario watched the oak tree's leaves flutter in the dry breeze. "All right. So you didn't have anything in the place that could cause any problems. Right?"

Danny didn't say anything.

"Right, Danny?"

"The gun I used to whack Missy Greiston and Tony? It's gone."

———————

When Jake, Alicia, Tom, and Peter arrived at Darien's house, Lelandi greeted them looking so anxious that Jake was afraid something more was wrong.

But Lelandi quickly asked Alicia, "Are you all right? Peter said you fainted at the bank."

Jake was glad that was all that was the matter.

"I'm fine." Alicia explained the situation about her father and the birth certificates, but although Lelandi listened, Jake could tell that wasn't what was concerning her.

"You look awfully pale," Lelandi said, and Jake suspected she knew Alicia was pregnant but was trying to prompt her to tell without being asked.

"Jake and I are going to get married," Alicia said, taking hold of Jake's hand and pulling him closer. "Right away. We'll get the justice of the peace to do it."

Lelandi's lips parted, but she didn't say a word, her gaze quickly shifting to Jake.

He tried not to react in any way, yet he tensed. He couldn't help it. His kind just didn't get married. And he didn't like the inference that he couldn't be faithful without a marriage license, although he had to remind himself that probably wasn't bothering Alicia as much as having a name for the babies. He planned for Alicia to be a Silver anyway. Once she was one of the Silvers, no one would question her about getting a new driver's license or anything else she might need in her life.

"Marriage? By the judge? No way," Lelandi said, her red brows furrowed.

Jake wasn't entirely surprised by her reaction. But he would marry Alicia in the judge's chambers, no matter what Lelandi or his brother said about it, since that was what Alicia felt she needed.

"But Jake said he would. And I won't feel right until it's done," Alicia insisted, determination in her voice.

Jake wrapped his arm around her shoulder, but before he could defend their decision, Lelandi raised her brows at Jake, smiled, and patted Alicia on the shoulder. "What I meant to say is that if we're going to go against tradition, we're going to do this right. We'll have a proper wedding."

Proper wedding?

Jake groaned before he could catch himself. Tom chuckled. Peter grinned but wisely didn't say anything. Even Alicia didn't look pleased with the notion.

"First, we need to get you a wedding dress. You've been married before, so a cream-colored dress would probably be better. Although, what the heck, since we don't do weddings, you can wear whatever your heart desires. No sense in sticking to a tradition we don't even have."

Lelandi took Alicia's arm and pulled her away from Jake and headed for the sunroom. "We do have a bridal shop for the humans in town. And the owner is a wolf, of course. She will be ecstatic to be our consultant. Her shop also carries formals for special occasions and Victorian ball gowns for our Victorian festival. The men rarely dress up except for that, so this will be fun."

"I didn't want to go through a whole lot of pomp and ceremony," Alicia said. "I just wanted to make sure we had a marriage license. And I *have* been married twice already so it's not like I feel the need to go through any kind of ceremony."

"Nonsense. It'll be fun. Silva and I can help you decide about the festivities afterward. Darien can give you away. We'll have a ball."

Jake felt for Alicia. She clearly didn't want to go this far.

Tom shook his head at Jake, his mouth curving in a small smile. "Darien will love to hear he's been volunteered to serve as the bride's father in a wedding when we've never taken part in one before."

"I'm not certain Alicia's any more excited about it than I am." Jake glanced at Peter, expecting news about the calls he made earlier.

"I called about the autopsy. The report on Ferdinand Massaro's body showed no signs that he'd had intercourse prior to his death," Peter said. "In other words, he couldn't have raped Alicia shortly before he died."

Jake felt a little light-headed and sat down on one of the couches.

"The triplets are yours," Tom said, smiling. "Who would have thought you'd find your mate before me, as picky as you've always been. And now you have a whole family on its way in record time. You're the first one to have a wedding too. I mean, for any members of the pack."

"They're mine," Jake said softly, still not believing it. He glanced up at Peter, who was smiling at him too. "You're absolutely sure?"

Peter spread his hands in a way that said there was no other possibility.

"I've got to get cribs and all that stuff. Everything that Lelandi's been stocking up for her babies when they're born." Jake had thought all her purchases and the way she'd been stressing over the upcoming event had been unnecessary. That half of the stuff she'd bought was not even needed.

But now he was rethinking his position. Now when he had his own triplets on the way. He rose to his feet, wondering why he was sitting around when he had so much to do.

"They're not going to be here for several months. You'll have time," Tom said, looking immensely amused. "My advice to you, though, is don't make the nursery pink *just yet*."

Jake dragged his fingers through his hair, ignoring his brother's teasing, and then took a deep, steadying breath. Hell, now he had to get married. In a real wedding, of all things.

Peter said, "The other news is that I had some men check out Danny's place. You should have seen the way he rigged up the place. Strands of hair stuck to drawers in the event anyone opened them."

The guy was nuts.

"We replaced them, though. Found a gun in a desk drawer and some papers having to do with racketeering that we sent to the feds—in a surreptitious way. They'll probably get a search warrant and nail the bastard."

"He's not a wolf?" Jake asked, surprised. If Ferdinand Massaro had been and Mario might be, he'd thought for sure Danny was. But Peter wouldn't have sent the feds incriminating evidence if Danny was a wolf.

"Nope. And no wolves had been in the house. So unless someone changes the equation, Danny's free to go to prison—for as long as he should live."

Darien entered the house with his cell phone to his ear, his expression grim and his brows raised as he acknowledged Jake, Tom, and Peter. Jake had the sneaking suspicion that more bad news was on its way.

Darien signed off with whomever he was talking to on the phone. "The police in Denver want to speak with Alicia about Ferdinand Massaro's murder again. They believe she witnessed the murder and want to put her in the witness protection program."

"They can't," Jake said.

His older brother sighed. "I know that, Jake. But you, Tom, and Peter will have to accompany her to Denver. Along with some men for backup guard."

"What if she shape-shifts?" Jake asked.

"Just pray she doesn't," Darien said, glancing in the direction of the sunroom, undoubtedly hearing some of Lelandi's conversation and probably wondering what that was all about.

Lelandi must have been talking on the phone as she said, "Oh yes, a real wedding. What do you think for bridesmaids' gowns, Silva? Alicia says she wants you to take part, too, and wanted your opinion."

Darien gave Jake a questioning look.

"We're getting married." Jake spoke as if he didn't want any discussion about the matter.

"Married? Bridesmaids' gowns?" Darien asked, his voice low.

"We were all set to just go to a justice of the peace, but Lelandi wouldn't hear of it." Jake shoved his hands in his pockets, almost wishing Darien would make Lelandi cease and desist. But he knew Darien wouldn't. "Guess who gets to give the bride away."

Darien looked at Tom, who was grinning big-time now.

"Don't look at me," Tom said. "*You're* the pack leader."

Darien groaned. "Hell, if it wasn't for Lelandi's temperamental condition, I'd put my foot down and say absolutely not. So when the hell is it scheduled?"

Jake sighed. "What do I know? The women have taken over."

"That's what happens when the women are pregnant," Peter said, although since he wasn't mated, he hadn't had to deal with all the ups and downs himself.

Darien's gaze swung back to Jake.

This time, Jake couldn't contain the delight in his expression or tone of voice. He sounded like a kid at Christmas. "Alicia's pregnant, Doc says. With triplets."

Darien was still frowning. "Yours?"

"Appears that way."

That was when Darien's smile first appeared. He said to Tom, "You're next, Little Brother. We'll have a boomtown here before we know it."

The next morning, on the drive to Denver to see the police about Ferdinand Massaro's murder, Alicia had a panic attack. Although it wasn't really a panic attack because the panic was for real. The moon was at its fullest, and although it was daytime and the moon wasn't easy to see, it was there all the same.

And Alicia knew, despite trying to stop it, that she was getting ready to shift. She was worn out from the discovery the day before about her father and learning she was pregnant with triplets, as well as Lelandi's rush to help her find a gown before Alicia couldn't wear one unless it was a maternity gown, and Jake loving her all night long. She'd been sleeping with her head in Jake's lap as Tom drove the SUV to Denver, while Peter sat in the front passenger's seat and remained quiet. Another SUV filled with four more pack members followed, making her feel safe and protected and totally overwhelmed by all the events of the past couple of days.

But all of a sudden, she began to get really, really hot. That brought back into focus how she wasn't herself anymore. The first thing she did was worry about the babies. Would the shift hurt them? Then she realized that werewolves had lived like this for a very long time, and they'd survived all these years, so everything would be all right.

But Alicia still had little control over her shifting, and she desperately needed to get out of her clothes. Lelandi had explained that stripping out of clothes in front of other pack members was a natural process, and the shift happened so quickly that no one got much of a look at anyone else anyway. But none of that made it any easier to swallow.

Alicia bolted upright, and immediately Jake stiffened. "What's wrong, Alicia?"

Peter glanced over the seat at her. Tom looked in the rearview mirror to see what the matter was.

"I've got to shift." She climbed in none too ladylike a way over the back of the seat to get into the rear seat, more hidden from the view of the bucket seats that Tom and Peter were sitting in up front. And then she began stripping out of her clothes.

Darien had tried to convince the Denver police that Alicia had been feeling too poorly to see them right away, due to her pregnancy, but because the police were investigating a murder and had no clues as to who had done the crime, they wouldn't hear of any delays.

They would treat her with care, they assured Darien. Jake and the rest of the pack hadn't been worried about her pregnancy but this business with shifting. By the time she got her clothes off, she was shifting.

Jake said, "You'll be fine when we're speaking to the police officers, Alicia. You can get it out of your system for now..."

She growled at him. She meant for it to be a grumble, but she wasn't sure how to make a grumbly wolf sound. It just came out an irritated growl and was a lot harsher to her ears than she had intended. Peter and Tom smiled. Jake reached over the back of his seat and scratched her between the ears.

She bumped his hand with her nose, trying to make up with him, and he smiled. "You'll be fine," he repeated, but the undercurrent of tension relayed a promise. The pack would take care of her—and the police officers if she screwed up.

CHAPTER 19

ALICIA DIDN'T WANT TO SCREW UP IN FRONT OF THE POLICE. She didn't want to always be a problem for the pack. Lying in the back seat of the SUV in wolf form, she tried to think of something other than the interrogation that awaited her.

But she was having a difficult time thinking of anything else. This time, like when she'd been questioned about the shootings at the Crestview Motel, she'd have to tell the truth, minus the wolf part of the tale. She'd discussed the wolf business with Jake and his brothers—and Peter because he had the mind of a cop. But she knew from past experience that no matter how prepared she might be to tell the police her story, one little bit of evidence she hadn't known about, one little thing like an eyewitness account could throw her version of what had happened into the sewer.

Instead, she tried to think about her wedding dress—a cream-colored, A-line gown with a corset-type bodice that had asymmetrical swirls wrapped around it, embellished with lace and pearls in a soft, shimmery satin. The full-pleated skirt that swirled out in full opulence below the slim-fitted bodice cupped her derriere and then extended out into an elegant train. The dress made her feel like a fairy princess, and Jake was definitely her fairy-tale knight.

Some of the younger women had clamored to take part in the wedding and would be wearing violet dresses as bridesmaids. Several girls would participate as flower girls, and Lelandi would be the matron of honor. Because of all the teasing Jake was getting over the whole affair, he had selected Peter, Sam, and four other men to be his groomsmen, while Tom was the best man. Darien would serve as the father of the bride. Others he had tasked to serve as ushers. Alicia had been amused because although most of the men tried to show they didn't care for the idea of a wedding, she saw another side of them—a sense of family, of celebration, of belonging—and their enthusiasm didn't go unnoticed.

The men participating would wear black tuxes with gray satin cravats and tuxedo vests. The best part? The woman in charge of the bridal shop said she'd have everything ready to go in a week's time, which was good because Alicia kept fretting that she might start to show and the gown wouldn't fit. She groaned. What if she shifted in the middle of the ceremony? First wedding ever for a *lupus garou* pack and first major disaster. She could see it now. No one would ever allow a wedding ceremony to take place again.

In her wolf form, she lay down on the back seat and closed her eyes. She hadn't told Lelandi the truth about having had weddings before because she'd been trying to get out of doing anything this formal. But Alicia had never had a wedding dress. Never been married in a church. Never had a bridesmaid or a father to give her away. Just a mother and her boyfriend to serve as her witnesses in front of a judge, *twice*.

She smiled at the thought of being a beautiful bride for Jake.

Then she sighed. He didn't want this. He probably wouldn't be happy with any of it, no matter how nice the ceremony was or how excited the ladies were about having it. She hadn't been able to read Darien. Apparently, he'd agreed to give her away, but he had seemed distracted, probably over this further police business. She suspected he was worried that she could get all the pack members who went with her in trouble if she ended up shape-shifting while being questioned. And that was when she began to worry about the interrogation again.

She must have managed to sleep for a couple of hours. When she finally awoke from a nice wolf nap, she was surprised that her head was in Jake's lap. When had he climbed into the rear seat with her?

He was stroking her back in a soothing way, and when she lifted her head, he said, "We're almost there. But if we have to, we'll just park somewhere until you can shift. We'll tell the police we were held up because of a flat tire, running out of gas, something."

She closed her eyes, cursed her inability to shift when she needed to, and tried to convince herself it was time to be a human. A few minutes later, she was hastily getting dressed in the rear seat, hoping the tinted windows were truly tinted enough so that no one could see into the vehicle while they were parked under a shade tree in a park.

Once she was presentable, Peter drove the SUV to Ferdinand Massaro's condo where the police were supposed to meet them.

"We're here," Peter said quietly a few minutes later, as if he was trying not to upset her and cause her to shift again.

She had no idea why the urge to shift came and went like it did. She suspected it had something to do with having not changed in so long since the last time.

"How are you feeling?" Jake asked, running his hand over her stomach.

"I'm all right. At least I hope I'll be." But she really wasn't. Every inch of her body was feeling the tension, and she was terrified she'd get their kind into trouble.

"Let's go then," Jake said, sounding like he wanted to get this over in a hurry, just like she did.

Her bodyguard detail stayed in the second vehicle, figuring that with the police here, she'd have no trouble. Jake took Alicia's hand and led her to the front door of the brick two-story condo, while Tom and Peter followed. An officer let them in while two others watched them, and then introductions were shared around the living room. Helm Sanderson was tall and stout and looked down at her like she was in for real trouble. John Kohn looked like he'd slept in his clothes, his face wearing a couple of days' growth of blond stubble, his eyes bloodshot. The last detective, Arthur

Connelly, was younger than the other two and kept looking at them as if reading their cues on what to do.

"Have a seat, Miss Greiston," Sanderson said, motioning to the couch where she'd seen Ferdinand's dead body.

If the detectives had wanted to see her reaction, to see if she'd actually witnessed Massaro sitting dead on that couch, they hadn't needed to do anything further.

"I–I don't feel well," she suddenly said, a cold sweat breaking out across her skin, her vision blurring as a fresh wave of nausea struck. She rushed for what she hoped was the kitchen.

She could smell the death in the room although they'd cleaned the place up. She could smell the colognes of the men who'd murdered Ferdinand. The odors were making her gag, bringing back the terror she'd experienced when the one man had come looking for her and she'd barely breathed beneath the bed.

She made it in time to throw up in the sink, as Jake drew close and rubbed her back gently. She noticed the youngest detective watching her, while the other two remained in the living room with Tom and Peter. Had Detective Connelly come to see if she was truly sick or just faking it? Or was he just not as jaded as the older detectives? She halfway suspected he was checking on her to see if she was faking being sick.

Jake got a paper towel and offered it to her. She cupped her hands under the faucet and rinsed out her mouth, not wanting to touch anything else in the condo, although they would have already dusted everything for fingerprints. And yes, had found her prints on the front door. Not that she had been thinking very clearly that night. Not when she had found Massaro dead, was afraid for her own life, and was trying to get over the fact that she'd turned into a wolf.

"Are you all right, Miss Greiston?" Detective Connelly asked.

"Yes," she managed feebly, feeling horrible.

"She's pregnant with triplets," Jake explained.

The detective quickly looked at Alicia's waist, back to her face, and turned pale. He put his hands out and motioned back to the living room. "Please, come in and sit down, if you think you can manage now."

Jake took her arm and led her back into the room. Once they were in the living area, he let her guide him to where she wanted to sit. When she was seated on a couch at a right angle to the one where Massaro had been murdered, Sanderson sat down only inches from where Massaro had been sitting and said, "Tell us what happened. From the beginning. Don't leave any detail out."

"I want a lawyer," Alicia said, tilting her chin up and staring Sanderson down.

Everyone stared at her in surprise.

"I don't feel well," she continued. "I haven't committed any crime, yet I feel I may be incriminating myself if I don't have a lawyer present."

"You're not a suspect, Miss Greiston. If you have nothing to hide…" Detective Sanderson said, spreading his arms wide as if trying to reassure her that talking to him wouldn't be a problem.

She shook her head. "I want a lawyer."

———

Jake could tell something was wrong with Alicia, more than just the pregnancy. He was worried she was fighting shifting again. "Is she free to go until we can get ahold of a lawyer?"

Detective Sanderson looked pissed off as he folded his arms. "We need to know what happened. She was in the condo. We have a warrant to get a blood sample from her. We have her prints on the inside doorknob. So what happened when Massaro was murdered? We want to know what she saw or heard, who was here, anything that could help us piece together what happened so we can catch whoever did this."

"And if she was here? And didn't report a murder? Then she could be charged with a crime," Jake said. "Is she free until we can obtain legal representation?"

"She's not a suspect. Just a person of interest. In fact, we suspect she was a victim, if the bloodstains are hers," Sanderson insisted. "We know she was here. We know she's afraid of them. That she was afraid they might learn she was here and would kill her for it. But whatever she can tell us can help us to nail them."

Jake helped Alicia to her feet. "We'll be in touch as soon as we get a lawyer."

"I could hold her for obstructing justice," Sanderson said, playing hardball.

"She's sick," Jake said.

"Pregnant with triplets," Detective Connelly said urgently, looking as though he was afraid she'd expire on the spot.

Sanderson looked at him as if the guy couldn't be that naive.

"If she were to miscarry," Jake said with dark promise, "every media source would hear about it."

For the longest time, Jake and Sanderson measured each other with steely gazes in a showdown of wills. Then Sanderson said, "All right. Get your lawyer. You've got twenty-four hours. Just let us know where you're staying until then."

Jake took Alicia's arm and started to lead her to the door.

"Who's her doctor, by the way?" Detective Sanderson asked. "Just in case we need to get in touch with him." He gave a sardonic smile.

"Dr. Weber can fax you a copy of her pregnancy test, if you need it," Jake said sharply, then walked her out the door as Tom and Peter followed close behind.

"What's wrong, Alicia?" Jake asked as he took her out of the building and toward the SUV.

"The smells in there were overwhelming. And the memories. I'm so sorry, but I had to get away. The wolf senses felt as though they were crushing me. I just couldn't think straight."

"Sanderson's a real bastard," Tom said. "I could smell that Massaro had died on that couch where he was sitting, the location where he had motioned for you to sit initially."

"Same ploy I would have used as a detective," Peter said. "Rattle the witness. Secure any kind of statement that would help me to solve my case."

Alicia cast him an annoyed look, but as green around the gills as she felt, she doubted her look was as annoyed as she wished to appear. "I don't believe you could be that mean."

He gave her a small smile. "Only with a nonwolf who was involved up to her hairline. In your case, no, I wouldn't have stooped so low. But then, I wouldn't have needed to."

She raised her brows at him in question.

"I'm not out to solve this crime for the city of Denver but to solve this crime so we can go after the killers themselves and stop them from getting to you."

She sighed and reached over to squeeze his arm. "Thanks, Peter. I didn't mean to say you were like Sanderson. You've been nothing but kind to me."

"It's been my pleasure, ma'am."

"What do we do now?" Tom asked. "We have no idea who might be a wolf lawyer who could represent us the way we need him to."

Alicia noted that Jake was awfully quiet as he opened the SUV door for her. He cleared his throat. "I know a lawyer."

Both Tom and Peter looked surprised. Alicia wondered if the man didn't like newly turned wolves. Why else would Jake seem so reluctant to mention him?

"Who?" Tom asked.

"Sherry Slate."

The only reason he could be reluctant about mentioning the woman was because she'd meant something to Jake. An awkward silence stretched between them.

Finally, Jake closed the door and looked at Tom, who was staring at him with incredulity. Alicia guessed Jake must have been seeing some women without his family knowing it. Peter looked just as surprised.

When he got in the SUV, Jake said to Tom, "Take us to Hill and Sanders. It's a law firm."

Peter set the GPS, and they were off.

Everything was so quiet in the vehicle that Alicia could hear everyone's heartbeats. She finally took Jake's arm and draped it over her, snuggling close to him as he tightened his arm around her. If she understood the ways of the werewolves, she knew he couldn't have been seriously involved with Sherry. They didn't have any sexual intimacy unless they planned to mate for life. Still, maybe this Sherry had expected something more of the relationship. And now instead of being Alicia's advocate, Sherry could seal her fate.

But she couldn't, could she? As werewolves, wouldn't doing something like that hurt all their kind?

She relaxed a little as Jake's hand caressed her shoulder. She didn't question him about the woman, figuring he didn't want to talk about her in front of Tom and Peter. But then he must have decided it was more important to get this out in the open before they met with the woman.

"We've seen each other a couple of times. Lelandi had talked me into coming here first to drop off some of my photographs at one of the art galleries, as you recall." He was speaking to Tom and Peter. "Sherry collects modern art. I was here alone, not knowing anyone. She was a wolf." Jake shrugged. "We had lunch. Then we took in a movie."

"Drive-in?" Alicia asked, hating that she sounded so suspicious.

He chuckled. "No. Nothing happened between us. She's very much in charge and loves her job, her life here in the city, and her wolf friends. She wouldn't have ever considered moving to a small place like Silver Town. There was never any spark between us. It was just a mutual friendship."

So why had Jake been reluctant to mention her to anyone?

"She thought it was more than that?" Alicia asked.

"Let's say she wanted more than that. But her fascination with me was more that I was someone new, an alpha, a challenge. I let her know I wasn't interested in anything more than friendship. She didn't like being turned down. I felt it was akin to her losing a case."

"You don't happen to know any male attorneys who could help me out, do you?" Alicia asked wistfully.

"She knows her role in our society. Protect the wolf kind. She won't do anything to get you into any kind of trouble."

At least not more than Alicia was already. Wait until Sherry Slate learned Alicia was pregnant with Jake's triplets!

———————

As soon as Jake called Sherry, she cleared her schedule for the afternoon, but when he told her what it was about, he could tell she was ready to rethink her afternoon plans.

"She needs your help," Jake said, pleading. Hell, Sherry was a professional. He wanted to tell her to act like it. "Unless you know another lawyer in the Denver area that might be able to help her." Like one of Sherry's partners, if any were wolf types and had the time.

He swore he could hear Sherry's spine stiffening. He imagined she did not easily give up difficult cases.

"I'll speak with her." Sherry's tone was clipped.

Jake was afraid Alicia was in for an even rougher time of it. But they didn't have a whole lot of choice.

When they arrived at the office, Jake assumed from the waiting room that the law firm was doing well. The luxurious seating was on leather couches and chairs, much more ostentatious than at the law offices in Silver Town. A pretty receptionist sat at the counter, with blond hair in curls down to her shoulders and bright-green eyes. She smiled at Jake and Tom, raised her brow at Peter, undoubtedly because he was wearing his uniform, and gave a cursory glance in Alicia's direction.

The first thing Jake noticed about her was her feminine wolf smell. Plus a number of wolf scents had been left in the reception area. Just the place Alicia needed to be, among their own kind where they would protect her with whatever they could.

"You're here to see Ms. Slate? She'll be out in just a moment. If you'd like to take a seat…" The receptionist motioned to the chairs.

Jake sat with Alicia on one of the couches while Peter and Tom took seats in nearby chairs. And then they waited. And waited. And waited.

After half an hour, Jake rose and walked over to the counter. "Maybe there's someone else who has more time and could see us?"

The woman glanced back at the door that led to the offices down the hall. "Let me check with Ms. Slate and see if that's acceptable." She punched in some numbers and said, "Ms. Slate, Mr. Jake Silver was asking if it would be much longer."

He was amused the receptionist didn't tell Sherry that he would seek another lawyer in her place if she didn't get her butt in gear.

"I'll be there," Sherry snapped over the phone.

Jake was afraid the animosity in her voice spelled more trouble for Alicia.

After a few more minutes, Sherry walked into the reception area, looking professional and long-legged and wearing an expensive-looking black skirt and jacket and black high-heeled shoes. A smile was pasted on her face for Jake. She took hold of his hand and held on as if momentarily claiming him and said, "So good of you to see me again." Then she glanced at Tom and her smile broadened.

Someone new to switch her attention to?

Her gaze slid to Peter, her smile never changing, and then she shifted her attention to the object of her annoyance, no doubt.

"Miss Greiston, I presume," Sherry said with chilly politeness, her smile instantly fading. She looked Alicia over as if trying to figure out why Jake had picked her over herself. "Come on back to my office, if you would."

Jake took Alicia's ice-cold hand and followed Sherry, who he swore swayed her hips more than she'd done the last couple of times he'd seen her. In fact, his impression of her had always been one of professional detachment, as if she was trying to maintain a businesswoman's appearance no matter where she was or what she was doing.

In sharp contrast, Alicia wore a robin's-egg blue skirt that softly swirled below her knees with her every step and a matching top of some kind of silky fabric that he enjoyed touching and sliding his fingers over. She wore heels, but not as high as Sherry's, and they were strappy, sexy, and much more appealing. And while Sherry's hair was pulled back in a severe twist of curls at the back of her head, Alicia's softly caressed her shoulders in an inviting way. Sherry was elegant in a professional way, while Alicia was enticing in a feminine way.

When they reached Sherry's office, she motioned to a chair in front of her desk. Alicia took the seat as Jake sat beside her.

"Well, as you probably know, Jake filled me in on your story. Quite a tale," Sherry said, with a biting edge to her words as she took a seat behind her desk.

"Your partners in the law firm are wolves," Jake said. Having smelled several in the reception area, he assumed the law firm was made up of wolves. But it was also a way of letting Sherry know that if she couldn't deal with this on a strictly professional basis, he'd look elsewhere for help.

She smiled coyly, immediately getting his drift. "For our

friendship, Jake, I won't charge anything for my services." She focused again on Alicia. "So exactly how did you get yourself into this mess?" She held a hand up, stopping Alicia before she could say a word. "Tell me from the beginning what happened."

CHAPTER 20

MARIO SWORE AT DANNY AS HE PACED AROUND HIS CONDO IN Breckenridge. "What the hell do you mean Rudy's in police custody? And didn't I tell you to...hell, disappear?"

"The police were keeping a tight lid on Rudy's arrest. Hell, I dropped by Alicia's apartment to see why Rudy wasn't answering his cell phone while he was waiting there to see if she returned. Not only were the police there, but Alicia was coming out of her apartment with three other men after the police left. One was wearing a uniform, but they all took off in two vehicles."

"And you followed them."

"Hell, yeah. From a safe distance. They drove to Silver Town, then out through the country and pulled off on a private paved road. I couldn't see it, but I imagine a house is tucked back into the woods."

"Why didn't Rudy use his phone privilege to call you so you'd tell me and we could get him a lawyer?"

"I checked with the police, and some sergeant informed me that Rudy had gotten his phone call."

Mario stared at Danny. "You didn't get a call."

"No, sir."

"Hell. I want him out of there before he says something he shouldn't. Did Celinas say he'd gotten in touch with Rudy?"

"No. I called the lawyer right away. He hadn't had any word, so he went down to the jailhouse, and they said Rudy already had a lawyer."

"Who?"

"Some guy named Alistair Gray. He's a lawyer in the area, and he convinced Rudy he'd save his hide."

"Tell Celinas I want him down there changing Rudy's mind. Now."

"All right. And, sir?"

Mario frowned at him.

"I got word Miss Greiston is being questioned by the Denver police. Seems she was at Ferdinand's condo when we killed him."

Mario stared at him, then shook his head. "Damn it, Danny. I told you Jimmy said Ferdinand had taken her before we terminated him. She must have been hiding somewhere in the place. So what did she see?"

"According to our source, she wouldn't speak to the detectives without a lawyer present."

Mario rubbed his chin, then stalked over to the window and stared out. "Was she still with the men she'd been with earlier at her place?"

"Yeah. They're sticking pretty close to her. Plus they had another SUV full of bodyguards protecting her."

"Hell."

"You want me to find where she's staying? It's probably in Silver Town. Celinas checked with the art gallery and learned Jake Silver is the artsy-fartsy lover boy."

"He's a dead man," Mario grumbled under his breath.

"He's got a home that's even more isolated than the house I followed them to. I could put some men on it and—"

"No. Just give me the location, and I'll check it out." Hell, the artist would not be able to stand up to a wolf. Mario would kill him and take Alicia for his own. And then he'd hide her away from the police, from humans—his trophy mate. She was a wolf now. And as much trouble as her mother had given him, and then Alicia, she would pay for it.

Danny was another story. Mario hated to eliminate his last cousin, but once the police learned the gun Danny had hidden in his house had killed both Missy and Tony, they were sure to link

Danny to him. He just had to think of a way to get rid of Danny so that no one would ever learn of it.

"We'll only do this with the promise Alicia Greiston will not have any threat of prosecution," Sherry Slate told Detective Sanderson while Jake listened in at Massaro's condo. Peter and Tom stayed with Alicia in the hallway until the detective had agreed to the lawyer's terms. "She saw nothing, heard voices, but that was all. She doesn't know who the men were who murdered Ferdinand Massaro. Although, like you, she suspects Mario Constantino had him killed."

"All right," the detective grudgingly said.

"Remember what I said about her delicate condition," Sherry repeated. "I don't want to have to go to your superiors if you make this difficult for her. She was the victim in all this."

Sanderson nodded once, his blue eyes hard. Jake could tell the detective didn't like being dictated to by a lawyer, particularly because she was a woman, Jake suspected.

After half an hour of questioning, Alicia appeared worn out. But she looked relieved, too, when Jake bundled her up in the car and headed on the long drive back to Silver Town. All he could think of was lighting a fire in the fireplace at his home, making her a cup of hot chocolate with whipped cream on top, and cuddling with her in front of the fire until he could coax her into bed. He wanted to make love to her, like he always did, but he wanted to comfort her if that was what she needed more for the time being than the lovemaking. They had a lifetime of that ahead of them.

"What are you thinking about?" Jake asked as he held her close and she snuggled against him in the middle seat of the SUV.

"How nice Sherry ended up being. I mean, she loathed me, but she really was very good at her job. Of course, I think she was trying to catch Tom's eye and probably didn't think she'd stand a chance if she didn't try her best to get me out of hot water."

"She had to or face the consequences. No newly turned wolf could be incarcerated without causing dire consequences for all of us," Jake reminded her, rubbing her shoulder in a loving way.

"Hmm." She turned her attention to Tom and asked, "What did you think of her, Tom? Possibilities?"

He shook his head. "She's just like Jake said. All business through and through. I doubt she has a seductive bone in her body."

"Sometimes all a woman needs is the right man." Alicia ran her hand over Jake's thigh.

He slipped his hand beneath her blouse and stroked a bra-covered breast, enjoying the way her nipple strained against the silky fabric with his touch. If they'd had more privacy, he would have taken her cue and had his way with her. Stopping at a hotel on the way was an idea too. But he couldn't inconvenience everyone with his insatiable need to have her.

Tom said, "Darien told me everyone in the pack is coming to the wedding. It'll be a feast to end all feasts."

"Lelandi said it would be in the clearing in the woods out back," Alicia said. "Is it big enough?"

"Yeah," Tom said. "We have pack games and other pack gatherings there." He turned to give Jake an annoyed look. "You realize that after this wedding is over, Lelandi's going to be on my case even more about finding a mate, don't you?"

Jake shook his head. "Her babies are coming soon. She'll be wrapped up in that. So you're off the hook for a little while."

Alicia was melting into Jake's lap, and he was getting damned hard as he continued to massage one of her breasts. "Tell Peter to drive faster," she whispered to Jake.

Tom shook his head, probably having overheard Alicia's words spoken in private to Jake. "Hell, I've got to get me a mate," Tom said.

Of all the damned things, Mario thought as he circled in his wolf form around the house that the artist lover-boy owned. Wolves lived in this area. Were they wolf-wolves or werewolves? He couldn't tell the difference. But never having met any other werewolf types except the bastard he'd killed and the ones he'd made, although only one still lived, he hadn't thought many more existed. They probably were regular wolves.

He sniffed the area and listened. No one was here. The place was quiet, and no one was guarding it. He figured that when Jake Silver returned with Alicia, he'd most likely have that bodyguard force with him. Mario was going to have to enlist the help of the one other man he'd turned if they had to fight a couple of wolves. Danny and a couple of others would have to be the firepower to serve as a distraction so he could grab Alicia and leave. Things were getting too hot for Mario in Colorado. A warrant had been issued for Danny's arrest, and he was a dead man once Mario got his hands on Alicia.

Not only was that damned police chief in Breckenridge breathing down Mario's neck, but the Denver police somehow had linked his name to Ferdinand Massaro's death. And the feds were looking into Tony Thomas's death, somehow linking him to someone named Antonio Frasero.

Mario was thinking of going someplace else. Somewhere in Minnesota, maybe. Up nearer to the Canadian border where he could slip away if need be. He'd heard there were real wolves in those parts. That meant he could blend in.

All his trouble had started with that damned Tony. If he hadn't been looking into Mario's business dealings, and then if Missy Greiston hadn't gotten involved, everything would have gone along like it always had. Their deaths had gotten Missy's daughter involved, and she had created even more trouble for Mario. One little woman. Wolf now. He'd show Alicia what it meant to mess with him.

He turned and loped off to his car hidden in the woods. Time to get reinforcements.

———————————

After dinner at Darien's and a much more relaxed atmosphere, except for Lelandi bringing up the wedding plans again, Alicia had had a wonderful time with the family and already felt as though she'd known them forever. When she and Jake returned to his home, guards were again posted outside. She hated that men had to stand guard detail all night, although Jake assured her no one minded doing what they needed to when they had to keep pack members safe. Even so, she did feel much safer knowing they were there.

Jake made her sit on the couch and watch the orange flames shoot up toward the chimney as he heated cups of hot chocolate. She could envision a winter-filled landscape out the big picture windows when the first snowfall began and how beautiful the woods would be. Just like her favorite poem by Robert Frost, "Stopping by Woods on a Snowy Evening."

"A penny for your thoughts," Jake said, stalking back into the living room with two cups of steaming hot chocolate.

"Did I tell you how much I love you? You've rescued me more times than I can count. Been my knight, my protector, never condemned me for having so many husbands when your kind never divorce." She took a deep breath, then sipped her hot chocolate, the rich, velvety flavor tantalizing her tongue and the aroma making her take another deep breath of it.

"That's because our animal senses help us to find the right mate the first time around. And our loyalty is inborn," he said, watching the way she curled her tongue around a dollop of whipped cream before it melted into the chocolate. He took a swig of his drink. "We don't go through a phase where we feel we're missing out if we don't ditch the old way of life and try out someone new."

She took another wondrous sip of the chocolate and whipped cream and sighed. She licked her lips, and his gaze switched to her mouth.

"We renew our love for each other in special ways to spark the old flame. It's important to our kind to stay together throughout our lives. Although if we lose a mate, we're free to find a new one. Some do. Some don't. Besides, Alicia, the men you ended up with were real jerks. I already told you so," Jake said, adamant about it. But then he smiled at her with a speculative gleam in his eye. "I can't believe anyone would prefer to watch ice hockey to watching you dance on ice like you do." He shook his head and took another sip of his hot chocolate.

She studied the chocolate and a speck of whipped cream on his lips, tilted her chin up, and licked both off his lips.

He set his half-finished cocoa on the coffee table and took her free hand in his. She hastily finished her cocoa, not wanting to give up a drop, and set her mug down with his, knowing he had other business in mind, and she was all for it.

His hands combed through her thick curls as he pressed her back against the couch with his body and kissed her hungrily. But then he took a deep breath, rose from the couch, and lifted her into his arms. "Although the men are watching the house to protect you, I don't want to distract them from their business. No drapes on the windows," he added.

"I noticed."

"Tom and I took the old ones down. They were worn and badly needed to be replaced. I actually had it in mind to leave the windows bare to show off the view. Living alone or with Tom, it wouldn't have mattered. But with you, that's another story."

"Hmm," she said, unbuttoning his shirt as he strode down the hall to the only furnished bedroom, carrying her tightly in his arms. "I didn't think any of your pack members would look."

He chuckled. "They're only human, Alicia. And a lot wolf."

He carried her into the bedroom, and before she even sank into her soft, comforting mattress, she thought of how wonderful it would be to make love again to Jake in her bed. Not in some unfamiliar motel room or in the forest, although anything would do, but still, she felt a certain possessiveness in knowing they weren't in a strange bed but hers. And he was hers. In her bed. And not just for a one-night stand.

The concept that anyone might want her forever still seemed foreign, but for this night and for as long as they would have each other, she knew her dream had come true. The home was quiet, too, unlike the noisy apartment she was used to. With her enhanced hearing, it would have been worse. But here...

She sighed as Jake sat her on the bed.

Here it was quiet and peaceful, the only sounds the faint rustle of tree branches fluttering in the breeze, the trickle of running water in a stream nearby, and Jake's heartbeat ratcheting up several notches. Comforting, pleasing sounds.

Jake was unbuttoning his shirt, watching her expression. "What are you thinking, Alicia? You have kind of a lost look on your face. Like you're a million miles away."

"I was thinking," she said, unbuttoning her blouse, "how I would have you in my bed again and how wonderful that notion is."

He smiled and lifted an arrogant brow at hearing her words. "Were you now?" He tugged off his shirt and tossed it on a chair. Then like a wolf on the prowl, he put his hands on the bed on either side of her hips, caging her in as his mouth sought hers, melded with hers, and caressed hers. His body pressed against her knees, forcing her to part her legs for him. Yet he kept his weight off her, all except his mouth kissing and loving hers, and now her thighs caressed his as he leaned between them.

All at once, she didn't feel as in control or that she had him in *her* bed, but that he claimed *her and her bed* for his own. The notion both excited and thrilled her.

Her hands went around his bare waist, loving his silky skin and hard muscles. Her bare thighs pressed against his soft stonewashed jeans; his thighs tensed beneath the fabric.

"You're so hard," she whispered, moving her hands down his waist to his lean hips, circling around to his buttocks, and then sweeping around to his crotch.

As soon as she caressed him, she felt him lose his measured control of the situation. He groaned and fumbled to remove her blouse, and she knew then that she had him right where she wanted him. He finally managed to pull off her blouse and toss it aside. Then he was searching blindly for the zipper on her skirt while he kept kissing her lips, maintaining the intimacy between them. She tugged to unfasten his belt, wanting to touch him skin to skin. But he clearly wanted her naked first. And she was still struggling with his belt when she heard her skirt zipper yield.

He was trying to tug her skirt down her hips while she was sitting, and he finally placed his hands on her shoulders, forcing her to lie on her back so he could slip the silky skirt off her. Then his belt gave! And she slid his zipper down, her fingers pressing the fastener against his arousal all the way down.

"Alicia," he groaned, half dying in agony, half pleading in ecstasy.

"Hmm?" she said with an uplifted tilt to her voice as she wiggled to help him remove her skirt.

She peeled his jeans down, but before she could slip her hand inside his boxers, he pulled off his jeans the rest of the way, then pressed his body against hers on the mattress, thwarting her, taking handfuls of her hair, and kissing her mouth again. She had the distinct impression he wanted to last, and if she kept touching him, he wasn't going to.

He rubbed his hardness against her skimpy red thong—the

one he'd bought her at the boutique in town—and she slid her hands up his boxers and caressed his bare buttocks. She thought she heard him curse under his breath as he plunged his hand into the front of her nearly nothing panties, found her sweet spot, and began to stroke her into a world of heightened pleasure she'd only been able to feel when he was touching her.

And now she was losing control, the tide of swelling pleasure rising in her as he took her higher and higher, her hands stilled on his buttocks, his tongue plunging deeply, erotically into her mouth.

He tasted of chocolate and whipped cream, his masculine scent and arousal arousing her, every sense heightened because of the wolf in her, every sensation more profound then she'd ever experienced. Before she could cling to the peak, the wave of ecstasy crashed over her.

───────────

Hot, wet, sexy Alicia, Jake thought as he stroked her into climax. He swore if she had stroked him like she was about to, he would never have lasted. She was a godsend, and he wanted to pleasure her like she should have always been loved. Like he'd always love her. With her body still shuddering with completion, he meant to strip out of his boxers, but she was already yanking them down.

He smiled as he nuzzled her cheek. Then when he was free of his boxers, he eased into her and pressed homeward. The bond between them would never be broken. Her hands roamed over his back and butt, caressing and stirring him into action, as he deepened his thrusts and claimed her again as if the ritual needed to be repeated to show her he meant to be here for her forever.

Her eyes were filled with wonderment as he gazed into them, her lips full, wet, and well-kissed, her breath light and barely audible, and then her eyes closed as she arched her pelvis against him, matching his thrusts, her fingers clenching tighter on his buttocks. She cried out, "Jake, oh, Jake," and moaned as she sank against the mattress, his seed filling her after that, and he collapsed on top of her in satiated bliss. He wrapped his arms around her, his whole posture stating she was his, and he blanketed her in his protective cocoon to ensure that.

She lay very still for several minutes while their hearts beat rapidly in unison and he continued to hold her close. Then she whispered, "They had to have heard me."

He kissed her cheek, rolled off her, pulled her against his chest, and covered them with the sheet and comforter.

"Hmm." He couldn't tell her no, when he knew they had to have, and she'd probably figure they had. He couldn't tell her yes and confirm what she had to suspect. So he'd just said *hmm*.

She let out her breath and toyed with his nipple. "Next time, if we have a bodyguard detail outside our windows, don't let me make a sound. All right?" She looked up at him with her brows creased.

He chuckled and ran his hand over her silky hair. "They already know what we're doing in here."

"I *know* that. But…at least they would have to guess when it came to the, um, end."

He laughed and wrapped his arms around her.

That was when they heard the sound of pops in the woods surrounding the house. Jake was out of the bed in a flash. For a second, he wasn't sure what to do—dress and grab his gun, or shift.

"Jake," Alicia said, sounding scared, her eyes huge.

"Stay here. I've got to see what's happening." Then he shifted and bumped Alicia's hand with his nose. After she ran her hand over his head, he turned and dashed out of the bedroom, intent on getting to his men and taking care of whoever was causing trouble.

Nothing had been unpacked, Alicia thought as she hurried out of bed, pulled on her bra and panties, and then looked for a box that might have a pair of jeans and a sweater. Frantically digging clothes out of one, then another of the boxes, she finally found a pair of jeans.

But before she could put them on, she heard footfalls headed in her direction down the hall at a full-out run. Her heart went into overdrive.

CHAPTER 21

JAKE SMELLED THE SCENT OF THE DAMN WOLVES BEFORE HE could locate them in the woods. Peter and three other members of his pack were looking for the men who had been shooting at them.

Sam had been hit, damn it. He was sitting in the grass, holding someone's bunched-up shirt against the leg wound. "Go," Sam said. The bearded, burly man's expression was one of barely suppressed rage. "Find them. Get rid of them."

Jake knew that the owner and bartender of Silver Town Tavern, a gruff man who looked like he lived as a mountain man in the wilderness most of the time, meant for him to go after the two wolves. The others were strictly human. Probably more of Mario's henchmen. Jake's men would be targeting them while in their human forms. He would bet Mario was one of the wolves.

Jake was worried about Sam's injury, though. If the bullet hit a major artery, Sam could bleed out and die before they could get him help.

"Darien's sending Doc," Sam growled. "Peter already called him." Sam detested being injured like this while everyone else got to hunt down the bastards. "Hell, Jake, I mean it. I'm going to live. Quit giving me them puppy-dog eyes."

Jake shook his head and tore off after the scent of the two intruding wolves.

Peter was the sheriff, and Heston was a new deputy. The rest of the men, even Sam, were deputized whenever they needed to go on a manhunt *or* wolf hunt. So there wasn't any need to call in anyone else to apprehend the human bastards. If they died in the shoot-out, they died. Simple as that. Lawmen had a right to protect themselves. In Silver Town, that was just what they did.

As for the wolves...

Jake was hot on their trail. Or at least one of them.

He finally discovered the wolf backed up against a pine tree and growling at him. Jake didn't know if it was Mario or someone else, but he didn't care. The wolf represented trouble for Alicia and for their kind. If he was ever arrested, and since he was either Mario or one of his men and eventually would be, he couldn't be allowed to live. Still, Jake couldn't, with a human conscience, just outright kill without the wolf first attacking.

They'd figure out something else to do with him, but what, Jake wasn't sure. It wasn't the first time he'd been glad Darien and Lelandi were the pack leaders. Tom and Jake and others of the pack advised them, but ultimately, decisions of this nature were left up to Darien and Lelandi.

The gray wolf continued to snarl and growl at Jake, his nose wrinkled in a hideous display of ferocity, his canines fully exposed, the fur on his back standing on end.

Another couple of shots were fired off some distance in the woods. Jake wasn't sure if that prompted the wolf to attack, or if Jake's failure to look ferocious made the wolf believe Jake was not someone to fear. But the attack came and Jake tore into him, showing the wolf he wasn't one to mess with as his teeth tore at the wolf's neck. The villain shook him loose and skittered away with a yelp.

Then he uttered a low growl right before he dove for Jake a second time. He wasn't a skilled wolf at attacking, which meant he probably hadn't used his wolf instincts in wolf-to-wolf combat much, if ever. Although some instincts would come into play in a fight to the death.

But the guy was much heavier than Jake, and the damned beast actually knocked him off his feet with the second charge.

Adrenaline coursing through his blood, Jake scrambled to get to his feet, knowing he could have been dead meat if the wolf had known how to attack him just right. Not wanting the wolf to learn from his mistakes or to put Jake in too vulnerable a position again, he attacked the bigger wolf this time. But it was like slamming into a damned brick wall. Jake dodged before the wolf could take a bite. The man reminded Jake of a bully with more brute strength than brains.

The wolf looked pleased, like he was smiling at Jake, and that pissed Jake off. Sure, the guy was a bigger wolf, but he wasn't going to win this battle. Not with Alicia's life at stake.

And with his attack on Jake, the deal was off. The pack leaders wouldn't decide this guy's fate. He was Jake's for the taking.

Jake lunged at the wolf, going for his throat again. The wolf's and Jake's teeth clashed in a wicked snapping of canines. Enamel hit enamel with resounding whacks, snarls ricocheting off the trees like a wolves' warning to others to stay away. Then like two fighters in the ring, neither of them making any headway, they both fell away.

Two wolves were out here, Jake reminded himself. Two wolves and he had to get the other too. He had to end this now. Easier said than done as he again attacked and the wolf matched Jake's skill with more brute force.

Jake whipped around in a circle, and before the wolf realized he was attacking again, Jake grabbed him by the throat. The wolf tried to yank away and nearly succeeded. But Jake held on, tightened his grip, and crushed the wolf's throat.

He didn't wait to see what happened next. It didn't matter whether Mario or the other man lay dead on the ground and would return to his human form. One was still on the loose as a wolf, as far as Jake knew. And his time to locate the bastard was growing short.

Jake tore off, trying to track the footpad scent of the other wolf who wasn't part of their pack. That was when he realized the wolf had gone straight to the damned front door! The shooters were the diversionary force. *Damn it!*

Alicia was alone and unprotected.

———

Not having time to dress any further, except for putting on the red panties and bra, Alicia dropped her jeans and looked around the bedroom for her purse, not remembering where she'd left it while everyone was still moving furniture. Kitchen? Living room? That was where her pepper spray and stun gun were tucked away.

Jake's gun! But where was it now? After he'd taken it into her apartment to use as protection, she didn't remember him doing anything with it. Had he returned it to the glove compartment?

With the sudden rush of footfalls toward the bedroom, it was too late to go for the gun. She raced to the window and had only managed to unlock it when someone barged into the bedroom.

She whipped around and stared aghast at Mario Constantino. He was naked, tall, and big, but mostly naked. She was so startled at the sight of him in the raw that she didn't react fast enough. He took two quick strides into the room and struck her in the temple with his meaty fist. A stab of pain shot through her temple before blackness cloaked her and she crumpled to the floor.

———

Jake whipped around to the back of the house and slipped through the wolf door, then raced down the hall to the bedroom where he heard someone rummaging around.

When he peered into the room, he saw a naked-assed Mario Constantino dumping all Alicia's things from the boxes onto the floor. Alicia was dead to the world, lying on the bed.

Jake growled low and threatening. Mario swung around, and Jake swore the bastard was about to have a heart attack. He quickly looked back at Alicia.

Yeah, you'll pay, bastard.

Mario's mouth dropped open as his attention returned to Jake. "Hell, you're a wolf? The artist?"

So Mario had thought Alicia had turned into the wolf. That was the reason for him looking back at her on the bed.

Jake growled even lower, pushing Mario to shift. But the bastard wouldn't. Maybe he couldn't. *Damn him.* Jake couldn't let him live.

Jake advanced, still growling, his hackles raised and his posture as menacing as it had ever been. Angry didn't begin to describe how he felt about Alicia and the way this bastard had hurt her. Or what Mario planned to do with her in the future, if Jake let him live.

Mario was scowling and livid, probably because he'd been caught, but he still didn't shift.

Jake drew closer, growling, threatening.

Mario grabbed one of the half-empty boxes and threw it at Jake. He dodged it and turned his focus back on Mario as he shifted into the wolf. Like the other wolf, he was bigger than Jake, but this time, Jake wasn't going to give him time to make the first move.

He went for the wolf's throat and sent him crashing into the closet door, but Mario somehow managed to scramble over one of the cardboard boxes and slip away. Relentlessly, Jake went after him again. Jake bit at him, got a mouthful of fur, and broke the skin on Mario's shoulder. Mario yelped and skittered away. For being a tough bastard as a Mob leader, he was a cowardly wolf.

He probably felt much more capable with a gun in his hand. Or having others doing his dirty work for him.

Jake leaped over the cardboard box in his way, and Mario tried to reach the door.

But there stood Alicia in her red push-up bra and silky red thong, her hand against her temple, unsteady on her feet, her face pale, her expression pained. Mario stopped for an instant. With her free hand, she shut the door, sealing his fate.

Worried Mario would hurt Alicia, Jake tackled him from behind. Mario whipped around with Jake clinging to his back, holding on with both paws, trying to get a better grip on his neck.

The voices of men hollering outside caught Jake's attention, but he remained focused on Mario and bringing him down. He heard the box springs squeak and figured Alicia had collapsed on the bed before she passed out again.

Mario was still trying to wriggle free, and Jake kept losing his grip on the massive wolf's neck.

"Where's Jake?" Darien hollered outside the back of the house.

"In the house," Sam shouted back. "He's fighting someone as a wolf."

Not for long.

Mario stumbled over a box and got his feet tangled in Alicia's jeans, and Jake bit him hard in the throat. Killing him. For Alicia. For her mother. For her father.

———

The next day, Alicia's temple was black and blue from where Mario had struck her. She was seated on the couch in Darien's home with Jake's arm around her. Darien, Tom, Lelandi, and Peter offered her moral support as two federal agents sat down to talk with her.

One was a pretty blond with a short bobbed haircut and a smart black suit-skirt and pretty hazel eyes. The man was dark-haired and dark-eyed, also wearing a black suit. Both were probably in their early thirties and both professional, yet instead of appearing as though they wanted to grill Alicia, they seemed…

She wasn't sure. Sympathetic, maybe?

That didn't make any sense to her, because she figured they would tie her to Mario's death and his henchman's too. Peter had rounded up the men who had been the diversionary force for Mario at Jake's home and turned them over to the federal authorities because they'd been involved in killings across state lines, racketeering, money laundering, and even lucrative Medicare scams. But a couple of the men had to heal from their bullet wounds before they appeared in court, Danny being one of them.

"Miss Greiston," the woman said, identifying herself as Agent White and the man as Agent Stone, "we want to commend you for bringing Constantino and his men down."

Alicia looked at Jake. He smiled at her and tightened his arm around her shoulder in a warm embrace.

"Your father, Antonio Frasero, started the work."

"He…was working for you?"

"Yes, as an informant. He was working for Constantino, but only to get the goods on him. That little black book you found in your mother's safe-deposit box? It had all the records we needed to put the whole lot away for life."

Again she looked at Jake.

"I gave it to Peter to give to the authorities," Jake said. "The sheriff must have turned it over to the feds."

"But helping you got my father killed," Alicia said to the woman agent.

"We gave him a deal. He was working for another crime boss when we caught up with him. We had enough on your father to give him a life sentence for his own crimes. He'd only been married to your mother for a couple of years, and you were not even two years old. They agreed he'd work for us so he'd stay out of prison."

"But my mother was dating other men."

"Only undercover. They were feds whose job was to make it appear Antonio wasn't her husband or too close to her while watching out for her. We knew Mario would go after her if he thought Antonio was selling him out."

Alicia frowned. "Which Mario did."

The woman took a deep breath and exhaled. "She loved your father and didn't want to see anybody else any longer. She wanted to pretend she was Antonio's lover when she was really his wife. We couldn't convince them how dangerous it was. Mario must have thought she knew about Antonio's working with us and had them both murdered. Then you came along. You wouldn't have anything to do with Antonio, so we figured you were safe. But then when your mother was murdered, you tried to arrest Mario and..." Agent White shook her head.

"Why didn't you protect Alicia when you must have known Mario would want her dead?" Jake asked, his voice sounding irritated.

"We couldn't keep track of her. We put bugs on her car four times, and each time, she located them and put them on other vehicles. We bugged her apartment, but she never returned home. She took off from the motel in Breckenridge and vanished. We only learned of it when you had the clerk contact the police to say she had disappeared. We assumed she had vanished on her own and figured she was safe."

"Until?"

"She was connected to Ferdinand Massaro's murder. We learned later that he was informing her as to Mario's locations. He was one of our informants until something happened. All of a sudden, he went rogue. We think it had something to do with Mario trying to have him killed." Agent White cleared her throat and said to Alicia, "In any event, we just want to say that even though your father started out on the wrong side of the law, he helped to put away several who would have continued their criminal activities by keeping all the records he did. And we have you to thank for handing over the little black book that made it all possible."

"My mother was the innocent in all this."

"Yes," Agent White said sympathetically. "But she loved your father and couldn't give up on him."

Alicia understood some of what had gone on while she was growing up. The men who had been her mother's boyfriends had only been feds pretending to be something they weren't. The ones who witnessed her weddings.

Had her father ever thought she was marrying the wrong men? Her mother hadn't. She must have thought the guys Alicia had married were good sorts because they didn't have anything to do with the Mob. But now Alicia understood why her father had wanted to maintain his distance from her, probably to ensure her safety but also to keep her from learning who he truly was—and all about his checkered past. And yet, somewhere deep down, she suspected he wished he could have been the father to her that he might have been, had things been different.

She cleared her suddenly gravelly throat. "Thank you for telling me about my father and mother."

Agent Stone stood. "Just for the record, Miss Greiston, Mario Constantino and another of his henchmen were found dead in a ravine over a hundred miles from here by a group of hikers. At least that's what the anonymous caller told us. Wild animals had eaten most of the remains. But we had enough to positively identify them. The initial coroner's report stated that they fell off the cliff to their deaths as they were attempting to escape prosecution. If you need anything from us," he said, pulling a card from his suit pocket, "don't hesitate to call."

Alicia took the card and smelled a slight scent of wolf. She looked up at the federal agent in disbelief. He gave her a wolfish smile back. But she hadn't smelled... The air was so still in the room, and with him being such a distance from her...

She rose and stepped closer to him to shake his hand and took a deeper breath. He was a wolf.

She looked at the woman, who gave her a conspiratorial wink. They were wolves. Both of them.

"Thank you," Darien said and led them out of the house as Alicia collapsed on the couch.

"It's over," Alicia finally said.

"For us, it's a new beginning." Jake took her hand in his and kissed it.

"They loved each other." Alicia swallowed hard. "I wish...I wish they could have been here to see me get married." Then she gave a small smile. "Actually, I know they will be watching over us as we get married. They'll always be with us." And with that, she tugged at Jake's hand. "Let's go home." To the first real home she'd ever known, ready to start her life all over again. Her father might not have been there for her, but Jake would be here for his own children, and that was all that mattered now. "Ready to hang some pictures?"

Jake smiled back at her. "Pictures?"

The look in his eyes said hanging pictures wasn't at all what he had in mind.

———

That day in the forest so long ago, when Jake had wiped off Alicia's feet with his good dress shirt before he put her tennis shoes on, had made her feel like Cinderella. And now on their wedding day—since their kind never married like this, he absolutely refused to believe he shouldn't see her before the wedding—he was helping her into her gown because, as he told her, he wanted to know how to get her back out of it as quickly as possible once the festivities were over.

She swore he was insatiable. And she loved him for it. But now he knelt at her feet dressed in his tuxedo, looking like the most handsome prince in the world while he slipped one pearl-white shoe onto her foot and then did the same with the other. When he was done, he slid his hands under her gown, up her calves and higher to her thighs, and looked up at her.

"This will be the longest day of my life," he said.

She smiled at him. "We'll sneak off early." At least she hoped they could.

The fragrance of flowers perfumed the air in the forest setting as Alicia cried at the wedding. Happy tears. She hadn't planned to. She blamed it on being pregnant. On being a sentimental sap. On wishing her mother and father could see her truly happy. But even Lelandi joined her with teary eyes, and Darien and Jake just looked at each other sympathetically.

Silva slapped Sam on the back, his gunshot wound all healed up. "Think we might do something like this someday?" she asked sweetly.

He grunted.

Lelandi laughed. "I'd be game to put on another one of these."

Darien shook his head.

Everyone glanced at Tom, who was tugging at his cravat. "Don't look at me. I haven't found a girl to date, let alone mate."

Lelandi smiled at him, the expression on her face one of calculation. Who could she find for Tom, now that Jake had gone off and found a mate all on his own?

Everyone was so busy grazing at the tables of food that no one saw Jake take Alicia's hand and pull her away from the festivities. Or maybe they did, but she was certain no one really minded.

"We never discussed going away on a honeymoon," Jake said, driving Alicia back to the house.

"You're kidding, right?"

He looked at her, his expression surprised.

"I have trouble with shifting," she reminded him.

"Ah. But you won't be able to during the new moon."

"Can you guarantee it?"

"Yes."

"Hmm," she said, running her hand over his thigh. "After all that has happened in the past several months, would you think me very boring if I said I'd just like to stay at home with you? Take walks in the woods where you can show me where you've taken such beautiful pictures of wildflowers. Enjoy a fire and hot chocolate with whipped cream and whatever else we have in mind to occupy ourselves."

"Skinny-dip on a night when the moon shimmers in the night sky."

"You mentioned doing that before. That sounds like fun. Do you have any drive-in theaters around here?" she asked as he drove down their long wooded drive.

"Forty-five minutes from here in Green Valley."

She smiled. "Looks like we have the start of a wonderfully delightful honeymoon scheduled, right here at home."

Home. It *was* home. And she had a man she could love just like her mother had loved her father. And a whole new family who loved her just as much as she loved them back.

And a whole mess of babies that would be here before they knew it. *Triplets.* She shook her head and cuddled next to Jake, her gown making her feel like she was cocooned in satin like a fairy princess. He wrapped his arm around her as they pulled into their driveway.

———

"What are you thinking now?" Jake asked, kissing the top of her head.

"When I first saw you, I thought you were one handsome, dangerously devilish man." She rubbed her belly. "Boy, did I have that right."

He chuckled, parked the truck, and carried her out of the

vehicle. "I wanted to kiss you in the worst way. And that was *my* undoing."

And the beginning of his life. He sighed, carried his mate *and bride* across the threshold, and vowed to give her the honeymoon of a lifetime, right here close to home. He would take pictures of her among the wildflowers, her hair freely flowing over her shoulders while she wore a tank top and short shorts, braless, barefoot, and pregnant, just as he'd envisioned so many weeks ago—except for the triplets part. And he couldn't be more pleased with the way the picture had changed.

Tangling with the Wolf

A Silver Town Wolf Novella

CHAPTER 1

IF THERE WAS ONE THING THAT REALLY ANNOYED HANNA Bridgeman—and as a red wolf, she could get really growly about it—it was when she asked a cute guy out to have a drink and he was late. She was all by herself, didn't know anybody in Green Valley, Colorado, and she was nervous about going for a job interview there tomorrow, so she was hoping for some company, or at least a distraction, not to be stood up.

Maybe he just hadn't had the nerve to tell her no. She'd recently lost her job at the local paper in Loveland, Colorado, and had just arrived in Green Valley when she had met the guy at a service station, pumping gas for his truck, and asked him where a good place would be to go for a drink. She'd needed one, and her hotel didn't have a restaurant, unfortunately.

He was human and had told her about this pub, so she'd asked if he would like to join her there at six and here she was. But the guy wasn't, and it was already six thirty. Traffic jams holding him up? Not likely in Green Valley. Hanna wasn't even sure whether she wanted to live here, but she needed work, and being a news reporter was her job. Rather...*had* been her job. If she hadn't asked the police chief in Loveland some embarrassing questions, she would still have her job.

She sighed. She could be a bit of a rogue wolf when she wanted to do real investigative reporting instead of writing fluff stories all the time.

At least the pub had some fun decorations: a stack of three jack-o'-lanterns on the bar, lighted pumpkins on each of the tables, orange and black lights hanging on the walls, and a sign that had a wood carving of Dracula with the words *Dracula's Pub* beneath it. The bartender was dressed like a pirate with a patch over his eye, and the servers were wearing a variety of costumes ranging from a sexy cat to Superwoman.

Hanna glanced out the window again. The colorful fall leaves were beautiful. Oranges, purples, reds, yellows, and a few evergreens and Colorado spruce trees really set things off. Crisp, cooler night temperatures were great for wolf fur coats and sweaters and jackets. She loved the fall. It was her favorite time of year.

She eyed the parking lot. No blue pickup truck. Lots of motorcyclists were showing up, though.

Then a guy caught her eye as he got out of a shiny, red Corvette. The car was cute. So was he. Or…sexy, rather. Except he had a military haircut. And she'd vowed to stay away from military guys. Two disastrous relationships had been enough for her. This guy was blond and green-eyed, tall and muscular with no fat, not a bodybuilder type but more the kind who could use his muscle when he needed to in a real combat situation.

When he came inside the pub, he glanced in her direction, and she quickly looked away. She wasn't here to pick up some other guy. Not that he acted like he was looking to hook up either. She motioned to the pirate waitress, who was busy visiting with some bikers sitting a few tables away. When the waitress came over, Hanna ordered a glass of chardonnay and a hamburger. She figured she might as well enjoy her dinner even if her "date" wasn't going to show up. Then she would head back to her hotel.

The military-looking guy sat at a table across the aisle and two tables away from hers. He ordered a soda and then pulled out his phone and read something. Maybe a text from a date or a friend he was supposed to meet. Maybe the person was late in arriving too. She couldn't imagine anyone who looked that hot being there by himself. At least she wasn't the only one sitting alone. She hadn't exchanged cell numbers with Joe, the no-show, but at this rate, she was glad she hadn't. She wasn't actually very outgoing. She'd had to work at learning to step out and meet people to interview them. It was something she always forced herself to do so she wouldn't backslide into her shell.

The motorcyclists were beginning to get unruly, catching her attention.

She took a sip of her citrusy wine and glanced at them talking among themselves, ordering beers, and glowering at the bikers at the other tables. The groups were members of different biker gangs, and she didn't think they would play well together. She frowned and eyed them more closely. They looked like some of the outlaw motorcycle gangs that were allegedly into all kinds of criminal activity. She checked her phone to see if she could identify them, and sure enough, there were members of the Bandidos, Hells Angels, Outlaws, and Pagans, all embracing the regalia of their motorcycle clubs.

Corvette Man looked up from his phone and saw her gawking at him again as if she were trying to catch his eye and get up close and personal. What was the matter with her? No matter how much she chastised herself for showing interest in him, she couldn't help it. She envisioned having asked *him* to have a drink with her. He would have shown up—on time even.

She glanced down at the navy sweater she was wearing that was covered in fuzzy pills or balls and pulls. It was her favorite sweater for fall, though she had told herself she should only wear it when she was raking leaves or shoveling snow, not to meet and greet people. Her jeans were just as worn, and her hiking boots had seen better days. Even her hair, clipped back in a French twist, had been tugged and pulled by the chilly breeze, leaving strands dangling about her neck and shoulders. She should have gone into the ladies' room and straightened it out. And why was she even thinking of that?

Hot and dangerous, Corvette Man was the reason. He looked

like he could handle any weapon known to man and then some. Her dad had always told her she needed to look her best when she went out because there was no telling who she might run into—relating his own experience when he had looked like the dregs, dropped into a pub, and met her mom. It hadn't turned out badly for them, though her mom always talked about how he'd been dressed in a grass-stained sweatshirt, jeans, and scuffed work boots and was wearing a scruffy, three-day growth of red beard. But she said his green eyes and wolfish smile had won her over, and she had overlooked his disheveled appearance.

Corvette Man left his table, and as he walked past Hanna's, he dropped his paper napkin on her table. She glanced down at it and read the scribble on the napkin: *Get out while you still can.*

Hanna raised a brow as he hurried past, and she smelled the napkin, finding the waitress's scent and a male red wolf's scent. She frowned as he left the pub. He was a red wolf too! Running into gray wolves was a rare enough occurrence, but running into a red wolf like her was unheard of. She looked out the window and saw him on his phone, talking to someone.

A biker at one table shouted something derogatory to a biker at another. Her first instinct should have been for self-preservation and getting out of there like the male wolf had done. But then she thought of her job interview at the local paper tomorrow. Wouldn't it be great if she could write this story and impress the editor? She had a front-row seat to a fight in a pub between biker gangs.

She pulled her phone out of her purse and began to record the beginning of the fight between the gangs.

Suddenly, the male wolf returned to the pub. She thought he was going to sit back at his table and finish his drink, despite the escalating fight between biker gangs and the fact that he'd warned her to leave, but he targeted her instead.

"Come on. You're bound to get yourself killed in here," he said gruffly.

Before she could object, which she fully intended to do, the wolf grabbed her arm and pulled her out of her seat.

"Hey! What do you think—"

"Saving your ass and keeping you out of jail."

Chairs started to fly. Two men unsheathed knives, and two others had their guns out.

All Hanna could think about was the story she could have written that would secure her a job!

"I'm an investigative reporter," she said, angry at the wolf for forcing her toward the door.

The guy looked skeptically down at her, which irritated her even more.

"Let me go!" she said.

Men were shouting above the piped-in mood music, making it sound surreal.

A chair flew at them, and the blond-haired wolf pulling her toward the exit threw his arm up and blocked it. The chair hit his arm and fell to the floor with a clatter.

"Are you okay?" Hanna asked. Even though he was a wolf and healed faster than a human, he could have broken his arm while trying to protect them.

"Yeah, I'm fine. I'll be bruised, but no problem."

As soon as they were outside, the cops pulled up in squad cars. Several got out of their cars and pointed guns at Hanna and the wolf.

"Get on the ground now!" one of the officers shouted.

"Great, just great. Instead of writing a news report about the fight, someone will be writing about me getting arrested!" Hanna couldn't believe what the guy had gotten her into. Though when she really thought about it, she knew the fight hadn't been his fault and he had been trying to rescue her.

Bryan "Phoenix" Wildhaven glanced at the woman lying on the pavement next to him. She was a red wolf like him—feisty, stubborn, bullheaded like he could be. Instead of being grateful that he had gone back inside to save her ass, she was pissed off at him. She was a tall, long-legged strawberry blond, with beautiful green eyes that had been watching him with interest when he had walked into the pub, looking away coyly after he'd caught her ogling him. And she hadn't even known he was a wolf like her at the time.

If he had just left her at the pub, he could have been well on his way to Silver Town without further incident. He'd been driving for so many hours that he'd just needed a break so he wouldn't fall asleep at the wheel. But she'd been a single woman, wasn't part of any of the groups of people causing trouble, and she was a wolf, so he had wanted to warn her to leave before she got hurt. When she had ignored him, he'd had to return and take matters into his own hands, which had irritated him. She didn't have the good sense to stay out of harm's way, and he couldn't believe a wolf would be that naive.

Now they were being handcuffed and put into a squad car until the police officers could sort things out, while the crisis inside the pub was escalating. Bikers were running out of the building. Police were taking them down. Except for rescuing the woman, Phoenix felt he should have just grabbed a soda from a convenience store and continued on his way to his sister's house.

"I'm Bryan Wildhaven, by the way, though everyone calls me Phoenix," he told the woman as they sat in the back of a squad car together. This was certainly his first time to be arrested, though he knew they would be released once the police had time to check them out. Well, at least he would. What if the she-wolf had had trouble with the law? That wouldn't be good.

"The phoenix rises from the ashes. All right. If I weren't tied up at the moment, I could shake your hand. Hanna Bridgeman, by the way."

Little Miss Hanna had tenacity; he would give her that. "So you knew the guys were going to have a fight in the pub, and you were there to report on it, if you didn't get yourself accidentally killed? Just because a bullet is meant for one target doesn't mean it won't hit another."

"And you know this from experience because you're military, or ex-military, right?" she asked, sounding a little sarcastic. So she didn't like guys in the military?

"Army Special Forces, Green Beret, retired."

"Figures. I wasn't at the pub expecting trouble. I would have had to be an undercover cop or FBI or something to know that." She gave him a sweet but fake smile. "When you dropped the note on my table, I thought it might have been your special way of trying to pick up a wolf."

"Hardly."

"I can't believe we left the pub, didn't cause any trouble, and aren't carrying weapons, but we got arrested. *You* must look suspicious," she said.

He cast her an evil smile. "So what were you here for?"

"A date, but he was a no-show."

"A wolf?" He couldn't imagine a wolf standing her up without good reason.

"Human. What were you doing here? And how did you know there was going to be trouble?"

"I'd been driving for several hours, and I was getting sleepy. So I stopped to get a soda and take a break."

"You're not from here?"

"No. I'm going to Silver Town to visit my sister and her new mate. As to how I knew about the trouble, I realized those were bikers from different gangs and there was bound to be difficulty between them. I smelled your scent when I walked past your table the first time and had to warn you. But you wouldn't heed the warning. So you're from Green Valley and work at the local paper?"

"Uh, no. Loveland, Colorado."

That didn't add up. "And you came all the way down here to get a story? Wouldn't the Green Valley news reporters do the story?"

There was something she wasn't saying.

"I told you. I didn't know the gang members were going to be in the pub."

A couple of gunshots went off inside the building. Both of them instinctively ducked.

Hell, he wished they were out of here now. More shots were fired, and then police were hauling bikers out of the pub with wrists zip-tied. They began loading people in a police van. Ambulances arrived to take injured bikers to the hospital. Then an officer opened the door to the squad car and helped Hanna and Phoenix out.

He questioned them about what had happened, removed their handcuffs, and inspected their IDs. Once he'd run a check on them, he said, "You're cleared. If you think of anything else, let us know."

Hanna rubbed her wrists. "What happened after we left the pub?" she asked the officer.

"Two of the gang members shot each other. Then others began shooting. Three were stabbed. We have to haul them all in for questioning to learn who was involved. Sorry about taking the two of you into custody. We didn't have time to do anything but try to get a handle on things."

"No problem," Phoenix said. "Are we free to go? I'm on my way to see my sister and brother-in-law in Silver Town."

"Yes, Mr. Wildhaven, you're free to go."

The police officer left to help gather evidence from the crime scene. Phoenix asked Hanna, "Are you going to be okay?"

"Yeah, I'm headed over to my hotel."

"Have you had dinner?"

"Uh, no. My hamburger hadn't arrived before all the trouble began."

"There's a place here that has great burgers. You have your own car, right?"

"Yeah."

"Okay, why don't I follow you to your hotel and take you to the restaurant so I don't lose you?"

She hesitated, then nodded. "All right."

They got into their cars and he followed her to the hotel. Once she parked, she climbed into his Corvette. "Beautiful car."

"It was a retirement gift for myself."

"It sure is nice."

"Thanks." He drove her to the hamburger place next. He hadn't planned to eat there, but now it was getting so late that he didn't want his twin sister and his brother-in-law to have to wait on him to eat. He called his sister on Bluetooth. "Hey, Carmela, don't hold up dinner for me. I'll explain when I get in, but it'll be another couple of hours before I get there."

"I hope nothing's wrong. No car trouble?"

"No, I'm good. I ran into a situation here in Green Valley, so I'm close. I'm just grabbing a burger and then I'll head out." He wasn't about to explain he was with a she-wolf, not while Hanna was in the car with him and listening in on the conversation.

"Okay, then we'll see you in a couple of hours."

They ended the call, and he pulled into the parking lot of the hamburger place.

"They have every kind of topping you can imagine," he said as they headed inside.

"Hmm, sounds good."

"They have wine and beer, too, if you wanted to try again at having a glass."

"And you?"

"I'm still headed to Silver Town after this, so I'll have another soda."

She glanced at the deck with its huge wood carving of Sasquatch holding a rope in his hand, attached to a woodcarving of a fish, and the orange lights draped across it and the building. They had all kinds of clay jack-o'-lanterns set in the windows. Inside, small cauldrons sat on each of the tables holding lit orange candles, and black cats decorated the whole restaurant.

The owner must have cats, he thought.

Hanna smiled at all the decorations. He had thought she might get a kick out of the nine-foot-tall Sasquatch. Plus, the food was great. The restaurant was farther from the main road that would take him to Silver Town than the pub was, which was why he'd dropped in there for a soda and not here.

"Were you going to have dinner with your family?" she asked.

"It's getting late. It would take me about forty-five minutes to drive to their place in Silver Town, and I don't want them to have to wait on me to have dinner." He opened the door to the hamburger place and stepped inside.

"Besides, you wanted to have a date with me," she quipped.

He smiled darkly at her. A she-wolf who wouldn't obey him when he was trying to be gallant and keep her safe wasn't a wolf he would seriously date.

So that begged the question—why was he having dinner with her?

CHAPTER 2

"This is the cutest place," Hanna said to Phoenix as she looked at the photos of black bears, brown bears, moose, wolves, elk, cougar, lynx, red fox, bison, and beavers in their natural habitats in Colorado, hanging on the warm, golden-oak-paneled walls. There were also pictures of black cats everywhere. "I love Halloween, so this is fun to see all the decorations."

She and Phoenix sat in a booth that featured a table and seats in the same warm oak as the paneled walls and a picture of two gray wolves howling. They didn't have anything like this in Loveland, and Hanna immediately felt her spirits lifted. Getting a good meal would help too.

"And the food is great," Phoenix said. "So are you dressing up for Halloween?"

"Always. I hand out candy to the kids, wearing something fun. A steampunk outfit this year. What about you?"

Smiling, he shook his head.

"Aww, come on. Don't tell me you don't have fun with the paranormal."

He chuckled. "We are the paranormal. That's good enough for me."

"What about when you were a kid?"

"Yeah, sure, but—"

"You're all grown up." And how.

Wearing gray, furry wolf ears, furry wristbands, and a tail, the waitress brought them each a menu and a glass of water and smiled. "Oh wow, a couple of reds. You're new to the area."

"Uh, yeah," Phoenix said, looking at the menu, but then he smiled at the waitress.

"Yes." Hanna knew the woman said *reds* and not *wolves* because everyone else here appeared to be human. The waitress, Carla, was a gray wolf. Hanna was surprised.

"Our leaders are a gray and a red," Carla said.

"Oh wow, really." Hanna smiled. Maybe it wouldn't be such a bad place to live after all. She wouldn't mind being part of a wolf pack, since they didn't have one in Loveland. "I'm going in for a job interview at the paper tomorrow." She hadn't meant for Phoenix to know anything about that or that she'd been fired from her other job. She shouldn't care, but she suspected he'd ask her more about being an investigative reporter and wanting to cover the story at the pub.

"Oh, great! I sure will be rooting for you. Maybe our leaders can put in a good word for you at the newspaper office."

"Wow, that would be super." Hanna told Carla her name and gave her cell-phone number to her.

"If the two of you have had a chance to look at the menu, what would you like to eat?" Carla asked.

"A soda and the Sasquatch Burger for sure." Phoenix handed his menu to her.

"Ohmigod, four pounds of hamburger and one pound of cheese?" Hanna looked incredulously at Phoenix. "For real?" The guy was muscular, but he wasn't bulky in the least. She couldn't imagine where he could pack all that protein away.

"Yeah, I worked up a healthy appetite tonight saving a red from out-of-control biker gangs."

Hanna rolled her eyes at him.

"Oh no, I can't believe they would come to Green Valley of all places," Carla said. "It's all over the news."

"Maybe that's why they did. Because they thought they could get away with it and no one would be able to react quickly enough," Hanna said, wishing she could have had the lead story.

"Ryan McKinley is our mayor, and he takes a personal interest in keeping the city free of crime. He's angry about it. He texted the pack members to ensure none of us had been there, and he's starting an investigation into the pub owner to see if he had anything to do with the biker gangs all appearing there at one time. Not that the pub owner was necessarily involved, but if he was, McKinley will deal with it."

"Wow, your leader is the mayor?" Hanna asked.

"Yeah, he also runs a private investigator business. So he really can check things out in a hurry," Carla said.

Hanna handed Carla her menu. "That's great."

"What would you like to order?"

"A glass of chardonnay and a blue cheese and mushroom burger." Hanna was glad she had come here for dinner instead of just eating the protein bar she'd packed in her bag.

"Okay, I'll have those right up." Carla gave them both a big smile and left.

A guy dressed as a Wookiee walked by them, nodding.

Hanna chuckled. "This is a much better place to have a glass of wine. And it's a lot of fun too. Thanks for recommending it and keeping me company for dinner."

Phoenix drank some of his water. "After what we experienced at the pub, I agree. When I hauled you out of there, you said you were an investigative reporter?"

"Well, a reporter for the paper in Loveland."

"But you're looking for a new job as an investigative reporter in Green Valley?" Phoenix asked.

"Yes."

"And you wanted the gang story to hand in to the editor to help you get the position?"

"That was the general idea."

"But then you were afraid you were going to be locked up by the police, and how would that look to a prospective employer?"

"That's the gist of it."

"Sorry about messing up your gig."

"No, you aren't."

Phoenix shook his head. "Your life is more important than an article for a paper. Believe me."

Changing the subject, Hanna said, "You told me you had retired from the army. Now what are you planning to do?"

"I'm checking out the pack in Silver Town, also run by a red wolf and a gray wolf. Lelandi Silver, the red wolf, is a cousin of mine, formerly with the last name Wildhaven. And, of course, my twin sister, Carmela, and her mate, Michael Hoffman, live there now. He is also special forces, retired. And so is Michael's brother, Daniel. He intends to retire there too. We were friends in the army."

"So you plan on settling in Silver Town?"

The waitress brought them their meals and a soda and glass of wine. "Silver Town is wolf-run, if you didn't know," Carla whispered to Hanna. "But we're trying to build up our pack here in Green Valley too."

"As in, turn it into another Silver Town...or so I've heard," Phoenix said.

Carla smiled. "We're working on it. We just need to get our people into all the key positions, running all the businesses, filling all the vacancies—as long as everyone who takes the jobs is fully qualified, of course."

"Sounds good." Hanna got the impression Carla was trying to sell her on Green Valley.

"I imagine you could get a job as a reporter in Silver Town, no problem, because of who runs the town," Phoenix said, "if things don't work out in Green Valley."

"Okay, so things could be looking up for me." Hanna had never realized two packs were out in this area of Colorado and certainly not that they would be able to help her get a job. She was so relieved.

"Without even having to report on biker shootings at a pub or anything that dangerous," Phoenix said.

"That was something," Carla said. "Were you really there during the fight?"

"Yeah, unfortunately," Phoenix said. "But we got out before the shooting started."

"That's good. I'm glad you weren't hurt. You're military, aren't you?" Carla asked.

Hanna frowned. It didn't matter that she wasn't with him on a date; she was still "with" the wolf, and she was ready to tell Carla to back off.

Phoenix smiled at Hanna, probably because she looked annoyed. "Yeah, retired special forces."

"Wow, cool. Then you were in good hands, Hanna."

Hanna smiled lamely at the two of them.

"Did you need anything else?"

"No, I'm good. Thanks, Carla," Hanna said.

"I'm good too," Phoenix said.

Then they began to eat their hamburgers. They were divine. When she wanted a burger, this was going to be the place to go if she ended up living here.

Once they finished their meals, Phoenix gave Hanna his cell number. "I've got to get on my way, but if I'm in the area and you ever need help or anything, give me a call."

"Like if I'm at another unscheduled motorcyclists' convention?"

"Hey, if you're going to be an investigative reporter, no telling the trouble you could get yourself into."

She chuckled. "So what? You're volunteering to be my bodyguard?"

"Something like that."

"Thanks for saving me tonight at the pub."

He paid the bill and she opened her mouth to object. She hadn't intended for him to pay for her meal.

"My treat. I invited you. Think of it as a first date, of sorts."

She scoffed. "I don't go out with military guys."

Her comment earned her a smile. "Bad experience?"

"Two."

He smiled again. "Okay, not a date. Just a…way to make up for you not getting the story to sell to an editor."

"Thanks then." She gave him her cell number as well. "Just in case you have a story you want to share with me that I can report on."

"I can guarantee you that won't happen."

They said goodbye to Carla, who told them to come back anytime, and left the restaurant. "What are you doing tonight?" Phoenix asked Hanna.

"I planned to see a movie about a woman with superpowers," Hanna said.

He pulled out his phone and scrolled through some pages. "That looks good. Do you want some company?"

She frowned. "Okay. But what about your sister and brother-in-law?"

"I'll send my sister a text telling her I have to keep a friend company and will be there after the movie ends. I can't think of anything worse than worrying about a job interview, staying in a hotel in a town you're unfamiliar with, and watching movies on TV. And then not being able to sleep because of worrying about the job interview."

"So you going with me to the theater will take the pressure off?"

"Yeah. It's a movie I was interested in seeing anyway, if you want the company."

"Are you sure?"

"Yeah. It's great when others have superpowers too."

"Your sister won't mind?"

"Are you kidding? She knows I'll be there after that, and I'm staying with them until I sort out what I'm going to do and where I'll be living. They'll be glad I'm not underfoot for too long."

He texted his sister and then drove Hanna to the theater.

She wouldn't call this a date per se, and she had the distinct impression that reporters weren't on his most favored list of people to get to know. But he was taking her to the movie, and he'd even bought her dinner. Things were looking up.

CHAPTER 3

"THAT WAS INTERESTING," PHOENIX SAID AS HE AND HANNA left the movie theater.

"You didn't like it." She didn't have to be a mind reader to know that. Because of their ultrasensitive wolf sense of smell, she could tell he had been annoyed with the woman in the movie—a reporter like her, who was following the lead on a story out of her assignment zone and got canned for even mentioning it to her editor. The woman ended up saving the world after learning about the trouble the world was headed for. See? Getting fired from a job was the best thing that had ever happened to the superhero *and* the world.

"It was all right," he said.

"But you didn't like it. Why not? I thought it was great. Because the woman got fired from her job, she saved the world."

As they climbed into his car, Phoenix smiled a little at Hanna as if he thought she was being silly for getting so into the movie, which annoyed her.

He drove her to the hotel, where she thanked him for taking her to the movie and buying her popcorn and a soda.

"You're welcome. I hope you have a good interview tomorrow and get the job."

"Yeah, me too. Thanks again." Hanna got out of his car, waved, and headed inside the lobby. Well, she didn't need to worry about getting interested in this guy who had been in the military. His obvious aversion to reporters was enough to make him *so* not her type.

She glanced back at the hotel's covered driveway and noticed he was still there, making sure she got in okay. That was nice of him. Finally, he drove off. She noticed a biker gang member take off from the parking lot headed in the same direction as Phoenix, and she saw another biker watching her. Hadn't the police arrested all of them?

As she walked into the hotel lobby, Hanna thought again about the job interview and sighed. She knew she'd have to tell the editor that she had been fired from her last job. She hoped he didn't hold it against her since she really wanted this job as an investigative reporter. She should have just found a different investigative-reporter job before she irked her former boss enough to fire her, though it was a little late for regrets. When she'd heard the police chief openly lying about money from the department that he had spent on home improvements—at his house—she couldn't help but call him on the carpet about it.

Hanna got on the hotel elevator and a man joined her—the gang member who had been sitting on his bike, watching her from the parking lot. He was dressed in a black leather jacket and pants and boots, his brown hair tied back in a tail and his beard well groomed. He eyed her with disdain, and she considered jumping off the elevator. His insignia indicated he was with the Hells Angels—a skull with wings on the helmet and *Hells Angels* written across the top of it.

"You called the cops on us," he said, his voice gruff and dark as the elevator door closed. She should have gotten off when she'd had a chance.

Her wolf instincts were dead-on, and she could smell his aggression, even though he seemed to be keeping his cool.

"If you're talking about the incident at the pub, I didn't call anyone."

"What about the guy you were with?"

"No. And if you didn't know, they stuck us in a squad car and questioned us too."

"But you aren't in jail. My brother is."

She wasn't the one who started the fight either. And she didn't have any warrants out for her arrest. She suspected some of the bikers armed with guns weren't supposed to be carrying them.

"Anyone in the pub might have called the police. The waitstaff, someone else who was there having a drink. It certainly wasn't me." She arrived at her floor and was ready to jump out. The door opened, and she put her hand out to stop it from closing, afraid he would react violently if she tried to bolt because he thought she had lied to him. Now she could have used a military guy as her boyfriend!

"You had your cell out."

Uh, yeah, recording the actions of the biker gangs. Hanna frowned. Despite still wanting to use the video recording in her interview, she supposed she should hand it over to the police so they got the culprits who actually started the fight.

"I was checking messages. Something that many of us do when we're waiting on someone to show up." She hoped he wouldn't realize she was lying. "This is my floor."

He grabbed her arm, and her first instinct was to turn into her wolf and tear into him. Of course there wasn't any way she could do that without stripping and shifting. And there wasn't any way she wanted to bite him and turn him.

"Let me go."

"You'd better not be lying. My friends and I will be watching you, and if we learn you've lied, you'll wish you hadn't." He released her, and she left the elevator, furious with the biker. He'd bruised her arm, not to mention threatened her! The elevator door shut, and she glanced back to see if the hallway was clear. Thankfully, it was. She'd been afraid he might follow her to her room. Wanting to make sure he didn't change his mind and come after her, Hanna raced down the hall, turned the corner, and ran to her room.

She used her key card to enter her room and then called the police.

"Hello, about the incident at the pub tonight? I have a video of some of what happened in the beginning, before my friend pulled me out of the place and he and I were falsely arrested."

"And you didn't tell us before now because?"

"I'm a reporter and I was going to use it for a story, but if it can help you get the right guys, I want to do my part."

"A reporter? That's a first."

Yeah. She sighed. So far, things weren't going well for her. And she wasn't sure Carla, the waitress, would call the pack leader to ask him if he could put in a good word for her at the newspaper office.

The investigative officer told her where to send the video. Hanna held her finger over the send button, sighed again, then pushed it. There went her story.

―――――

Phoenix should have known that as soon as he arrived at his sister's home in Silver Town, he'd find her waiting up for him, curious about who had delayed him.

"We thought you might have stayed overnight in Green Valley." Carmela gave him a warm embrace, her green eyes smiling. "What kept you so long?"

He was glad to see her, but sometimes having more privacy was welcome when it came to his love life. Phoenix hugged his sister back. He heard the shower going and figured Michael was getting ready for bed.

"She's a wolf." A wolf who was hiding something. He was wary of her, maybe because of the issues he'd had with reporters before—shoving mics in his face, wanting to know how his team members had died on a mission, how he felt about being the only one who had survived the missile attack.

"And?"

"I'm not staying with her because we're not courting." He explained to his sister how he had met her.

"Ohmigod, we heard all about that on the news. Of course, we thought of you since you were in Green Valley, but we had no idea you would have been in the midst of all the trouble. Why didn't you tell us you had been there? Forget it. I know why. You're special forces and you don't need anyone's help."

"Not that time anyway."

"We'll have to have her over to the house for lunch or dinner. What's her name?"

"Hanna Bridgeman, and no to having her to the house for lunch or dinner."

His sister's jaw dropped. "Okay, so things didn't work out. I'm sorry. Do you want to talk about it?"

"No."

Thankfully, Carmela changed the subject. "Well, I'm so glad you retired from the army and are here for good."

"Thanks. I'm glad I'm out of the rat race and can settle down."

"Right. Well, it's late and we were headed to bed when I heard your car pull up. We'll see you in the morning."

"Thanks, Sis." He hugged her again, and she walked to the master bedroom while he carried his bags to the guest room on the other side of the house.

He couldn't believe disliking a movie had rubbed Hanna the wrong way. Was there a deeper reason? Ever since he first saw her, he had been attracted to her, to her feistiness and yet vulnerability. Despite giving him grief, she had seemed relieved he'd wanted to take in the movie with her. She was a mystery, and he was intrigued with her. She was new to the area, no attachments, it appeared, and he was new to the area and wasn't seeing anyone. And they were both red wolves. It certainly wouldn't hurt to get to know her better.

He thought again about the reporter in the movie who had

been fired from her job. Phoenix frowned. Had Hanna been fired from her job—and it was personal? He pulled out his laptop and looked her up at the newspaper office in Loveland.

He wondered about the guys she'd dated before and why that had caused her to swear off military men.

He found the web page for her newspaper in Loveland, but she wasn't listed. He frowned. But when he searched for stories with her byline, he discovered she'd written tons of newspaper articles. None of them were investigative in nature. He found an article about her asking the police chief some pointed questions concerning spending department funds for his own home improvements.

Hell, she probably had been fired!

He smiled. She was a bit of a rogue. Like he was. He could imagine himself doing the same thing.

After giving the police her video, Hanna paced across the hotel room floor, unable to stop worrying that maybe one of the motorcyclists had followed Phoenix to his sister's house. Maybe he would be okay because he was retired military, but she needed to at least give him a heads-up. She tried calling his cell number, but it went to voicemail. Afraid he might be in trouble, she found the Green Valley pack leader's phone number, since he was the mayor. She didn't know the names of the pack leaders in Silver Town who would know Phoenix's sister.

"Hi, I know it's late and I'm not a member of your pack, but this is Hanna Bridgeman."

"You're calling about the job at the paper?" Ryan asked. "Carla left a message for me about you."

"Uh, no. Do you know Phoenix Wildhaven? He and I were at the pub tonight that was in the news—the one with the biker gangs causing a shoot-out. One of the gang members approached me at my hotel. He wanted to know if I had called the police, and when I said no, he asked if Phoenix had. I'm worried about another gang member who headed in the same direction as Phoenix on the road to Silver Town. I thought the man might follow Phoenix all the way to his sister's place. I wanted to warn Phoenix, but I haven't been able to reach him. I hoped you would have his sister's number."

"If one of those bikers knows where you're staying, he could be back. I'm sending someone over to pick you up right now. You'll stay with Carol, my mate, and me just to make sure you're safe. I sent word earlier to the newspaper that I was recommending you for the job they have posted. I'll get in touch with Carmela, and she can tell her brother about your concern."

"Thank you."

"Max Browning, one of the private investigators who works for me, will pick you up. He's a retired Navy SEAL so he can offer you good protection."

"Okay, thank you, Ryan. I'm in Room 411."

"I'll let him know. And I'm forwarding you his picture so you will know who he is."

She couldn't believe this was all happening, though she was glad that Ryan had a guy with some muscle picking her up and that the pack leader would make sure Phoenix knew the trouble he could be in. She packed her bags and hoped she wouldn't have any further trouble tonight.

———

Phoenix heard his sister's footfalls as she hurried toward the guest room, and he got out of bed to see what the matter was.

"Ryan McKinley called. He said Hanna, the woman you were with at the pub, was threatened by a biker gang member at her hotel."

Phoenix was already yanking on his jeans, ready to go into rescue mode and bring her there.

"Ryan said he's sending Max Browning, one of his PIs and a Navy SEAL, to pick her up, and he's taking her to Ryan and Carol's house. She'll be safe there. But Hanna worried that someone from the gang would follow you here. She said something about the gang member thinking you or she had called the police on them. Ryan said she couldn't get ahold of you." Carmela raised a brow.

"I was in the shower. A Navy SEAL is watching out for her? Hell."

Carmela frowned at him. "Are you sure there's not something more going on between the two of you?"

"No, and just so you know, she doesn't date military men."

Carmela smiled. "You never let that stop you before."

Phoenix ran his hands over his hair. "She's a reporter. Well, she *was* a reporter. She was fired from her job for questioning the police chief about some illegal money transactions."

Carmela frowned.

"*Fired*," he repeated, in case she hadn't heard that part.

"Not that you never questioned your former commander when you felt the situation was necessary."

"Not in front of the press."

Carmela raised a brow.

"Okay, so once."

She folded her arms and cocked her head, indicating she was waiting for him to fess up.

"Well, twice."

"And those are the two times you told me about. No doubt there were others. And your commander didn't fire you because you're good at your job, but someone else? Probably would have been court-martialed. Anyway, Ryan McKinley has it covered. And he said he told her he contacted the newspaper about the job she's interviewing for tomorrow. She—and he—just wanted to give you a heads-up if any gang members showed—"

They heard a couple of engines rumbling as two motorcycles drove into Carmela's driveway and parked.

"Speak of the devil. I'll wake Michael and call the sheriff. Don't answer the door until the cavalry arrives." Carmela hurried off down the hall to her bedroom.

Phoenix finished getting dressed. Hell, he never thought a gang member would go after Hanna at the hotel. He should have walked her to her room at the very least.

Michael was soon heading into the living room, shirt and shoes and a couple of Glocks in hand. He set the guns on the back of the couch and pulled on his T-shirt. "Hey, Phoenix, good to see you. This reminds me of some of our earlier days." When Carmela rejoined them, Michael kissed her and said, "Go back to our bedroom, honey. We'll take care of this."

"Don't the two of you dare do anything. Wait for the sheriff and his men to arrive!" Then Carmela headed back to the room.

Phoenix watched her and realized his sister had gained a bit of weight since the last time he had visited with them, six months ago. "Is she—?"

"Yeah, she is. Babies are due next year." Michael pulled on his boots.

"She never said anything to me about it."

"She miscarried after three months the first time, so she didn't want to say anything this time until she was more sure they'd be okay. She's five months along now."

Phoenix slapped Michael on the shoulder. "Congratulations, man. How many?"

"Twins. We're thrilled."

Someone banged on the door, as if telling the occupants they'd better open up or their callers would huff and puff and blow the house down. The problem was that the wolves were on the inside, and more of the pack would be arriving shortly.

Michael handed Phoenix one of the Glocks. "Let's do this."

Just as Michael was about to pull open the door and jump aside so Phoenix could confront them, the sheriff and a couple of deputies were running their sirens and headed straight for the house.

The next thing they knew, the motorcycles had taken off and were racing out of Silver Town.

"Well, now you see firsthand what a great pack this is," Michael said, and then he and Phoenix went out to meet the sheriff and deputies.

"Good to see you have finally come to stay," said Peter Jorgenson, Silver Town's sheriff, shaking Phoenix's hand.

"Yeah, I'm glad to be here." But all Phoenix could think about was the she-wolf in Green Valley who'd had to face a gang member all on her own when he should have protected her.

CHAPTER 4

AT THE MCKINLEYS' HOME, HANNA HAD JUST SHOWERED AND thrown on a long, purple T-shirt featuring a black cat sitting in a pumpkin. She was climbing into bed when she got a call. She grabbed her phone from the bedside table and saw the call was from Phoenix. Worried about him, she said, "Hello, are you okay?"

"Hell, I was worried about *you*."

She smiled. "I'm fine. I'm staying with the Green Valley pack leaders while I am here to do the interview. Did you have any trouble with the bikers?"

"They were just here. Good thing you called us about them. The gang must have had someone follow me to my sister's house in Silver Town, then wait until another biker joined him to provide more muscle. They both drove up into the driveway. But our sheriff's department was here in no time to back us up."

"Oh good. I tried calling you."

"I was in the shower. I got your message after the fact. I'm sorry. I should have walked you up to your hotel room."

"It wasn't necessary. At least I didn't think it would—" Suddenly, the door to her bedroom opened. Hanna eyed it warily, then saw Carol's tabby, Puss, saunter into the room and jump onto the bed. She laughed and started petting the cat.

"Is everything all right?"

"Yeah, Carol's cat, Puss, decided to come join me in bed."

He chuckled. "Well, I'll let you go then. Tell me how the job interview goes."

"I will. Thanks."

They ended the call. A few minutes later, he called her back, surprising her. "Do you want to have breakfast with me before you have your interview?"

She closed her gaping mouth. She figured she would be having breakfast with Carol and Ryan in the morning. So why did she tell Phoenix sure?

"Okay, I'll meet you at the Waffle Makers on First Street. My treat. They have all kinds of different food if you don't like waffles—omelets, sausages, hash browns. All kinds of breakfast foods."

"My interview is at ten. So at nine?" She was stroking Puss, who was happily purring, her little motor rumbling under her supersoft fur.

"Yeah. I'll meet you there then."

"Night."

They ended the call and she set her phone on the bedside table, smiled, and closed her eyes. Maybe she could give another military man a chance.

———

Phoenix rested his head on his hands on his pillow as he thought about dating—really dating—the she-wolf. Hell, Hanna was a reporter! And reckless! But damn if she didn't fascinate him on several different levels. What if the Navy SEAL Ryan had sent to pick her up at the hotel and take her to the pack leaders' home had already caught her attention?

He closed his eyes, determined not to borrow trouble. Before long, it was time to get up and tell his sister and brother-in-law he was having breakfast with the woman he told his sister he wasn't interested in getting to know. He knew she had figured differently. Carmela always seemed to know him better than he knew himself.

"Hey," he said to his sister as he walked into the kitchen and gave her a hug. "Congratulations on the twins."

"Thanks! We're excited."

"I'm going to get breakfast in Green Valley."

Carmela laughed. "But you're sure you don't want to invite Hanna home for lunch or dinner?"

"Lunch is okay. Let me ask her. We're having breakfast together, and then she's having her interview. After that, I'll bring her home for lunch if she would like it. She may need to return to Loveland to take care of business."

"Does she have family?"

He tilted his chin down and looked at his sister with exasperation. He had no idea. He and Hanna hadn't spent time with each other as if they were really getting to know each other. But now he did want to know about her.

"Oh, right, you aren't dating her."

Michael came in to get some coffee. "Give him a break, Carmela."

Phoenix chuckled. He was going to like having his brother-in-law in his corner.

"Remember who you're sleeping with," Carmela said, giving Michael a kiss and then starting to scramble some eggs.

"Okay, I'm off. I'll check in with you later, one way or another," Phoenix said.

Carmela seasoned the eggs with lemon and pepper spices. "Ask her what she likes or doesn't like to eat."

"Right. See you both later." Phoenix drove off to Green Valley, hoping Hanna got the job there. Though if she ended up in Silver Town, that would be good too.

What he hadn't expected was to see Max Browning with Hanna at the Waffle Makers restaurant, and he realized his mistake. Phoenix should have told her he was picking her up at the pack leaders' house and brought her to the restaurant. Though he had assumed she would drive herself. He was ready to go tell the retired Navy SEAL to take a hike.

Phoenix went inside, and Max smiled at him as he approached the table. "I'm here, per Ryan's orders, to watch out for Hanna, but if you're going to be with her until she has her interview—"

"I am. You can leave. Thanks for watching out for her." Phoenix was more abrupt than he had meant to be.

"If you want to stay and have breakfast with us, Max—" Hanna said, giving Phoenix a look that said he was being way too wolfishly possessive.

"I'm sure he's got important PI business to conduct." Phoenix lifted a brow at Max, signaling him to go and he would take care of matters.

Max smiled at him. "I want to wish you well on your interview, Hanna. I do have some urgent business to take care of. Otherwise, I would stay and have breakfast with you." He glanced at Phoenix as if to tell him the Green Beret wasn't chasing off the SEAL.

"Thanks so much, Max, for watching over me."

"My pleasure." Max said goodbye to both of them and then left the restaurant.

Hanna glanced at the menu. "You could have been nicer to him and let him stay to have breakfast with us."

"I *was* being nice. I didn't want us to keep him from his urgent business and stress him out."

Hanna laughed.

He smiled, glad she wasn't annoyed with him for sending the SEAL away.

They both ordered blueberry waffles and blueberry syrup.

"So why don't you like reporters?" She drank some of her coffee and then took a bite of her waffle.

"Who said I don't like reporters?"

"Oh, I don't know if you realize this about me or not"—she leaned across the table and spoke low for his ears only—"but I'm a wolf."

He laughed. "Okay, so you sensed it. Honestly, I want you to have every success in your field of endeavor."

"What happened to you that makes you not like reporters?" She was tenacious and not dropping the issue. She might just make a good investigative reporter.

"On one of our missions, all the members of my team died except me. It was bad enough that I had to deal with inquiries from all over from military officials about how I managed to survive, but reporters had a field day with me. After it happened, I was numb. I couldn't get over what had occurred. I couldn't believe my buddies were all gone. I'd been injured, too, but once I had recovered, I kept wondering why I had lived when they had died. For months, reporters hounded me. You can see why I'm not that fond of them."

"Oh, I'm so sorry. That must have been horrible for you."

"It was. What about you and military guys?"

"Not as devastating as your story. The first guy had a secret wife and was seeing me when he went to training in Colorado. His wife was in Florida."

"A wolf?" He didn't think she would be shook up about a human she'd been seeing, but he was surprised the cheater had been a wolf.

"Yeah. Unreal, right? We mate for life."

"Very few of us are like that. Most of us believe in the wolves' ways." He drank some of his coffee. "What about the other guy?" He cut into his waffle and took a bite. "What was his problem?"

"Oh wow, well, he acted so into me whenever he returned from an overseas assignment, and we weren't supposed to be seeing others while we were dating. We had an agreement. If we decided to move on, we would. I kept my part of the agreement. He didn't."

"So you think all military men are cads."

She smiled. "I'm beginning to think I might give one more guy a chance, if I find one who—"

"Wants to date you? Hell, put me on the list before any other military guy gets there."

She smiled brightly. "I don't know any other military guys—"

"Max."

"Oh. Him. Yeah, well, if you hadn't saved me from the motorcycle gangs fighting at the pub, he might have been on my list."

"I knew I had done something right when I went back inside to drag you out, no matter how pissed off you were at me. So I'll be waiting for you at the newspaper office, and my sister wants us to have lunch with her and Michael later. If you're agreeable, I'll let her know."

"Yeah, I would like that. I, um, need to tell you that I was fired from my last job for going against my boss's instructions."

"I got lucky with my boss. If I hadn't been so good at my job, I would have been fired any number of times."

She chuckled. "I doubt that."

"Oh hell yeah. I'm a bit of a rogue wolf."

"Like me."

"Yeah, that's exactly what I was thinking." He glanced at the clock. "Are you ready for your job interview?"

She let out her breath. "Yeah." She was going to pay for their breakfast, but he did. "Thanks."

"Is there anything you would like or don't like to eat at my sister's house?"

"No, anything is fine."

"Are you nervous?" he asked.

"Yeah. They always say to have a job to get a job, and being fired from a job isn't the same as leaving it. I have to be honest with the editor, though."

"I agree. You wouldn't want that to backfire on you." He walked her out to his car. "I guess Max brought you here and didn't follow you from the pack leaders' home."

"Right."

Phoenix drove her over to the newspaper office, and she took a deep breath before they went inside. He sat in the lobby while she went to the receptionist, spoke with her, turned and gave Phoenix a small, worried smile, then headed to an office.

Phoenix texted his sister: We're on for lunch. Noon?

Carmela texted: Sure. What would she like to eat?

Phoenix: Anything is good with her.

Carmela: Okay, see you then.

Phoenix figured he would show Hanna around Silver Town and check with the newspaper office there if she didn't get the job at the Green Valley newspaper. He watched the door to the office, hoping she did well with the interview, and he swore he felt as nervous for her as she had been.

———

Hanna shared her résumé with the editor, who frowned at her work. She didn't have a good feeling about this, even though the mayor had spoken on her behalf with the editor.

"I have to tell you that I was—"

"Fired from your last position? We're a newspaper office, Ms. Bridgeman. We are all about the news." He didn't smile, and she figured this wasn't going anywhere.

"Yeah, I saw where the police chief is under a lot of scrutiny now. Maybe they'll make him pay for his crime," she said, hoping the editor would realize she was right.

"I have to be honest with you. I have three other candidates applying for the job," he said.

Oh, naturally. Why hadn't she realized she wouldn't be the only one?

"Two have worked as investigative reporters for a few years with larger newspaper offices. They wanted a slower-paced town like this one to relocate to... Families, you know." He flipped through her résumé, as if he was really seriously looking over all her journalistic awards and other credentials. "You don't have any investigative experience."

"I'm a quick learner."

The editor smiled.

Okay, just end the interview already. There wasn't any sense in prolonging the inevitable.

"I have another interviewee in just a few minutes."

"Of course. Thanks so much for your time." She rose from her seat and shook his hand, smiling graciously.

"If you don't get this job…"

As if she would—

"Don't give up on your dreams, Ms. Bridgeman."

"Thanks, I won't." When she left his office, she saw Phoenix seated in the reception area, but he immediately rose to his feet. She didn't smile. She couldn't help but be disappointed. A rejection was a rejection. Then she thought of Silver Town. There, she might get a fair shake because it was wolf-run.

"Hey," Phoenix said and drew her into his arms.

"Sorry." She wiped away a tear, damn it. She hadn't wanted to fall apart in front of him just because she didn't get the job.

"Max told Ryan I'd brought you here, and Ryan knew you were in the interview, so he called me."

"Yeah, well, now I have to tell him I'll have to try in Silver Town. Ryan and Carol really want me to stay in Green Valley."

"That's what he called about. He said if the editor didn't hire you, he would."

Hanna stared up at Phoenix. "Doing what?"

"Communications staff. He learned the mayor in Knoxville was hiring newspaper veterans to be his communications staff, and Ryan thought it would be a great idea. He didn't want to mention it to you unless you didn't get the job because he knew how much your heart was set on being an investigative reporter. And the icing on the cake?"

"Yeah?"

"He wants you to help him with his PI agency—doing some

investigative work. You'll have to get some additional training for that, but what do you think? A communications officer for the mayor's office and a PI so you can do some investigating to really help him out?"

"Ohmigod, yes." She threw her arms around Phoenix and kissed him as if *he* had hired her and put her out of her misery.

He kissed her back, but it was much more of a heated and passionate kiss between wolves than a glad-you-feel-better kiss. And she was really beginning to warm up to the idea of dating the Green Beret and taking the chance that he wouldn't be anything like the last two military wolves she'd dated.

"We're supposed to go to the mayor's office next, if you liked the idea of working for him. I think he was afraid Silver Town would hire you in a heartbeat, when he's trying to increase the wolf population in Green Valley."

Hanna smiled. "Let's go see him, shall we?" She was thrilled. And she was glad Ryan had called Phoenix to have him give her the news so she wouldn't feel bad if she didn't get this job.

When they arrived at the mayor's office, Ryan ushered them right in, even though Phoenix didn't need to be with Hanna to learn about the job. But Ryan said, "I can offer you a job too, Phoenix."

Phoenix raised his brows.

"If you're looking to join our pack. I know your sister is in Silver Town and you might want to get a job there, but we are really trying to expand our pack and our influence over the town. If you want to work here, we would be delighted."

"What's the job I would be doing?" Phoenix asked.

"Private investigator, communications, anything you could do that would help the pack."

"Okay, sure. I'm interested." Phoenix glanced at Hanna as if telling her he was sticking around, so they could do some things together.

"As for you, Hanna, if you want to be one of my communications officers and work on getting your PI license and do investigative work, I would be glad to help you out."

She smiled. "Yes, thanks so much. I would love it."

"You can stay with us until you can find a place to live. Phoenix, you too. We have plenty of room for guests."

Hanna thought Phoenix might want to stay with his sister and brother-in-law since they were family.

But he just nodded. "That'll be great. Then I won't have to commute."

She couldn't believe it.

"We have a fall festival going on tonight, if the two of you would like to join us. Hayrides, cornfield maze, pumpkin patch, face painting, costumes, food, and fun," Ryan said.

Hanna smiled. "I would love to go."

"It has been set up on the acreage behind the house. And we have plenty of woods to run in as wolves, so you're welcome to strip and shift and run at any time."

"All right." Hanna thought this was just what she'd needed. A real change of pace. She hoped she would do a good job for Ryan.

"Sounds good to me. I'm going to show Hanna around Silver Town, and we're having lunch with my sister and her mate. After that, we'll come back here," Phoenix said.

Ryan shook his head. "Don't convince her to stay there."

Phoenix smiled. "No problem. I think she's looking forward to her job here, and I wasn't sure what I wanted to do so this works for me. We'll get out of your hair then."

"Thanks to both of you for joining our pack." Ryan rose and shook their hands. "We'll see you when you return. Feel free to pick any guest room to stay in at our house when you arrive, Phoenix."

"We'll be there," Phoenix said.

"I'll need to pack up my things and move them," Hanna said, not wanting to delay getting moved. Her apartment lease was coming up for renewal, and she needed to clean out her place.

"You can have all the time in the world to get moved. We can help you."

"I can help you too," Phoenix said. "Being in the military, I have moving down to an art."

She smiled. "I don't. So thanks."

CHAPTER 5

"I can't believe Ryan hired both of us at the same time," Hanna said as Phoenix drove her around Silver Town to see the sights in the downtown area and then took her out to the ski resort.

"I do. My sister, Carmela, had told me Ryan was checking out the Silver Town pack to see how he could make Green Valley more like it, more wolf-run. Silver Town had the advantage of being built by wolves from the ground up, and they didn't let others settle in their town unless they were wolves. Ryan took over the pack in Green Valley and has been trying to change things ever since."

"That's great. We need more wolf-run towns. I love Silver Town. I love all the wood carvings of wolves at the entrances to several of the establishments. And that old ghostly Victorian inn is pretty neat. Too bad somebody hasn't renovated it."

"I agree. Do you ski?" Phoenix drove her to his sister's house.

"I do. So the resort will be close enough to Green Valley to go skiing. What about you?"

"Yeah. That's another reason I liked the idea of moving into the area. By the way, my sister's going to think there is more going on between us than there is, so ignore her if she makes any mention of it."

Hanna sighed. "Here I thought you took the job in Green Valley and are staying with me at the pack leaders' house because there *is* more between us."

He chuckled, but he didn't agree or disagree with her. He needed a job. He got a job. What more could he ask for? Dating the she-wolf? Once he had met her, that was inevitable, despite all his denials to the contrary. He couldn't imagine dating a shy, retiring wolf. If he had any say in it, Hanna was not dating Max, the Navy SEAL.

She smiled as if she knew just what he was thinking.

When they finally arrived at the house, Carmela welcomed Hanna as if she were her long-lost sister. "I'm so glad to meet you. I was worried about what happened to you and Phoenix last night at the pub. I'm relieved he was there for you."

Hanna sighed. "I had hoped to get a news story out of it."

"Oh, sure. If I was in your line of business, I would too. How did the job interview go? If you didn't get the job, I was going to contact our own editor and see if he needs an investigative reporter," Carmela said as she set plates of spaghetti on the table and Michael brought them glasses of water.

"Thanks so much, Carmela. In truth, I didn't get the job, but Ryan McKinley gave me one instead. I'm really looking forward to working for him. And he gave Phoenix a job too."

Her mouth agape, Carmela abruptly shifted her gaze to Phoenix. He smiled, knowing just what she was thinking. He'd taken the job to be with Hanna.

"Ryan wants to expand his pack," Phoenix said.

"Well, I'm glad about it. We were going to ask the Silvers what kind of jobs they had that you could do, but that works too. You'll be close by anyway." Carmela set a platter of garlic toast on the table.

"And we're staying with the McKinleys while we find a place, um, places to live," Hanna said.

Carmela smiled brightly and brought over a bowl of salad while Phoenix poured them glasses of tea. Then they all sat down to eat.

Michael finally said, "That sounds like a really good deal."

Phoenix knew they would have been happy to have him stay with them, but he was eager to start on a new job and get settled in, especially with his sister expecting twins.

"So where are you from?" Carmela asked, and Phoenix knew poor Hanna would get the third degree.

"Fresno, California, but my parents and my sister and I moved to Loveland, Colorado, when I was three. My dad is still in charge of the post office there. My twin sister, Susan, runs a day care. She loves it in Loveland and doesn't plan to move. My parents are the same way. There are no wolf packs in Loveland, so I'm excited about joining the Green Valley pack."

"It would be a good pack to join," Carmela said. "You must be a royal."

"Yeah. I take it you are too."

"Yeah, we were all in the military, no time to take off for shifting when we didn't want it to happen," Phoenix said.

"Oh, I bet. Same with me as a reporter. The meal is delicious," Hanna said.

"Thanks. I figured I would make it because it's both Michael and Phoenix's favorite dish," Carmela said. "I'm glad you like it too."

"Well, we're really glad you both got jobs," Michael said as they finished up their meal.

"We are too," Hanna said. "We're going to the fall festival that the pack leaders, Ryan and Carol, are putting on for their wolves. Do you want to go with us?"

"Oh, I would love to, but the cooler fall weather and nausea from the pregnancy are keeping me from doing a lot of extracurricular activities right now," Carmela said.

"How wonderful. Do you know how many? Their sex?"

"Twins, but we don't know the sex yet. I think Michael is sitting on pins and needles more about it than I am."

Michael and Phoenix chuckled.

"When are they due?"

"February next year."

Hanna smiled. "Congratulations to both of you."

"Thanks," Michael and Carmela said.

They cleaned up after lunch, and Phoenix repacked his bags

in the guest room where he was staying. He couldn't believe he would take Hanna to a job interview and end up with a job of his own and a new pack to join.

Before he left, he gave his sister a hug and shook Michael's hand, then gave him a warm embrace. Carmela hugged Hanna, too, and she looked like she appreciated it.

Then Phoenix and Hanna drove back to Ryan and Carol's house in Green Valley. "Are all your things out of the hotel and at Ryan and Carol's place?" Phoenix asked.

"Yeah. I checked out completely." Hanna frowned. "I wonder who called the cops on the motorcycle gangs at the pub. And why they thought we had something to do with it."

"I phoned them."

"What? You never mentioned it to me when we got arrested. I told the biker you hadn't notified the police."

"Anyone at the pub could have called the police." Phoenix let out his breath. "So you're irked that you didn't tell the gang member the truth?"

"Of course not. I thought that *was* the truth. I wouldn't have said you had, if I had known. You could have told me that you called them, though."

"You had your phone in your hand when I pulled you out of there. I thought you had called the police and that's why the biker came after you and me, because I had been with you. Wait, you were recording the fight, weren't you?"

"I'm sure several people were."

He passed another car on the road to Green Valley. "And you're irritated with me for calling the police. What if one of the gang members had seen you documenting their illegal activities? And captured their faces in the event the police had warrants out for their arrest?"

"I had to get my facts straight."

"And you didn't turn it in to the police when they questioned us."

"No. I did later, though."

"And?"

This time, she let her breath out in exasperation. "They were grateful."

"What did they say about the delay in turning it over to them?"

"I told them why I had and they understood. You know, if you're going to date me, you're going to have to get used to being with a—"

She hesitated to say anything further, and he figured she remembered being a reporter was no longer her job.

"Well, you're just lucky I'm not," she said.

He smiled. "Sorry." He didn't comment any further about her taking the video.

She smiled. "Okay, now that's been said and done, I like your sister and her mate. That was fun. And I can't wait to go to the fall festival."

"With me." He wanted her to be with him. Yeah, he'd done about a one-eighty from the first time he met her, but she was the kind of woman who made things exciting for him. He'd been waiting a long time for someone like her who could keep him on his toes.

She chuckled. "Yeah. With you."

"Maybe we could get a place to rent together so we won't be on top of Carol and Ryan at their place," Phoenix said. "I mean, when we feel we like our jobs well enough and plan to stay."

She glanced at him. "You're moving awfully fast."

"I've waited a very long time to meet a she-wolf like you. You're the one I never saw coming."

She smiled. "Thanks, Phoenix. I guess you saw me ogling you at the pub when you first arrived."

"I did."

"So tell me, why do you have the name Phoenix?"

"Uh, that. When I was on a mission, a bomb hit a building we were checking out, and when it did, the place exploded in flames. Everyone but me had made it out, and when I finally managed to get to my feet and exit—luckily—I got the nickname Phoenix, for rising from the ashes."

"Wow. Okay, I truly need you by my side if I have any trouble with bikers or anyone else. Let's see about the rental after we've been at the jobs for a while. I feel like we don't want to overstay our welcome."

"Yeah, I agree."

They arrived at the pack leaders' house, and she helped him move his bags in.

It was brisk outside, and they pulled on their jackets and were ready to have fun at the festival.

"What do you want to do first?" he asked.

She looked like she was excited about this, her gaze glancing around at the pumpkin patch, the sign for the cornfield maze, the booths of food, the bobbing for apples, craft booths, and a bounce house for the kids. She grabbed his hand and hurried him to the maze. "I have never been in a cornfield maze before."

He laughed. "Then the maze it is."

"Bobbing for apples after that."

He smiled. "I want the apple with the longest stem."

"You're a Green Beret. You can have the shortest one."

Then she was pulling him through the maze at a run.

"We'd better slow down or we'll find our way out of it too quickly."

"The sooner we're out of here, the sooner we'll get to bobbing for apples."

He had to admit he was having fun with her and felt more light-hearted, like when he'd been a kid on an adventure. He was having nothing but pure fun with a she-wolf, and he felt he was making memories with one who might one day be his mate. He pulled her to a stop and kissed her.

Hanna couldn't believe she was kissing such a rare, mythical bird as Phoenix again. He was cupping her face and kissing her mouth in a way that was both precious and memorable, and it made her think that perhaps moving into a shared apartment sooner rather than later would be something they would have to do.

She was giving the kiss her all just as passionately. Well, maybe she pushed for more, making sure that he knew she was all in when it came to showing him some intimacy. They heard voices of people coming toward them in the maze. She pulled her mouth away from his and kissed his cheek, then took off running with him, her hand in his.

Phoenix smiled at her. "I think we're going to have to get our own place very soon."

"Oh yeah, I believe so too." The way their pheromones had jumped in to tell them just how much they were interested in each other was a clear sign of their deeper attraction.

While they were racing through the maze, they ran into several dead ends, entered another path, turned a corner, and found yet again a dead end. Others behind them somewhere in the maze were laughing at their own folly. If others had found the right path and stayed on it, they all could have gotten right out of there just by following the first wolves' scent. But everyone was having as much trouble making their way out of the maze, and Hanna loved it.

"This is so much fun."

"Yeah, I don't think I've had this much fun in a good long while." Phoenix seemed to be enjoying this as much as she was, which was important to her.

No stick-in-the-mud wolves for her.

When they finally found the exit to the maze, she hugged and kissed him. "Yes! We made it."

He laughed and kissed her back. It was chilly out, though they were wearing jackets, but she was full of energy, and he was warming her right up. "Bobbing for apples next." She took his hand and led him to the activity's station.

He let her go first, and she tried and tried and finally got hold of an apple and pulled it out of the water. When he tried, he had to struggle to get his apple out of the tub for much longer than she had. Hanna was glad that she outdid the special forces guy, and then they were off to ride the horse-drawn hay wagon that took them all over the property while they sipped hot apple cider and were covered in a pretty green-and-black-plaid blanket. She snuggled up next to him, his arm wrapped around her shoulders.

"I'm glad I went to the pub," she said.

"Because it led to a job."

"Because I met you."

He smiled. "Yeah, you know I had thought of just stopping to get gas and grabbing an energy drink there, but I saw the pub and something just drew me in."

"Me?"

He laughed. "I couldn't help but notice you sitting there all alone, looking like you needed some company, but then I saw the bikers, learned you were a wolf, and things worked out differently than I had planned."

They ended the ride, and he asked her what she wanted to do next.

"We should have worn costumes. But I didn't bring mine with me," she said as she looked at participants dressed as everything from superheroes to cats, witches, elves, and warlocks.

"Yeah, I don't have one either yet. So what's next?"

"They have guided trail tours. Since I've never seen the property, I'd love to do that. How about you?" she asked.

"Sounds like a great idea. And then we'll know where to run."

"Oh, and they're having a howling contest. I want to do that too." She saw little kids making wolf masks on paper plates, with others face painting or striking at a wolf piñata.

They took the walk on the hiking trails hand in hand, which was fun, the trail lined with battery-operated candles in orange sacks, while their tour guide gave them a nature talk about how long the property had been owned by the wolves and how they had expanded the acreage to allow for their pack members to run.

Hanna loved the river and all the forested land. "We can come here and run later tonight."

"Yeah. That would be good. After we have apple cider, turkey legs, and pumpkin pie, or whatever else appeals to us, we'll have to work some of those calories off."

They headed back to the main activity area and watched a man dressed in a skeleton outfit being dunked.

"Have you got a good arm?" she asked Phoenix.

"Yeah, the rest of me is good too."

She chuckled. "Go win something for me."

"You got it." He started throwing the ball at the target and knocked the skeleton into the water.

"Betcha can't do that again," the skeleton taunted.

Phoenix smiled and threw another ball. He hit the target and sent the skeleton into the dunk tank again.

Hanna clapped her hands. "Yes! I want the big stuffed wolf."

"Ten shots without missing," he warned.

"I'll go home with you tonight if you get it for me."

He chuckled since they were staying at the pack leaders' home together already. He threw the next ball and sent the skeleton dropping into the water.

"You can't make the next one," the skeleton said, climbing back out of the water.

Phoenix threw the next four balls and dropped the skeleton every time.

"Okay, give someone else a chance," the skeleton said. "Sheesh."

Phoenix smiled and threw another ball. A crowd was gathering to watch now and cheered when he dunked the skeleton an eighth time.

Ryan joined them and folded his arms and smiled. "Next time we choose teams for baseball, you're on mine."

Phoenix laughed. Two more times, he hit the target and won the prize for Hanna.

"My hero." She hugged and kissed him and then took her stuffed wolf in a hug. It was four feet long and she loved it. The wolf toy would make it an even more memorable night.

Everyone clapped, and the skeleton said, "Anyone else? You there, Robin of the Hood. Why don't you try?"

Robin Hood looked like he was about five. The skeleton must have needed a break from being dunked in the water.

Phoenix and Hanna grabbed some turkey legs and wandered around. They saw the ladies and their handmade quilts and the maple-syrup booth where pack members were demonstrating how to produce syrup from the maple trees. They watched a man doing hand-tooled leatherwork and a woman carving small animals, predominantly wolves, from wood. Another man was carving animals from soapstone.

Others were carving pumpkins, and Hanna and Phoenix had to try that. He carved a phoenix flying. She carved a bear, to do something different. They carried their pumpkins to the McKinleys' deck and set them there to decorate it. Afterward, they stopped by a booth for sugary pecans, bottled water, and pumpkin pie. Hanna had thought of leaving her stuffed wolf on the deck, but she didn't want it to wander off, and she was enjoying cuddling it. Though while she ate her treats, Phoenix was good enough to tuck Wild Thing under his arm so she could have her hands free.

They finally sat by the bonfire where a man was telling ghost stories.

"This is the best." She had her wolf on her lap, and she was snuggled up to Phoenix.

"Yeah, I agree, but it wouldn't be this much fun without you." He leaned down and kissed her cheek.

Hanna should have known that it was all too perfect and trouble would turn up.

Some of the pack members had motorcycles, so Hanna really hadn't paid attention to the sound of additional motorcycle engines rumbling out in front of Carol and Ryan's house and cutting out.

Soon, they saw that six members of the Hells Angels had come to their pack fall festival. Only the wolves were allowed to be there. Their wolf-pack parties weren't open to the general public. Hanna worried the reason the members of the biker gang were there was because of her, and maybe Phoenix too.

Sure enough, the men began walking through the activities, looking like they owned the place, and headed straight for the bonfire where Phoenix and Hanna were sitting.

Phoenix was on his feet in an instant.

She was worried, but she needn't have been. Women and children had suddenly slipped away like wolves in the woods seeking safety, all but her. She was sticking by Phoenix. If she had brought the trouble here, she didn't want to lead any of these men to the women and children.

Ryan and several armed men in the pack headed to the bonfire to speak with the gang members. "This is a private party," Ryan said, his voice razor sharp. "You're trespassing on private property."

"I want to talk to that woman and her boyfriend," one biker said, pointing at Hanna and Phoenix.

Phoenix moved forward to confront the biker. "You've already spoken to her, threatening her. We have security video of it. We know who you are—your background, your brother's, and the reason he's in jail—and you and your gang are under surveillance at all times while in Green Valley."

She loved that Phoenix would be a PI and could do that kind

of work, even though he hadn't been involved in it yet. She knew Ryan would have had his men on the case from the moment she'd called about the trouble.

The man looked like he wanted to kill Phoenix right then and there. But one of the men slapped him on the shoulder. "Come on. We can't afford to end up like your brother."

The blond was still staring Phoenix down as if he hated to give up the confrontation, like one alpha wolf to another. But Phoenix wasn't backing down, and more of the male wolf-pack members showed up with guns to emphasize the point that they had the firepower to end this confrontation in their favor.

"Come on," the other man said to the blond again. "Anyone could have called the police on us. And your brother knew what would happen this time if he got caught."

The blond scowled at Phoenix and Hanna. Then he growled, turned on his booted heel, and left with the other men. Ryan's men followed them to ensure they left the property peacefully.

The party resumed after that, and Ryan said to Phoenix and Hanna, "I'm glad you told them the PIs have been investigating everything there is about those men. Rest assured, the sheriff is just waiting for any excuse to throw them back in jail. None of this group are innocent, and we don't want them harassing anyone, wolf or otherwise, in Green Valley."

"Thanks," Hanna said. "I was worried they might have been after me because I turned over the video to the police that showed who started the fight."

Ryan smiled. "You two will fit right in."

CHAPTER 6

WITH THE FULL MOON SHINING BRIGHTLY IN THE NIGHT SKY, orange lanterns lighting all the paths and trails, a couple of wolves getting a start on being wolves by howling in the woods, a band playing in the background, and the man telling stories as Phoenix warmed Hanna up at the bonfire, this couldn't be more perfect. Not to mention he'd really lucked out when he'd managed to knock the skeleton into the tank ten times in a row without a miss to win Hanna her stuffed wolf. He knew he'd made her night.

Hanna made his. He hadn't done anything like this since he was a kid, and certainly not with a she-wolf wrapped in his arms. He couldn't think of a more special way to spend the night with her in Green Valley.

He was glad that they had Ryan for a pack leader and the whole pack to back them if they had trouble with motorcycle gangs or anyone else who might cause trouble for them in the future.

"Hey, are you ready to run as a wolf?" Things would be winding down soon, and he really wanted to run as a wolf with her before it got to be too late. He realized they hadn't even talked to Ryan about when they would start work.

"Oh yeah, I'm ready," she said.

He stood and helped her up, then they walked to the house and she dropped off her stuffed wolf in her guest room.

"You're staying with me, aren't you?" she asked.

"Yeah, sure." Hell yeah.

He began stripping off his clothes, and she was doing the same. They were eyeing each other with small, appreciative smiles. Then she shifted, and she was a beautiful red wolf with white fur legs, chest, and under her chin. He had a black fur band around his chest, red and gray fur under his chin, and a darker tail. But she was just beautiful.

She licked his face, and he nuzzled and licked hers. Then they pushed through the wolf door and ran toward the woods where they heard other wolves barking and playing.

At first, they ran and were just having a great time, and then they began play fighting, nipping each other, tussling with each other, biting, growling, having a blast. He couldn't believe his timing in meeting Hanna like he had.

She liked to play rough, but he was easy on her, not wanting to injure her.

She suddenly stopped playing and lifted her chin and howled at the moon. He smiled at her and howled with her. Now he knew her lovely wolf voice. They'd missed the wolf-howling competition, but this was just as much fun.

Then she tackled him again—when he was off guard. Phoenix wanted to laugh. They were suddenly joined by other wolves, and he could smell Carol's and Ryan's scents, Max's, and the others he didn't know. But they greeted him and Hanna, welcoming them to the wolf pack, and he was really glad to be part of a pack after not having been for so many years while moving around with the army.

Hanna nudged Phoenix and then raced off. He chased after her and figured she was heading to the house.

As soon as she barged through the door, he followed her inside, and they raced to the bedroom. She shifted and shut the door behind him.

He shifted and pulled her into his arms and began to kiss her.

Her hands were all over his back, her body rubbing against his growing erection, their mouths fusing together with long, dreamy kisses. Her green eyes had darkened, and she kissed his neck and cheek. He pulled away to kiss and lick her taut nipples, her breathing growing ragged.

He breathed in her sweet, wild scent: the fresh woods, apple cider, and cinnamon. Their tongues tangled together again, stroking, passionate, wanting more. Her hands ran through his hair, and he combed his fingers through hers, their bodies rubbing against each other.

"I knew you were hot the first time I saw you," she whispered, licking his chin.

"Did you 'see' me like this then?"

"Hmm, in my dreams that night after the pub incident." Then they were kissing again, and he slid his hand down her backside and pulled her against his thigh, raising her leg a bit over his.

He began stroking her between her legs and she was groaning. He stopped and she moaned, but he wanted her in bed with him. He released her and jerked back the covers, then swept her up in his arms and set her on the bed. He followed her there, stroking her again, and she was practically purring as she arched against his fingers. He enjoyed this with her, everything he'd done with her, but this ended the night perfectly.

———

Phoenix was all lean muscles, his erection reaching out to her, and she wanted him to bury himself in her, but for wolves, it was a mating for life. So for now, they had to be satisfied with going as far as they could without consummating the relationship.

His strokes on her feminine nub were magnificent, his tongue entering her mouth and dueling with hers intoxicating, and she was wet with arousal. He smelled musky and feral, a wild wolf ready to mate. Heat filled every cell in her body as he kept stroking her nub until she felt the end coming. Relief, anticipation, expectation, and then mind-blowing release.

"Ohmigod, yes!" She kissed him and he kissed her back, as if she was the most important wolf in his life.

She rubbed her body against his steel-hard erection.

"Are you ready?" she asked, as if she needed the confirmation.

"Hell yeah. For you, yeah."

She chuckled and began to stroke him, his breath hitching. She was kissing his mouth at the same time, his hands gently combing through her hair. He had such a wonderfully, kissable mouth, and his hands were strong yet gentle too. His body was taut with need, beads of sweat forming on his brow. She smiled, loving how she could make the tough Green Beret sweat.

She ran her free hand over his nipples, then leaned over and licked one and gently nibbled it. His hand tightened on her hair, and he lightly groaned. Then she kissed his other nipple and licked it.

But she didn't let up on stroking his erection. The way he was tensing, she knew he was about to come, his face grim, his green eyes darkened, lust-filled, and then he exploded.

"Hmm." She kissed him soundly. "Should we check the shower next?"

He chuckled darkly. "Yeah."

She'd heard Carol and Ryan head for their bedroom earlier, so she and Phoenix grabbed some nightwear, and naked, they raced each other to the bathroom. They were trying to be quiet about it, but they were laughing when they got there.

This was just what she needed in her life. A hunky military guy.

CHAPTER 7

A MONTH LATER, PHOENIX WAS SERVING AS A PRIVATE INVESTI-gator for Ryan in his firm and loving his job. He'd had a four-year criminal justice degree when he went into the army, and now he could finally use it for something. He and Hanna were trying to agree on an apartment to rent, so they were still at Ryan and Carol's house. The McKinleys were glad to have them stay there, but Phoenix and Hanna needed their own place.

Phoenix had decided they were getting a house, instead of bothering with an apartment, if Hanna would agree to it.

She was working as a communications member of Ryan's team, and she was loving her job too. Best of all, they'd had so much fun with the pack activities. It was nearly Thanksgiving, and Phoenix had lots to be thankful for. Hanna topped his list.

He left the PI office and headed over to the mayor's office to pick up Hanna for lunch and drive her to the house he thought she might like. She'd shown him pictures of homes that really appealed to her, but they wouldn't know until they actually walked through it whether the home was the right fit for them.

Ryan was releasing her early from work, though she didn't know it, so she and Phoenix could look at homes. He was getting tired of their indecisiveness in finding an apartment. Phoenix knew they couldn't decide on one because they really needed a home, one with a wolf door. A place near Carol and Ryan's vast acreage. Someplace where they would feel safe as wolves. They could always go to the pack land and run no matter where they lived, but wouldn't it be better if they could just run through a wolf door and be in the woods?

There was one place that would border pack land once Ryan had bought up more of the land, and it had just gone up for sale.

"Hey, honey," Phoenix said, "are you ready for lunch?"

Hanna smiled at him. "I sure am. I'm starving."

"Okay, great."

She got into his car, and he drove her out toward the pack's land. "Wait, there aren't any food places out here."

"There's a house that I wanted to look at with you. It's on the border of the pack's territory." He was certain Ryan was hoping they would buy it to keep the pack's territory more secure, but no one else in the pack needed a home. Phoenix had even wondered if Ryan and the pack had had anything to do with the people wanting to sell the property.

"Really? Is it what we wanted?"

He motioned to his phone. "You can look at all the pictures and the specs of the place."

Hanna lifted his phone and found the house he'd been looking at on the Google search. "Oh, this is nice."

"With my salary, retirement, and savings…"

"And mine," she said.

"We can get it, if it suits us."

"The property butting up to Ryan and Carol's property is great, and it does have ten acres with it," she said.

"Just think, anytime we want to run as wolves, we can. No driving to the pack's lands."

She sighed. "We have to feel connected to the house. We've looked at so many apartments, and all of them were—"

"On top of other apartments. That's not how we live."

"Okay, well, I hope this is it then."

When they finally reached the property, they found a pretty log home, about twenty years old, treed property, a wraparound deck, big windows, and a two-car garage.

"I don't know about you, but I like the look of the house and the property already," Phoenix said, hoping they could agree on something.

"Don't mention you like it to the owners."

He glanced at her after he parked.

"So we can get them to come down on the price."

He smiled and took hold of her hand and squeezed. "Right."

Then they got out of the car and headed for the front door. "It's for sale by owner, so the owner said he'd be here when we wanted to look at it."

"Okay, great."

They walked up to the front door, and Phoenix smelled Hanna's nervousness.

"I want to like it. I really do," she whispered. But she was frowning.

"What's wrong?" He hoped she wasn't already feeling bad vibes about the house.

"I smell a familiar scent that I've smelled before." Then she snapped her fingers, and just then the door opened and she said, "Joe."

When Joe, the human who had stood her up her first night in town, saw her, his jaw dropped.

Phoenix was frowning at the two of them, having no idea what was going on.

"Hey, uh, I'm sorry about missing seeing you at the pub that night. Something came up." Joe sounded like he hoped he hadn't screwed things up with them buying the house because of that little incident a month ago. "Then I heard about the motorcycle gang incident there, and I was glad I hadn't gone."

She arched a brow.

"I mean, well, sorry."

Yeah, the guy was sorry all right.

"Can we take a look at the house?" Phoenix asked, ready to sock the guy for standing Hanna up. He figured if he hit him, it wouldn't help in asking Joe to reduce the price of the house if Hanna loved it.

They looked at the large living room area and the stone fireplace, and Phoenix was already thinking of setting up a Christmas tree near it the day after Thanksgiving, if they could get moved in that quickly. The place was devoid of furniture and household goods, so it looked like it was ready for the new owner to move right in.

"So why are you selling the place?" Hanna asked, looking over the kitchen.

"My mother died years ago, and my dad just died. I inherited the property three months ago, but I had to have it probated, sell everything else off, and then put the place up for sale."

"I'm sorry about your parents," Hanna said.

The cabinets in the kitchen were honey oak, and the appliances all had wood-grained paneling. The counters were granite and the floors tile. And they even had a wolf door. Well, large dog door, but it would be their wolf door.

At least Phoenix was ready to settle in. All his furniture was in storage. Hanna had moved her household goods into the same storage unit, so they would just need some muscle to help them move it all, and they would be all set up in their very own home.

One wall in the den was covered with built-in bookshelves, a nice touch. The master bedroom had a walk-in shower and a Jacuzzi tub. Hell, Phoenix was sold on the house already.

But Hanna was looking into closets and frowning, glancing out the windows and frowning. She hadn't said one nice thing about the house. He was dying to buy it.

"She and I haven't agreed on anything so far," Phoenix said, sounding like this was another lost cause. He hoped his words would convince Joe to push to sell it to her by lowering the price.

"It's not exactly what I want," she said, peering into the fridge. "I mean, we'd have to replace all the appliances."

"They're only two years old," Joe said, sounding exasperated.

"She loves to cook, and she knows just what she wants in a home," Phoenix said, though she really hadn't cooked much, not at Carol and Ryan's house. Carol and Ryan both loved to cook.

Joe folded his arms. "Okay, make me an offer."

He'd listed the property at $295,000. Phoenix was going to offer $280,000, but Hanna took hold of Phoenix's hand and said, "We've got some other homes to check out."

Phoenix looked at her in disbelief. What if some other interested couple saw the property and bought it outright? He would still be dreaming about being with Hanna in this house, making it a home for Thanksgiving.

"Two hundred and eighty thousand," Joe said.

Hanna looked at the kitchen again, frowning, and let out her breath in exasperation. "Two sixty-five and you have a deal. I can use the money we didn't spend on the asking price to renovate the kitchen, and you aren't going through a real estate agent, so you don't have that cost."

Joe rubbed his bristly chin. Phoenix knew he was dying to sell the house as much as Phoenix was dying to buy it. But would he drop the price that much?

"You think about it. We're going to look at the other homes now," Hanna said and pulled Phoenix toward the door.

Hell, if they missed the opportunity to buy this house and the land that went with it—

"Okay, two seventy."

"When can we move in?" she asked.

Joe smiled. "Now, today, any time. I just need a down payment—"

"Let's get a contract written up. We have the funds for a home, so we'll be good to go," Phoenix said, relieved beyond measure. "We can move in now, if you allow it, and we'll get the title transfer and all the other paperwork done as soon as we can." He knew it could take thirty to sixty days to close on a home, but they weren't taking out a loan, and Ryan had told them one of their wolves owned the title company, so they'd expedite the transfer of title.

Hanna smiled at him and squeezed Phoenix's hand. He realized she'd played both of them. Here he was a PI, and she was a con artist! He loved her.

CHAPTER 8

HANNA AND PHOENIX WERE SO EXCITED TO MOVE IN THAT once they had paid the down payment, signed the contract, and had the appointment for the title company, they were ready. Joe had deposited the check and left them the keys to the home, glad to be rid of the property after the house was signed over.

Phoenix called Ryan with the good news. They needed pack help to move their belongings to the house, but the title company had already let him know that they were closing next week. The pack couldn't be happier that the property would belong to pack members.

"I've already made arrangements for a moving van, a driver, and a bunch of guys to help you get moved."

"Thanks, Ryan. For everything," Phoenix said.

"Thank you for adding that land to our property. You can be one of our outer guard posts."

Phoenix laughed.

"But really, thanks for buying it. And I know you'll love being there."

"We will." Phoenix rubbed Hanna's back.

She was smiling up at him. When they ended the call, she laughed and twirled around with exuberance. "It's ours. Don't you just love it?"

"I love you. And yes, I love the house too. I didn't think you cared for it all that much." He pulled her into his arms and hugged her.

"That was the ploy. Pretend it wasn't exactly what we wanted and we were going to look at other places that might suit our needs better. But oh, this is just beautiful."

"No renovations on the kitchen then?"

"No way. We probably will need to get some furniture, but I couldn't have said that to help convince him to reduce the price on the house."

"True. You really like it?"

She kissed Phoenix. "Yeah. I know you were totally exasperated with me when you thought I didn't like it. I could smell your tension and saw it in your face. It was a good thing Joe didn't recognize it."

"It wouldn't have mattered. All that mattered was what you wanted. He was sure you wore the pants in the family."

She laughed. "We both do. Come on. We need to get our bed moved here and then we need to—"

"Mate?"

Smiling, she nodded. "I was beginning to think we would never agree on a place to live and this wouldn't work out between us."

"Are you kidding? An apartment? No. We needed a home in the woods. And we'll make it *our* home. I love you." He was even thinking about when they had kids and how this would be perfect for them. The home had five bedrooms and three and a half baths. Perfect for a family. And no more moving. He was ready to settle down permanently.

"I agree. And I love you too. Let's go and get our stuff."

After moving their belongings to the home, they spent the rest of the afternoon setting up their house, but they didn't have any groceries to make dinner. It would still take them days, weeks, to get everything the way they wanted and to find things too.

"Let's go to the pub where we met and celebrate," Phoenix said, "and we can buy some groceries in town after that."

"Let's invite the pack, in case we have trouble again there."

He laughed. "It wouldn't be a celebration without them. Besides, if any motorcycle gangs show up, we'll be safe. I'll invite my family too."

That evening, they had dinner and drinks at the pub with close to thirty pack members, several of whom had brought them housewarming gifts. Both Hanna and Phoenix were overwhelmed by the generosity of the pack. Michael and Carmela were there, too, promising them a housewarming gift in a few days.

"We'll have everyone over for a barbecue one of these days," Phoenix said, though they needed to get set up for it first.

"In the spring," Ryan said. "You two need to get your household set up the way you like it."

A couple of motorcyclists drove up and parked at the pub, and Phoenix and Hanna eyed them speculatively through the window, but they didn't belong to any gangs and grabbed a booth inside. Hanna sighed with relief. Not much later, Joe drove up in his blue pickup and entered the pub with a woman. When he saw Hanna and Phoenix, he almost looked like he wanted to leave.

They smiled and said they were getting all moved in, and he looked relieved.

After dinner, a number of pack members piled plants and small appliances and other presents into Phoenix's car and wished him and Hanna the best on their first home together. Phoenix and Hanna drove to the grocery store for one last trip before they settled into their house for their first night out in the country.

He got steaks; she got fixings for s'mores.

"I thought you were going to dump me if I didn't agree to buy the house," she said while they were trying to remember everything they needed to set up housekeeping.

He was pushing the basket, and she was grabbing flour, sugar, and spices. "I should have known you really wanted the house. You would make a terrific poker player."

She chuckled.

Then they were finally home, ditching their jackets, scarves, gloves, hats, boots, and socks, unpacking their groceries and gifts. Other than putting the refrigerated goods away, Phoenix figured none of the rest of the stuff mattered for now. Not when they had other business they needed to attend to.

They still hadn't hung pictures, boxes were filled with their household goods, and they had to make their bed. But when he swept her up in his arms and headed into the master bedroom, he discovered she'd found the sheets and made the bed just for them.

He'd figured they would be making love on the bare mattress, floor, anywhere would do, but he was glad they had a made bed for their mating.

"You planned this all along, didn't you? Seducing me?" he asked, kissing her cheek.

She laughed. "Yes, while the guys were putting the bed together and you were helping to unpack the rest of our furniture and household goods, I was frantically searching for our sheets and pillows, and when I finally found them, I made the bed. Just for this."

He glanced down at the green comforter decorated with pink hearts and the pink sheets and smiled.

She shrugged. "We can get something else later. This will have to do for now."

"Pink works for me as long as you're the one in between the sheets."

"Hmm, and you're there with me."

He started removing her sweater and pulled it over her head and kissed her cheek. "At the rate we were going, I never thought we'd get to this."

She laughed. "Of course we would. I know, I know, we couldn't agree on an apartment, but that didn't mean you and I weren't meant for each other." She smiled at him, pulled his shirt out of his waistband, and ran her hands underneath and up his shirt and over his ripped abs. "I wouldn't give you up for anything."

"The same here with wanting you. Hell, if we'd had to live with Ryan and Carol forever…" He kissed her cheek, his hands rubbing over her shoulders.

"No. Way."

He chuckled. "My feeling exactly."

———————

She found his nipples and gently tweaked them with her fingers. He moaned deep in his throat, then kissed her mouth, leisurely, lovingly. His large hands tenderly rubbed her shoulders, and he made her feel amazing. *He* was amazing. His mouth was incredible on hers as he brushed kisses against her lips, his green eyes mesmerizing.

She sighed as he unbuttoned her blouse and found she was braless. His masculine lips smiled against her mouth in a predatory way.

She shrugged. "If you weren't going to ask me to mate with you, I was going to ask you…and fewer clothes work better."

"All day at work—"

"I had a shirt and sweater on." She smiled up at him.

"Vixen." Then he lowered his head to kiss the swell of her breasts, one and then the other. He kissed a nipple with his hot mouth, then licked and moved across, pressing kisses against her skin, leaving a sizzling path in his wake before he began to lick the other nipple, suckling.

Heat enveloped her and her breath grew ragged. She breathed in the scent of him, her wolf forevermore, maleness personified, hot testosterone, enticing pheromones, the human and the wolf, desire filling her with each passing second. Wet with need, she pulled off his shirt. She began to work on his belt, unfastening it, unzipping his trousers. Reaching down as he was kissing her mouth, she ran her hand down, and what she found shocked her.

Her heavily lidded eyes shot wide open as soon as she touched his penis and short, curly hairs, and her mouth curved up. "You weren't wearing boxer shorts today?"

"I was going to ask you to mate with me, and the fewer clothes, the better."

She laughed. She loved him. "Great minds." She hurried to pull his trousers down his lean hips and kissed the tip of his penis before his trousers fell to the floor and he kicked them off.

He hurried to pull off her trousers and he smiled, ran his hand over her lacy boy-shorts, and pulled them off.

She wrapped her arms around his neck and pressed her naked body against his. She loved the feel of his hard, muscled body against hers as he ran his hands down her back and cupped her buttocks and squeezed.

"You're a wild one," he whispered against her cheek. "Wild and mine."

"Shy and retiring, in truth." Of course she was teasing him. He did bring more of the wildness out in her, though.

"No way. You're just the one for me." Then he was kissing her again, and she let him in all the way, tongue to tongue, greeting him in a way that said there would be no holds barred this time.

"Hmm, so hot and wolfish." She rubbed against his arousal and he groaned low.

She savored every bit of him: his touches, groans, scent, taste. He was just divine, and she was so glad they had a place of their own where they could be themselves, be a couple, enjoy the intimacy in total privacy, and become mated wolves.

He slipped his hands under her buttocks and lifted her so that she wrapped her legs around him, and he carried her to the bed. She already felt the white-hot ache for his touch. Then he was finding her wet, swollen nub with his finger, teasing the center of her pleasure. He pressed his advantage, stroking her, making her feel wondrous, lusty, and in love.

Scarcely breathing, she felt awash in rising pleasure, the need for fulfillment, the craving to have him inside her now filling her with urgency. Her heart and his were beating wildly, and she was heading for the stars and the moon, ready to release. And then she shattered in the most exquisite way, cried out, howled, and clung to the love of her life.

He was pressing the head of his shaft between her thick, slick folds and began to thrust after that, not waiting for an invitation, her howl enough to say she was all in on the union between wolves. "Love you so much, honey."

She kissed him with drive and enthusiasm. "I love you right back," she said, breathless. He took her breath away, filled her with joy, and meant everything to her.

She wrapped her legs around his waist, deepening his penetration, wanting him desperately to climax inside her this time. This was what it meant to be wolf mates, the consummated sex between wolves, the driving need to be as one, a mated pair forever.

She couldn't be any happier as his body slammed into hers, thrusting, undulating, sexy, hot, and hers. Seeing the tension on his face, the straining of his neck muscles, the way his body tightened, his ragged breathing, and lust-filled, beautiful green eyes, she knew he was near completion. But so was she. Again.

He growled as he filled her with his wet heat, and then he howled like she had done, thrusting until he was finished, but she ground out, "Not yet." And he smiled and slid his hand between them, coaxing another climax out of her, stroking, kneading, bringing her to the precipice and orgasm.

She cried out, feeling wondrously fulfilled, satiated, hearts beating as if they'd been racing through the woods as wolves, and that was just what she wanted to do next. As a newly mated wolf pair.

She pulled him to her, held him tight, her legs still wrapped around him, hers forevermore.

"Hmm, you aim to keep me," he said, his voice rough and sexy, needy even.

"You bet," she said. "I'm only letting you out of my grasp to run as a wolf tonight."

"I was hoping you would say that. Running with you as a wolf means we'll be ready for more bed play when we return home."

"I knew you were the only one for me." She shifted and he chuckled. He should know that about her by now. She could be totally unpredictable.

He shifted and she raced down the hall. He raced right after her, though they had to maneuver around a few packing boxes before they reached the door. They'd unpack more tomorrow, but for now, they were going to enjoy their newfound mated status.

Wolves in lust and love—the only way to be.

EPILOGUE

THE HOLIDAYS WERE UPON THEM. INSTEAD OF VISITING Phoenix's family or Hanna's, their families came from Loveland and Silver Town to see them for Thanksgiving, and so did the Green Valley pack leaders. Phoenix and Hanna were so grateful for all Ryan and Carol had done for them.

"You know we love having families join the pack in Green Valley," Ryan said to Hanna's parents and Hanna's sister, Susan.

"We're sure you could take over the post office here as soon as the postmaster retires, and Susan could be a teacher for our wolf children if you ever want to move out here and be part of our pack," Carol said.

Hanna smiled, but Phoenix knew her family had no interest in uprooting themselves from Loveland, as much as she hoped they would. He thought if they could convince Susan to move here, the sisters' parents would follow.

That was when Max Browning arrived late to dinner. It was Carol and Hanna's idea to have the retired Navy SEAL come to dinner, in hopes he and Susan might hit it off. But Michael had the same idea with his Green Beret brother, Daniel, who was visiting him and Carmela, so naturally they brought him to Thanksgiving dinner too.

"Sorry I'm late. I got a flat tire on the way over here," Max said, making a detour to the kitchen to wash up first.

"No problem at all," Hanna said as Max took his seat at the table next to Susan and introductions were made.

Maybe something would spark between Max and Susan. Or Daniel and Susan. All that mattered to Phoenix for now was that *he* had found his mate in Hanna during one big motorcycle-gang brawl close to Halloween.

———————————

Hanna was thrilled all the families could be together. Michael's twin brother was sitting on the other side of Susan, and Hanna hoped one of the two men, Daniel or Max, would interest her. She truly wanted her family to move to Green Valley before she and Phoenix had kids, but her parents wouldn't move unless Susan did.

Hanna squeezed Phoenix's hand and smiled at him. No matter what happened between her sister and the men, Hanna had her own loving mate. Dating a military guy had finally worked out, and she'd ended up with the job and a pack that she couldn't have been happier to be with. She and both their families and, of course, her mate couldn't have been more pleased or thankful for this holiday season.

Acknowledgments

I want to thank my family for always believing in me. And thanks to my Rebel Romance critique partners who, more than just being critique partners, are friends who understand the ups and downs of the writing experience—Vonda, Judy, Pam, Tammy, Randy, Carol, and Betty. And I so appreciate Deb Werksman for helping me to write the best book that I can, for believing in werewolves, and for being a dream editor to work with. Most of all, thanks to my fans, who inspire me with real wolf tales, the joy mine bring to them, and the hopeful inquiries as to who will find romance next.

About the Author

USA Today bestselling author Terry Spear has written over sixty paranormal and medieval Highland romances. In 2008, *Heart of the Wolf* was named a *Publishers Weekly* Best Book of the Year. She has received a PNR Top Pick, a Best Book of the Month nomination by *Long and Short Reviews*, numerous *Night Owl Romance* Top Picks, and two Paranormal Excellence Awards for Romantic Literature (finalist and honorable mention). In 2016, *Billionaire in Wolf's Clothing* was an *RT Book Reviews* Top Pick. A retired officer of the U.S. Army Reserves, Terry also creates award-winning teddy bears that have found homes all over the world, helps out with her granddaughter, and is raising two Havanese puppies. She lives in Spring, Texas.

Also by Terry Spear

RED WOLF
Joy to the Wolves

WOLFF BROTHERS
You Had Me at Wolf

SEAL WOLF
A SEAL in Wolf's Clothing
A SEAL Wolf Christmas
SEAL Wolf Hunting
SEAL Wolf in Too Deep
SEAL Wolf Undercover
SEAL Wolf Surrender

HEART OF THE SHIFTER
You Had Me at Jaguar

HEART OF THE JAGUAR
Savage Hunter
Jaguar Fever
Jaguar Hunt
Jaguar Pride
A Very Jaguar Christmas

BILLIONAIRE WOLF
Billionaire in Wolf's Clothing
A Billionaire Wolf for Christmas
Night of the Billionaire Wolf

HIGHLAND WOLF
Heart of the Highland Wolf
A Howl for a Highlander
A Highland Werewolf Wedding
Hero of a Highland Wolf
A Highland Wolf for Christmas
The Wolf Wore Plaid

WHITE WOLF
Dreaming of a White Wolf
Christmas
Flight of the White Wolf

HEART OF THE WOLF
Heart of the Wolf
To Tempt the Wolf
Legend of the White Wolf
Seduced by the Wolf

SILVER TOWN WOLF
Destiny of the Wolf
Wolf Fever
Dreaming of the Wolf
Silence of the Wolf
A Silver Wolf Christmas
Alpha Wolf Need Not Apply
Between a Wolf and a Hard Place
All's Fair in Love and Wolf
Silver Town Wolf: Home
for the Holidays

FIERCE COWBOY WOLF

Ranchers by day, wolf shifters by night. Don't miss the thrilling Seven Range Shifters series from acclaimed author Kait Ballenger

Sierra Cavanaugh has worked her whole life to become the first female elite warrior in Grey Wolf history. With her nomination finally put forward, she needs the pack council's approval, and they insist she must find herself a mate.

Packmaster Maverick Grey was reconciled to spending the rest of his life alone. But he needs the elite warrior vacancy filled—and fast. If Sierra needs a mate, this is his chance to claim her.

For these two rivals, the only thing more dangerous than fighting the enemy at their backs is battling the war of seduction building between them...

**"Kait Ballenger is a
treasure you don't want to miss."**
—Gena Showalter, *New York Times* bestselling author